TOUR
of
DUTY

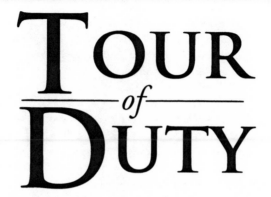

TOUR
of
DUTY

JAN D. HENDRIX

Tour of Duty

iUniverse books may be ordered through booksellers or by contacting:

iUniverse
1663 Liberty Drive
Bloomington, IN 47403
www.iuniverse.com
1-800-Authors (1-800-288-4677)

ISBN: 978-1-4759-2453-4 (sc)
ISBN: 978-1-4759-2455-8 (hc)
ISBN: 978-1-4759-2454-1 (e)

Library of Congress Control Number: 2012908352

Printed in the United States of America

iUniverse rev. date: 11/04/2012

Praise for
"Tour of Duty"

"In Hendrix's debut novel, an unlikely romance develops between two people on opposing sides of the war. They must decide if they can dare to defy their families, their obligations and their cultures in order to be together. Told in a straightforward, well-paced style, this love story comes across as universal and timeless."

—*Kirkus Reviews*

*To Curt and Dan and the 4th Ordnance Company,
Miesau, Germany: 1959—1962.*

Also by Jan D. Hendrix

The Blue Hole and Other Stories
A collection of stories depicting life-changing events.

CHAPTER 1

JUST ONE DAY OFF A troop ship at a north German port, Cpl. Mark Bergner waited along with two other replacements before an inner office door marked "Capt. John M. Williams, C Company." It was August 1950, and their new assignment was to the US Army post at Grahfenvern, Germany, a military installation located a few kilometers southeast of Frankfurt.

One of the new men, PFC Dave Myers, a sandy-haired youth from Wisconsin, spoke. "I've got a bad feeling about this outfit. I've heard this CO has requested combat duty, and that's too gung ho for me."

"Yeah, that says a lot about him," the second man, PFC Sam Wade, said. "Also, I've heard he has some wacky ways of indoctrinating new personnel," he continued in a slow Texas drawl. Wade had grown up on a ranch in Texas. All three men had joined the army right out of high school and had already completed a year of their military service before being shipped to Germany.

"Good or bad, we're here for two years," Mark, a slim six-footer with dark hair and a serious face, said. "Let's not screw up here at the beginning . . ." At that moment, the door opened to the inner office, and a sergeant appeared.

"The captain will see you now," the sergeant said.

The three men entered the office, formed a line before the captain at his desk, and waited for instructions. Dressed in olive-drab, Class A uniforms with Ike-Jackets, they appeared youthfully fit and stood erect with a precise soldier's bearing.

"Report," said the captain. He spoke calmly, nodding at Mark.

Mark came to attention and saluted. "Corporal Mark Bergner reporting as ordered, sir," he answered.

"At ease, Corporal," Captain Williams said, returning Mark's salute. "Welcome to Charlie Company."

"Thank you, sir," Mark said, standing at ease. A first sergeant stood to the left and slightly behind the captain. His lean figure and stern demeanor presented a formidable image of order and discipline. Mark took note of the ribbons on his chest, especially the silver and blue Combat Infantryman Badge, which said a lot about the man.

"I see from your record you've been in the army only twelve months and already a corporal. Coming from stateside, that's unusual," Williams continued. The captain sat behind a plain brown desk covered with paperwork. Positioned directly behind him stood two large flags on staffs, which dominated his background. Over his right shoulder loomed the American flag and over his left the regimental flag. Positioned at oblique angles and unfurled slightly, the flags provided an authoritative setting for the captain at his desk. "How do you explain that?"

"Mostly luck, sir," Mark said. "I fired 'expert' on the firing range, and after advanced infantry training, they needed instructors and made me an acting corporal. My CO worked to get me the full promotion before I shipped out."

"Luck or not, it speaks well of you, Corporal. Firing expert interest me . . ." The captain paused a moment as if considering that situation. "Yes, it interests me very much. You'll be hearing from me on that," Williams continued, setting Mark's personnel file to the left of the stack and turning to the next man.

Williams faced each man in a similar fashion and then leaned back in his chair as if studying the three men. When he continued talking, he sat upright and spoke in a commanding tone, "Men, you've been in the army long enough to know military regulation and procedures, so I won't bother with that. What I will cover and emphasize is a special requirement I have of men in my company." He again paused a moment, looking at each man. "And I can best convey this requirement by a demonstration I've prepared." He turned to the sergeant. "Set up and execute the demonstration, Sergeant."

The first sergeant left the room and immediately returned followed by a PFC who had been waiting in the outer office. The PFC carried a bucket of water, which he set on a metal chair before leaving again.

The first sergeant turned to the new men. "For this demonstration, you will remove your jackets and roll up your right shirt sleeves."

When this was done, he continued. "Now each one pass by the bucket you see there on that chair, put your hand down to the bottom, and pull it out." He stood rigidly before the new men as they passed by the bucket dipping their hands in the water.

The first sergeant then formed them up and called attention. They stood stiffly, right hands dripping. The captain walked to stand before Mark, who stood first in line. He equaled Mark's six-foot height and appeared wiry and fit looking. His tanned facial features conveyed a no-nonsense attitude. His uniform was tailored and well fitted, and his stance conveyed authority. The silver captain's bars on his collar stood out brightly against the olive green of his uniform. "Corporal Bergner, what did you notice about the water when you removed your hand?" he asked Mark, staring directly at him.

"I noticed nothing in particular, sir," Mark said, his eyes fixed on the regimental flag behind the captain's head.

The captain nodded slightly and walked to stand before the next man. "What did you notice, Private?"

"Nothing but the same water, sir," PFC Myers said.

After the three men had been questioned by the captain, he returned to stand behind his desk, flanked by the two flags. He began to speak: "None of you saw any difference in the water before or after you put your hand there. You know why?" The captain paused briefly. "It's because you made no difference," he said sharply. He paused again, looking from one to the other. "What can we learn from that?" he continued.

None of the men spoke. Mark knew it was an orientation ritual designed by the CO to introduce new personnel to company policies. Many company commanders had their own way of indoctrinating new personnel. In spite of the unusual demonstration, he knew to just play the game and get on with it.

"What we can learn is that individually we make no difference. Is that true from this demonstration?"

"Yes, sir," all three men said, simultaneously.

"Now, what if all three of you plus the other five that will be in your squad put your hands in the bucket at the same time? What will happen?" Captain Williams stepped back, folding his arms and waiting, his face serious.

"What about it, Corporal?" he said finally, addressing Mark again.

"With all our hands there, it'll displace the water, and some will spill out," Mark said.

"Exactly," the captain said. "Now, what can we learn from that?" No one spoke.

"What we have learned from this demonstration is that individually we make no difference. On our own, we are insignificant," the captain repeated his previous statement. "Is that true?"

"Yes, sir!"

"But working together in our squad, in our platoon, and in our company, we can make a difference. Is that true?"

"Yes, sir!" Mark said, along with the other two men.

The captain's face then took on a firm, authoritative look. "Very well, keep that in mind," he said. "We're an infantry company in the field. To our east we have the Soviet Bloc with a hundred and fifty divisions poised to attack any day; and, as I speak, we're getting our buts kicked in Korea by superior communist forces. At any time we can get the call to go one way or the other." He paused briefly, looking keenly at each of the three men, and then continued. "Needless to say, we stay combat ready. So work with your NCOs and platoon leader and stay out of trouble." He paused again as if to let his words sink in. "I repeat," he continued, "don't bring trouble to my company. If you do, you've got trouble with me." With that, he ordered First Sergeant Andrade to dismiss the men.

CHAPTER 2

T HE FIRST FEW DAYS IN Charlie Company, Mark didn't experience anything he wasn't familiar with from his stateside duties. The daily routine usually started with a two-mile run before chow, followed by classes on subjects such as first aid techniques or weapons familiarization, and finally training exercises on the parade grounds or in the nearby countryside. There was one unscheduled alert at three o'clock in the morning where NCOs suddenly burst into the barracks shouting, "Alert! Alert! Fall out, fall out!" They drew their weapons and, after falling out and into formation, were immediately dismissed back to their barracks like nothing had happened. Nothing in the training schedule was unusual until the following Thursday when one of Captain Williams's special training tactics was scheduled.

Early Thursday morning, their platoon sergeant called the new men aside and briefed them. "This particular training is the captain's idea of physical training while providing an opportunity to study the skills of his platoon leaders and NCOs in directing their men in competitive situations," he began, speaking as if he were before a class giving a lecture. "Most of the time this consists of a soccer match where the platoon leaders of each team direct their teams as if winning is a mission of importance. These matches are played with enthusiasm," he continued in his monotone voice. "There may be muscle strains and bruises or an occasional trip to the first aid station for some. But in most cases, a red facial scratch or purple bruise will be carried as a badge of honor in the days following the matches."

Mark learned later that in reality the platoon leaders were intentionally using controlled aggression as a training method to teach teams to work together with a goal-oriented objective. It was another form of training applicable to combat maneuvers, and Captain Williams insisted the games be taken seriously. He and the first sergeant would stroll about, watching the games and taking note of how the platoon leaders and NCOs handled their teams.

Mark fit right in with this activity. He had both played soccer and boxed in high school sports, and he was hard and fast and used to being knocked about. Lieutenant McBride, Mark's platoon leader and an officer with high regard, commented on his skills right away, saying, "Good man. I'll use him often." As the game progressed and Mark's game spirit running at a high level, McBride sent him back in with the hopes of slowing the other team, who had moved ahead by two points.

Both Wade and Myers were also playing at that moment. Myers, running fast and attempting to steal the ball from an opposing player, inadvertently got his legs tangled up with the other, and they both went tumbling forward, sprawling out face down in the grass. The opposing player, angry at the inadvertent fowl, quickly jumped to his feet, spitting dirt and grass. "You tripped me!" he shouted angrily at Myers. He then threw a punch at Myers's face. The hastily thrown punch missed Myers's face but caught the top of his shoulder, knocking him back down onto the field.

The man was much bigger than Myers, and Mark instinctively moved in to help. He was a few steps away, and moving fast, he hit the angry player with a running body block that sent him rolling back across the lawn. This act created a major skirmish where both on-field teams began pushing and shoving, and the men on the sideline began shouting and stomping about and shaking their fist in the air at Mark's team. Before the referees, who were heavyset sergeants of appropriate size to handle such melees, had pushed the two teams apart and declared a timeout, Mark noticed that Wade had been just behind him, protecting his back.

As the teams retreated back to their respective sidelines, the man that Myers had tripped and Mark had body slammed walked close by Myers. He was muscular with a thick neck and a deep and powerful-looking chest, and his face was red and grimy with black dirt and grass smears from the tumbles on the ground. "I'll get you, you little jerk," he said to Myers.

"Take it easy, man," Myers said. "It was an accident."

"Says you," the angry man said. He then turned to Mark, his face set with rage. "You're on my list, too."

"Lay off!" Mark said, meeting the man's stare. "He's much smaller than you."

"You're not!" the soldier quickly spit back at Mark. "And your day's coming as well," he continued while walking away and pointing back at Mark. "You can count on it." He was a little shorter than Mark but heavier set and had long, powerful-looking arms.

Mark ignored the gesture and turned and walked toward his sideline. He knew that such confrontations occasionally flared up in spirited matches and in most cases were quickly forgotten. As he worked his way through the maze of men returning to their respective teams, a soldier walked close to Mark. "Watch that guy, Soldier," he said, shielding his voice with his hand. "His name's Ricco, and he's a bad one."

"That right," Mark said calmly.

"Yeah, he's in my platoon, and he's already beat up two guys there," the soldier continued. "Hurt them bad."

"Thanks for the tip," Mark said.

"That guy hates everybody," the soldier went on as he walked away. "He'll be coming after you, so watch your back."

* * *

After the day's training exercises had ended and retreat had passed, the Charge of Quarters caught Mark as he left the chow hall. The CQ told Mark to report to the orderly room, because the captain wanted to see him.

"Corporal Bergner reporting as ordered, sir," Mark said as he entered the captain's office.

"At ease, Corporal," Captain Williams said, returning Mark's salute. He paused a moment while placing some papers into a folder on his desk and then looked up at Mark.

"I'll get right to the point," he continued. "I saw that fracas you were involved in this afternoon."

"Sir, I just lost my head," Mark stammered, unsure of his position with the situation but ready to defend his actions.

"No, you didn't lose your head," Williams said. You were reacting instinctively, and PFC Wade was in there too. You three men came over together and have already developed a strong camaraderie."

"Yes, sir."

"I liked what I saw," Williams said. "You put yourself at risk to protect one of your own, and in doing so, you were supporting your team, your platoon. That's what I like to see—team players."

"Yes, sir," Mark said. He began to relax.

"My congratulations to you," Williams said. "And pass the same along to PFC Wade."

"Yes, sir."

"In my outfit, I want team players with a team spirit," he began. "I want my men willing to sacrifice for the common good. There's no place for individuals in my outfit."

"Yes, sir."

"That'll be all, Corporal."

Mark saluted and left the captain's office. As he walked back to his barracks, he felt good about the interchange with the CO. But just as he approached the barracks door, it dawned on him that the captain's emphasis on team spirit was the same idea behind his bucket-of-water demo: *forget the self, think of the team,* the demo implied. He gave a little chuckle, shaking his head, and then entered the barracks. He was tired and needed a shower.

CHAPTER 3

A T FORT JACKSON WHERE MARK had been stationed before shipping out to Germany, he had sometimes found himself at a loss for things to do in his off-duty time. At first, he hung out in the post gym and lifted weights or played basketball. In high school, he had boxed and was good at it, and with that experience, he often sparred around in the boxing ring whenever a friendly match could be arranged. He enjoyed these activities somewhat but became bored with them after a time. Then, when another soldier invited him to the photo lab and taught him to develop photographs, he discovered a new interest.

Photography was a far cry from the rough, hard-hitting male sports he was used to, but once he began to shoot and develop film, he was hooked. At first, his interest in photographic subjects focused on people and activities in his army life, but in time, he began to develop an esthetic interest in life away from the army post. He would notice something special about the gleeful abandonment of children playing in the park or the graceful way a covey of pigeons glide in flight with legs down and ready just before landing in the square. He would see such scenes and feel the urge to capture the image, as if there were something important about them. He didn't understand this creative force, and he didn't think much about it; he merely went along with the impulse as opportunities developed.

On the weekend of his third week in Charlie Company, Mark secured an off-post pass and caught the train into Frankfurt. On the troopship shipping over, he had made up his mind to focus on two things during his two-year tour in Europe. He was going to do his best at soldiering, and he was going to continue his hobby of photography during his off-duty time. He reasoned there would be too many important sights and experiences encountered in his two years in Europe to not have some of it recorded in photographs that he could look back on after he returned home from the army.

Arriving in Frankfurt, he visited several camera shops, hoping to find a certain model Leica camera that he had read about. The third shop he visited had a small sign over the entrance that stated "The Camera Shop." Entering the shop he could see cameras, camera accessories, and posters advertising film and photography equipment displayed on the back wall. In front of this wall, a glass-top counter containing many types of cameras ran the length of the room. While leaning over the counter intently examining a Leica, he first saw her reflection appear in the glass countertop as she approached him. The pale white, reflected image of her face appearing suddenly in the glass interrupted his study, and he looked up to see a young woman with blue eyes and blond hair that fell loosely across her face and down onto her shoulders. His attention suddenly changed from the Leica to the youthful woman before him. *Wow! Some Fräulein!* he thought.

"Can I help you?" she asked in a quiet, professional voice.

Surprised by her English, and wondering how she knew he spoke English, Mark took a moment before speaking. "Uh, yes . . . how much is the Leica?" He guessed that she knew him to be a GI because of his youth and tentative mannerism. That disappointed him. In spite of deliberately acting casual and wearing his recently purchased dark blue sport coat and gray trousers that were the stylish look of young German men of the day, he stood out as an American. In fact, his close haircut, sun-tanned face, and trim frame pegged him as an American soldier with extensive outdoor training.

"Three hundred fifty marks," she answered as she took the camera from the glass case and held it out for Mark to see. Her look then went from the camera up to Mark's face. Mark's eyes met hers and stayed there momentarily. It was a direct and unassuming look and merged softly with his gaze. "The price has been reduced because it's last year's model. Newer models are already on the market."

He looked at her, sensing her sincerity and feeling the warmth of her eyes on his. He held his look without realizing he was staring.

"It's been a popular model," she said, dropping her attention back to the camera. "And it's a good buy with the discount."

Mark, in recovering from his sudden fascination with the young *Fräulein*, was both surprised and embarrassed. With some awkwardness, he said, "This is close to what I'm looking for, but I'll have to think about it."

"It's the last of this model we have," she said, her expression earnest, her casual demeanor applying no sales pressure, and her look soft and direct. "It'll soon be hard to find."

He thanked her and left the store, feeling embarrassed for staring. *Get hold of yourself,* he thought. *It's just another pretty face.* The encounter left Mark in a pleasant but puzzled mood. The salesgirl in The Camera Shop was attractive, but he had known many attractive young women in high school. He dated some, taking them to ball games and movies with friends, and he had experienced all the emotional sentiments young men have for the attractive girls with whom they have close relationships. But at that time, his attention had moved from one to another with no particular interest to any one single person.

There was something unexplainably different and exciting about this young *Fräulein* that left him perplexed. He couldn't forget her pleasant, calm face or the quiet, modest way she looked at him when she talked. *It must be the excitement of being in a foreign country and first meeting an attractive girl,* he told himself. *It will soon pass.* He not only expected the allure to pass, but he looked forward to being free of it, because the strength of the feeling was a new experience for him. Such a strong attraction had never happened to him before, which left him mildly uncomfortable.

*   *   *

In spite of Mark's expectations, the brief meeting with the young woman continued to dominate his thoughts. That night the aura of the event had not weakened but stayed with him, leaving him fretful and restless. He had trouble drifting into sleep, his thoughts returning time and again to The Camera Shop. He remembered vividly every detail of her face and hair—the fair texture of her skin, the way her hair fell forward as she leaned over the counter pointing out the various cameras—and her soft, feminine voice resonated throughout his thoughts. An image of her youthful face, clear blue eyes, and unassuming expression appeared ghostlike, materializing and evaporating several times in his dreams. He tossed about awkwardly and awoke in a sweat, feeling strange and apprehensive.

By the following weekend, he had made up his mind to return to The Camera Shop. He had thought of little else the entire week and was determined to buy the Leica. When he arrived, she was there as he had hoped, and the camera was unsold. He asked her about a flash attachment, the range of the shutter speeds, and the cost of an appropriate filter. She answered each of his questions with patience and showed him all the details of the camera. *She really knows cameras*, he thought. When the conversation moved to photography in general, she lost her sales clerk professionalism, and they talked with a quiet enthusiasm.

"Black-and-white shots are my favorite," Mark said.

"Mine too!" she said, as if surprised. "Black and white can reveal the character of the scene so well."

"Yeah," Mark said, pleasantly pleased with the tone of the conversation. "It's fascinating how a snapshot can capture a unique event in time and place."

"Have you had any of your shots published?" she asked, obviously curious of Mark's status with photography.

"No," he said. "I'm just an amateur. But I can look at some of my old shots, and it's like I'm there again," he continued, laughing self-consciously, hoping she understood his meaning.

"Yes, photographs are a bit of life frozen in time," she said. "They're our way of holding on to what we value in our past." Mark didn't answer immediately, surprised with the quick way she picked up his meaning and the depth of her understanding. He had never thought of photography quite the way she described it, and it left him momentarily silent.

It turned out they had much in common, and she agreed to continue the conversation over coffee on her afternoon break. They met at a nearby café, and while sipping sugary coffee, they talked about their experiences with photography. After each had told their favorite stories about pictures they had taken, the conversation naturally turned in a personal direction. He told her he was nineteen years old and had grown up in the Queens Borough of New York, the only child of a second-generation Jewish couple who owned a moderately successful construction company. Her name was Lauren Werner. She had just turned seventeen and had grown up in Ellenbach, a village a short train ride west of the city. She attended school and worked and lived with her father who was a school master.

"I'd like to see you again," Mark said, walking her back to The Camera Shop. She didn't answer but studied him closely before looking away. When he left her at the shop, she politely thanked him for the coffee. Although she didn't acknowledge Mark's offer, her smile and warm handshake left him feeling good.

*   *   *

On the train ride back to post, Mark's thoughts turned inward, ignoring the other passengers and the passing scenery, brooding over the brief time with the young Fräulein. To think of her and dwell on her was very pleasant and left him with a good feeling. But in spite of this, he was growing more uncomfortable with the way he couldn't stop thinking of her. He instinctively resisted the obsession, telling himself he needed his focus to meet the demands of army life. *It'll soon pass*, he told himself. *I'll just look at it for what it was—a brief encounter.* But this young Fräulein was a compelling and bewildering experience that he didn't understand. He wanted to see her, but at the same time, he wanted to be free from constantly thinking of her.

Mark's life in general was going too fast. Several events had his head spinning and mired in confusion. When he considered the problems nagging him, he was astonished at what had transpired in the first month of his tour. This included a tough commanding officer who was planning something unknown and probably unpleasant for him; a confrontation with another soldier who swore to get him and do him harm; and finally, to fully complicate matters, he had met a beautiful young woman whom he couldn't get out of his mind. In the first few weeks of his two-year tour, his life had changed from that of a carefree young man to one burdened with bewildering situations he had no control over.

CHAPTER 4

"ONLY TWENTY-TWO MONTHS TILL ROTATION," Dave Myers said, laughing, holding his beer mug up for Herr Kuntz's attention. Dressed in his only civvies— jeans and a University of Wisconsin sweatshirt—he held the mug up until Herr Kuntz acknowledged the order. "We must drink to that!" he continued.

It was Saturday night, and the CO had kept the company on duty until mid afternoon as punishment for not performing well on a field exercise the previous day. The extra duty had built up a little tension, and Mark and his friends were letting off steam.

"So little time, so much beer," said Wade in his southern drawl, his face reflecting amusement with Myers's high spirits. They were at the *Gasthaus* Zumeck, an inn in a hill country village about forty kilometers from post. The village was called Brockmulbach and was a place introduced to them by their German soccer friends. The village had become their favorite off-post hangout. The proprietor, an older German named Herr Kuntz, always seemed glad to see them. They paid their bills and were reasonably well behaved—most of the time.

"No hurry," Mark said. "We don't have to drink the country dry this early in our tour." Although they were drinking freely, they were all well in control. After the CO's extra duty, they had played soccer for a time and worked up a thirst. They then drove up the mountain to Herr Kuntz's place for a meal and relaxation. Herr Kuntz's daughter kept polka music going on the juke box and had danced with Wade and Myers a couple of times. Mark had said he didn't feel like dancing, but he offered to keep the juke box going to maintain a party atmosphere. One of the German youths had challenged Sam Wade to a foot race, and everyone went out of the *Gasthaus* for a brief time to watch the race. With all the activity and food, the drinking had only a cheering effect on the group.

"A beer for my friend Dave," Herr Kuntz said, walking up with a mug of beer in one hand and a plate of cheese and sausages in the other. "Beer for comrade Mark?" he asked, looking at Mark's near-empty mug.

"No, not quite ready," Mark said. Although he usually matched the others beer for beer, he was drinking slower. After the demanding activity of the soccer game was over, leaving his thoughts free, he had become preoccupied. His moodiness had begun a few days before, and it left him without the raucous spirit of the others. The *Fräulein* at The Camera Shop was a growing presence in his thoughts, and no matter how he tried, he couldn't get her deep blue eyes and quiet smile out of his thoughts.

Today he would have stayed in the barracks, but Myers reminded him of his promise to play soccer with their German friends. He had given in to their pleas only after they said they wouldn't have enough players if he didn't come along. The camaraderie developed among his fellow soldiers exerted upon him a strong sense of obligation to the platoon. He welcomed and enjoyed the camaraderie, but at the same time, he felt a pull at his sense of independence. It was hard to deny the will of the group when you soldier together, he had come to realize.

"I'll drive back to post," Mark said to Myers after Herr Kuntz announced closing time. "I know you're exhausted from lifting all those mugs." Myers had bought a secondhand Austin Healy just two weeks prior with money saved from his army salary and a pre-army job as a grocery delivery boy. Although Mark's father would have staked him the price of a car, Mark didn't feel he needed one. Being from New York City and accustomed to subways and busses, the German train system was all he needed.

"Are you kidding?" Myers said, frowning. "Me tired? Never! I just need one more to clear up my night vision." He looked around for Herr Kuntz. "And don't worry; I've trained my Healy to drive itself."

The road back to post was narrow and winding and at one point came down out of the hills to intersect at a crossroad in a village of a few houses and one *Gasthaus*. It was a moonlit night with only occasional clouds obscuring the moonlight, and descending down from the mountain into the lowlands, patches of fog hung in random spots along the way. The road would be clear and visible in the headlights one minute and the next be hidden by patches of white vapor. The patches were generally just brief white clouds that came and went quickly. As Myers drove, Mark was relieved that he let up on the accelerator when entering one of the fog patches and then resumed normal speed when coming out of the mist.

"Driving through these fog patches is like driving through a snow storm," Wade said, leaning forward from his backseat position to peer through the windshield. "Slow down when you enter one, Dave."

"Yeah, I'm doing just that," Myers said, his attention focused sharply on the road ahead. "Problem is you can't see them until you right up on them" he continued.

They exited a section of the mist and drove on for about ten minutes without encountering another one. Myers had resumed normal night driving speed, and they were almost out of the hills and getting close to the *Gasthaus* at the intersection when Mark spoke up: "Here comes another one, Dave."

Myers immediately let up on the accelerator as they were enveloped by a wall of white mist. The smoke-like mist clung around them as they moved through the night. Suddenly, a vague image appeared in the tunnel of illumination created by the car's headlights. It was only an instant blur that came out of the fog and appeared for a split second in the road before them. The blur came from nowhere, only a flash, then came a jarring crash with the sound of windshield shattering and glass flying around them and into their faces.

Mark shouted, "We hit something! Stop the car, Dave!" But Myers drove on, not slowing down. Looking around, from the glow of the dash lights, Mark could see small, bloody cuts developing on Myers's face. He seemed dazed and unfocused. The windshield on Myers's side of the car had caved in back to the steering wheel and had cut his hands slightly, and a small amount of blood was appearing there as well. "Stop the car!" Mark shouted again. Myers didn't seem to comprehend what had happened or what Mark was saying.

"He's stunned!" Mark shouted. "I've got to stop the car!" Myers stared straight ahead, gripping the steering wheel and blinking his eyes as he drove on.

They were approaching the crossroads without Myers slowing the car when Mark reached over and turned the ignition key. "Stop the car!" he shouted again.

By the time the car rolled to a stop at the intersection, smoke and steam were boiling out from under the crushed hood and grill. The acrid smell of burnt rubber and antifreeze permeated the air. Mark stepped out of the car, assessed the situation, and shouted at Wade to check on Myers while he went for help.

Going to the *Gasthaus* and calling back to post for help only took Mark a few minutes. Returning to the car, which was still releasing white steam from its damaged front end, he found Wade and Myers standing outside. Myers's face and hands were bleeding from several small cuts. "Are you okay?" Mark asked.

"He's coming out of it now," Wade said. "I think he was in shock."

"Yeah, but he needs medical attention," Mark said. "I called the company CQ; he's sending an ambulance and the MPs."

"What happened?" Myers asked, still dazed. Other than facial and hand lacerations, he didn't appear to be seriously injured.

"We've hit something," Wade said. "Probably a deer."

After he looked Myers over and felt that he was going to be all right, Mark asked Wade to stay with Myers while he went back up the road to see what they had collided with. He had gone several hundred yards without seeing anything in the road when it occurred to him that anything like a deer or cow would have been knocked off the road into the ditch. Retracing his steps and scanning each side of the road, he finally saw a form lying off to one side in the short grass.

Mark could see the form to be that of a man, his upturned face reflecting the moonlight but his body twisted and motionless, one leg turned oddly back beneath the other and an arm bent weirdly over his chest. In the bright moonlight, he could see a black area in the dirt and sparse grass around the body. Knowing the black area to be blood leaving the man's body, Mark stared at the motionless form a few seconds, struggling to get his thoughts together and hoping the scene wasn't real. Finally, the countless hours of military training kicked in, and his mind raced with emergency and medical procedures. First he considered the position of the body as being out of further harm from another oncoming vehicle; next, first aid procedures came to mind. But when he checked the neck pulse, he could only stand up and stare down helplessly at the lifeless form, knowing there was nothing he could do. Wade and Myers came running up.

"What was it?" Wade asked. "A cow?" He then paused as he stared at the body lying on the ground.

"No pulse," Mark said, looking from Wade back to the dead man.

They stared at the lifeless body without speaking for a moment. "What can we do?" Myers asked. He turned and walked a few steps from the scene, as if blotting it out of sight and mind.

"Nothing now," Mark said. "I wish there were, but there's not."

"There's another!" Myers said suddenly, looking around and pointing to a shadowy image twenty feet away in the shallow ditch beside the road. This one was face down in the dirt, and like the other, there was a black area forming around the body.

Wade hurried to the spot and bent over the body. He then turned back to the others. "No pulse here either!"

"Can't we do anything?" Myers said again, his voice breaking. "My God, I did this! It's my fault!" he continued in a shrill voice.

"Get hold of yourself, Dave," Mark said sharply. "It's nobody's fault. The best we can do is stay calm."

"Mark's right," Wade said in a firm voice directly to Myers. "Stay calm!"

"As much as I'd like to, there's nothing we can do," Mark repeated. "All we can do is wait for the ambulance and the MPs."

Wade was silent for a moment and then asked, "I wonder who they were."

Mark walked back to the first body that lay face up. In the clear moonlight, he could see the face of a young man, the complexion of the once fair face turning to the gray of its death color in the yellow moonlight. *He looks familiar*, Mark thought. *Could he be one of the boys we played soccer with this afternoon?* He quickly turned away, angrily forcing the thought from his mind, his subconscious defensively rejecting any familiarity with the dead men. Wade and Myers were silent, as if dealing with the situation in their own ways.

The three men then stood fixedly on the mountain road, talking quietly in the moonlight, waiting for help to arrive. The air had chilled, and the night closed in around them. On all sides was darkness and silence. Without intentionally doing anything out of the ordinary or harboring any ill will, fate had just laid out a new and unknown path for their lives to follow, and there was no changing that.

CHAPTER 5

THE FOLLOWING MORNING AS REVEILLE was breaking up, First Sergeant Andrade told the three men to report to his office. He had already received the MP's report and wanted to question each man about the accident. He had them wait outside the orderly room and then brought them in one at a time so each could state his view of what happened. After questioning the three men separately and together, he seemed satisfied that the incident was unavoidable and told the three his morning report to the CO would reflect that.

"But don't think this matter is over," he said before he dismissed them. "There will be an investigation forthcoming, and it will be methodical and exhaustive," he emphasized.

As they left the orderly room, the mail clerk, who was sorting mail in the outer office, said, "You three have letters. Might as well get them now."

Mark was beginning to put together the events of the night before. His mind-set accepted the reality that they had killed two men but had in no way, other than being on that road at that time and place, caused the accident. He felt sympathy for the victims and a dark foreboding concern for what was to come, but he knew there was nothing more that could be done. They had followed all required procedures following the accident, and now he and the others must carry on the best they could with what lay ahead.

He took his letter, and telling Wade and Myers he'd catch up with them later, sat down on the running board of a weapons carrier parked nearby. The letter was thick, and he knew there would be much news from home. It was the first response he'd received from a letter he had written home describing the many sights he'd seen since arriving in Germany. He had mentioned in this letter that he had found the Leica he had been looking for and also that he had met an attractive, young German *Fräulein* in the shop where he had found the camera.

The letter from home began by telling him of family happenings and news from the neighborhood. His mother mentioned a Greek family had moved onto their block, and she was concerned because their neighborhood had always been Jewish. "They're nice people," she had said, "but they're so different."

The next page was a section his father had written. He was concerned for Mark's future and had it all laid out for him. He said he had had several conversations with the chancellor at NYU and was assured that Mark would be given all considerations possible for enrollment the year his tour of duty was up. Mark sensed his father's humor coming through when he continued with, "Of course, the contribution I made to the College of Business and Economics didn't influence his decision, I'm sure." The letter continued, "The point is, you're set at NYU, and we'll be proud to have our son attend this great university."

"Right now education is the least of my problems, Pops," Mark said to himself. He smiled as he thought of his father. He'd always had a warm relationship with him, and an image of his serious, lined faced with heavy eyebrows and kind eyes lightened Mark's mood.

The following page was again from his mother. She wrote: "Mark, you wrote that you have met an attractive German girl in a camera shop. We realize that you have to get along with the citizens of that country, but please don't get involved with them. They are not our kind."

Just below these lines was taped a faded black-and-white photograph so that the photo could be flipped up to read the words beneath it. Mark looked at the photograph. There was an elderly man at the center, and grouped around him were a young man and woman with two children who looked to be six or eight years of age. No one was smiling. All had solemn looks and stared intensely at the camera. Their faces and posture reflected no emotions or attitudes, the one exception being the body language of the young couple where each clutched a child, holding them close. Mark had never seen the picture before and did not recognize any of the people photographed there. He studied the picture a moment and then chuckled quietly, judging the picture from the perspective of his own photographic experience.

"They could have used a better photographer to cheer up their pose," he said under his breath as he flipped the picture up to continue reading.

He had read but a few lines before his lighthearted mood vanished. He looked away for a moment before continuing. "There are things we have never told you about my family," his mother had written. "But now we feel you should know. This was my father and my youngest brother and his family. They lived in Warsaw. In the last letter we received from them years ago, we received this photograph. Treasure it greatly, for they were your family." Without reading further, Mark sat on the running board of the truck and stared blankly at the distant sky, his feelings cold with the knowledge of the way life was.

CHAPTER 6

THE FOLLOWING WEEKEND MARK RETURNED to Frankfurt. He had struggled all week, unable to decide if he should try to see her again after she refused his first offer. His thoughts had gone back and forth between telling himself to forget the whole thing and the more pleasant thought of seeing her. He would go for a time with the idea of getting over his infatuation and feeling the relief of a free mind, and then he'd remember details of their brief encounter and wanted to see her again. He wanted to stop thinking of her but wanted to see her. He had never before experienced such a confused and paradoxical state of mind.

Since Saturday was the only day he had enough free time to go into the city while she was working, he decided he had to make his move and try again to get together with her. On the train ride into the city, Mark kept telling himself that nothing was going to work out, while on the other hand, he had counter thoughts that wondered what he had to lose. He went straight to The Camera Shop from the train station. Lauren was working as usual, and he busied himself studying a photography magazine while she finished with a middle-aged man buying a camera strap. When it was time for Mark to be waited on, she came to the magazine rack.

"I happened to be close by and stopped in to get some film," he said.

"We have film," she said smiling, her eyes reflecting a familiarity that made him feel good. She was dressed in a gray skirt that emphasized her slim, feminine figure and a blue sweater that accentuated her fair complexion and blond hair. Her smile was encouraging.

The store was empty of customers, and Herr Clause, the store owner, was hanging a display on the wall across the room. Mark and Lauren struck up a conversation about the grainy effects of blowing up negatives to bring in the subject. He had timed his arrival to be just before her afternoon break, and when he asked if she would have coffee with him, she agreed. They drank coffee at the usual place; the café waiter recognized them from their previous visit and greeted them pleasantly. They sipped the coffee and chatted casually as if they were old friends.

During the previous week, Mark had considered topics he could bring up with her to enliven their conversations. Photography was already working for him, but he wanted to broaden the subjects they could talk in order to help them get better acquainted. He had read widely since being in the army and decided that books might be one she would relate to. When their conversation slowed, he mentioned, "I've been reading a lot lately."

"Oh," she said, showing interest. "And what are you reading?"

"Well, I'm reading a German author now," Mark said. "Remarque's *All Quiet on the Western Front*."

Lauren remained silent, looking at him with a blank face.

"Well, I guess you haven't read that one," Mark said, immediately sensing he had said something wrong. "Let's see, what did I read before that one?" he continued, struggling to think of a book she might have read.

"I've read Remarque," she said suddenly. Her face remained blank. "But I prefer not to discuss that one. It brings bad memories."

"I'm sorry," Mark said, unsure of what he had done wrong. He struggled to think of some book that would give them something to discuss. They sat without speaking for a moment.

Finally Lauren spoke. "Have you read *War and Peace?*" She spoke quietly and timidly, as if she were unsure of herself when asking that.

"Oh yes! Yes, I've read that!" Mark said, relieved they had found something in common. "I had all this free time on the ship coming over, and I read that long book."

"You've read *War and Peace!*" Lauren said, laughing happily. She smiled with surprise and pleasure in her eyes. "You're the only other person I know who's read that book!" she continued, still laughing freely.

"Yep, every page," Mark said, feeling good now that she seemed happy. "I will admit, though, I sometimes got bored with some of the long passages of things like battlefield terrain and scenes of the countryside."

"Yes," Lauren said, "but those same descriptive powers of Tolstoy were so effective in portraying the tenderness and love of Natasha and Maria as they cared for the dying Prince Andrei."

"I agreed," Mark said, taking note of her instant recall and critical opinion of the story.

They both grew silent for a brief moment, silently sipping their coffee, their faces reflecting the relief and pleasure they felt by finding common ground in the reading world. Finally, Lauren said, "I should get back to the shop now. I've enjoyed our time together, today." Her eyes had a warmth and brightness to them as she spoke, and that cheered and encouraged Mark.

"Lauren, wait," Mark said as she pushed her chair back to stand. "There's something I'd like to ask you."

"Yes?"

"Lauren, I know a restaurant that has good food and soft jazz music," he said, leaning forward slightly. "Go with me tonight."

She looked at him a moment before letting her eyes drop. After deliberately taking the table napkin from her lap, folding it, and carefully placing it on the table, she looked up. "I'm sorry, Mark," she said slowly. "I have plans."

Again, Mark felt deeply disappointed, but he worked to appear normal. "Maybe some other time then," he said casually. When they parted back at her shop, she paused at the shop door, chatting happily. Her smile and lingering handshake consoled him, and he left with a resolve to keep trying.

The following week Mark went through his duty hours with Lauren on his mind, as usual. None of the military duty taxed his energy or spirit to the point of distracting his thoughts for long. The morning runs and calisthenics, the military classes, endless field training—he performed them all precisely and appropriately without thought. After duty hours, barracks wisecracks and friendly pokes were a constant occurrence, and most evenings Mark, Myers, and Wade spent a few hours drinking and cutting up with others at the Enlisted Men's Club. But unless they were in a scheduled alert, where all personnel are restricted to post and combat ready, Mark's Class A Pass gave him free weekends. He planned to spend most of his weekends in the city.

The following Saturday he again went to The Camera Shop, and he and Lauren had coffee and spent some time talking. But just as before, when he asked her to have dinner with him, she refused, saying she had plans.

This became a routine for Mark. Whenever he could get away from post, he would find some excuse to visit her shop, and each time, Lauren would consent to spend her break with him. Their brief times together were always pleasant; they were both well-read and could discuss books easily, and with their common interest in photography, they never ran out of things to talk about. But she continued to decline his offer to get together after work. Mark was perplexed. She seemed to enjoy his company; he could see it in her face and smile and hear it in the way they talked. She showed it and he sensed it, but it didn't seem to matter. *Why won't she see me after work?* he asked himself over and over.

Finally, Mark decided he was never going to get any closer to Lauren than their trips to the coffee shop. He greatly enjoyed their time together, but he wanted to take their relationship to the next step, and now that seemed less and less likely. *She must be committed to someone. Just her good looks would mean she would have many admirers,* he told himself. *I'll just have to move on.* Dejected and feeling angry and foolish, Mark decided he wouldn't go back.

*   *   *

His resolve to get past Lauren stood firm through the following week. Instead of catching the train to Frankfurt on Saturday, he went with Myers and Wade to the village of Freiberg, which was celebrating a *Fasching* Fest. The village was small but had two *Gasthauses* that had the ancient fests going strong with some of the citizens dressed in colorful costumes and everyone having a good time. They went from one crowded *Gasthaus* to the next, enjoying the merriment while drinking beer and taking photos. It just so happened that during one particular polka, as an energetic couple twirled about, they bumped the table where Mark had left his camera unattended, knocking it to the floor. The fall broke the camera's shutter mechanism, and he was faced with finding a shop that could repair a Leica camera.

At first, Mark refused to go back to The Camera Shop. He tried the Post Exchange camera department, and they said they would have to send it back to the factory to get it repaired. Knowing sending it out would mean he'd be without his camera for a month, he decided to return to Frankfurt to find a shop that repaired cameras. The following Saturday he made the trip back to the city to the address the PX sales attendant had suggested. Once there, the salesman looked at the camera and said it was still in warranty, but to benefit from the warranty's policy, he would have to take it back to the shop where he had made the purchase. Mark now had no choice but to return to The Camera Shop.

When Mark entered the shop, Lauren was tending to two young German men who were examining a tripod. It had been several weeks since he had bought the camera and had first asked Lauren to go out with him in the evening. It had been two weeks since he had last seen her. She glanced at him when he entered but didn't speak or acknowledge his presence. When the two men left carrying the tripod, Mark approached the counter. He was determined to do what he had to do and leave.

"I've had an accident with my camera," he said, setting the camera before Lauren, his face showing no emotions.

Lauren's eyes stayed on Mark's face for a moment before they dropped to examine the camera. She clicked the mechanism and turned the device around one time.

"The shutter mechanism is broken," she said softly, holding the camera up to Mark. "We can replace that."

"Okay," Mark said, casually. "I'll pick it up next trip in." He was intent on getting the camera business over with and catching the next train back to post.

"Okay, I'll tag it 'rush,'" she said. She then gave him a receipt, and he turned to leave. As he opened the door, Lauren called out, "Mark, wait!"

Mark turned, waiting. He thought she needed more information for the repair work. He knew it was too early for her afternoon break.

"It's about time for my afternoon break," she said, obviously ignoring her regular break time. She paused a moment, and when

Mark didn't speak, she continued. "Would you go with me to the coffee shop?"

"Yeah . . . yeah, I have time," he said, casually. Mark was uncomfortable with her request. He had his mind set that he was going to get the camera work started and leave, but common courtesy overcame his feelings of rejection, and he agreed to go with her.

They went back to the same café that was only a few doors from her shop. As they sipped their coffee, Lauren made cheerful small talk, but Mark said little and only nodded occasionally to show he was listening. He noticed she had a quizzical look at times, but he didn't think much about it. Lauren carried the conversation the entire time they were at the café. Soon they left and returned to her shop.

"I'll pick up the camera next Saturday," Mark said as he held the door for her to enter the shop. "I need to get back to post now."

Lauren nodded and entered the shop. She paused a moment and then turned back to Mark, as if she wanted to say something. But when she turned, Mark had already walked away and was striding up the street.

CHAPTER 7

Although Mark, Wade, and Myers knew the accident was being investigated, they agreed to keep it as quiet as possible, expecting the Investigation Board to declare it as an unavoidable event. The first sergeant told them that Captain Williams was furious but was waiting the outcome of the board before he gave his opinion on the incident. In spite of this, not knowing what was going on still weighed heavily on the minds of the three men. This was especially true in the case of Dave Myers, who had been driving the car at the time of the accident.

Several days following the meeting with the first sergeant, Lieutenant McBride ordered Mark, Wade, and Myers to stand fast as he dismissed the platoon at morning reveille. "You three men have been ordered to report to the provost marshal at 1000," McBride said. "Take one hour and report back here at this spot with starched fatigues. Look your best!"

"Sir," Mark said, "may I ask what this is all about?"

"It's about the accident you were involved in awhile back," McBride said. "You're to be questioned by the provost marshal's office."

"But, sir, we have already given the MPs our statements," Myers said. "Has something new developed?"

"I don't know," McBride said. "I've been ordered to bring you to the provost marshal's office, so get moving. I'll have a jeep waiting." He turned to leave but then turned back to the three. "Whatever you do, don't make my platoon look bad," he said. "If you do, you've got trouble with me."

Mark and the others went to the barracks and dressed in the fatigues they kept in reserves for impromptu inspections. They brushed their boots to look the best they could. They were not only worried about the upcoming interview but about Lieutenant McBride as well. Their platoon leader had the reputation of being very tough on any soldier who made him look bad. He would make life miserable for anyone in his outfit who screwed up.

The provost marshal's office was located at Regimental Headquarters, a fifteen-minute drive from Charlie Company. When they entered the outer office for the provost marshal, they found two MPs sitting at desks that had only one clipboard atop each. The nearest MP stood up and approached them with his clipboard when they entered the room. He was dressed in Class As with boots bloused and white sidearm holster and web belt. He asked their business in a clipped, business-like voice. While McBride explained their purpose there, Myers whispered to Mark, "Parade MPs."

"Yeah, but let's not get them on our case," Mark whispered back. "We have enough problems already."

The provost marshal was a lieutenant colonel, and he sat behind his desk unsmiling as McBride reported for the group. He was a thin, dark man who wore glasses that looked like something a grandfather would wear. But underneath the comical glasses, his eyes and overall demeanor were coldly serious. He had each of their 201 files on his desk. He told them he had already examined their records and found them in order. He then talked to them in a conversational manner, asking questions that were seemingly unrelated to any serious investigation. Then he talked to each of the three separately. He spent most of his time with Myers. After a few minutes, he dismissed them but asked McBride to remain a moment.

"That was easy," Myers said on the way back to Charlie Company. Myers sat in the backseat with Mark, while Wade drove and McBride sat to his right.

"What'd he ask you, Dave?" Mark asked, turning to Myers.

"We talked for a while," Myers began. "At first, it was just ordinary talk. Then he had some serious questions. He asked me how I was getting along after the accident, and I told him I was very sad and was having trouble sleeping at night. Then he asked something strange. He asked if I had ever been a member of a gang or if I had ever been arrested before I joined the army. Did he ask you guys any questions like that?"

"Not with me," said Wade as he maneuvered the jeep around a truck. "All he asked me was if I played sports in high school. I told him I played football, and we talked about that for a couple minutes. That's all."

"Yeah, all he asked me was what I planned to do after the army," Mark said. "I told him I hoped to get into NYU."

A worried look came across Myers's face.

"He was checking you out," McBride said. "He wanted to get a sense of what kind of people you are. I'm really surprised with this procedure for an accident."

"Checking us out?" Myers asked, his face showing more concern. "Why's he interested in what kind of people we are?'

"The real question is, why is the provost marshal himself conducting an inquiry?" McBride said. He stared straight ahead in deep thought as Wade drove through the street traffic. Finally, after a couple minutes, he suddenly spoke again. "This is highly irregular, this provost marshal interview and all. Auto accidents are not that unusual. They're investigated, and if no fault is found, they're closed out. That's it! There has to be something involved with this case we don't know about."

"What could that be?" Myers asked. "And why did he grill me more than you guys?"

"I don't know," McBride said. He grew quiet for a moment and then added, "He told me that one of the victims was the son of the *Bürgermeister*."

The three enlisted men grew silent with this news. Finally, Mark spoke. "Being a *Bürgermeister*, he might be making demands."

"I don't like it," McBride said quietly. No one else spoke.

CHAPTER 8

AFTER THE INTERVIEW WITH THE provost marshal, Dave
Myers became more and more despondent over his
situation and the situation in general. His sadness over the
death of the two men in the accident was depressing him and not
knowing how the army viewed the incident at higher levels worried
him also. He became withdrawn and moody and was easily irritated.
After duty hours, he wouldn't go to the EM Club or off post with
Mark and Wade, telling them he'd rather stay in the barracks and
write letters or read. When he did go out, he preferred to be alone
and would avoid the bars closest to the main gate, the gate First
Battalion used. He did this because he didn't want to run into
anyone he knew. He told himself he would get through this, but
until then, he just wanted to be alone and think.

Two blocks to the west of their main gate was gate two, another
post gate that was used by Second Battalion and other elements of
the post. Outside this gate were several bars frequented by personnel
from these outfits. Dave knew that he wouldn't run into anyone he
knew in this area, because most First Battalion personnel used the

main gate to come and go from post. He also knew that Mark and Wade almost never frequented these noisy GI bars; they preferred the German *Gasthauses* in the villages away from the post. On a Friday night after a busy week in Charlie Company, Dave decided to walk the few blocks to the gate two area and have a few beers by himself.

He entered the first bar he came to and found it packed with soldiers sitting at tables and standing around in clusters. The room was well lit but filled with gray smoke that colored the air like fog. The reverberating chatter of many voices rose and fell and merged with music from the juke box that typified GI bars on a busy night. After working his way to the bar and ordering his first beer, Dave stood and looked about the room. A few of the soldiers there were dressed in civilian clothes, but most were in OD uniforms or fatigues, as if they had just gotten off duty.

A spirited conversation was coming from four soldiers sitting at a table just to Dave's right. Through the noise he could make out that they were arguing over the difference between the New York Yankees and the Brooklyn Dodgers. One soldier was waving a five-dollar bill in another's face as if trying to get a bet going. A cluster of soldiers stood just beyond this table, and one guy said something that had the rest laughing loudly. Dave felt good that he didn't recognize a single face before him. He was away from it all now—the accident, the provost marshal's interview, the not knowing—everything seemed a little less important now. He relaxed and let his look drift about the room.

He ordered his third beer, and after a few sips, he turned back to watch the activity in the room. A group of soldiers had moved before him on his right, blocking his view in that direction. He then turned his attention to the left side of the room. In this direction, there were many tables crowded with soldiers who were drinking and talking. There were no standing clusters, so Dave had a clear view across the room to the front entrance. As he stood looking across the room, a Doris Day song came on the juke box. He like the song, and with half his beer gone, he was beginning to relax. Just as the melodious song lyrics were reaching "whatever will be, will be," Dave suddenly froze. While his glance was casually drifting about the room, his look had locked onto a familiar face that left him cold. He quickly looked away and tried not to look back. But soon he was compelled to look again. There before him in the crowd was the man from the soccer match a few weeks before who had sworn to get him. Dave remembered his name as Ricco.

Dave quickly turned away, knowing he best get out of the bar. Ricco was sitting near the front entrance, so he knew he couldn't exit that way. Instead, Dave walked around the bar and down a hallway where the latrines were, hoping to find a back entrance. He found a back door and stepped out the door into an alleyway. The clean, cool air felt good as he walked toward the front of the building. He didn't think Ricco had seen him, but Dave didn't want to take any chances. He would avoid anyone he might meet in front of the bar. On the street, Dave had to walk back by the front entrance to the bar in order to head back to the main gate and Charlie Company. There was light at the building's entrance, and he didn't see anyone ahead of him on the sidewalk. He hurried forward, intent on getting past the bar's entrance as quickly as possible. But just as he reached the circle of light before the building, Ricco suddenly stepped from behind a sign into the light facing him.

"I've got you now, you little jerk," Ricco said, a small, twisted smile developing on his face. He stood directly before Dave, his shoulders hunched, his stance ready. "I knew my time was coming."

"Stay away from me, you creep," Dave said. Dave was angry but afraid; he knew he was no match for the bigger man.

"I've got you now, and I'll get your friends next," Ricco said again, his lips curling farther back on his teeth as his sadistic grin grew.

"Stay away, you son of a bitch," Myers said, his heart pumping, his thoughts racing to escape. His mind said run, but somehow he didn't.

Ricco quickly move forward and clutched Dave's shirt. Dave swung hard, getting in the first punch. But he hardly saw Ricco's counterpunch before he went unconscious.

* * *

When Mark and Wade entered the aid station, Lieutenant McBride was already there. They had just returned from off post when the CQ told them Myers had been beaten up and was at the post hospital. McBride was standing at the entrance to the emergency room talking to an MP when they walked up.

"So what did this witness say?" McBride asked the MP.

"He said he was across the street from the ruckus when he saw this big guy hitting this little guy," the MP said. "Said the little guy was trying to hit back but was overpowered by the big guy."

"Did he see who the big guy was?"

"The witness said by the time he and his friends could get across the street, the big guy had just walked away, leaving the little guy unconscious."

Mark and Wade went into the room where Myers lay propped up in a bed. The injuries on Dave's face had already been dressed and covered in white bandages. The bandage across his forehead had a red smear where some blood had leaked through. Both his eyes were swollen almost shut and were purple and blue. The hair on the left side of his head was shaved to the scalp where a cut had been treated and stitched up. The doctor was giving Dave a shot as they walked up.

"You've had a bad time, but this will make you feel better," the doctor was saying as he finished with the hypodermic and laid it in a tray by the bedside. "You're going to be okay," he continued as Mark and Wade approached the bedside. "I'm putting you in the hospital, and we'll see how you do for a few days." He then nodded at Dave and walked out but stopped to talk to McBride.

"What happened, Dave?" Mark asked immediately. "Who jumped you?"

"Yeah, who did this?" Wade asked, going around to the other side of the bed.

Dave tried to smile but stopped, the act obviously causing him pain. "All present and accounted for, sir," he said finally as he made a mock salute with his good arm. His attempt at humor came as a pleasurable result of the morphine the doctor had just given him.

"Cut the clowning, Dave," Wade said. "Who did this?"

"Well," Dave began. His mouth was swollen, and he had difficulty talking. "Well, you won't believe me when I tell you."

"Try me!" Mark said quickly.

"Remember that guy at our first soccer match in Charlie?"

"What guy?" Mark asked.

At that moment, McBride came back into the room. "The MP said that no charges could be filed, because it was an off-post altercation," he began. "On post, it's a court-martial offence, except in self defense, but that is not the case here. I'm writing this up as an unprovoked attack by this jerk Ricco in Second Battalion."

"Ricco!" Mark said, looking from McBride back to Dave.

"And I'm going to get with his platoon leader on this," McBride continued. "I want to know more about this guy."

"Yeah, Mark, it was Ricco," Dave mumbled. He was almost incoherent, his voice weak and his eyes nearly closed from the morphine shot. Then just before he went under, he added, "And he's coming after you or Sam next."

CHAPTER 9

Lauren's reluctance to be with Mark beyond work came not only because he was a new and intense experience that she hadn't had time to get used to but also because of her father, Herr Werner, and the way he had brought her up. The war had cost Herr Werner and his family much. At the beginning, there were five of them. By the time it was over, he only had Lauren. She was his life, and he wanted to pass on to her all the advantages his training and intellect could offer. Further, he had lived in the village of Ellenbach his entire life, and he couldn't imagine Lauren not doing the same.

"Someday I hope you will marry a young German man and live close by," he told her one night at supper.

"Oh, Papa," Lauren said, laughing while drinking her milk. "I want to marry a prince and live in a castle." But when she noticed her father's look of disappointment, she quickly added, "But it will be a German prince, and we will live close by." She learned early how to please her father.

Herr Werner had a peculiar background. As a young boy, he had almost severed his left leg while chopping wood. Being inexperienced and standing awkwardly as he worked, he had let a glancing blow catch his leg, sinking the axe blade down next to the bone. The sharp blade had severed muscles and tendons, leaving him unable to walk for a long spell and with a permanent, shuffling limp. Not being able to get about and do normal chores and interact with others, he became a near recluse and spent most of his time studying his schoolwork and reading widely. This studious exposure during his formative years developed an intellectual nature within him that, as he grew older, put him above those around him in intelligence and insight. For this reason, his parents encouraged and educated him to become a schoolteacher.

His physical handicap and his teaching position exempted him from military duty, and he spent the war years working as an educator. At first, he spoke out against Germany's militarism, but he soon learned that speaking against the government put him and his family in danger, so he kept his political opinions to himself. Not being able to prove his patriotism militarily, he immersed himself in German culture exclusively and expounded it openly.

When Lauren entered high school, he avoided her classrooms so as to give her room to grow both socially and scholastically. But when they were home together, he constantly encouraged her to read and to think. And his tendency to expand a dialogue on the greatness of Germany was not limited to the schoolhouse; he brought it home to Lauren.

"Who was the greatest composer?" he would sometimes quiz Lauren when she was a young girl.

"Why that would be Beethoven, Papa," Lauren would quickly answer. She not only knew her history, but she knew what her father wanted to hear. "But don't forget Bach and Wagner," she would continue, giggling. Lauren grew up under such constant tutorship, relentlessly playing studious games that taught her facts and concepts of history, philosophy, and most any subject related to Germany.

"And who were the greatest philosophers?" He might surprise her with questions at odd times, such as walking home from school or at the dinner table. But even if they were unexpected, his questions were always asked in a cheerful and playful manner.

"Why that would be Kant and Nietzsche," Lauren would promptly answer, ready to play his games. "And don't forget Leibniz, Papa," she might continue while laughing, as if to tease him back.

"And what about Kant and Nietzsche," he asked her one day, as if to test her further. "What can you say about these great Germans?"

"Well, I can't say a whole lot about them," Lauren answered, looking thoughtful and thinking deeply. "Except I prefer Kant's explanation that things can be better explained using experience and reason than the negative ideas of Nietzsche."

After responding to his questions in these scholarly sessions, Lauren would then wait, smiling, as if happy at the pleasure she saw on his face. This process of perceiving her father's reasons and motivations early in life later developed insight and understanding of others that provided her intelligence and maturity beyond her age. Such exposure to scholarly pursuits also produced two distinct characteristics in her personality: she developed a strong sense of duty to family and country, and she became a brilliant student.

From the beginning, Herr Werner taught her to not fraternize with soldiers. In fact, he not only taught her to not associate with soldiers, but he adamantly forbid her to do so. "The soldiers are from a different background, a different culture, and a different way of life," he told his young daughter. "Stay with your own; they are more likely to be your friend and protector."

In spite of this early education, Lauren had her own opinions about people outside her friends and family, instinctively knowing there were good and bad in all groups and cultures. Her reading was wide and thought provoking, and her day-to-day contact with people in the city, at work, and on her commute reinforced this knowledge. But she cared deeply for her father and always wanted to please him. And she knew exactly what it took to do this. "My friends are those at my school and my family," she told him many times.

"That's right," he answered her each time. "They are more likely your friends, because they are German and have the same heritage as you."

After meeting Mark, Lauren began to think more about Americans and how they lived and how they were different from Germans. Most of the American soldiers that came into The Camera Shop were much the same as her German customers. As a matter of fact, she mused, they were just as polite but didn't seem to argue as much about the cost of things as the Germans did. One night at the evening meal, Lauren decided to discuss the difference between Americans and Germans with her father.

"Papa," she began, "why don't you like Americans? They are polite and fair when they come into the shop."

"Oh, I don't dislike Americans in general," he said, putting the paper he was reading down and looking at Lauren. "They're about the same as other foreigners."

"But, Papa, just because they're foreigners and from another country doesn't mean they're so different, does it?"

"Yes, they're different," he said looking at her closely. "They're different because they're not German."

"But wouldn't I be one of them if I lived in their country and spoke their language?"

"No," he said adamantly, frowning seriously at Lauren. "You'll always be German, and they will always think of you as German. That is your heritage, and you can't escape your heritage."

CHAPTER 10

Mark's last visit to The Camera Shop had left Lauren confused and troubled. His polite but formal attitude was a change from his usual easygoing and attentive manner, and she felt responsible. Mark had been persistently pursuing her for two months, but she was afraid now that her repeated refusals to join him for a movie or dinner were beginning to discourage him. In spite of liking him considerably, thinking of him often, and always enjoying his company, she remained hesitant. Lauren was hesitant not only because her father forbid her from fraternizing with the soldiers. As much as she cared and respected her father, she would have disobeyed him—such was the strength of her feelings. She was hesitant because of the way Mark made her feel. It was such a new and powerful experience that she was afraid she wouldn't deal with it properly if left alone with him.

Thus, Lauren wanted to be with him but was afraid to be alone with him. This emotional paradox troubled her and left her worried and insecure. But as the days went by, a situation developed that presented her a chance to be with him in the safety of a crowd.

In her language class, where for some time they had been studying English, her teacher, Frau Keller, had promised the students she would find someone whose native language was English to talk to the class. In explaining the reasons for bringing in someone, Frau Keller had said it was an effective teaching technique that would offer the students an opportunity to exercise their English speaking skills in a real-life situation. Lauren said she knew such a person and could invite him to visit their class. Frau Keller said she trusted Lauren's judgment and agreed to her proposal. She went on to say that she'd been unable to find someone whose native language was English and was willing to take the time to come to their school.

A few days later, Mark came by The Camera Shop to pick up his camera. While he examined the shutter operation, Lauren carefully began her plea for help. "Mark, there's something I want to ask you."

"Yes?" Mark said, looking over the camera.

"At my school, we're studying English," Lauren continued. She stopped, unsure of herself.

"Yes, go on."

"My teacher, Frau Keller, has promised the class she would find someone whose native language is English to speak to the class."

"Good idea," Mark said casually, as he clicked the camera shutter a couple of times.

"She's promised this, but she has not been able to find anyone who will come and speak to us."

"That's too bad," Mark said as he open the camera and peered inside the mechanism.

"Mark, would you come and speak—" Lauren became embarrassed then and didn't finish her sentence. She could tell by his formal, businesslike manner that he was still offended by her repeated rejections.

Mark looked up from the camera. Lauren's face had turned red, and her eyes dropped for the moment. "Are you asking me to speak to your class?"

"Yes," she said earnestly, her look now staying with his. "I promised Frau Keller I would ask someone I knew." Her request for help was sincere and convincing. "If you could come and visit for just an hour, it would mean very much to me and my classmates. All you would have to do is let the class talk to you in English to exercise their language skills."

"Well, yes, I'll visit with your class," Mark said, smiling and laying the camera aside, obviously forgetting his feelings of rejection and determination to stay away and wanting to help Lauren. "Of course, that depends on me getting permission to leave the base on the day you choose."

*   *   *

Mark's request to be excused from duty for a day to participate in an intercultural exchange at Lauren's high school was granted. Captain Williams told Sergeant Andrade that Mark's request was a worthy cause and that the US Army was always interested in improving relations with the German citizenry. Early the following Friday Lauren met Mark at the train depot in her village. Mark wore Levis and his green varsity sweater that had the letters *FG* on the left front and three stripes on the sleeves indicating he'd played varsity sports at Forest Grove High School in Queens.

"What do the letters on the sweater mean?" Lauren asked as they walked out of the depot. "The letters *FG* and those stripes?"

"Just a school sweater," Mark answered. "It means I played sports."

"I like it," she said, smiling.

"I'll give it to you," he said, and he meant it. He had forgotten his anger and hurt feelings and felt good that he could help Lauren.

"Nooo," she said, laughing. "I can't take your sweater. But I like it." As they continued toward the school, Lauren briefed him on questions he may be asked by the students. Mark was a little nervous but happy to be with her.

Once at Lauren's school, Mark first met Frau Keller outside the classroom. After Lauren introduced them, they talked for a few minutes, giving Mark a chance to adjust to the situation. Mark found Frau Keller to be a plump, middle-aged lady with a pleasant demeanor and a quick smile. He liked her immediately, and she seemed pleased with his visit. Frau Keller then entered the classroom and introduced Mark. She told the class that for the next hour or so they were free to discuss anything they wanted to with their American guest. She then exited the room, leaving Lauren in charge.

Lauren asked Mark to sit in the middle of the room and directed the other twenty-three students to gather around. There was an excited mumble of voices and a loud scraping of desks as they formed a circle around Mark. The school had a uniform dress code, and the girls wore blue dresses with white collars. The boys often violated the dress code, but all at least wore something blue of their required uniforms. The young students were sixteen or seventeen years of age, and they surrounded Mark in a circle of blue with bright, expectant faces. Mark sat amused and grinning atop a desk in the center of the students. Lauren moved to the rear of the circle and sat quietly.

Mark's spoken German, which was closely akin to the Yiddish he had grown up with, had developed quickly after coming to Germany. He took initial charge of the discussion: "*Was spreche ich?*" he began, smiling and hoping to get a conversation going.

"No! Speak English!" a clamor of voices immediately came back at him. "We want to speak English."

"Okay," Mark said, laughing. "That's certainly better for me."

At that point, the students began to talk, and the questions began to fly: "What state are you from?" "How old are you?" "How many are there in your family?" "Who is your favorite movie star?" "What are your favorite songs?" The questions came at Mark in a barrage of broken English, intermixed with giggles and laughter.

He answered as many questions as he could while laughing and joking back at the class clowns and smiling at the shy ones. He watched closely anyone who didn't seem to be talking and asked them questions. He would then wait patiently and attentively while they stumbled out with some answer. Mark soon had every student talking, and it turned out their favorite subject to discuss was American music. He was surprised at the knowledge some of the students had of American songs, and he related his favorite ones to them. For more than an hour, the room resounded with high-spirited and cheerful conversations in English, both directed at Mark and between students.

Frau Keller came back once and stood in the hallway unobserved. She listened a moment and then continued down the hallway with a pleased look on her face. She reported to the headmaster that she had an invited guess speaking to the class. Herr Werner nodded his approval, unaware of who the guest was or who had brought him to his school.

Lauren sat quietly at the outer edge of the group. She never stopped smiling, and her eyes never left Mark.

The time passed quickly, and Mark said his good-byes, saying it had been a pleasure being with them. As he walked out of the room, there was a loud and resounding "Good-bye! Good-bye!" While Mark headed back to the train station, Lauren went by her house to dress for work and then joined him at the depot. On the train ride back to the city, they both talked excitedly about the event. Mark was pleased with the interchange with her classmates and told her several times. Shortly before the stop where Mark would leave the train, Lauren became quiet and pensive. She seemed to want to say something but didn't know how to say it. Finally, just before they were to separate at the next train stop, she turned to Mark.

"Mark," she said, her voice low, her face sincere. She held his eyes momentarily before continuing. "I've been thinking about something—something I hope you . . . or we . . . can do." She paused a moment and then spoke in a shy voice. "Would you like to go on a photo tour?"

"Photo tour? . . . Sure!" Mark said with interest. "Where? When?"

"A good place to study the outdoors and shoot landscapes is at a village called Martinschule. It's a small village in the hills and surrounded by low mountains. I can meet you there Sunday morning."

"Great! What time should I be there?" Mark asked.

"My train will get there around ten o'clock in the morning," Lauren said as she wrote the name of the village train depot and the time on a slip of paper.

"I'll be there," he said. Mark was elated. *Now I'm going to be with her, and it'll be just the two of us,* he thought. His already good mood soared.

"Color is best for landscape," she said, her eyes bright with pleasure, which, in turn, pleased Mark. The image of her face never left his thoughts on the train ride back to post.

CHAPTER 11

"ANOTHER DAY ANOTHER LETTER," MARK said, walking into the barracks. An air mail letter lay glaringly white at the head of the blanket covering his bunk. Ignoring the letter, he unlocked his locker and began stripping down.

Mark was tired and gritty and smelled of gun oil. He had recently been assigned to a three-man, .50 caliber machine gun team, and today his team had performed a field qualification test, including qualifying on the firing range. The qualification process required a full day's work with a disassembly of the gun, a three-mile march with each man carrying the various parts of the heavy weapon, and a drill where they set it up and fired. The day's events lingered in Mark's thoughts. He was surprised how well he had done on the firing range. After they target fired, acquiring some familiarity with the weapon, the instructor took them to another section of the range where they set the gun up before a large, open field that rose up to a hillside in the distance. Midway up the hill sat a disabled tank used for target practice.

The range master gave his initial instructions: "Down range you see an armored vehicle. Imagine that is an enemy tank approaching your position. You must place your fire on the tank, or it will annihilate your position."

"How do we know when our rounds are hitting the tank?" Mark had asked.

"You watch your tracers," the instructor began. "If they just disappear in the distance, you're missing your target. If they're hitting the target, the tracers will ricochet off in all directions."

At the fire-when-ready command, Mark carefully pressed the trigger and felt the big gun come alive. He focused on the tracer stream, judging that it fell just below the target tank. Adjusting upward slightly, he was surprised to see his fire envelope the tank and ricochet about like fireworks at night.

"Excellent!" the instructor had shouted. "We've got us a gunner here!"

Then, on returning to Post, disassembling, cleaning and oiling, and checking it back into the armory took the remainder of the day plus a couple of hours. In spite of being tired, Mark felt good; his team had done well on the firing range, receiving "well done" and looks of approval from the range master.

As they were unloading the gun and equipment, First Sergeant Andrade had approached them saying the range master had reported an excellent grade for Charlie Company's team. "Heavy weapons teams that perform well make a company look good," he went on to say as he inspected the gun for cleanliness before it was signed in. "It'll look good not only on record but at Battalion level. As a matter of fact," he continued, looking at Mark. "That's why the captain was so interested in your skills on the firing range that first day you reported into Charlie. He's watching you closely, and he'll be pleased with this day's report."

Mark had nodded his understanding to Andrade but remained uncomfortable for being singled out and closely scrutinized, the same as he was on that first day.

*　　*　　*

After his shower, Mark began to put the day's firing range experience behind him. He returned to his bunk and straightened up his locker. He continued to ignore the letter. Myers watched him a moment then asked, "See your letter?"

"Oh, yeah," Mark said casually. But he didn't pick up the letter.

"I picked it up when I got mine," Myers said. The three men had become good friends. Their circumstance of shipping over and arriving in Charlie Company together and their proximity in the barracks promoted a strong camaraderie. They looked out for each other in many ways, and Myers bringing Mark's mail was just the usual procedure.

Myers seemed disappointed that Mark continued to ignore his letter. Both he and Wade had been off duty a couple of hours and had already had chow and a shower and were just relaxing. Myers had read his letter several times. "Aren't you going to read your letter, Mark?" he asked.

"I don't have to," Mark said. "I already know what it says. I just want to relax now."

"How do you know what it says?" Wade asked, laying aside the book he had been reading.

"I know, because it'll say the same thing as the last one," Mark said. "And the one before that."

"What do they say?" Myers asked.

"Well, they're from my mom," Mark began. "She's always and forever worried about family. Since I was a kid, she's told me over and over about her father, his father, and his father, and so on."

"Why's that?" Wade asked.

"She afraid I'll forget my roots—my Jewish heritage, whatever that is," Mark said, dropping his field jacket across his footlocker and peeling off his fatigue shirt.

"Ah, she's just another fussy Jewish mother," Myers said. "Be glad you've got family back home."

"That I do, but . . ." Mark's word's trailed off as he spoke.

"What's the problem?" Wade asked.

"This family thing," Mark said. "It's . . . I don't know."

"Families are suppose to be close, Mark," Wade said, turning a page in his book.

"Gentiles are different, they would say," Mark continued. "Stay with your own. Always stay with your own."

"How about Gentile girls?" Myers asked, an amused smile forming on his face.

"Especially Gentile girls," Mark said, neatly hanging his field jacket in his locker. "I mentioned Lauren in a letter, and they became very upset. My father wrote back that they objected to me getting involved with a German girl."

"That is close," Myers said, laughing. "When it comes to girls, there are no limits." He was still laughing as Mark lay down on his bunk.

"That's not funny," Wade said to Myers after Mark didn't respond. "There's a deep-seated hatred in some Jewish communities for Germans."

"Oh, I didn't know that," Myers said. "I hope I didn't offend you Mark."

"Don't worry about it," Mark said. "I'm use to it."

"Yeah, that's good," Wade said to Mark. "But I hope you don't get too serious over this *Fräulein*. If you do, I'm sure you'll create big problems on the home front."

"I know," Mark said quietly. He rolled over and closed his eyes as if he wanted to be left alone; he was worried about Andrade's news regarding the captain's close scrutiny and his growing situation with Lauren.

CHAPTER 12

AFTER LAUREN HAD SET UP the photo tour with Mark, she began to have some misgivings about the situation. On the train ride home from work that day, her thoughts dwelled on their differences. He was an American soldier of the Jewish faith from a culture that had, in the recent past, been in opposition to that of her own. He would serve his military tour in Germany and then go home to pick up his life there. She was a German Catholic from a family that had lost much. With vivid memories of huddling in the dark of their cellar, she felt unquestionable and absolute loyalty to her family who had held her close, consoling and comforting her from the rumbling noise and trembling walls. She now had only her father, and he remained keenly protective and had strong traditional views of the German culture and its past and current state of affairs.

Still, Mark was different from all the other boys and men she had met. Many men, both young and older, had showered her with attention, but their attempts at a relationship were always met with a polite but dispassionate indifference. Of all these men, Mark was the first to hold her interest. She first felt something special about his easygoing mannerism, and he had a certain indefinable look when he made eye contact that left her a little excited. Although she was attracted to him from the beginning, she didn't trust her feelings and refused to see him beyond the coffee shop, thinking that special feeling would pass. But after numerous weeks and their many friendly encounters, Lauren found her interest growing and saw no harm in the upcoming meeting to photograph the countryside.

By the time the train reached her village and she had walked the distance to her father's house, Lauren had a plan forming in her mind. During dinner that night, she would bring up the fact that an American soldier had bought a camera from her, and during the transaction, they had an interesting conversation about photography and about the United States. She would mention this casually and study her father's reaction closely.

They were halfway through their meal when Lauren began to talk to her father about things that went on with her at school as she often did. Her father, in spite of being a headmaster, often read assignments deemed exceptional and passed on to him by the teachers. He was always on the lookout for that future scholar. While they had their dinner, he was reading a student's paper. As Lauren talked, he would look up occasionally to show he was listening to her.

"My French teacher says I have a strong talent in language," she said.

"I know," he said, looking over his glasses at her. "I'm proud of the way your language skills have developed from German to English and French."

"Maybe I'll become an interpreter for the UN," she said, smiling at him across the table.

"I'd rather you emphasize the German language and become a schoolteacher," he said, his look returning to the paper before him.

"And what would you want me to teach?" she asked, her smile and demeanor taking on a knowing look. She already knew his answer.

"Why, German culture, of course," he said as he made a mark on the paper. Herr Werner believed in his country's greatness and felt strongly patriotic. "German history, language, literature—" he continued.

"But I like photography," she said, continuing to smile across the table at him. "Why can't I have a career in photography?"

"Germany needs schoolteachers more than photographers," he said without looking up. "You're still young, and your interests are still developing. You'll see I'm right as you get older."

"Speaking of photography," she began while watching him closely. "I sold a camera to an interesting customer awhile back."

"Uh huh," he said, still concentrating on the paper.

"He was an American soldier," she continued, her glance going to his face then back to her plate. "We talked about photography and the United States for some time."

Her father stopped reading and, while remaining silent, looked intently over his glasses, as if waiting for her to continue.

"He was very nice and interesting," she said as she took a sip of water and continued to look down at her plate.

"Lauren," her father began slowly. He paused a moment until she looked up. "You know I don't want you fraternizing with the soldiers."

"Why not, Papa?" she asked. "This one was very polite and nice."

"You should keep to your own."

"But I have to work with whoever comes into the shop," she said. "And except for his short haircut, he looks no different from us."

Herr Werner laid his pencil down and leaned back in his chair. He looked at her for a long moment without speaking. When he did speak, he spoke quietly and in a serious tone. "Lauren, we've lost so much."

"I know, but we have to forget, Papa," she said quietly, her look going to his face then back down to her plate. "Times are different now."

"Forget? No, we can never forget!" he said. "We must remember all that has happened. We must remember our triumphs and our failures and learn from them. We must remember those we have lost and honor them. We must know that what has happened is our unique place in history—our destiny. It was not something we chose but something prearranged by fate. We came along at this time and this place, and that's where providence has placed us. With what we faced, we did what we could with what we had and with the knowledge and understanding we had before us. We had no options, no alternatives, and no choices. Forget? Never! To forget would mean our sacrifices were for nothing."

Lauren looked at her father a long moment before she spoke. She understood him completely, and her loyalty and sympathy were with him. "Yes, Papa," she said, her eyes remaining lowered. She then rose from the table to begin her after-dinner chores. She didn't mention her plans for the photo tour with Mark. And although she still looked forward to the trip with him, she felt some guilt for defying her father.

CHAPTER 13

S UNDAY MORNING, MARK'S TRAIN ARRIVED at the village of Martinschule a short time before Lauren's train. It had been almost three months since that first day in The Camera Shop, and he paced the platform nervously in anticipation of their first meeting for something more than a cup of coffee. He was prepared to be on his best behavior and as cheerful and entertaining as possible.

When she arrived, Lauren stepped from the train car next to where he waited. He had a moment to watch her as she paused on the platform and looked around. Seeing him through the crowd, she waved and turned his way. Dressed in tan walking shorts and a white cotton shirt and carrying a knapsack, she worked her way through the train crowd toward him. He had only seen her in formal work clothes, and her casual look now accentuated her youth and striking good looks. Her blond hair was combed neatly back from her face, and her confident walk caused Mark to smile and reach for his camera. *She's like a young model,* he thought. Remembering how she had once said that photographs were like our memories and could freeze things we value in time, he quickly shot two pictures of her as she walked toward him from across the station platform.

"Starting already!" she said, laughing, her voice pitched slightly higher over the din of the train's bells and revving engine. She handed Mark the knapsack, and they left the train station, walking close together.

They walked about the village, taking shots of an ancient church and a covey of pigeons bursting into flight as they approached the village square. Mark stayed close to Lauren, making small talk and finding himself a bit captivated by being with her away from her work for the first time. As they neared the square, they came upon a statue mounted on a pedestal. Lauren pointed out the advantage of shooting a picture of the square standing on the base of the statue. She said the slight downward angle would give the shot a broader view to better represent the small square with its walkways and park benches. Mark helped her step up on the statue's pedestal, and her touch and close presence in holding her arm while she climbed up left within him strong feelings that lingered pleasantly. Lauren panned around the scene through the camera lens before taking the shot. Mark hardly noticed the square. He was finding it hard to take his eyes from her.

Finally, Lauren said, "Would you like to do some landscapes? We could walk up the mountain a ways."

"Yes," Mark answered. "That'll be a nice change." He could see the green foothills of the mountain looming over the low buildings in the distance. He had a strong desire to be alone with her, and he looked forward to the quiet of the open countryside. In reality, he had hardly noticed the shots he'd taken in the village.

They walked up into the hills beyond the village where the air was cool and pleasant and found a spot where they could oversee the countryside beyond the hills. A wide valley spread out before them—a patchwork of brown and yellow and green squares forming the valley floor. A narrow black roadway twisted and turned as it worked its way up to a small, doll-like village that lay midway up the valley. Beyond the village, the roadway split and went in different directions, each narrow black path disappearing into separate parts of the distant gray mountains. In the pale, blue sky, occasional patches of white clouds drifted southward, their gray shadows moving slowly across the valley floor.

During the climb, the sun had warmed them, and the uphill walk was a little tiring, so they rested in the shade under a tree at the crest of the hill, sitting close together and sipping a mild red wine from Lauren's knapsack. The air had a stimulating freshness about it. The faintly sweet wine cast off a pleasant aroma, like newly turned spring earth, that warmed and cheered both of them. They quietly talked about the photo scenes the valley below presented and the best camera settings for shots. But even with the colorful valley and the panoramic scene before them, Mark couldn't think about landscapes. As they laughed and talked, each glance into her face when he caught her eyes that would quickly drop away or accidental touch brought a keen and compelling awareness that held his attention.

"We really need color film with a slow ASA to shoot these landscapes," she said, looking around to find his look on her.

"Yes," he said and he glanced down to the valley and then back to her.

"Notice how those two clouds are drifting close together," she continued. "If they merge, it will make a colorful foreground for the mountains in the distance."

"I think they're coming together," he said. "It will make a fine shot." Each time he looked away, he quickly found his eyes drawn back to her.

"I'll set the camera," she said, picking up the camera.

"The best scenery is here," he said, now holding her eyes with his.

"A good view, no?" she said, grinning and pointing to the valley below.

"A good view, yes!" Mark said. He wasn't looking at the valley but at her. He held her eyes.

"Down there!" she said pointing again, her blue eyes laughing. "We're supposed to be studying landscapes." But her laugh trailed off and her look stayed with his. She laid the camera down without making adjustments. They looked at each other for a moment, both awed and captivated by the compelling reality of their closeness, both yielding to feelings that longed to be released.

"I've found the perfect shot," he whispered as he pulled her to him, feeling her warmth and the exquisite pleasure of holding her close for the first time. They embraced eagerly and kissed repeatedly, both releasing long-suppressed desires and each responding to the other's warmth and touch and feel. They then lay back in the grass and made love with a quiet, deep passion that consumed every thought and feeling.

Later they lay close together in the shade of the tree, neither speaking. They found themselves quietly captivated by their feelings, each trying to understand what had just happened and neither able to remember such an intense and powerful experience before.

CHAPTER 14

INFANTRY OUTFITS HAVE FIELD MANEUVERS in their training schedules where they periodically train in the field performing tactical exercises. An upcoming exercise had First Battalion scheduled to start off the program. The battalion commander designated Charlie Company to be the first company to begin the exercise. The location for the maneuver was in a forestry area east of a small town in central Germany called Landsthule. It was approximately one hundred and fifty kilometers from the Grahfenvern Post. Not only were Charlie Company personnel not familiar with the terrain at this location, but they were not familiar with the route they would take to get there. Getting a convoy across country and to a designated area can be a problem. Some of the small villages on the route are hundreds of years old and have ancient stone houses so close to the road that large military vehicles would have problems passing through them. For this reason, Captain Williams was ordered by Battalion to send a simulated convoy of a few trucks to find the best route for the larger convoy that would come later. Williams selected Lieutenant McBride and his Second Platoon to take on this mission.

McBride was highly regarded and had an interesting background. Six feet tall, slim, and wiry, his steady, penetrating gaze said he meant business. When he was just sixteen, his widowed mother had died, leaving him homeless and an orphan. Having nowhere else to go, he lied about his age and enlisted in the army. Catching the final phases of combat in '45, he got the right amount of action to whet his appetite for the army life. After Officers Candidate School, he volunteered for a line outfit anywhere in the world and was sent to Europe. He had the rare quality of being brash while at the same time knowing when to back off to avoid trouble. He also had a reputation of getting things done.

"McBride," Williams said as he briefed the lieutenant. "Your mission is a crucial one. In a few weeks, there will be two full companies in convoy traveling to the exercise location. That's approximately four hundred men with about forty vehicles. Any screw up could make a nightmare of this operation. Make a trial run and map all obstacles."

McBride organized his scout convoy to consist of three five-ton trucks with a jeep leading and a three-quarter-ton ammo carrier bringing up the rear. He and his driver would be in the lead jeep and would run back and forth from front to rear of the column of vehicles to make sure there were no stragglers. Being a simulated combat operation, all personnel would carry their weapons and combat gear, but no ammunition. An exception to the no ammunition policy was the officer in charge. It was standard operating procedure for an OIC of a convoy to be armed with a sidearm. Lieutenant McBride carried a loaded Colt .45 automatic at his side.

Mark had been in Charlie Company for six months and had become proficient in handling all the vehicles the company had available for its use. He was assigned to drive the lead five-ton with a PFC James Spells as his assistant driver. As the small convoy left their post in the early morning, everyone expected a routine exercise. The weather was good with only small patches of morning fog as they traveled southeast on the autobahn to Kaiserslautern. All went well until after Kaiserslautern when they left the autobahn and took to the back roads across open country.

Some of the narrow farm roads were unmarked on his map, and Lieutenant McBride had to go on his sense of direction and gut feeling at some of the crossroads. He knew the map location of their destination, and at unmarked crossroads, he would take the road that appeared most likely to take him in that general direction. He marked each turn on his map with notes of obstacles such as narrow bridges and washed out roads. He would pull over occasionally to see that all his vehicles were close behind him. If all trucks were not in sight, he would have his driver turn the jeep around and backtrack until the straggler was located.

McBride was on one of these backtrack trips, and Mark's truck was leading the convoy when they entered a small village. The village had stone houses situated right next to the road. It was very old and had grown up along the narrow road long before automobiles were used. People could walk out of their brown-and-gray stone houses right into the street. If there was a Volkswagen parked next to a house, Mark would have to drive the five-ton very carefully, watching both sides lest he hit the car on one side or a building on the opposite side. He had progressed halfway through the village when the road and the buildings curved slightly. Just around this curve sat a small car whose owner had carelessly parked out into the street a short distance. This would not have presented a problem for the normal traffic through the village, but it blocked the way for the large military vehicles.

Mark and his assistant driver dismounted and stood in the street trying to decide what to do next. There was no one in sight to ask about the small car. The other trucks backed up behind the lead truck and stood motionless, their motors idling. McBride's jeep was stuck at the rear of the column. Presently, other soldiers from the following trucks dismounted and came up to see why they had stopped. In a few minutes, the entire Second Platoon was standing around in the street talking about the stalled convoy. Finally, Lieutenant McBride came hurrying up demanding to know what was going on. When Mark pointed out the car blocking their way, McBride immediately went to the first door and pounded loudly with his fist. A woman opened the door.

"Whose car?" McBride demanded, pointing to the car.

The woman gasped when she saw the commotion in the street and disappeared back into the house. A short time later, a large man appeared in the doorway, pulling suspenders over an undershirt that covered a set of wide, powerful-looking shoulders. He appeared irritated as he stepped out into the street to face the soldiers.

"Your car?" McBride asked, again pointing to the car.

"*Ya!*" came back an immediate answer from the man.

"Move it!" McBride demanded.

The man burst into a rapid discourse, speaking harshly and pointing to the military vehicles. His face was glowing red, and he glared menacingly at McBride. He was bigger than McBride, and he leaned toward him as he talked.

"Move it!" McBride shouted, speaking just as loudly and harshly as the German.

The German stepped farther out into the street, waving his arms and pointing to the trucks and turning back to McBride.

"Sir," Mark said, "he's saying military vehicles are not supposed to be here in his village."

"Tell him to move that car or we will," McBride said, ignoring Mark's comment. Mark relayed the message in a formal respectful manner, saying it was necessary for the convoy to pass through the village. He apologized politely.

This seemed to infuriate the man even more. He began to shout and glare down at McBride who stood firmly, facing the larger man.

The more the German shouted, the angrier he become until finally he lost control and pushed McBride back violently against the lead truck. This was a mistake on the German's part. For no sooner had he touched McBride than McBride's .45 appeared in his hand, pointed directly at the German's face.

"Sir!" Mark said quickly as he heard the metallic click of the hammer going into single action mode. "Sir, we can work this out!"

"Tell him in German to move that car," McBride said again. His voice was cold, and Mark knew something terribly wrong was about to happen. Mark spoke quickly, pleading to the German to move his car. He used his most formal and polite language to plead with the man.

With the .45 in his face, the large man quickly backed away, throwing up both hands with palms outward as in compliance. He mumbled something, and shaking his head as if in agreement, he turned and walked quickly back into the house.

"Sir," Mark said, "I think he said he's going to get his car keys."

"To hell with him," McBride said, waving the automatic. "You men gather around that car and move it against that house."

The soldiers of Second Platoon quickly and easily picked up the car and set it up against the building, clearing the way for the trucks to pass. McBride then ordered PFC Spells to go back with his jeep driver, saying he would ride in the lead truck until the jeep could work its way back to the front of the column. He de-cocked and holstered the .45 and stepped up into the five-ton. "Let's get moving!" he said to Mark.

As they were pulling away, Mark could see the German had returned to the street. He was clutching his car keys and staring at his car setting against the wall of the house. After they cleared the village and before the jeep could regain the lead to pick up McBride, Mark turned to the lieutenant. "That was a close one, sir. Would you have shot him?"

"I don't know," McBride said. He had been studying the map and making notes at the village location. At Mark's question, he paused and looked straight ahead in deep thought.

"But that could have created a serious problem for you, sir," Mark said, shifting gears as the truck's speed picked up. "Was it that important?"

McBride didn't answer immediately; he stared straight ahead as if studying the ancient oak trees that lined each side of the road. Finally, he turned to Mark. "It's my outfit and my mission," he said. "That's more important than my welfare." With that, he went back to studying the map and marking out a route that would bypass the village.

Mark thought about what the lieutenant had said. There was something familiar about it. At first, it didn't come to him, but then he knew what that something was: *It's that damn bucket-of-water thing again,* he finally realized. *Sacrifice the self for the mission. Is there no let up from that way of thinking?* The thought spun around in his brain as they continued down the narrow road lined with ancient trees.

CHAPTER 15

THE UPCOMING FIELD MANEUVERS WERE considered crucial to the company commanders' reputations, and Captain Williams worked hard to make his company look good. He met often with his platoon leaders to plan out and address all preliminary work that should be done before the date of departure. Knowing that one of the first concerns for the exercise was to get his company to the designated location with as few problems as possible, he set the training schedules around preparing for the exercise. Mark and the other men assigned as truck drivers were given a long list of maintenance tasks to perform on their assigned vehicles in preparation for the exercise. This involved several days with most of their time spent doing preventive maintenance on their trucks. Since the motor pool was some distance from their company chow hall, they would have noon chow at the battalion's consolidated mess, which was closer.

They were in their second day of their motor pool detail and had arrived at the consolidated mess for chow just after noon. The line was long, as usual, and Mark, Wade, and Spells entered the line and slowly worked their way toward the serving counters. The consolidated mess was a large facility and could accommodate a couple hundred soldiers at any given time. There were several serving lines that exited into different areas of the chow hall. Each of these sections had several smaller sections containing rows of tables and chairs and drink containers of milk, water, and tea situated at the rear of each section. KPs hurried about refilling drink containers and keeping the area clean. There was a constant flow of soldiers entering and exiting each section. Some entered to look for an available table, while others exited after finishing their meals. A din of low talk and laughter and the clanging of trays, plates, and drinking mugs filled the room. It was a routine noon chow in a large army mess hall.

After exiting the serving line with loaded trays, Mark, Wade, and Spells entered the nearest dinning section in search of a free table. Spells found a table for them, and Wade was ahead of Mark as they entered the section, working their way toward his table. Mark's tray was loaded to capacity. He was hungry after the heavy physical work of replacing the rear tires on his five-ton. It had taken him all morning, and he had been so intense in the work that he had skipped both coffee and water brakes. Moving carefully through the narrowed entrance, precariously holding his loaded tray, Mark was suddenly jolted by a body shoving hard against his back. The blow drove him stumbling forward and caused him to spill his tray across the floor and splash drink on the nearest soldier's boots and fatigues.

"What the hell?" exclaimed the splashed soldier, coming to his feet.

After Mark controlled his forward stumbling and could collect his sense of presence, he turned to see a soldier standing behind him with both hands spread outward as in surprise and apology. "Sorry, Soldier," he said. "I stumbled and lost my footing."

Although Mark didn't recognize the man, there was something vaguely familiar about him. Partially stunned from the blow and embarrassed by the commotion he had created, Mark didn't concern himself with identifying the man. His food, tray, and utensils were scattered across the chow hall floor. The normal chow hall noise had ceased, and everyone was looking at him. Wade and Spells hurried up to see what had happened. In his confusion, Mark stood quietly, trying to collect his composure.

"I'm really sorry," the man said again.

The mess hall sergeant in charge walked up, poised as if ready to jump on anyone or everyone. "Okay, what's going on here?" he demanded in an angry voice.

"It was my fault," the man said, turning to the mess sergeant. "I stumbled and bumped into him. I'm really sorry."

The mess sergeant looked from Mark to the other soldier suspiciously. He seemed undecided momentarily and then turned to the nearest KP, saying, "Clean up this mess and mop down the area."

"I'm really sorry," the clumsy soldier said again to the mess sergeant. "I just stumbled."

"Okay, okay," the mess sergeant said. "If you've eaten, get out of here!"

"Yes, Sergeant," the man said respectfully before turning and leaving.

"I don't know if that was an accident or not," the mess sergeant said, turning to Mark. "But I do know I won't tolerate any altercations in my chow hall." He then turned and walked away.

Mark said nothing. He was angry but dazed, embarrassed, and unsure of himself or how to feel about the incident. He didn't know whether to apologize to the soldiers who had gotten splattered with food or just leave the area. He no longer felt hungry—just humiliated.

"What a mess," Spells said, looking down at the floor as one KP began to pick up and another walked up with a mop and bucket.

At that moment, the soldier who first had his boots splattered approached Mark. "I saw the whole thing," he said. "That soldier came hurrying up from behind and hit you like a fullback going through the line. That wasn't an accident. He did that on purpose."

"Mark," Wade said, as if just realizing something, He stared hard in the direction the man had disappeared. He glanced at Mark and then back in the man's direction. "That was that creep from the first soccer match. The one they call Ricco, and the one who jumped Myers."

"Ricco!" Recognition and anger flared on Mark's face. He quickly turned and headed after the man. He was already outside the mess hall and looking left and right when Wade and Spells caught up with him.

"Slow down, Mark!" Wade said, taking his arm. Mark jerked his arm away, turned, and walked hurriedly toward the open street, moving forcefully as he looked for Ricco.

"Wade's right," Spells said as he came running up beside Mark. "This is more than it seems. Don't let him sucker you in!"

Mark ignored their words and their caution. He was furious. He had been waylaid, ambushed, and embarrassed. He was blindsided and set up for humiliation and discredit. It was an open and obvious insult to his self-respect. His individual integrity was destroyed, and the deed had been executed and accomplished and then excused by a false act of contrition and apologies. To regain his personal honor, he must have a settling of scores. And that's what he meant to do.

"You know the rules," Wade said, clutching Mark's arm. "Anyone fighting on post is subject to court-martial except in self-defense."

"This is self-defense," Mark said angrily.

"No, it's not self-defense!" Wade said quickly. "If you go after him, you're the attacker, and you'll be the one who'll receive a court-martial."

"And you're the one who'll spend time in jail," Spells added, grabbing Mark's other arm. "Don't you see? He'll act innocent, claiming you attacked him because of the accident in the chow hall. He's got you set up!"

With Wade and Spells both holding Mark's arms, he began to settle down and see the logic of their words. As Mark begin to relax and the tension went out of his arms, Wade let go. "Don't worry, your day will come," he assured Mark. "I know his type. Sooner or later, he'll give you the opportunity you want." Wade then paused a moment before continuing. Looking hard at Mark, he added, "But, Mark, you've got to be ready. He's a bad dude!"

CHAPTER 16

I
N ALL OF MARK'S LETTERS from home, no matter how
disagreeable his parents might have been with him, they
nevertheless ended their letters by encouraging him to call
home collect anytime and request anything he might need. Mark
had never called home or requested anything until after visiting
Lauren's school. He was so impressed with the student's fondness
for American music that he thought of a plan on his return trip to
post. He set his plan in motion the next evening by missing retreat
so he could make a collect phone call from the company phone
in the orderly room. He made his call at retreat time because he
wanted privacy, and the first sergeant and the company clerk would
be in formation at that time.

After the initial greetings and small talk with his parents and
after his mom got control of her excitement, he made his request.
He began by telling them that he had made several friends playing
soccer, and he wanted to give them a gift. He asked that they
purchase twenty-five sets of the top-ten selling 45 rpm records and
package them with each ten-record set individually wrapped so they

could be easily distributed. He also asked his mom to include in the package two of his best old soccer shirts that were well worn and were soft and cottony. He asked them to address the package to "L Werner" and gave them Lauren's address, saying that was where his closest soccer friend lived. His mom eagerly agreed and said the package would be sent the following day and would be posted air mail, special delivery. His parents smiled at the request, telling each other they were happy that their son still needed them.

*   *   *

Several days after Mark's parents posted the package, Lauren came home from work to find a box sitting in her doorway. The package was addressed to her using only the letter *L* for her first name. She was a little confused, and her confusion increased when she opened the box and found the packages of records and the two shirts. Because of the New York address, she guessed it might be something Mark had initiated. She hadn't seen or heard from him since their photo tour to Martinschule. The situation that happened there had been completely unplanned by her, and it had left her awed and perplexed. Neither of them had easy access to a private conversation by phone and communicated only when together, both trusting the other to be in touch whenever possible. Her confusion, along with some anxiety, increased into the following day when she gave in to the pressure and placed a phone call to the number Mark had previously given her.

The phone number Mark had given her was to C Company's orderly room, and this required the company clerk to send his runner, PFC Myers, in search of Mark and bring him in to take the phone call. It was a long wait before Lauren heard someone on the line.

"Charlie Company, Corporal Bergner, here," a crisp, sharp voice finally came back at her. She recognized Mark's voice but didn't relate to the way he expressed himself. She had never been around him when he was in his military persona, and the formal, military tone of voice that came back at her confused her even more. She explained to him about the package and asked if he had sent it.

"Affirmative," came back a quick answer. Then, in a softer voice, he added, "The individual packages are for each member of the class, and the other items are for you know who." Lauren was hesitant to talk further, sensing he didn't want to continue the conversation. She could hear a loud, angry voice in the background, and that caused her more concern. What she didn't know, or couldn't relate to, was that First Sergeant Andrade was chewing out the company clerk for spilling some coffee on his desk and that Mark was talking the way he always did when on duty and on the phone. She hung up the phone feeling more insecure, as if she had not done something right. But at least she knew what to do with the packages.

The following day when Frau Keller reported to class, Lauren told her she had gifts from the American who had talked to the class a few weeks earlier. Lauren passed out the individual packages to each student and one to Frau Keller as well. There was much excitement as the wrappings came off the packages and the records spilled out onto each desk. Soon the room was filled with excited talk: "This one's 'Sixty Minute Man' by the Dominoes." "This one is 'Mona Lisa' by Nat King Cole." "Look at this. 'Cry' by Jonnie Ray."

The excited chatter went on and on with a complete disruption to the normal class activity. Finally, as it came time for the class to end and after Frau Keller had examined her ten records, she called for the class's attention. "These records of American music offer us a good opportunity to study the language," she said. "In one week, I will give you a test. The test will be to translate each of these English language songs into German." With that, she dismissed the class, and the students rushed out, hurrying to find a 45 rpm record player so they could play their new records.

Lauren was in a mild daze. So many things were coming at her: She felt uneasy about being given credit for the gift of records when all she did was deliver them. Her ongoing confusion about the event on the mountain at Martinschule was causing her to lie awake at night. The fact she hadn't seen Mark since that day troubled her. And, finally, the odd and distant quality of her phone conversation with Mark the day before set her to wondering if he was pulling away from their relationship.

What she couldn't know was that Mark's post had gone on a standby alert where all passes are pulled, all personnel are restricted to company training schedules, and no off-post communications are permitted. With all that happening, she wasn't sure how she stood with Mark.

It took her a minute to collect her thoughts after the other students left. When she came back to the present, she realized she had to hurry to catch her train into the city and to her job at The Camera Shop. In her haste, she spilled all ten of the records as well as her books onto the floor. As she was picking them up, she looked up to see Frau Keller watching her with a smile on her face. When their eyes met, Frau Keller said, "It was nice of you and your American friend to give the class a gift."

"Oh, I had nothing to do with it, Frau Keller," Lauren said, her face turning crimson and showing her hidden emotions. "It was done by the American alone."

"Maybe so," Frau Keller said, shaking her head patiently, as if she understood the situation better than Lauren.

"But, Frau Keller, it's the truth," Lauren said with a serious face and tone. "I had no idea—"

"Maybe so," Frau Keller repeated, interrupting Lauren. "I'm sure you didn't plan it or do anything directly. But you're responsible."

"I don't understand," Lauren said, confused with the direction of the conversation. "I'm just as surprised as anyone."

"Lauren, I saw the way he looked at you," she continued with a smile. "You're the one he wants to impress. It's you the class owes thanks to."

Lauren didn't say anything further. She looked at Frau Keller a moment, and then her face colored even more and her eyes dropped.

"In any case," Frau Keller said quickly, as if sensing Lauren's discomfort. "The gift from the American is a nice gesture. And I might add," she paused a moment as if considering what to say and then spoke quietly, "your modesty becomes you."

CHAPTER 17

LTHOUGH THE AUTO ACCIDENT HAD stayed on the minds of everyone involved, nothing was heard about it and little was said about it for some time. After the trip to the provost marshal, the event seemed to have been forgotten until one day the CO received word from the battalion commander that an investigation board was being formed to look into the accident. In spite of the fact that it had been more than five months since the event, the army hadn't shut down the investigation. What at first seemed to be an unfortunate but unavoidable accident was now becoming a bigger issue for some reason. And this reason continued to be a mystery to everyone in C Company.

Captain Williams had received a preliminary report from the provost marshal's office. They had finally decided the event was a serious matter and escalated the investigation to a higher level. This escalation would bring C Company under investigation in addition to the accident. Charlie Company itself had an outstanding record and had nothing to fear from an investigation. Nevertheless, in the records at higher echelons, it would be noted that the company had been investigated, and that would be a noted mark that would stand out to someone looking at the records. Williams was furious; he had worked hard to lead and manage his company and men, and this situation was the only questionable mark on his company's record. He called each of the three men involved to his office separately to again grill them on the minute details of that night. Mark was the first one he questioned.

"Yes, sir, that's the way it happened," Mark said, standing at attention before Williams and giving his account of the accident. "After the impact, PFC Myers was in a state of shock and wasn't aware enough to stop the car." Mark related the entire story to Captain Williams but left out the fact he had to turn the ignition key off to stop the car. If they knew Mark had stopped the car instead of Myers, the captain and the investigation board would think Myers was trying to leave the scene of the accident. Then, wanting to reemphasize why Myers had not stopped immediately after the impact, Mark continued with his false story: "And, sir, he stopped on his own when he regained his senses."

Williams was so upset about the situation he was having trouble controlling his anger. "Do you realize what this will do to C Company's reputation, Corporal?" he said to Mark, his face solemn with anger. He stood leaning over his desk toward Mark as he spoke. "Do you realize the seriousness of killing two German citizens? It doesn't matter that they were drunk and walking down the middle of the road on a foggy night."

"Yes, sir, I realize this matter is serious."

"Just the investigation will be a black mark on the company. Do you realize that?"

"Yes, sir."

Captain Williams stood with white knuckles pressed into the desk, glaring at Mark. He seemed to be considering his options. "You and PFC Wade can't be held responsible for this," he began, as if not sure what to do. "But the investigation will look closely at Myers. They'll want to know if he's a reckless driver, if he has any speeding violations, if he was drinking heavily, if he performs his duties." He paused a moment as if to collect his thoughts and then added, "They'll look at everything they can find on Myers, and for his sake, he'd better look good."

"Yes, sir."

"I'll say this now," Williams said, as if concluding the meeting. "You men are in my company. If your story is the truth, I'll do what I can to help you. But if you're holding back something, you're on your own."

"Yes, sir."

"Dismissed! Get out of here!" Williams said, returning Mark's salute and picking up the phone.

Mark returned to the barracks and told Myers and Wade about his confrontation with the CO. He stressed to them not to mention that it was he who had stopped the car by turning off the ignition key. "Dave was in shock when he drove on," he said. "We know that, but the investigation board may look at it differently. Let's simply say that he stopped on his own when he regained his senses and take that issue off the table." They all agreed.

Each of the other two had their meetings with Williams, and the ordeal was the same with each man. The three of them agreed it best to keep it quiet as long as they could and not discuss it with any of the other soldiers. All was quiet for a couple of weeks. The routine during duty hours was the same. After hours, they continued as usual, going to the post movie or having beers with other members of the platoon at the post EM Club. Mark even managed to get away to Frankfurt on Sunday as had become his routine. The break in silence came when the company clerk overheard the captain talking to Regimental Headquarters about the accident on the phone. The clerk told Wade that he had heard an investigation board had been formed and that the investigation was officially underway. When Wade heard this news late one afternoon, he immediately went to the barracks looking for Mark.

"Have you heard the latest on the accident?" he asked as he hurried up to Mark, his silver dog tags hanging outside his fatigue shirt and swinging freely about his chest. Myers had been assigned to work at the motor pool and was still on duty.

"Nothing since last week," Mark replied, working with a shoe brush to remove dust and dirt from his boots.

"Not good," Wade said, shaking his head. "Not good. The company clerk just told me the investigation is already underway. He said he heard the CO talking on the phone, saying they're taking this case very seriously. Says they've brought in legal officers from the adjutant general's office at Army Command, Europe."

"But why? It's still just an auto accident!"

"Yeah, you know that, and I know that," Wade said. "The clerk said they're investigating for a hit-and-run, saying the driver didn't stop until the car was disabled at that intersection. Also, the local German government is pressing the army for answers."

"If the local government is pressuring the army, that may explain why the investigation is being shifted to a higher echelon."

"Yeah, and the fact he drove on after the impact looks bad."

"But Dave didn't know what he was doing. He was injured and dazed by the crash."

"The clerk said we'll be sent to Regiment to testify individually," Wade continued. "Maybe we can help Dave if we keep our stories straight."

"Yeah," Mark said. "But our stories have to be more than straight. They have to clear Dave of any wrongdoing."

"Yeah, and we need to get with Dave and make sure we're all on the same track on this," Wade said.

"If we don't handle this right, we're in serious trouble," Mark said.

CHAPTER 18

THE MOTOR POOL HAD REQUESTED help from Charlie Company to attend to work they needed done, saying they couldn't spare their available personnel for a particular detail. First Sergeant Andrade, knowing that accommodating their request would obligate the motor pool to reciprocate in the future, had offered to send them a man for temporary duty. He chose Myers and relieved him of his duties as company runner in order to take on the assignment at the motor pool. With Myers working at the motor pool, and knowing their conversation shouldn't be overheard, Mark and Wade decided the motor pool would be a good place to discuss their accounts of the accident. The back lots were isolated with few people around to hear their conversation. Rather than wait for Myers to return to the barracks, they headed for the motor pool to discuss their plans.

Once there, Mark and Wade entered the small building at the gate. The entrance was marked with a sign that read "457 Regimental Motor Pool: Sergeant Riley, SIC." When they entered the small office, they found the sergeant in charge at his desk reviewing a stack of trip reports. The sergeant had a sizable beer gut and was smoking a cigar. He looked up at the two men suspiciously when they inquired of Myers. At their inquiry, he pushed himself back from his desk and said in a no-nonsense tone: "He's in the back lot. I've got him stenciling numbers on some tracks back there. I want him to finish today, so don't distract him for long."

The tracks the sergeant referred to were M4 Sherman Tanks, and there were several rows of these large vehicles lined up such that each two rows faced each other with their seventy-six-millimeter guns forward and pointing downward. All the tracks were painted dark army green and parked in perfectly straight lines with their large guns at the same angle. As the two men approached the back lot, they could see that the rows of Shermans were as organized and symmetrical as columns of troops on parade.

The sun was getting low in the sky, and gray shadows were developing in the lot as Mark and Wade walked down the lane between the rows looking for Myers. From a distance, they spotted him kneeling before a track at the far end, working with his paint. With his green fatigues blending with the army green of the tracks, he appeared small and insignificant next to the thirty-two-ton vehicles.

"Hurry up there, troop," Wade said as they approached Myers, surprising and slightly startling him as he focused on his work.

"Yeah," Mark said, laughing at catching Myers off guard. "You don't want to miss chow."

Myers stood up holding a stencil in one hand and a paint brush in the other. He regained his composure quickly, and grinning at the two intruders, said "Quiet, can't you see Picasso's at work!"

They joked around a minute or two, both Mark and Wade criticizing Dave's work unmercifully as most close friends did in such situations.

"Hey, Dave, you need to go back over that zero there," Wade said, laughing. "It's a shade lighter than the other numbers."

"Yeah," Mark said. "Sergeant Riley will give you hell for that."

Finally, Mark stopped joking, his face becoming serious. "Dave, we need to talk," he said, laying his hand on Myers's shoulder. "We've heard the investigation board is about to convene."

"Yeah," Wade said. "We need to get our stories straight."

"So? We all know what happened," Myers said. "Just tell it like it was."

"Not good enough," Mark said, seriously. "They're investigation for a hit-and-run."

"And who knows what else," Wade said.

"Um . . ." Myers said, as if thinking about Mark's statement as he looked from one to the other. Then, as if to allay the seriousness of the situation, he waved his paint brush dramatically in the air. "They wouldn't dare question Picasso!" he declared.

Mark and Wade looked at each other and then back to Myers. "Glad you've still got your sense of humor," Mark said.

"Yeah, as long as you've got that and keep your head, you'll be okay," Wade said.

"Sure I'll be okay," Myers said, continuing with a little nervous laugh. "I'll probably get a Good Conduct Medal out of this."

"You little shrimp," Wade said, grabbing Myers affectionately around the neck in a headlock, as they often did while clowning around in the barracks. "You don't understand the judicial process that will be coming at you. Take this serious, now."

"Look, Dave," Mark said. "Sam's right. We've got to take this seriously. This will be an official inquiry, and we need to be ready. We've got to give the same story, and it's got to be one that exonerates you.

"Yeah, Dave," Wade began. "If they're looking at this as a possible hit-and-run, we stand a good chance of beating it if we all say you stopped on your own accord after you regained you senses. We won't mention that Mark turned off the ignition key." He paused a moment as if in thought and then continued: "And we need to say you were not drinking. If they think you were drunk, they could press for negligent homicide."

"Let's decide here and now what our story will be," Mark began, "and let's stick to that at all costs."

"Okay, then," Wade said. "Our story is that Dave had not been drinking, is a good driver, and stopped on his own accord as soon as he regained his senses and became aware of the impact."

"No, wait!" Myers said. "I was drinking! And I didn't stop immediately. That had nothing to do with the accident, but it would be a lie to say something different. We'll be testifying under oath, and lying under oath is perjury—a serious offense." As Myers continued, he grew serious for the first time. "I'm not going to let you guys run that risk."

"Dave's right on the issue of not drinking," Mark said. "There were many witnesses at the *Gasthaus* Zumeck who saw him drinking."

"Okay, you're right," Wade said. "He was drinking in public, so we can't say he wasn't. The question then is how can we mitigate that fact?"

"Try this," Mark began. "There's nothing wrong with drinking a beer. Every GI in Germany and every German citizen drinks beer. So we shouldn't say he wasn't drinking but that he had only one beer."

"Wait a minute," Myers said. "Herr Kuntz knows he served me more than a couple beers. I drank a lot, and they'll surely question him."

"Okay, so he did serve you many beers," Wade said. "But you didn't drink them. You passed them on to us after drinking only one."

"That should do it," Mark said. "We'll say Dave bought several beers to pass around to keep the party going, but he didn't drink any after the first one."

"It'll be our word against whoever might contradict that," Mark said.

"It's shaky," Myers said. "I don't want you guys to take the risk."

"Maybe so," Mark continued, "but we're not going to let you take this alone. Individually, we're not very effective, but together and with a consistent story, we can make a difference."

"Listen, Dave," Wade said, pushing Myers back slightly with his hand to his chest. "If they nail you with a negligent homicide, you'll do time in an army prison."

"And you two may do some time if they prove you're lying," Myers said. "I just ain't going to let you guys do that. This is my mess, and I'll deal with it—somehow."

"No, Dave," Mark said. "Sam's right. Like it or not, we're in this together. And if we don't stick together, we'll surely go down. Individuals don't count in this situation. It's only when we stick together that we'll be okay."

The three men stood silently for some time. They glanced down at the ground and at each other and up at the darkening sky, but no one said anything for a short time. Their situation was like being the losing player in a chess game. Their king was in check, and only one move would avoid capture. In their minds, that one move was to all agree on a viable and credible story that would clear them of all wrongdoing and then present that story convincingly at the inquiry. It didn't seem to matter to Mark and Wade that there were no charges against them and that all they had to do was give testimony of their versions of the accident. The army had taught them not to think of themselves but of the group, the unit, and the mission.

"There's no other way," Mark said, finally. "We're innocent of any wrongdoing, but we're in a tough situation where we have the burden of proving that."

"That's right," Wade said, shaking his head. "And a clean, consistent story from the three of us will head off any incriminating charges."

The two men then looked at Myers and waited for his decision. The sun had dropped farther in the sky with the temperature falling slightly and the light between the rows of Sherman tanks fading rapidly. They stood in the graying shadows surrounded by the olive drab green of the army vehicles. "Okay," Myers said finally. "If you guys are sure this is the best way, then I'm with you."

They went over their story several times, considering every detail. Finally, all agreed on the specific details they would relate to the board of inquiry. When they were sure they all had the same story, Mark and Wade helped Myers clean up and shut down his paint work for the day.

CHAPTER 19

WHILE MARK WAITED FOR THE call to testify about the accident, army life continued as usual. He performed well at the various jobs he was assigned, staying in good standing with his platoon leader and the first sergeant. He secured a weekend pass and, as previously arranged, had planned to meet Lauren in her village. She had told him it was time to meet her father, and Mark knew this would be a crucial point in their relationship. It had been almost eight months since that first day at the camera shop. They'd had many pleasant and fun rendezvous since then, but it was the first time Lauren had offered to bring him to her home. He had wondered about this often but had never mentioned it to her. He was soon to discover the reason she was reluctant to introduce him to her father.

When she told Mark of her plans, she had warned him that her father was firmly set in his ways and might not be friendly at first. But she went on to say that if her father could meet him, he might begin to like him. This would be the first step on the path to friendship. She told Mark she had carefully planned out the meeting. To eliminate the chance of her father misunderstanding Mark's conversations, she asked him to speak only English so she could interpret. This in spite of the fact that Mark's spoken German was fair and getting better by the day.

"It's easy when speaking a foreign language for something to get lost in translation," she told Mark. "I don't want to take any unnecessary chances that he'll mistake your meaning. I know how to handle him," she continued, smiling. "If I translate, I can be sure he'll hear nothing that will offend him."

When they reached Lauren's house, she knocked on the front door as opposed to entering as she usually did. "We don't want to appear unannounced and possibly disturb him," she explained to Mark.

"Mark Bergner," Mark said, holding out his hand and facing an elderly German man with a full head of black-and-gray hair and a dark, aging face. Mark and Lauren stood in the doorway of Lauren's home, facing her father. Standing there, Mark noticed two red indentations on the bridge of the man's nose. *Reading glasses,* he thought. *We've interrupted his reading.* "I'm pleased to meet you, Herr Werner."

Lauren immediately translated the greeting into German for her father, who shook Mark's hand firmly but didn't smile. Dressed in rumpled, faded gray trousers with black suspenders and a well-worn brown shirt buttoned to the neck, the elderly German man displayed no hospitality in dress or manner, and his cold blue eyes bore into Mark. Lauren continued speaking to her father and then turned to Mark. "I've told him you're an American soldier, that we met a few months back and discovered we both liked photography, and that I wanted him to meet you."

Mark smiled and held up the Leica he had purchased from Lauren. "I bought this camera from Lauren," he said, speaking slowly and clearly. "I had been looking for this model and found it in her shop." Lauren's father continued watching Mark, not speaking, leaving Mark more uncomfortable.

On the train, Lauren had explained that her two older brothers had died in the war, and a short time later her mother had also died, leaving just her and her father. Mark sensed the closeness between Lauren and her father and knew that he must sell himself for the sake of their relationship. "We plan to tour your village today and take some pictures," Mark added.

Lauren translated and continued speaking in German to her father. His face remained sternly fixed, staring at Mark intently. He was obviously surprised by the unannounced visit and needed time to adjust. A flicker of understanding then came into his eyes, and Mark could see his mouth tighten and his face grow tense.

"Ber-ge-ner!" he finally said, mispronouncing Mark's Jewish name and looking from Mark to Lauren. His glance went back and forth for a moment before he grunted, turned, and disappeared back into the shadows of the house, leaving them standing in the doorway.

"But, Papa!" Lauren said, her voice reflecting anxiety and humiliation. "Don't go!" She took a step as if to follow him but then stopped and faced Mark. "Oh, Mark," she began but then turned and disappeared into the house following her father.

Mark was unsure what to do, so he remained at the entrance. He could hear voices coming from inside the house. Although he couldn't make out what was being said, he could detect the anguish in Lauren's voice. The voices came back at him going back and forth from Herr Werner to Lauren. At one point, it sounded like Lauren's voice turned from pleading to anger, and Herr Werner's voice grew silent.

Soon Lauren returned to the front entrance with Mark. Even with a troubled face and eyes brimming, she still showed anger and determination. She took a moment to compose herself before she spoke. "I'm sorry he's that way. Some of the old people can't change." Lauren took Mark's arm and led him back out into the street. "I'm sorry I got you into this. I had hoped it would go better," she continued angrily as they walked away from her house.

"My parents are the same way," Mark said, thinking he had to get control of the situation and comfort her. He desperately wanted to relieve her of the embarrassment and distress of the unintended situation and struggled to think of what to say. "Their attitudes are shaped by the past . . . It's hard for them to change"

They continued walking down the main street of the village. Lauren seemed to have gotten over her anger and had settled into a quiet, pensive mood. Mark knew that she had brought him there hoping he could win over her father. She often spoke of him in a loving, respectful tone. Finally, many months into their relationship, she had told Mark the time was right and set up the meeting. He not only knew that he had failed but sensed that not being accepted by her father and not being able to be a part of her family would pose a serious problem. The fact that he was Jewish and she German Catholic didn't concern Mark or Lauren. If anything, their separate backgrounds offered them an attraction of differences.

Forcing the incident from his mind, Mark focused his attention on Lauren. He attempted to distract her by discussing the scenery and snapping random pictures of the winding, narrow streets with occasional shops and ancient gray-and-brown buildings that hadn't changed for centuries. He had her pose before a small church that had one steeple and was set back a ways from the street. The shot framed her, demure and smiling, with the cross atop the steeple above her in the background. Even though she smiled, her face seemed to lack its normal youthful radiance. She said little.

In the village square, they came upon a war memorial of cast iron and bronze sitting atop a concrete base. Mark stopped and studied the memorial for several minutes. The bronze monument consisted of several life-sized figures that had initially been a light bronze color but with age had become dark gray with black streaks. At the memorial's head walked a German soldier in full battle dress, followed by a woman with oxen at plow, followed by two young children. Lauren broke her silence: "It represents sacrifice and duty," she said, her voice low and reverent. "We are told this in school . . . It's our heritage."

"Yeah, fate played a dirty trick on that generation," Mark said. "People like your father and my parents didn't ask for what they got."

"No they didn't," she said, "but we all have to make the best of what life gives us." Turning her back to the monument, she walked a few steps away. "And like it or not, we are all a part of our heritage," she added, as if speaking to herself.

Mark looked at Lauren closely, puzzled by her statement. *She's sorry she brought me here,* he thought. *I must keep her talking, so she can talk it out.* Surprised by her mature understanding and amazed that someone so young could be so perceptive and worldly, he continued with the same line of conversation. "Their lives were affected by powerful forces beyond their control." He wanted to relieve her pain and disappointment. "Our parents are among the many who are victims of something they had nothing to do with."

"Yes," she said, turning to him, touching his arm again. "You understand, don't you?"

"Yes."

"I mean, about my father."

"Yes, I think so."

"It's important that you understand."

"And I do understand."

They then settled on a bench in the small park in front of the war memorial, and each grew quiet for a few minutes. Mark gazed distractedly at the memorial, thinking what a grave and profound heritage to have to live with.

Lauren remained quiet and pensive for a brief time but then continued with her previous conversation. "It's not something against you personally, or that he's against anyone, for that matter. It's just that to change his thinking now would make his life and sacrifices pointless."

Mark again was puzzled and thought deeply about what she said. He felt he was missing something and not fully relating to what she meant. He tried to put it out of his mind, but it continued to bother him as they sat before the monument. The phrase "to change would make his sacrifices pointless" stuck in his mind. Reflecting on this idea and finally coming to realize its meaning not only helped him understand her father but his own parents as well. He shifted the camera strap on his shoulder.

"That's the older generation," Mark finally said. "Our parents, in spite of being survivors, are still victims of the war and their sacrifices."

"I won't be able to take you there again," she said quietly, looking up into his face.

Mark didn't answer, but as they sat there, each holding the other's gaze, he nodded his understanding. He knew what this meant, and he knew she knew he understood. Finally, he said, "We should go. I need to catch the next train."

They left the park and walked arm in arm back down the cobblestone street toward the train station. Just before the depot Lauren suddenly stopped, pulling Mark around to face her. Then with a solemn face, she asked: "Mark, do we know what we're getting into?"

CHAPTER 20

WITH THE STORY THAT MARK, Wade, and Myers had formulated for the investigating board firmed up in their minds, the three men began to relax on the accident situation and focus on the upcoming training schedule. The time was nearing to execute the tactical maneuvers that followed up Second Platoon's earlier scouting trip. This was an important field maneuver exercise where each company would demonstrate their capabilities and efficiency in both offensive and defensive tactics in the field. These maneuvers were performed under the close observation of tactical referees from division headquarters, and the company commanders were graded on how well their companies performed, as rated by these referees. Knowing their reputations and future promotions were at stake, the COs of each company worked their men hard to perform well. Most of their waking hours were spent in preparation for these maneuvers.

Days before Charlie Company mobilized to convoy to the designated area for the maneuvers, the platoon leaders and NCOs put their men through numerous and detailed inspections to make sure they were ready for field duty. The night before the move, an inspection was executed that required each soldier to lay out his field gear for the platoon leader's scrutiny. Steel helmets, bayonets, gas masks, shelter halves, mess kits, canteens, entrenching tools, web belts with first aid pouch, and assorted personal clothing items were displayed under the watchful eye of platoon NCOs and then packed away immediately for a quick departure the following day.

Because Mark was team leader on a .50 caliber machine gun, he had an extra detail after all the other details were finished. When in convoy, the .50 MGs were mounted on firing stands on the five-ton trucks for air defense. Mark, Myers, and a soldier name Jackson (the other two men rounding out Mark's three-man team) had to check out the gun and other associated equipment from the armory and then mount the gun on their assigned truck. It was close to midnight when they finished all of their work and had showered and prepared for sleep.

On the following day, the convoy made it to the designated area without incident, a result of the route carefully planned out by Lieutenant McBride and his Second Platoon's scouting trip. The area planned for the field maneuvers was in a forest area some 150 kilometers from post. At first, all was quiet as they began to set up their bivouac. But in the midst of unloading equipment, putting up the mess tent, and establishing a defensive perimeter in the heavily wooded area, aggressor forces began their harassment tactics.

Mark was in the process of handing down the barrel of the heavy gun to Myers and Jackson from the firing stand of the five-ton when several aggressors came running through the bivouac area shouting and firing blanks and setting off bomb simulators. It was a planned exercise by the tactical referees to catch a company off guard in order to test how quickly they could react and organize into a defensive posture. Even though this was just war games, it had a sense of reality and presented a challenge to the just-arrived company. There was mass confusion. Platoon leaders were shouting at their NCOs to get their men prepared, and the sergeants were running about assigning men to positions on a defensive line.

Lieutenant McBride quickly organized his platoon and began walking the imaginary line, making assignments for key positions and special weapons. He dropped a man off with a 2.5 rocket launcher and followed that with several rifle positions. Continuing to walk rapidly along, he commanded Mark to follow him with his MG team. He selected a spot and then said, "Set up the MG here. Dig it in good and proper. You can fill sandbags later." McBride then hurried on his way, shouting at a sergeant to get some men and fill in a vacant position on the left side of the line.

Mark immediately began to set up the gun. He had been in Charlie Company ten months now, and he knew his job well. "Okay, guys, let's do it," he said. "Let's play the game." He selected a spot for the tripod and attached the gun. With the gun assembled, he picked up a stick and marked off the line for the machine gun pit to be dug. "Dig, you slaves," he said to his amused team members.

Myers went to work immediately with his entrenching tool. "I'm in the army now," he began to sing as the soft dirt began to fly.

"I believe you like this work," Jackson said to Myers as he worked on the opposite side of the gun pit.

"I'm not behind a plow," Myers continued singing, laughing at Jackson.

"You lifer," Jackson said back at Myers. Both men worked feverishly to get the pit dug. Mark had told them they could take a break after they finished setting up the gun emplacement.

As they worked, Mark noticed a soldier standing a few meters behind them. He carried no weapon and wore no steel helmet atop his helmet liner, as everyone else did. His helmet liner had a white line around it, and Mark knew he was a tactical referee. These men were not allowed to talk to those they were observing, but Mark noticed just a hint of a sneer on his face and got his unintended message. As the referee turned and walked away, Mark thought, *There's something wrong. He's got us on something.*

Looking around, Mark began to assess their location in the wooded terrain. He saw before him and to his right a wooded area with much undergrowth that he hadn't noticed at first. To his left, the trees and undergrowth thinned down to a sparse growth, and a short distance farther laid a flat, open field that extended several hundred meters out in front of the defensive line that was being set up along the tree line. "Hey, guys," he said, "we're gigged already!"

"How's that?" asked Jackson.

"Our position in this terrain is wrong," Mark said. "It's wrong for this gun."

"How's that?" Jackson repeated.

"There's a heavily wooded area before us, to our right we have no field of fire, and we can be flanked easily on our right because of the undergrowth giving cover for an aggressor," Mark said as he studied the area. "It wouldn't matter as much with rifle positions, but it's not a good location for our MG."

"It looks that way," Myers said. "But we were ordered to set up here."

"I'm going to find the lieutenant and see what he says," Mark said. "He was in a hurry when he selected this location." Mark left but returned shortly. "Can't find him or the platoon sergeant," he told the others. "They're all back at the command post or scattered out somewhere."

"We best continue setting up here," Jackson said. "That was our order."

"I know," Mark said. "That would be the safest thing for us to do."

"What's bothering you, Mark?" Myers said. "We're in the clear since we were ordered to set up here."

"Yeah, I know," Mark said, studying the terrain toward the open field. "But it's bigger that just us."

"How's that?" Jackson said for the third time.

"You sound like a stuck record," Myers said to Jackson, giving him a scornful look. "What do you mean?" he said, turning back to Mark.

"The company will get a serious gig for this," Mark said. "It's an obvious mistake, and the tactical referees have already taken note."

"What do you suggest?" Myers asked.

"Let's set up to our left just off the corner of that open field," Marked answered, his mind already formulating his defense for relocating the gun and disobeying McBride's order. "There we have a complete enfilade of all that open space."

"And the wooded area will give us better flank protection from armor on our right," Myers said, agreeing with Mark.

"Plus, there'll be a rocket launcher to our left to cover armor," Mark said, his eyes sweeping the area for the third time.

"It's best we don't disobey orders," Jackson said. "Besides, more than likely an aggressor force would infiltrate through the wooded area where they have cover."

"That's true, Jackson," Mark said. "But with the MG covering that huge open area, many of those riflemen there could be relocated to strengthen the line before the wooded area."

"Maybe so," Jackson said. "But disobeying Lieutenant McBride's order can bring big trouble."

"Mark's ranking man at this moment," Myers said quickly to Jackson. "He's giving the orders."

"I'll take the responsibility and whatever trouble that comes from it," Mark said. "Let's get moving and get set up before the line's firmly established. The referees will soon be taking their final look at our initial positions."

It took several trips for the three men to move the gun and the other equipment to the corner of the open field. Two men digging rifle positions there were told to relocate back to the old MG location. They complained, as usual, but moved immediately, thinking the orders had come down from the lieutenant. The MG was set up and the gun pit half dug when Mark saw Lieutenant McBride walking along the line surveying each position critically. He walked to meet him some distance from the gun emplacement. Mark reported and immediately explained the move and the reason.

"What?" McBride said. "You didn't follow my orders!"

"But, sir," Mark said, "I assessed the situation, and I looked for you to discuss the weakness of that location. Where it is now, it can cover twenty times the ground and not easily be flanked. On top of that, I was getting negative looks from the tactical referees. When I couldn't find you or our platoon sergeant, I made the decision to make the move."

"I gave you a direct order," McBride said, frowning. He looked critically around the entire area, walking back and forth and then returning to the gun emplacement now nearing completion. "We'll discuss this later," he said in a sharp tone. "And make sure those grenade sumps are at standard operating procedure," he continued as he walked on down the line, checking each position. He obviously realized the superiority of the new location, or he would have come down hard on Mark for not following orders. Just the fact that he didn't order Mark to move the gun back to the original location meant he agreed with Mark, but officers don't admit mistakes to enlisted men.

Mark knew McBride to be a good officer, and he felt that when he had time to study the big picture and not be burdened with minute details, he would see the advantage of the new position. A gun with such firepower facing a clear and broad enfilade in the direction an enemy would approach would be a tactic hard to deny. In spite of this, Mark felt he hadn't heard the last from McBride for disobeying his orders. The first gun position was clearly a mistake made by an officer in the haste of the moment. But disobeying orders was a serious offense if those in command wanted to push it. Mark knew he was walking a risky path, but he also felt it was something he had to do. He could have stayed at the first location with no risk to himself or his team, but that would have set up the company for a severe gig. Thus, he felt the issue relative to the good of Charlie Company bigger than the personal risk he would face. *I know I'm in trouble,* he thought, *but this is bigger than me.*

Shortly after they had completed the initial phase of the gun emplacement, Mark left the position to retrieve a notebook and writing pen from the five-ton located some distance behind the now well-established lines. He wanted to make a firing chart of the kill zone for the gun, showing boundaries and approximate distances in meters. He left word for Myers and Jackson to take a break while he was gone. He chuckled to himself, knowing they would take a break in any case once he left.

Jackson sat down on the edge of the gun pit, took off his steel helmet, and laid it beside him. He took a cigarette from his fatigue pocket, lit it up, and took a long, slow draw. Looking at Myers while exhaling, he said, "I wouldn't want to be in the corporal's boots right now."

"Why not?" Myers asked, staring at Jackson, as if ready to defend Mark.

"These are simulated combat maneuvers," Jackson said. "He could lose a stripe or get company punishment for a long time."

"You think so?" Myers asked with a concerned face.

"Yeah, the lieutenant can be one tough hombre when he's riled," he said. "And the corporal disobeyed a direct order."

CHAPTER 21

F OR WEEKS, MARK AND WADE felt the accident issue was covered, but as more time passed with no word from the investigation board saying the issue had been resolved and the investigation dropped, their concern resurfaced. This was partially based on the first sergeant's statement that the investigation was taking an unusually long time. "These matters are usually over in a few weeks," the first sergeant had said. "If it takes longer, it means they have reasons to continue studying the case."

The three men had been in Germany roughly eleven months now, and Wade had managed to save enough money from his pay to buy a secondhand car. It was an old French Citron that was slow to start, but it got them around once it was running.

"Mark," Wade said one afternoon as they were getting off from duty, "let's ride back up to that intersection where the accident happened."

"Yeah," Mark said. "I kind of hate to go back there, but it's not a bad idea. We should be clear and consistent in our statements in case we're questioned further."

They skipped chow and drove back to the mountain road. It was the first time they had been on that road since the incident. The day was nearing toward dusk, and the sky was overcast when they parked the Citron by the *Gasthaus* at the intersection where Myers's car had finally stopped. Knowing they had only a little daylight left, they immediately began to retrace their steps from the night of the accident. It took them some time to walk the distance back to the point of impact. A truck drove by as they walked, and they stepped off the narrow road into the shallow ditch while it passed.

"The distance Dave drove after the collision is farther than I thought," Wade said as they finally arrived at the spot where the crash occurred.

"Yeah," Mark said. "It must be close to a quarter mile."

"That's not good," Wade said. "If only he'd stopped immediately, it would look much better to the investigation board."

"But after the impact, he was stunned," Mark replied. "He didn't know what had happened or what he was doing."

"There's the spot where the first body laid," Wade said. "Is it my imagination, or is there still a slight depression in the grass." The short grass alongside the road revealed a spot that was sparser in growth.

Mark stared at the spot for a long moment, reliving the events of that night and recalling details. The sound of the crash echoed in his memory, and he could hear and feel the impact and the glass fragments shattering back into his face. "Why's the dirt black there?" he asked, just now noticing the discoloration of soil under the grass.

"You know!" Wade said, looking hard at Mark to emphasize his point.

"Yeah, I guess so," Mark said. "Damn, I feel bad about this!" He continued, turning away.

"Me too," Wade said as he stared at the dirt beneath the grass. "Blood in the dirt—it's like giving your blood to your country."

"Yeah," Mark said, "but without a cause." He stared at the dark spot as if mesmerized. For the first time, he was beginning to empathize with the victims. Although, to his knowledge, he had never met them, he somehow began to connect with their passing and felt a deep sense of loss. In time, he regained his equanimity, but the moment had left him embittered. "But in the end, does the cause or the reason or anything else really matter to the individual? I mean, to this person, what matters at this point?"

"What?" Wade said, looking oddly at Mark.

"I mean, life can be short for any of us. The question is how should we live it?"

"Easy, Mark," Wade said. "Brace up, man, we can't afford to let our feelings go at this point."

"Oh, hell. You're right," Mark said. "I'm getting morbid. Let's get out of here."

"You sure are," Wade said. "Let's go back to that *Gasthaus* and have a beer and maybe something to eat. We'll feel better."

They left the scene and walked back to the *Gasthaus*. Entering the inn, they found it nearly empty. Except for a middle-aged couple having dinner and an older gentleman reading a newspaper by the kitchen door, there were no other customers. The room was well lit in a warm, yellow glow, and a small bar at the opposite end had a row of clean beer steins atop it, offering the possibility of cheer to both men. A slightly plump but young and attractive *Fräulein* stood behind the bar, drying glasses with a towel and placing them atop the bar. She immediately approached them and asked in English what they would like to have. She spoke with a strong German accent, some of her words coming out in English and some in German. She obviously knew they spoke English, because Mark and Wade were still in their fatigues. They had wanted to get to the scene of the accident before it got dark and had not taken time to change into civilian clothes before they left post. Wade asked the waitress's name, and she said it was Ursula.

"Two beers, Ursula," Wade said. "Big ones," he added, making a sign with his hands to indicate something large. The *Fräulein* smiled and returned to the bar. She wore glasses, and as she drew the beer, she glanced several times back in Wade's direction.

"She's got you in her sights," Mark said.

"Okay with me," Wade said as the *Fräulein* returned carrying two one-liter mugs with heavy white foam on the top. Both men began to drink. They had not had evening chow, and the room-temperature beer lifted their spirits almost immediately. Wade started a conversation with Ursula. They talked back and forth in halting English mixed with German.

Mark, who spoke reasonably good German because of his background and his contact with Lauren, remained silent; his mood and spirit had not recovered from the accident scene. He wondered about the families of the two victims, how they were handling their grief and what they thought about American soldiers. As he drank his beer, only half listening to Wade and the Fräulein's conversation, he suddenly turned to Wade.

"Sam, do you realize what she's asking you?" He said, glancing at the *Fräulein*.

"Not really," Wade said, laughing. "I only know she's talking about the accident."

"She asking if we're investigating the accident."

"Why would she be asking that?" Wade said.

"There must have been others here investigating," Mark said. He then turned to Ursula and spoke to her. They conversed in rapid German for a brief time and then Mark stopped talking and was thoughtful for a moment. He turned to Wade and started to speak but turned back to Ursula. "Two more beers, please."

When Ursula left their table, Mark turned to Wade. "She says this place has been crawling with investigators—mostly Americans and mostly officers. Says they've talked to her several times, but they've also spent much time up and down the road."

"That's not good," Wade said.

"Not good at all," Mark said. "If they're putting so much manpower and time into the investigation, it means they're trying hard to find something. This thing is getting bigger by the minute."

"I just thought of something," Wade suddenly said, getting up from his chair. He then went to the bar where Ursula was drawing their beers. After speaking to her a few minutes, he returned to the table. He sat down a minute before he spoke. "I very gently asked Ursula if she knew the men who were killed. She said she did and that they were in here just before the accident."

"Did she say anything else about them?" Mark asked.

"She said they were celebrating after a soccer match and had drunk quiet a lot that night," Wade answered. He paused a moment before continuing. "She said they were two fun-loving, young men who had left the *Gasthaus* singing. Said one was the son of the local *Bürgermeister*."

"Yeah, we know that."

"She said they had been playing soccer?" Mark asked suddenly. "My God, Wade, they might have been two of the boys we played with that afternoon."

"But we don't know that," Wade said quickly. "And it's best we don't know."

Both men grew silent. Mark's thoughts went back to the soccer game. He could clearly see the boys on the opposite team running about, kicking the ball, and playing enthusiastically, their faces flushed and red from the strenuous exercise.

When Ursula came back with the beers, they ordered food. They had a fine dinner of venison, salad, and peas and potatoes—a meal that went well with the beer and lifted their spirits. As Wade's high spirits returned, he kept a conversation going with Ursula. As awkward as the exchange was, they seemed to be connecting with one another. She invited him to the juke box to help select some music, and they stood over the machine for several minutes, laughing and pointing at different songs. They danced briefly to some number. Wade stopped suddenly, laughing at his awkward steps. He asked her if she would be working the coming weekend, and she said she would. Wade promised he would return Saturday afternoon.

Mark, in spite of his command of the German language, was mostly ignored by Wade and Ursula. They were hitting it off and seemed preoccupied with each other as they played the juke box, danced, and laughed at each other's attempts to communicate. That suited Mark just fine. He remained preoccupied with the death scene and the events of the day. And although the food and beer made him feel better, in the back of his mind, a black mood nagged away at his consciousness.

CHAPTER 22

L AUREN HURRIED ABOUT THE KITCHEN, stirring pots with a critical eye and opening and closing the oven door to keep a close watch on the roast. Dressed in jeans and T-shirt Mark had bought for her from the Post Exchange and covered with a blue apron, she hurried about her work. Between stirring pots and frequently checking the roast, she set plates on the table and sliced a loaf of freshly made bread from the local bakery. She had gotten permission from Herr Clause to leave work a few minutes early and had taken an earlier train to beat her father home. As she put the bread slices on a plate and covered them with a clean white towel, she rehearsed the points of the subject she planned to discuss with her father after he had his supper and was in a good mood. She was well aware of the difficulty of what lay ahead of her, but she felt the issue had to be faced by both of them.

"You've prepared an excellent meal," Herr Werner said as he finished his meal and looked across the table at Lauren. Usually he beat Lauren home to enter a dark and cold house. But today, after Lauren's preparation, he found the house warm and bright and the delicious smell of cooking greeted him at the door. "The roast was cooked just right, and the potatoes and cabbage went well with the roast."

"Thank you, Papa," Lauren said, smiling across the table at him. "I knew it was your favorite meal. That's why I prepared it." She then rose and quickly began to pick up the dishes and leftover food. "Don't leave the table just yet," she continued as she worked rapidly. "I have a surprise."

"A surprise?" Herr Werner said. He started to say something else, but Lauren had disappeared into the kitchen. When she returned carrying coffee cups and saucers, he continued. "What kind of surprise?"

"Just you wait," she said before disappearing back into the kitchen. When she returned the second time, she was carrying a disk neatly covered with a clean table napkin. Placing the dish between them on the table, she removed the napkin. "It's your favorite desert, Papa. Plum pudding," she continued. "I asked the baker to make it this morning, and I picked it up coming in from work today."

"My, my," Herr Werner said. "How good you are to me—my favorite meal and my favorite dessert." He looked at Lauren with a warm smile.

"My favorite also," Lauren said, avoiding his look and trying to appear casual. "Try the pudding. Is it just right?" she asked as she took a bite of the dessert and a sip of coffee.

"It's perfect," Herr Werner said as he began to eat the pudding. After finishing the dessert, he pushed the plate to the side and leaned back in his chair, holding his coffee saucer in his left hand and the cup of coffee in the other. "Now," he began, a smile growing on his face. "After preparing my favorite meal and my favorite dessert, what does my one and only child and the one most important to me in this world have to say to her Papa?" He then took a small sip of coffee and waited for Lauren to answer. His eyes rested affectionately upon her, and his demeanor was sympathetic.

Lauren was just bringing her cup up to sip the coffee when Herr Werner posed the question. Surprised at her father's perception in seeing there was more to her fine meal than the meal itself, she slowly replaced the cup back on its saucer. She looked submissively at him for a long moment before speaking. "Papa, I know that you know I prepared this meal you like so well because I wanted to talk to you." She paused a moment before continuing. Her look was dutiful but steady and determined. "Papa, I want to talk to you about something very important to me."

"Yes," Herr Werner said, his patient smile slowly fading into a look of concern. "You can always talk to me about anything."

"Papa, what I want to talk about is—" Lauren paused a moment, her eyes flickering, wavering for a moment, but then resuming a steady and firm look. "Papa, I want to talk to you about Mark."

"Mark?" Herr Werner said. "Who's Mark?"

"Mark," Lauren began. "You remember—the soldier I brought to our house awhile back."

"You mean that American soldier?" her father said, his look turning serious.

"Yes, that's who I want to talk about."

"I thought we settled him some time past," Herr Werner said. "Why do you want to discuss him now?"

"Because," Lauren began, again pausing as if she were thinking about how to say what she wanted to say. When she continued, her voice was very low but clear. "Because he's the one, Papa," she said slowly, slightly nodding once, her look direct and unwavering. "He's the one, and he's the only one, and nothing can change that."

With that statement, she had set her challenge—her manifesto, so to speak. It was all out in the open now, and she was ready to defend her position on the matter. She sat waiting—waiting for what she had said to be fully understood. Her respectful look rested on her father's face. Herr Werner sat quietly, not speaking for a moment as if thinking about what she had said. For a long moment, neither spoke as they looked blankly at each other, each waiting for the other's reaction.

"Humph," Herr Werner finally uttered. With that, he rose from the chair and turned to walk away. Lauren remained seated without saying anything, her look dropping to the coffee cup in her hands. Just as Herr Werner was about to leave the room, he suddenly turned and walked back to the table. "Lauren," he began in a soft, controlled voice. "Don't you remember what I said before? What I said about honoring all those who have sacrificed for us? What it would mean to forget what they have done for us?"

"I remember, Papa. I haven't forgotten."

"Lauren," Herr Werner continued as he leaned forward from across the table, his voice serious and nearly pleading. "I've lost my sons to the cause of Germany. I could never not support my country's cause. To do so would mean I don't support the honor and purpose of their sacrifices."

"But, Papa!" Lauren said, rising to her feet and facing her father across the table. "To accept Mark doesn't mean you reject your ideals or dishonor the memories of your sons, my brothers." Her voice initially rose, but she quickly regained control and spoke in a quieter tone. "Can't you see that?"

"Why does it have to be this American soldier?" Herr Werner asked as if he were trying to understand but couldn't find an explanation. "They go home after their tour is over, and where would that leave you? You're just seventeen years old and can take your pick of many. Wait for a young German man. You'll be glad you did."

Lauren stood before her father, firmly positioned in her stance, her attitude, and her frame of mind. She slowly shook her head, looking at her father with weary, sad eyes. "Papa," she began in a slow, measured tone, "as my father, I love and respect you. I know my obligations to you, my school, and my work and will honor them. But as a man is to a woman, he's the one. He's my first, and he'll be my last. I have no illusions about him going home either. The time may come when we'll go our separate ways. But even with this knowledge, I can't imagine a time when he won't be the one."

"But it doesn't have to be this way."

"But it is this way!" she said with emphasis and finality. "We're just two people whose paths have crossed, and that has started something much more than us individually. I agree it doesn't have to be this way, but you must understand, Papa. It is this way."

"I can never forget their sacrifices," Warner said again, holding to his old argument.

"Neither can I, Papa!" Lauren said, her voice breaking as she stood before him and held the table for support. She paused momentarily, struggling to control her feelings. Then, with her face pained, her eyes brimming, she spoke in almost a whisper. "They were my family too, Papa, and every day I miss them."

Herr Werner stared at his daughter in disbelief. He had often told her that his dream was for her to marry a young German man and have many grandchildren for him. He slowly turned from Lauren and went to his room without another word.

CHAPTER 23

"**B**ERGNER," LIEUTENANT MCBRIDE SHOUTED AS he dismissed Second Platoon from Monday morning reveille. "Report to the orderly room now!"

Mark mumbled his disappointment under his breath as he headed toward the orderly room. Since returning from the field maneuvers, he had found little time for himself. With the exception of the trip he and Wade had made back to the location of the accident, he hadn't been off post. He hadn't seen Lauren either. By the time he got off duty and could get into the city, she would already be home. And going to her home was out of the question. To make matters worse, he had applied for a three-day pass immediately after returning to post and was denied. He missed seeing her and was growing edgy and tense.

The war game scenarios had been stressful. The games were conducted under the watchful eye of tactical referees, and that kept the pressure on the officers. The careers of company commanders and platoon leaders can hinge on the grades received from these exercises, and they kept the pressure on the men. For this reason, the men were carefully scrutinized and constantly prodded by their NCOs to perform to the standard operating procedures of the tactical games. There's no letup after duty hours when a soldier can go to the EM club and relax and have a beer. It's a twenty-four-hour-a-day exercise that lasts for the duration of the maneuvers.

As Mark entered the orderly room, First Sergeant Andrade looked up and without saying a word nodded Mark toward the CO's office. Mark entered the office and stood waiting while Captain Williams completed a phone conversation. *What have I done now?* he wondered as he reported to the captain and was told to stand at ease.

"Corporal," Williams began and then paused a moment as if collecting his thoughts. "We've been watching you closely these past few weeks, especially during the field maneuvers."

Mark remained silent, not knowing what to expect and wondering how he'd screwed up. *It has to be that gun emplacement incident with McBride,* he thought. *I disobeyed his orders, and now I'll have to pay for that.*

"We were particularly interested in how well you would conduct your MG team in various situations." Williams paused again, picking up a sheet of paper and holding it up as if to base his statements on the document. "One of the incidents mentioned here in Lieutenant McBride's field report states that when the company was attempting to establish a defensive perimeter under harassing circumstances, you took it upon yourself to move your gun emplacement from its original location to one that provided a superior advantage in case of a frontal attack.

"Sir, I can explain that," Mark said, ready to defend his decision to move the gun but feeling his cause was already lost. "After reconnoitering the area, I could see the first location was not the best one."

"Lieutenant McBride has briefed me on that action and has made some strong recommendations."

"Yes, sir," Mark began as he braced himself for what was about to come. "I tried to find the lieutenant to discuss—"

Williams stopped Mark's speech by holding up one hand while he read and used the other to move down the page with his finger. "And it says here that the tactical referees gave this position an excellent grade because of clear enfilade for hundreds of meters in front of the line." Williams stopped reading again, glanced up at Mark momentarily, and then continued his reading. "It goes on to say the new position had strong rifleman support on both flanks and a 2.5 rocket launcher in the tree line to cover potential armor approaching across the open field." He again stopped and looked up at Mark, nodding his head as if pleased.

Mark remained silent, still unsure of his situation.

"This event was the main one that rated C Company tops in the battalion in these exercises," Williams continued, laying the report down and leaning back in his chair. "The tactical referees checked your record on the firing range to make sure you were qualified with the .50 MG before they made their report. After they saw you fired expert, I'm told they were so impressed that one of them said that your team alone with that gun could hold off an entire enemy company at that position."

He studied Mark, frowning somewhat and nodding his head in a positive way. After a moment, he leaned back over his desk. "And there's more," he said, selecting another sheet of paper. "Lieutenant McBride's personal evaluation describes you as controlled and disciplined, well liked by members of you platoon and a strong team player." Williams then dropped the paper and leaned back in his chair, again studying Mark. After a moment, he asked in a quiet voice, "What have you got to say for yourself, Sergeant Bergner?"

"Well, I was just trying to do my . . . Sir, I'm a corporal not a—"

"You were a corporal," Williams interrupted Mark. "You're now a sergeant."

Mark's surprise at what the captain had said left him speechless for a moment. "Thank you, sir," he finally said. "I'm honored." He couldn't think of anything else to say.

Williams nodded his head, obviously pleased with Mark's record. "That'll be all," he said. "Well done!"

As Mark was leaving the outer office, Sergeant Andrade stopped him. "Congratulations, Sergeant," he said.

"You knew!" Mark said. He had not fully recovered from the news.

"Yes, I knew," he admitted, smiling slightly. "It's been in the mill for some time now. We all consider you good army material—disciplined and duty minded."

"Thanks," Mark said. He didn't feel like discussing the promotion at the moment. Although he had always tried to do his assignments well, he had never once thought about being promoted. "What about Wade and Myers?" he asked.

"Always looking out for the other person," Andrade said, smiling. "That's one of the reasons we all pulled for you to get the sergeant's stripes." He paused a moment as if to let that sink in. "I'm working on Wade's paperwork now," he continued. "He's a good man and deserves a promotion."

"And Myers?" Mark asked

"I think Myers is a good man also," he began. "He's does his job, and everyone likes him. But when I bring his promotion up to the CO, he says not until that accident mess blows over." He paused for a moment. "I don't understand why the investigation hasn't cleared him by now, but it hasn't."

Mark left the orderly room thinking he couldn't mention the promotions because Dave was, for the moment, left out.

CHAPTER 24

B Y THE END OF THE week, Mark and Wade's promotions were common knowledge. Most everyone congratulated them, not only because they had earned the honor but also because of what was expected after a promotion. When anyone got promoted in Second Platoon, tradition had it the promoted soldier would buy a keg of beer to celebrate. Mark and Wade made it known they were combining their promotion parties, and two kegs would be bought. The party was set for Friday night at the Rocket Club, a bar just outside the main gate to the post.

Friday night the party was already underway when Mark, Wade, and Myers arrived at the Rocket Bar. The uniform for the day had been khakis, and everyone had left post immediately after retreat to get in on the free beer. Entering the bar, the three men found it packed with khaki uniforms and a cheerful atmosphere of loud, pulsating voices and lively polka music. Not only were there the usual customers, but at least twenty-five members of Second Platoon were there as well. The bar was a hullabaloo of noise with soldiers laughing and talking in groups or milling about looking for laughs or their next beer. The effect of the free beer that Mark and Wade had prearranged with the bar owner created a cheerful mood of raucous celebration. As they entered, several soldiers lifted their mugs in acknowledgement with some shouting off-color but good-natured salutes.

Myers didn't seem disturbed by missing out on the promotions; he shrugged it off, saying his time would come. Nevertheless, both Mark and Wade made a concerted effort to keep him in good spirits. Mark wouldn't let Myers's mug get near empty before he would have it refilled. He bribed the young *Fräulein* working the bar with a five-mark note to talk and joke with Myers as she found time between customers. She got his attention right away by asking him where he was from and then seeming to be very interested in his hometown of Madison, Wisconsin. Each time she passed him at the bar, she would stop for a moment to carry forth the conversation. Wade did his part as well; he challenged Myers to an arm wrestling contest, and in spite of being far stronger, he let Myers beat him. After a time, Myers swaggered away, obviously feeling good and saying he wanted to speak with someone he saw in the crowd.

Mark was impressed with the young woman and the attentive manner she used in cheering up Myers. He passed her another five-mark note and thanked her for helping out. She responded with a smile and moved on down the bar to wait on another customer. Mark had turned back toward the crowd looking for Myers when suddenly Lieutenant McBride appeared before him. He had entered the club unnoticed and had found Mark and Wade standing at the bar. They both showed surprise, for it was seriously frowned on by command protocol for officers to fraternize with the enlisted men.

"Gimme a beer," he shouted across the bar in a mock command voice. He then turned to Mark and Wade and laughed, offering his congratulations and a handshake.

Mark and Wade both liked and respected their platoon leader. As they shook hands, Wade ordered three beers back over his shoulder. The *Fräulein* working the bar was quick with the beers and began filling mugs and passing them over the bar. McBride grabbed the first mug and turned it up immediately. He took the beer and, between long sips, he told the two they had done well. He took another long pull from the mug, emptying it completely, gave a little half salute, and was gone. No one seemed to notice there had been an officer in the bar.

Wade looked at Mark, shrugging his shoulders and laughing. "Good officer," he said. He then saw someone in the crowd and walked away to talk to them.

Mark nodded his approval and laughed also. The *Fräulein* was suddenly back by his side.

"I don't need this." she said as she held out the five-mark note. "You've already paid me enough." She was looking at Mark directly, and he sensed her sincerity.

"No, keep it," Mark said. "You helped out."

"My pleasure," she said. "I like the way you stick up for your friend."

Mark only nodded, acknowledging her words.

"And how about you?" she asked. "I can see in your face that you're missing someone. Are you homesick?" She didn't give him time to answer but moved off to wait on a customer down the bar. When she returned, she had a new mug of beer and placed it before him. He had not ordered the beer, and he nodded and smiled his thanks. She stood close and smiled back at Mark. He could feel her eyes and her closeness. She was young and attractive, and he instinctively responded to her closeness.

"I am missing someone, but she's not far away," he said.

"Oh, so you have a German girlfriend," she said. Mark didn't answer her.

At that moment, the tempo of the noise in the room changed noticeably, and a loud roar went up at the other end of the room. Mark turned toward the noise but wasn't particularly concerned; it wasn't unusual for some groups to burst out in loud laughter or into some raucous drinking song. But as he was turning back toward the *Fräulein*, he distinctly heard above the crowd noise, "Hit him, Myers!"

He immediately knew this wasn't good and began pushing his way through the crowd toward the commotion. When he broke through the crowd, he saw Myers being held against the wall by another soldier. Mark quickly moved forward and jerked the soldier around and away from Myers. The man lurched around and faced Mark, a smile slowly developing on his face. It was Ricco. He was drunk, and it was obviously a mean drunk.

"Well now," Ricco said, a sneer crossing his face. "I've got both you jerks at last."

Even though Mark had long ago gotten over his anger for the chow hall incident, he still wanted a go at Ricco for what he had done to Myers. He instantly set his mind to fight. When he saw Ricco's body crouching slightly, he knew he would come at him swinging. As Mark braced for the confrontation, focusing on the man's body movements, he saw someone break out from the circling crowd and viciously push Ricco just as he started his move toward Mark. The shove caught him off balance and threw him stumbling awkwardly into the crowd. The man bounced back and faced the newcomer. It was Wade who had just worked his way through the crowd, sized up the situation, and made his move. Wade now faced Ricco with a cold smile. The soldier was heavier than Wade, but Wade had him beat on height, and his cold glare sent a message.

"I don't have a beef with you," Ricco said, "but I can start one."

"You're in the wrong crowd, friend, to be making threats," Wade said, ready for anything but talking calmly. "Look around you."

Ricco glanced around, seeing only Second Platoon faces. As this fact and Wade's cold stare sunk through the haze of alcohol and hate, the man's face reflected a changing attitude. He hesitated a moment and then turned and lurched through the crowd and out the door.

The crowd dispersed immediately, going back to their routine as if nothing had happened. Wade looked at Myers, grabbed him playfully in an headlock, and mussed up his hair. "You little shrimp," he said laughing. "Can't I keep you out of trouble?"

"I could have handled him," Myers said. "I was ready for him this time."

"Sure you could," Wade said, winking at Mark. They both laughed, and the three of them headed back to the bar. Turning to Mark, Wade added, "Sorry to interfere, but this is not the best place for this. Ricco could have said you started the fight."

Just before they left the Rocket Club, a soldier that neither Mark nor Wade recognized approached them. "I saw what happened earlier," the man said. "That soldier's in my platoon, and he's a bad one."

"Yeah?" Wade said.

"Yeah, he's got everybody in our platoon afraid of him," the man said. "Rumor has it he came into the army running from the cops because he killed a guy."

"Thanks," Mark said. "I know he's bad."

"He's an animal, so watch your back when he's around," the soldier said as he turned and walked away.

CHAPTER 25

THE BACK AND FORTH OF letters from home had increasingly become more strained and demanding to Mark as time went on. He had been proud of his promotion and wrote all about it to his parents. He mentioned the nicer aspects of the promotion party and how Lieutenant McBride had broken protocol to come to the party to congratulate him and Wade. He had ended the letter saying the party was fun, but it had caused him to miss seeing Lauren for the weekend. That had been his mistake, he realized later. In the shortest time for an airmail letter to complete a round-trip, he received a reply from his mother. She was direct and to the point.

"Mark, you must realize," she wrote, "both your father and I are adamantly opposed to this relationship with a German girl. And we always will be."

At first, Mark was angry and said to hell with it. But as he thought about it more, considering their background and history, he could only conclude that their mind-set was understandable in many ways. But this understanding didn't bring him peace of mind;

it only made his situation worse. He firmly disagreed with them, but he could understand their point of view. On the one hand, they were justified in being fearful, while on the other hand, Lauren was in no way responsible for the cause of their fear. By accident of birth, nationality, and time in history, she was being labeled and categorized with something she had nothing to do with. This dichotomous situation weighed heavily on his mind.

Mark struggled with his dilemma throughout the week. It wasn't something he wanted to talk about with Wade and Myers, and he certainly couldn't talk about it with Lauren. He tried not to think about it and consoled his angst with the thought of seeing Lauren on Sunday. But on Saturday when he called her at The Camera Shop, she said she was obligated to attend a school function with her father on Sunday afternoon. He was being honored in a village ceremony for his community work, and it was only right for her to be there. She reminded Mark she had previously mentioned the obligation to him, and then he remembered she had. It was something she couldn't get out of, she said, and she would have to wait until the following weekend to see him.

Mark understood that she had her obligations, and he resigned himself to not seeing her for another week. But as Saturday afternoon moved on to Saturday night, he grew more restless and annoyed at everything around him. He couldn't relax in the barracks, and he didn't want to go out drinking with the other guys. He knew he couldn't sleep, and he considered going for a long walk about post but changed his mind before heading out. Then he thought about going to the post gym and working out with weights or maybe sparring a few rounds with someone to work off the tension. The thought of putting the gloves on and pounding the punching bag brought some relief, but then he remembered the gym closed early on weekends to give the staff working there time off.

Finally, it occurred to him that Lauren might be free for a while Sunday morning, and he decided to go to her village. Since her father had no phone, he would have to go unannounced. He knew this was unwise, that going to Lauren's home at any time would create a serious problem with her father. But his restlessness and tension and the desire to be with her was so strong that he couldn't think straight.

Trains ran infrequently in the early morning hours, but after several hours of waiting, he finally made connections that put him at her train stop just before the sun broke through the trees surrounding the village.

As he walked toward Lauren's house, Mark began to have misgivings about trying to see her. It was highly irregular for anyone to visit at this early hour. Her father didn't like him in the first place, and he certainly wouldn't permit him to see Lauren at this hour of the morning. *I must be crazy,* he thought, and within a block of her house, he turned and walked back to the train station. At the depot, he saw the next train scheduled in his direction was three hours away. He paced up and down the station platform for some time before he decided again to go to her house. He arrived at her front door before he again felt it was too risky to knock. Mark knew that if Herr Werner answered, Lauren would be in trouble. He turned and again walked back to the depot.

Finally, after more pacing in the train depot, he decided, *To hell with it. The worst Herr Werner can do is call the polizei.* The thought of writing home about being arrested and thrown into a Germen jail brought Mark a perverse pleasure. The sun was up but still too low to light the early morning, and it was semidark in the street as he approached the Werner house for the third time.

He knocked on the door with a deep dread growing, fearing the worst was about to happen. His anxiety couldn't overcome his desire to see Lauren, though, and he waited. He knocked and waited, his anxiety mounting, and then knocked again. Nothing happened, so he knocked a little louder. When no one answered he wondered, *Could it be there's no one home?*

Finally, after knocking several more times, the door opened just an inch or two. At first, Mark could not see who had opened the door. Then it opened wide, and Lauren stood in the opening. She wore only an oversized, faded blue jersey that he had given her months before. The words "Forest Grove Soccer" stood out clearly on the jersey. She was barefooted, and her legs were bare and white in the shadows of the doorway. Her hair was uncombed but still neat with one strand falling across her face. The dim morning light fell far enough into the room to clearly define her soft features and flaxen hair.

Dressed only in his jersey, she obviously had just gotten out of bed to answer his knock. Neither spoke for the moment, both awed and astonished in their own way at the sight of the other. As she stood before him, her facial expression didn't change, and she didn't speak. Both stood quietly for a brief moment and then, in an instinctive, reflexive, and unconscious move, she quickly walked into his arms. They embraced silently and eagerly, relishing their contact and clinging tightly for a long moment, each feeling and savoring the other's closeness and experiencing the other's unique warmth and scent.

Soon Lauren pulled free, saying softly, "Wait here!" She disappeared back into the doorway and was gone barely a minute. When she returned, she had slipped on shoes and wore a coat over the jersey. "Let's walk," she said, now fully composed and smiling up at him. Undisturbed by his unplanned and unexplained early morning visit, she seemed only glad to see him.

"I wanted to see you," he said. "I didn't want to wait until next weekend."

"I'm glad," she said, taking his arm and walking up the street. "There's a bakery that opens early. We can get coffee."

The man at the bakery greeted Lauren cordially as they entered the warm, well-lit shop. His face was rosy red from working the ovens, and he had a towel thrown across his shoulder that he used intermittently to wipe white flour from his hands as he prepared their order. As Mark and Lauren were leaving the shop with two large mugs of steaming coffee and a sack of sweet rolls, the baker asked, "And how is my favorite schoolmaster, your father, today?"

Lauren laughed, saying, "I don't know. He still sleeps."

They sat on a bench in the small square in front of the bakery and sipped the hot coffee and ate the rolls. For a while, they didn't talk much, each perfectly comfortable with the surprise visit and happy to be together. The sun was behind them and finally broke over the distant buildings, warming their backs and chasing away the night shadows.

"Wish you were free today," Mark said as a covey of pigeons circled the square, slowing in their flight to settle down lightly in the grassy area before them.

"Me too," she said.

"Couldn't you have a headache or something?"

"Yes, but it wouldn't be right."

"Would be right for me," he said, turning to face her.

"But, Mark . . ." she said, setting her mug down and facing him. She was silent a moment, studying his face. "Mark," she continued, finally, speaking softly, "is there something wrong?"

"No . . . no, there's nothing wrong. It's just that I'd like to be with you today."

"And I with you," she said.

"So, is there some way?"

Lauren didn't answer. She glanced at him and then looked down at the napkin in her lap. After folding and unfolding the napkin twice, she looked back up at him. "Mark, is this so important?"

Mark didn't answer her but glanced vacantly down the street where a middle-aged woman had just left a doorway and was walking toward the bakery.

"If it's so important, can't you tell me what it is?" she asked.

"I'd rather not talk about it now," he said, glancing at her then back at the woman's slow plod toward the bakery.

Lauren sat silently. She refolded the napkin and put it back inside the sack before turning back to Mark. "Mark," she began in a quiet voice, "if it's so important to you, I'll find a way to get out of it. But it won't be right of me to do so. This event has been planned for some time, and my father will be very disappointed if I don't go with him. It's not that I don't want to be with you. It's that I'm obligated, and it's only right that I fulfill my obligations. Nevertheless, I can see you're troubled, and I'll stay with you."

Mark turned to study Lauren. He could see in her face the anxiety he was causing her. He then realized he was being inconsiderate and selfish. He was putting her in a difficult position and making her uncomfortable, and he was doing it without explaining his reasons. He felt bad and immediately began to make amends. "No, no, it's not a big deal," he said. "It's just that I thought it would be nice if we could be together all afternoon. But I understand that this is something you have to do."

"Are you sure?" she asked, looking at him indecisively.

"Yes," he said quickly. "You have your duty, the same as me." He smiled, nodding his assurance.

They finished their coffee and returned the mugs, thanking the red-faced baker for the loan of them. They then strolled about the village, seeking out the cobblestone streets that caught the early sunlight. They walked along slowly, holding hands and talking quietly. After a time, Lauren said she should return home to get ready for the day. With that, she giggled lightly, saying, "I'm still in my bed clothes."

Mark felt better as they slowly walked back to her father's house. At her front door, she stood close to him and asked, "Are you okay now?"

"Yes, I'm fine," Mark said.

She embraced him and then entered her father's house.

On the train ride back to post, Mark suddenly felt very tired. He had not slept at all the previous night, and the letter from home made him realize there was a severe and growing disconnect between his parents and himself. He had never before felt such a divide, and this began to weigh heavily on his mind. He understood the cultural conflicts that separated his parents from Lauren, and he sympathized with them. He even, at times, felt sorry for them. He knew that, in their minds, they were doing what was right, and he knew they could not change his mind about Lauren. In spite of this understanding, he was becoming increasingly uneasy with the mutually exclusive aspects of the worlds in which he and Lauren existed.

CHAPTER 26

FOR SOME TIME, WADE HAD been uneasy about something. He couldn't explain exactly what was bothering him; it was just a feeling, a kind of restless foreboding that left him repeatedly looking over his shoulder. Whenever he was having a beer in the EM Club or in a *Gasthaus* or just walking around on post, he found himself watching those around him, always aware of who was behind him and constantly studying faces. This unusual and uncomfortable feeling worried him until he finally figured out its cause. It had all started with the confrontation with Ricco at the Rocket Bar.

Wade also noticed that Mark had grown distant and withdrawn and didn't seem to have much interest in anything. He saw this change in his personality and knew something was bothering him. He knew it was serious when Mark let their tour anniversary date pass without showing interest. He tried to prod Mark. "Say, Mark, we just passed the one-year mark," he said. "We're over the hump, man! Shouldn't we celebrate?"

"Not me," Mark said. "You guys go ahead."

"But this is an important milestone," Wade said. "We can start our countdown now."

"No thanks," was all Mark would say.

Wade first thought Mark might also be concerned with the Ricco incident. He talked to Myers about Mark's moodiness, saying that something was bothering him and he might be concerned with the soldier Ricco.

Myers didn't think so. "I don't think Mark's troubled about Ricco," he said with a thoughtful look. "For all his easygoing mannerisms, he's a pretty tough guy. I've heard he boxed some at Fort Jackson and some in high school and even had some Golden Glove bouts when a young teen. He can take care of himself if he gets riled up. Besides, I remember how he stood up to Ricco in that first soccer match."

"Boxing!" Wade said with interest. He spoke as if that idea was something he hadn't thought of but should have. "That might be just the diversion to shake him out of his funk. Maybe we can get him to the post gym and get him boxing again."

Wade's excitement at getting Mark back into boxing came from a twofold interest in the sport. The strenuous exercise and competitive activity might help him come out of his gloomy moods. But also, with Mark's knowledge of boxing, Wade might spar around with him and pick up some techniques of his own. He and Myers had been going to the post gym a couple times a week to work out with weights or play basketball. While there, Wade would sometimes watch guys sparring in the boxing ring and wish he had those fighting skills, thinking they might be needed some time.

After much encouragement, Wade and Myers talked Mark into going to the gym with them after evening chow. The gym's boxing ring was set up at one end of the major room. Adjacent to the ring was a mat-covered area designated as a sparring area. A sign on the wall next to the area said, "No boots on mats." A bench sat next to the wall for spectators, and there were usually a couple guys sitting around watching the boxing activities.

Wade mentioned to Mark that he would spar a little if he could find a willing partner. Mark offered to be his sparring partner but said he didn't want to do any serious boxing. Wade not only found Mark a skillful boxer, but he seemed to enjoy teaching the techniques of boxing.

Boxing soon became their favorite gym activity, but Mark, in spite of being adept at boxing, didn't want to mix it up and get into serious matches. He would bob and weave and focus mostly on defensive tactics and only occasionally throw a light punch. Wade, as a result of ranch life and football, was tough, but at first he didn't have sufficient skill to be an effective fighter. He would throw a punch and then leave himself open to Mark's light but quick left jab to the chin. When Wade would attempt such a move, Mark would stop and correct him. He would hold his gloves up, hands open, and then point out to Wade how after throwing a punch, he should protect his stance for the counter punch that would come back at him. With such technical pointers Wade soon began to show a marked improvement.

Mark continued to coach Wade, and Wade took his coaching seriously. And as he picked up more and more techniques, he became a more skilled competitor. They worked hard, and Wade soon developed sufficient skill to spar with other soldiers. He and Mark would often box with anyone who wanted a friendly match. Soon they both became known around the gym as good boxers. But it was Mark who caused the most talk, and this talk was usually centered on the question of just how good he was.

The sergeant in charge of the gym had been watching Wade and Mark's bouts for some times. He approached Wade one evening as he headed to the water fountain. Mark had agreed to give a soldier some pointers on footwork and was busy in the ring. The SIC waited until Wade had finished at the fountain and then said, "You know, I've been watching you guys spar around for some time now. Your friend there is good."

"Oh yeah," Wade said. "Yeah, he's okay . . . much better than me."

"No, I don't mean he's just okay," the SIC said. "I boxed competitively back at Fort Bragg, and I've seen a lot of this. Bergner is really good; he's just not showing it."

"How can you tell?"

"The way he moves, the ease of his motions, and his quickness; he's a natural," the SIC said. "He's as good an amateur at defensive sparring as I've seen." The sergeant waited a moment before continuing. Then he said in a serious tone, "He's holding back, you know."

"Holding back?" Wade said. "What do you mean?"

"Yeah, when you and the other guys spar with him, he blocks and rolls away from your punches like he's playing, and it's effective," the SIC said. "I'd like to see how he fights when he really wants too."

"We've all wanted to see that," Wade said, "but nobody has been able to get him to go all out."

"If you want to test him, go at him really hard and see what he does. His instinct might kick in. If it does, we'll see what he's got."

"Um," Wade said, as if considering that approach. "I might do that. He might show his stuff if he gets under pressure."

The next time Wade and Mark sparred, Wade fought as usual, moving around Mark and throwing left jabs while trying to set him up for a quick right. He tried this a couple times, but when he thought the time was right to tag Mark with a quick right, his jab would somehow miss. Mark seemed to always anticipate his moves, and when Wade threw his punch, Mark would bob or weave, and the punch would find nothing but air.

Knowing the SIC was watching and growing frustrated with his missed punches, Wade decided to really go after Mark with a battery of punches that would throw him off guard. The first time he did this, Mark backed up and pushed Wade away from him with a surprised look on his face. With this move, Wade thought he had found Mark's weakness, and he immediately bore in again, both arms flailing away. This time, something seemed to click in Mark. He dodged a couple of blows and then his left flicked out straight into Wade's face. Wade never saw the right punch that followed and landed squarely on his headgear. He just suddenly found himself somewhat dazed and sitting on the ring mat.

"Hey, Sam!" Mark said immediately. "You okay? I didn't mean to clip you so hard. Here, let me help you up." Mark reached down to help Wade up. He was genuinely concerned for Wade.

"Where'd that punch come from?" Wade asked groggily, struggling to get up. "I never saw it coming!"

Later, when Mark saw Wade was okay and had headed for the water fountain, Wade caught the eye of the SIC. The sergeant had a little smile on his face. As Wade stepped out of the ring, he walked by and said quietly, "I told you so!"

Wade's only comment was, "Now we know."

At the end of their session and while walking back to the barracks, Mark said, "You know, I've been feeling a little down lately, but these workouts are making me feel better."

Wade smiled. *Yeah, and we're getting ready for what's coming*, he thought.

CHAPTER 27

THE SITUATION WITH THE UNRESOLVED investigation concerning the accident continued to worry not only the three involved, but Captain Williams as well. He had said that in his opinion, the accident was unavoidable and the soldiers involved were innocent of any wrongdoing. Still, any situation involving the death of civilians was a serious matter and could cast a bad light on Charlie Company. Williams had, on several occasions, inquired about the event at Regimental Headquarters and with the provost marshal. But all he could get from these sources was "no word on that at this time." First Sergeant Andrade had promised the three men he would let them know something as soon as he could, but his main source, the battalion's sergeant major, couldn't find out anything through his sources. No one seemed to have any idea what was holding up the process. Finally, a lowly corporal, Cpl. Sam Wade, lucked out and ran across some information that could explain the hold up.

Wade's luck and information came through Ursula, the young *Fräulein* he had met and befriended when he and Mark had revisited the scene of the accident several weeks back. He and Ursula had been together often since their first meeting and had developed a close relationship. When Ursula learned that Mark and Wade were involved in the incident, she talked to him seriously about the accident. After Wade explained the way the fog had developed on the mountainside that night, emphasizing that Myers was using all caution as he drove, she considered the situation carefully. Ursula then told Wade that she well knew of the frequent heavy fogs in that area and the tricky road conditions they created coming down the mountain. Considering all aspects of the situation, she agreed that the accident was unavoidable and that the three soldiers in the car were in no way at fault. And because of her fondness for Wade, she wanted to help. At Wade's request, she kept her eyes and ears open to anything she could learn about the investigation. As the military investigators and some civilians continued to show up in her *Gasthaus* asking questions, she began to piece together some important details and to pass these on to Wade.

She informed Wade that the man who had lost his son was important, a *Bürgermeister*, and that he had organized several of the *Bürgermeisters* from the surrounding villages to protest to the army at the highest level. She had learned this from what she had overheard from a meeting the group had held in her *Gasthaus*. She also told Wade that this *Bürgermeister* had political ambitions and was using the accident as a rallying point. He had given speeches at different villages to important local people, saying the American soldiers were responsible for the death of two Germans citizens. He never mentioned that the accident was unavoidable, and if anything, the two victims who were drunk and walking down the middle of the road were the cause of the accident. His repeated mantra was, "We must demand punishment when our citizens are harmed."

Wade had been on a weekend pass visiting with Ursula when he learned this. He and Ursula were having a pleasant time driving around to local sites and meeting and talking to her friends when she told him about the *Bürgermeisters*. He interrupted his holiday to return to post early Sunday morning to talk to Mark. He caught Mark just as he was leaving the barracks to catch a train into the city. Mark was dressed in gray slacks and a dark blue sport coat and was going through his wallet when he stepped from the barracks.

"Mark, hold up!" Wade said with some urgency. "We need to talk."

"Aren't you supposed to be on pass?" Mark asked, obviously surprised to see him back on post.

"Yeah, I came back with news about the accident," he said, shaking his head. "And it ain't good."

Mark listened to Wade's explanation of what was transpiring among some in the local population and how the one *Bürgermeister* was campaigning on the issue. He immediately suggested they find Myers and get together with Sergeant Andrade. "He may be able to analyze it better than us," Mark said.

Andrade listened to Wade's story then exclaimed: "Damn! If these *Bürgermeisters* have been protesting to the army and we haven't heard anything about it, it means one thing." He paused a moment in thought. "These guys must have connections, and they have submitted their protest to a level higher than any we have access to. They must be protesting at USAREUR level."

"What level is that?" Wade and Mark asked simultaneously.

"USAREUR is the command organization for the United States Army in Europe," Andrade explained. "Its headquarters is located at Heidelberg, and it oversees all US forces in Europe."

"Why would this particular accident elevate to that level?" Mark asked. "There are often such accidents that happen around Germany, I'm told."

"Yes, there are," Andrade said. "And they happen often. But these *Bürgermeisters* must have connections. I'm going to brief the CO on this. I'll let you know what he says."

* * *

"What!" Captain Williams exclaimed after Andrade briefed him on Wade's information. He had been sitting at his desk rereading the report of C Company's excellent performance during the field maneuvers. "We're getting attention from USAREUR. After scoring so well on the field maneuvers, we're getting hit with a black mark from an unavoidable accident that has created an unsolvable situation."

"It's beginning to look that way, sir," Andrade said. "Of course, this is only hearsay at this point, but I've got a gut feeling it's a fact."

"I've got the same feeling, Sergeant. It would explain why this case hasn't been closed already. At USAREUR, they haven't decided what to do yet," Williams said. "I'll report this to Battalion and see what they think. It's certainly more than we can handle here at company level."

"It's beginning to look like this situation is getting bigger than any of us," Andrade said.

"And you know what happens to little fish when they get into big waters," Williams said, tapping his pencil on his desk.

"Yes," Andrade said with a frown. "They're eaten alive!"

CHAPTER 28

H ERR CLAUSE, THE OWNER OF the shop where Lauren
had been working for some months, was just as ardent
a patriot as Lauren's father. Both he and Herr Werner
had been schoolmates in their youth and had remained close friends
since then. In their professional lives, Herr Werner had become a
schoolteacher and Herr Clause had become a journalist. After the
war, Clause immediately began doing what he could to help in
reconstruction. His background in journalism helped him get work
with the rebuilding newspaper, *Der Stern*. A confirmed bachelor
and with his livelihood taken care of, he devoted his spare time to
volunteer work. He worked for the International Red Cross, doing
whatever they could find for him to do.

After he stopped working as a journalist and started his business
with The Camera Shop, he still found ways of doing his part. Like
his old friend Werner, he felt the hope and future of the country
was in the development of its youth. One of his goals was in finding
and promoting those special individuals who had the talent and
enthusiasm to make a difference. He had already guided two gifted

young men into engineering and worked to get a brilliant young woman into medical school. He received great satisfaction in watching his protégés grow in whatever fields they chose, and he knew the country would benefit from such talent. In this mentor role, he felt he had found his true calling. It was this aspect of Clause's personality that had led him to hire Lauren to work in his shop.

It had started when the two old friends were having lunch together one day on one of Werner's infrequent visits into the city. "So what's new with you, my old comrade?" Clause had asked Werner. "And how is your young daughter doing in school?"

"Fine, fine," Werner had said as he sat back and sipped his coffee. "My school is doing well, and Lauren is growing up. She's turned sixteen now, you know."

"And how is her schoolwork?"

"Excellent," Werner said. "She has excelled beyond everyone's expectations," he continued, while pulling his pipe from his coat pocket. "And she's so mature. She told me just yesterday that her schoolwork was not that challenging and she should also work during her final year of high school."

"Well, that's interesting," Clause had responded. "I may have something for her." It just so happened that his camera shop business was doing well. Also, he needed more free time from routine sales chores to pursue activities such as advertising and researching new camera lines. He was well aware of Lauren's excellent school record and her dedication to her duties. He offered to give Lauren a trial run as a sales clerk. He made the offer not only to help his friend and to acquire some help in his business but also because, in Lauren, he sensed a talent with potential. At the time, he knew there was no way of knowing how Lauren's talent would develop, but he was prepared to watch for signs that showed promise and to exploit them gainfully.

When Lauren came to work for him, she picked up the routines of sales work immediately. She then began to learn photography so that she could better present the equipment to prospective buyers. In a short time, it became evident that photography was more than just something she did at her job. After her first week at the shop, she said to Herr Clause: "How long will it take me to earn enough to buy a camera?"

"So, you want to buy a camera," Clause had said casually at the time. He was keenly interested, but he didn't show it. He wanted to see how her potential would unfold if left alone. This way, her true interest would reveal the direction she should pursue. "Why, that depends on the type camera," he said patiently.

"Just any camera, Herr Clause," Lauren persisted.

"Um . . ." Clause began, as in deep thought. "Did I not tell you that one of the perks of working here in my shop is you have access to a camera? And not only that, you can develop your film in the lab."

Lauren looked at him with excited eyes. "Oh, that would be wonderful, Herr Clause!" she exclaimed. "I so much want to take photographs of things I see."

"But you must buy the film and take good care of the camera," Clause said with a serious look. "And you must only develop shots that you're sure are good. It costs money, you know," he lectured.

After she got the camera, Lauren told Clause that she carried it wherever she went whenever possible—on her train commutes and even at school in case the right shot appeared on the walks back and forth. At first, she had told him, she would often stop and focus the camera on a subject, studying the image without taking the shot but relating to herself the best camera angle and lighting effect and other technical aspects of the shot. In time, he knew, she would become more discriminatory in selecting subjects to study through the camera lens, her sense of composition and image relevance would develop, and she would learn the concepts of lighting and exposure and the relationship of film speed. In her spare time at the shop, she read photography magazines eagerly, and he was pleased that she could discuss with the customers aperture settings, focal lengths, and shutter speeds with a skill equal to his own.

It was only three weeks from the day Clause had loaned her the camera that he first took note of her photography skills. She had been working in the darkroom developing a customer's film and had also developed a roll of her own. Clause poked his head in the door and asked if she could help with some customers out front. As she left the lab, he noticed she was carrying a stack of developed pictures in each hand.

"I'll finish these as soon as I finish with the customers," she'd said, laying the pictures on the counter in two neat stacks.

Clause finished with his customer, thanking the lady and saying she could pick up her pictures on Friday. He then decided to finish the stacks that Lauren had left on the counter. The first stack he inserted into a customer package and labeled and filed it in the "ready" file. Picking up the second stack to package, he took notice of the first picture, which was image side up. The picture revealed a small child sitting on the ground and looking up at the photographer. The child's face was smeared with dirt, and her bright, wide-open eyes and unpretentious look showed no fear of the photographer.

"Someone has captured the essence of childlike innocence," Clause said smiling. "This photo most effectively reveals the child's simple joy of play and peaceful contentment with her place there in the dirt," he continued, smiling as he shuffled the stack to fit them into an envelope. Just before slipping the stack into the envelope, he paused, looking again at the picture. He studied it a moment longer and then said to himself, "A really good shot! I wonder what else this person has done."

He looked at the next picture and studied it for a long moment. It showed a middle-aged woman sitting, half lying, in the street with a pained and shocked expression on her face. Beside her lay a torn open paper bag containing what looked like grocery items. Some of the items were scattered about the street around and behind her. Next to her stood a man who was bending over with his pant leg pulled up as he examined a dark spot on his leg. Other people stood around them, and all were looking at the lady in the street with serious faces. The image of the lady was at the bottom of the frame. A fire hydrant and storefront with various items in the window occupied the background, along with several people in various poses, either standing or moving, and looking down on the reclining lady.

"Another good shot," Clause mumbled to himself. "This person knows photography." He continued glancing at the remaining pictures in the stack but suddenly stopped when he came across a picture of Lauren's father. That's when he knew the stack of pictures belonged to Lauren.

After they were caught up with the customers and a lull had developed in the shop's activity, Clause asked Lauren if the pictures belonged to her. When she answered yes, he asked if he could look at them to judge her techniques. She agreed, and Clause began scuffling through the pictures, as if he had not seen them before. When he came to the street scene with the reclining woman, he asked, "This looks interesting. What happened here?"

"Oh, that shot," Lauren began. "That's when I happened upon an accident while on my break last week. A young man on a motorbike lost control as he approached a crosswalk full of pedestrians and ran right through the people. A couple of people were injured, but no one seriously."

"Did you take just one shot? If so, it's a lucky shot—it's good," Clause said, watching Lauren as she continued looking at the picture. "By that, I mean angle and overall composition."

"Yes, I think I got lucky," Lauren said. "But I didn't just snap the shot," she continued. "I worked my way around in the crowd to get the best angle. I knew my film speed was right and that I didn't have time to use the light meter. I quickly set the f-stop and stooping down slightly to get a background with the injured lady at the bottom of the frame, I snapped the shot between two bystanders."

"It's good no one was hurt too badly," Clause said, politely taking the picture from Lauren and holding it up to study it more closely. "What f-stop did you use?"

"I think I used an f/2," Lauren said casually. "There's another shot that goes with that one, if you're interested," she continued as she shuffled through the stack. She came to a picture and held it up for Clause to see. "I took this one a short time later after a policeman arrived on the scene."

In this shot, a policeman stood before a youth sitting on a motorbike. The youth was obviously the one who had crashed through the pedestrians and was being questioned. The image portrayed the policeman towering over the young man with hands on his hips: he was leaning forward and glaring down as if severely admonishing the youth. She had used a low, side angle shot that placed the policeman at the top of the frame and the youth at the bottom of the frame, as in submission.

"I had more time with this shot. When I finally took the shot, the policeman gave me a stern look. I took the shot and got out of there. I didn't want him after me with the mood he was in," Lauren said, laughing.

"Any reason why you stopped at these two shots?" Clause asked.

"Yes, I only wanted to show the event—its cause and effect," Lauren said.

"How's that?"

"Well," she answered. "The cause is the irresponsibility of the youth on the motorbike, and the effect is the injured pedestrians and the youth being arrested."

"So, you try to tell a story with your shots," Clause said. He was looking at Lauren intently, and a small smile was developing on his face.

"Yes. To me, it's the responsibility of the photographer to tell a story with the scenes chosen to shoot," she said. "If the scene doesn't have meaning, why waste the film?"

At the time, Clause was amazed at this interchange with Lauren and how quickly she was developing her own style and technique in photography. She had been with him only a few weeks, and already her interest and aptitude had manifested itself clearly. "She's only sixteen and already a promising photojournalist," he whispered under his breath. He remembered being very proud and thinking, *I've now found my next protégé.*

CHAPTER 29

WITH THE INVESTIGATION UNRESOLVED AND hanging over C Company's head and no word from either Regiment or the provost marshal's office, all Captain Williams and the others could do was wait for some word from higher up. Williams ordered McBride and First Sergeant Andrade to keep the three men out of trouble and to make sure they had impressively clean records.

"I agree, Captain," Andrade said. "With clean records, the three men involved, and C Company, stand a better chance of avoiding further investigation."

"Yes," Williams said. "If worse comes to worse, we don't want some minor record flaw to put us in a bad light. The fact that the investigation continues unresolved might mean that USAEUR is giving it a chance to blow over."

McBride, being one to confront problems head-on, had even broken out the Army Manual, searching for some clause that might designate a time limit on investigations such as this one. Andrade said the thing to do was to stay calm and see what happened. The fact that something was going on but they didn't know what it was continued to distract Charlie Company. Finally one morning Captain Williams got a phone call with orders from Battalion Headquarters. He was ordered to put PFC Myers under barracks arrest pending further investigation.

Williams met with McBride and Andrade and ordered them to prepare the three soldiers for the worst. Also, in spite of Myers's clean record, he had no choice but to place him under barracks arrest and confine him to the company area. The limits of Myers's activities, pending further orders, would be his barracks, the chow hall, and the Charlie Company orderly room. Myers took the news calmly. The incident obviously had been weighing heavily on his mind, and to have it out in the open seemed to bring some relief. The captain also ordered First Sergeant Andrade to find work details that would keep Myers busy and out of trouble.

"Myers is a good man," the CO said to the first sergeant. "We want to keep his record clean and get him through this. If he's court-martialed and found guilty of something, it's not only going to be hard on him; it's going to reflect on Charlie Company as well."

Although Andrade's sympathies were with Myers, he was dismayed with the order. He was swamped with his normal responsibilities and the hated paperwork, and to be burdened with overseeing work details was something he didn't look forward to. After getting the order from the CO, he sent for Myers.

"Myers," he began with his initial pep talk. "I'm going to personally oversee your work details. You do your job well, and things will work out." He paused a moment before continuing. "Unfortunately, at the moment, I can't think of anything constructive for you to do that will show you're a good soldier and a credit to your outfit, so here's what I want you to do. Take a little time, talk it over with others, and then come up with some project that will make you look good, make me look good, and make Charlie Company look good. When you dream up this detail, let me know. Now get out of here."

Myers seemed okay with the order. He talked it over with the company clerk and some others and reported to the first sergeant early the next morning. "Sergeant, I've got a suggestion for my work project."

"Yes, Myers, what have you dreamed up?" Andrade asked.

"A worthy project would be for me to keep the company area policed up and looking neat," Myers said.

"Not worthy enough," Andrade said, looking at Myers skeptically. "Company area already looks neat. Work on it some more. Now, out of here." As Myers left the first sergeant's office and Andrade went back to work on his pile of papers, an amused smile developed on Andrade's face. He obviously was becoming fond of the congenial nature of Myers, who always seemed to be in high spirits.

That evening in the barracks, Myers talked it over with Mark and Wade. "I don't have the slightest idea what he wants," he said. "He wants me to come up with something that makes us all look good."

After discussing it back and forth, Mark and Wade came up with the idea of putting a sign at the orderly room entrance that designated it as C Company. "It's something needed, and the CO will see it every time he approaches the orderly room to get to his office," Wade said. "This will give C Company some distinction and make the captain look good."

"And you might put the company's motto underneath C Company," Mark suggested. "That should impress the CO even more."

When Myers suggested such a project to the first sergeant, Andrade looked at him frowning and nodding his head, as if pleased. "Hmm," he said, "not a bad idea. A sign that reads C Company with the company's motto underneath. I like the idea. There's only one problem."

"What's that sergeant?" Myers asked, his face showing his relief that he was getting somewhere with his project.

"The company has no motto," Andrade said. "So, that will be the next step in planning this project. Come up with an appropriate company motto, and it has to be good. It has to reflect the spirit and attitude of C Company in a noble and military way." As Myers was leaving the office, he added, "And don't forget we're an infantry company in the field and combat-ready."

Myers was gone only an hour before he returned to report that he had an idea for the motto. Andrade was on the phone when Myers entered his office. Putting his hand over the speaker and looking at Myers impatiently, he asked, "What now, Myers?"

"The motto, Sergeant," Myers began. "'How about 'Kill Them All'?"

Andrade looked up to the ceiling and rolled his eyes. He spoke into the phone. "Just a moment, please." Then, once again covering the phone with his hand, he turned his attention back to Myers. "What the hell do you think we are? Genghis Khan?" he said. "Get the hell out of here and don't come back until you've got something better than that."

Myers left the sergeant's office but returned two hours later. "Sergeant, I've got something softer this time," he said. "How about 'Peace, Love, and Friendship'?"

"Now what do you think we are?" he shouted at Myers, "A bunch of Bohemian vagabonds? Out!" With that, he pointed toward the door.

Myers didn't go back for the rest of that day. That night in the barracks, he again brought the subject up with Mark and Wade. They tossed various ideas back and forth, and after awhile, they all seem to center around "duty." Before lights out, they decided on "Duty Before Self" and dropped the subject.

The following day, Myers presented his new motto to the first sergeant. "Hmm," Andrade said, his eyebrows lifting and a thoughtful look coming over his face, "this one might work."

JAN D. HENDRIX

Andrade dismissed Myers and presented the idea to Captain Williams. The captain liked the idea also but said he wanted the motto to be a bit more concise and military.

"How about 'Duty First'?" he suggested to the first sergeant.

"Excellent suggestion," the first sergeant replied.

"Duty First" then became the motto of C Company.

Myers got his project underway. With work orders from the first sergeant, he got the post carpenters to construct and install the sign. He also had a planter built around the base of the sign where he planted a thick growth of red, yellow, and white tulips. It added an attractive fixture to the unadorned entrance to the orderly room of Charlie Company. When anyone approached the building, he could easily see the white sign surrounded by tulips. It read: "C Company, First Battalion, 457th Infantry Regiment." And in the lower-right corner, the motto stood out notably in red markings: Duty First.

CHAPTER 30

AFTER MARK FULLY REALIZED AND accepted the fact that his parents were openly and adamantly opposed to his relationship with a Germen girl, he stopped writing home. The incident when he had gone to Lauren's in the early morning hours was unlike him. The letter had upset him so much that it had caused him to put Lauren in a situation that could have been very difficult for her with her father. It had worked out, but if Herr Werner had answered the door instead of Lauren, it would have been a far different situation.

Previously, he had been dutiful in his letter writing to his parents, even sometimes writing letters when he didn't have one to answer. But after his mom's last letter, he, for the first time, came to the realization that they would never change. Their mind-set was so firmly entrenched that accepting Lauren was not within their capabilities. It was something he knew intuitively all along but had never consciously accepted. In the back of his mind, he always felt that he could convince them that Lauren was right for him, but the last letter made him realize this could never be.

Not only did Mark stop writing home, but he stopped opening letters from home. When he received a letter from his parents, he merely added it to the growing stack in the back of his locker. In time, the letters came more frequently, as if a sense of desperation was developing back home. Mark's day-to-day training routine, along with his after-duty time at the post gym and off-post trips, kept him so occupied that he didn't give much thought to the letters. His life and frame of mind were becoming more and more focused on the army and his life in Germany and less on his past. Thus, he simply disregarded the frequent letters until one morning the company clerk approached him and said the CO wanted to see him.

*   *   *

"Bergner," Captain Williams said after Mark reported in. "I'll get right to the point. Why have you stopped writing home?" He was holding a letter and waved it at Mark as he spoke.

"Stopped writing home?" Mark asked, surprised by the directness of the captain's question. It took Mark a moment to realize what had transpired. The letter the CO was waving at him must have been from his parents. And the letter must be a request for information about Mark's welfare and revealing that Mark had quit writing home.

"That's right," Williams said. "It's none of my business except that morale is my responsibility, as well as military matters. And I smell a morale problem here," he continued, looking at Mark sternly.

Mark knew there was no way to explain his reluctance to write. He also knew that the quickest way to get through this situation with the captain was with compliance. "No morale problem, sir," he said. "I guess I've just been busy and have neglected to keep up my letter writing. I'll do better."

"Very well," the captain said, dropping the letter and glancing at the stack of papers on his desk as if he wanted to get on with the next issue. "Don't neglect the home front," he continued. "You have a duty there as well as here in Charlie Company."

"Yes, sir," Mark said. He could tell that the CO was preoccupied with other problems. "Will that be all, sir?"

"That's all, dismissed."

Mark soon forgot the incident and continued to ignore the letters that were coming in almost daily now. As the pile of letters grew and occupied more space, he thought about throwing them away. But when he gave it further thought, the idea seemed so insensitive and irreverent that he continued to file them in the back of his locker, unread. It was several weeks after the CO's morale talk that the company clerk approached him as he was leaving evening chow with Wade and Myers.

"Bergner," he began with some excitement in his voice. "You've got a phone call. Come to the orderly room, quick!" Individual phone calls were almost unheard of in the outfit. Mark had gotten only one in his entire time in Germany. That one was from Lauren, and he suspected the one now was from her as well.

"It's probably a paternity suit lawyer," Wade said, grinning at Mark.

"Maybe you've won the lottery," Myers said, smiling as his eyes went wide.

"Was it a female voice on the line?" Mark asked the clerk as they walked away from Wade and Myers.

"Oh, man, yes!" exclaimed the clerk, turning his head toward Mark. "And did it sound sweet!"

"Um . . ." said Mark, sure now it was from Lauren and wondering what the call was all about. The chow hall was two buildings away from the orderly room, and it required a few minutes to get there. "I think it's a friend calling," he continued as they hurried along. "Hope everything is okay."

"Yeah!" the clerk said. "It was the sweetest New York accent I've heard since leaving the states," he continued, obviously pleased with the rare contact.

"New York accent!" Mark exclaimed, catching the man's arm and stopping him.

"Yeah," the clerk said. "It's the New York operator connecting a person-to person call." He looked at Mark quizzically. "Don't keep her waiting."

Mark stood firm without moving. He looked confused for a moment and then said, "Look, I don't want to take this call."

"What? You're the only one in this outfit who gets a call from the states, and you don't want to take it?"

"That's right. I don't want to take it."

"Well, what should I tell them?"

Mark thought a moment. "Tell them I can't come to the phone."

"That's not good enough, Bergner; it makes you sound like a jerk."

"I can't help that," Mark said, looking down at the ground. "Just tell them I'm on duty and can't come to the phone."

CHAPTER 31

AFTER LAUREN'S DECLARATION TO HER father regarding Mark, Herr Werner was deeply concerned. His dream had been to rebuild his family as close as he could to the way it was through Lauren and a man of her choosing. He knew his daughter as being practical and highly intelligent, and he had never doubted that the one she chose would be anyone other than a sound young man of German heritage. And even when she began to have occasional overnight absences that she covered well by stating she was spending the night with a girlfriend in the city, he didn't object. He consoled his anxiety with the thought that she was growing up and needed her own space and time. He further calmed his fears by telling himself that she was capable of making sound decisions and was confident that she would. But now, the way things were developing, that dream would not be realized. In spite of this new development, Herr Werner knew that Lauren had her own nature and feelings to deal with, and he was smart enough to know that he could not change that.

After their confrontation, Herr Werner had lain wide awake until the early morning hours, worrying about the course their lives were taking. At first, there seemed to be nothing he could do to bring Lauren back to his way of thinking. But just before daylight, an idea came to him, and he finally dozed for a brief time.

The following day, Herr Werner hurried through his routine obligations as headmaster. It was nearing the end of the term, and he quickly looked through the grade reports coming in to see if there were any unusually good or bad students developing. He then met with a history teacher who had requested a new compliment of books to inform her that the school did not have the funds to accommodate her request. But, he went on to say, if she was willing to teach a subject from a particular time in German history that he favored, he would solicit funds from outside sources and contribute some of his own as well. As soon as he was caught up with his pressing duties, he closed the door to his office and placed a call to his friend, Herr Clause, at The Camera Shop. He asked Clause if he could have lunch with him. "I have something urgent to speak to you about," he said. "And it's important to both of us."

Herr Werner left his schoolwork early and took the train into the city to meet with Clause. They met for lunch at a restaurant a good distance from The Camera Shop to avoid a chance meeting with Lauren who would be working at the shop in the afternoon. Werner immediately began to tell Clause about his concern for Lauren and her relationship with the American soldier.

"I know that soldier!" Clause said, showing his surprise. "Lauren sometimes goes on her afternoon break with him, but I didn't know their relationship was serious."

When Werner told him of Lauren's announcement the previous night and her blunt statement that Mark was the only one for her and nothing could change that, Clause also became concerned. "With such a serious relationship, he might take her with him when he returns to the States!" he said, as if amazed at the very thought.

"That would spoil my plans for her to add to those working for the good of Germany."

"It would break my heart to lose her," Herr Werner said sadly. "I wouldn't want to live."

"Yes," Clause said quickly, as if to console his friend. After the old comrades had discussed Lauren at length, he added: "Yes, this is a serious problem. But what can we do? Tell me, and I will help if I can."

"I know what's needed," said Werner, returning Clause's grim look. "I gave it much thought last night, and now I think I know."

"What is it?" Clause asked. "What can we do?"

"Although I think I know what's needed," Werner said, "I'm at a lost to know how to bring it about."

"Well, what is it, Comrade?" Clause asked, showing his impatience.

"What's needed is a distraction," Werner said as he took a sip of his coffee, his eyes never leaving his friend. "Yes, a strong and attractive distraction—that's what's needed." As he spoke, Werner looked gravely at Clause and slowly nodded his head. He then began to tell Clause what he was thinking. Before he finished, Clause stopped him.

"Yes, I'm beginning to see what you mean," Clause said. "And I have an idea. Let me get back to the shop and make a phone call." With that, he stood up and dropped his lunch napkin onto his half eaten lunch.

*   *   *

The following day, Lauren was busy adjusting cameras and other equipment in the front counter when a young man walked in and asked to see Herr Clause. Lauren showed him to Clause's small office and then returned to her work at the front counter. A short time later, Clause and the young man emerged from the office. Clause was laughing and saying for the young man to give his best to his friend, the editor of the newspaper. He then introduced Lauren and the young man, saying that he was a reporter from *Der Stern* and that he had a list of items he needed for the newspaper.

"Take good care of Dieter," Clause said, smiling. "He's from the newspaper, and they're one of our best customers."

"Of course," Lauren said, smiling at Dieter. "Let's see your list."

"I mostly need film, but there are other items," Dieter said. He was tall with sandy brown hair, kind blue eyes, and a relaxed mannerism. "I have an assignment to do an article on Bingen on the Rhein."

"Sounds interesting," Lauren said, continuing to smile. "What's the assignment about, or am I being too nosey?"

"I'm to write about interesting sights, restaurants, accommodations, and such," Dieter said. "It's to be from a human interest angle designed to attract tourists." As he spoke, he smiled back at Lauren. He talked in a quiet, soft voice and looked intently at her. He was obviously pleased with what he saw in Clause's good-looking assistant. "The paper promised the Bingen Travel Bureau they would reciprocate for advertisement space they were buying in the newspaper."

"What an exciting profession," Lauren said, not hiding her awe and not able to suppress her interest in Dieter's work. "It would be so nice to work on assignments like that, taking photographs and interviewing people."

"Some assignments are better than that," Dieter said with a serious face. "Then again, some are worse." Both he and Lauren had a good laugh at the comparison.

"I see you two are getting along very well," Clause said, walking again from his office, carrying some inventory papers. "You know, it's about your break time, Lauren. Why don't you two go for coffee and talk over the newspaper business?"

"But I need to collect these items for Dieter," Lauren said.

"Oh, I'll do that," Clause said. "You young folks take a break."

"Yes, Lauren," Dieter said. "It would be very pleasant to continue our discussion over coffee. I can always use good advice on the camera."

As Dieter opened the shop door for Lauren to exit for the coffee break, Lauren was saying to Dieter, "If the sky stays overcast like it is now, you should use color and a slow speed film for those river scenes at Bingen."

Clause watched them go. He paused a moment in thought and then hurried to his office to make a phone call: "Hello, Headmaster Werner," he began formally, working to suppress his glee. "I'm happy to report that phase one of our master plan is underway, and it looks very good so far."

CHAPTER 32

"SERGEANT BERGNER, DO YOU UNDERSTAND that what you say before this board of inquiry may have bearing on the decision resulting from this investigation of the incident where German civilians were struck and killed by a vehicle driven by one PFC Dave Myers?"

Mark stood at attention before two captains and a major who formed the board of inquiry appointed by the command adjutant's office. He was dressed in the olive-drab Class A uniform of the day and held his service cap in his right hand. His hair was cut close, military style, and his face was relaxed and controlled. He stared just over their heads, his look serious and respectful.

"Yes, sir, I do."

"Proceed with what you observed during the night of the accident and relate any information that might lead up to the incident."

Mark began his story. He related how the three of them had met several German youths at a soccer match and made friends with them. The German youths had subsequently invited them to their village for a Saturday afternoon visit. They met at a *Gasthaus* in the village of Brockmulbach and had a few beers along with a meal of bratwurst and cheese and bread.

"What was the general gist of your conversations during this time?" the senior officer, Major Davis, asked, interrupting Mark. His eyes bored into Mark, and he leaned forward slightly.

"Sir, it was just ordinary conversation," Mark said. He spoke evenly and remained controlled. He sensed their first concern would be a security breach. "It was mostly centered around their interest in our everyday life in the US. It consisted mostly about movies and music, I would say. They seemed particularly interested in Hank Williams."

The three officers paused momentarily, seemingly satisfied with Mark's answer toward that line of questioning. "Proceed with what you observed, Sergeant," Major Davis said.

Mark continued relating events on the day of the accident but was stopped by questions from one of the investigating officers. "At the *Gasthaus* in Brockmulbach, how much alcohol did PFC Myers consume?"

"Only a little," Mark answered. "Best I remember, he drank maybe one glass of beer through the entire evening." He made this statement as naturally and relaxed as he could and then continued relating the events of that evening. He emphasized the peculiar characteristics of the fog patches they encountered that made the drive back from Brockmulbach extremely tricky. And he stressed Myers's dazed and disoriented state after the collision, knowing they would be keenly interested in why he didn't stop immediately after the impact. When Mark finished, the three officers seemed satisfied and looked at each other for further questioning.

When there were no further questions, Major Davis said, "That will be all for now, Sergeant. But remember, our mission here in Germany is not just the defense of NATO but a mission of rebuilding nations and that of goodwill between the United States and the nations of Western Europe." He paused briefly before continuing. "And our mission here in Germany is far bigger than any of us individually."

Mark left the adjutant's office and walked to the PX cafeteria where he was to meet Wade after his appearance before the board. In his mind, he went over the affair at the inquiry. He had covered every exonerating point he had planned to work into his answers to questions he knew would be posed by the investigating officers. He felt good about his testimony, recalling nothing that would incriminate Myers and much that would head off any accusations of irresponsibility. On the short drive back to post and Charlie Company, they both agreed the inquiry went well.

"We've done all we can do, Mark," Wade said as the MP motioned them to enter the front gate to post. "Let's hope Dave can get off barracks arrest soon."

"I'm satisfied with the way things went," Mark said. Although he felt good about the inquiry, his thoughts returned to Major Davis's last words several times. What did he mean when he said "Our mission is bigger than any of us individually"? Was he talking in a general sense, or was he specifically referring to the situation of the accident? Mark knew that if he was referring to the accident and the situation created by the deaths of the two young men, it was not good. His thoughts returned to the bucket-of-water analogy that means the individual don't count.

*   *   *

Returning to their barracks, Mark and Wade had to give a blow-by-blow account of the inquiry to the other members of the platoon. When they finished their story and answered all questions, the other soldiers began to return to their bunks. As Corporal King walked away, he stopped and turned back to Mark and Wade. "By the way, have you guys heard today's rumor?"

"What's that?" Mark asked.

"A friend of mine is the company clerk at Battalion Headquarters," King said with an air of importance. "He says he's heard a rumor that our battalion is one that's being considered to rotate back to the states."

CHAPTER 33

CAPTAIN WILLIAMS JUMPED FROM HIS jeep and entered Charlie Company's orderly room in a hurry. As he walked passed First Sergeant Andrade, who was busy working on the weekly training roster, he said, "Come into my office, Andrade."

Andrade followed his CO and stood waiting as Captain Williams flopped down behind his desk, picked up a pencil, and began tapping the desktop. He mumbled something under his breath that Andrade obviously didn't understand: "What was that again, Captain?" he asked.

Williams ignored him momentarily, continuing with the pencil tapping. Finally, he looked up to Andrade and said, "Why me?" Before Andrade could say anything, Williams began relating to him what was on his mind.

"Just left a meeting at Battalion. All the company commanders were there. And out of all the companies in the battalion, the colonel picks mine for this detail." He looked up at Andrade as if he should have an answer to his dilemma.

"I don't understand, Captain," Andrade said. "I'm out of the loop here."

"Off course you are, Sergeant," Williams said. "I apologize for my thoughtlessness," he continued while presenting a more formal military manner. "Let me brief you on my latest assignment. Somewhere down south of us is a large ammo dump. It's supposed to be the largest military ammo dump in Western Europe. It's guarded by a full company of MPs and a detachment of Polish guards used by the US Army for such purposes. Well, someone has been breaking into the remote bunkers and stealing certain types of ammo, mostly small arms type such as 30-06s and .45s. They've requested help in patrolling their fence lines to stop the intruders."

"Where's this ammo dump?" Andrade asked.

"It's on an army post near the village of Miesau," Williams replied. "The military compliment there is small, and the storage bunkers are spread out through a forestry area that is so vast that current personnel can't patrol it effectively. They've requested help to patrol certain critical areas until the intruders can be stopped."

"Who do they think is stealing the ammo?"

"Black marketers, I'm told." Williams said. "They say they can sell such munitions in Africa at great profits. That's why they'll run the risk of getting shot to get weapons and ammo." The captain then paused as he jotted down a quick note on the notepad before looking back up to the first sergeant. "The order came down from Regiment, and Battalion plans to rotate platoon-sized detachments through there until they can stop their operation."

"Why only a platoon-sized detachment?" Andrade asked. "Why not company-sized detachments and shut them down immediately?"

"Because they want bodies for information," Williams said. "With company-sized reinforcements, the intruders are sure to notice and back off their operation. It's hoped that fewer men will allow the intruders to continue their operation and give our guys a chance to capture one or more."

"Sounds like a good plan," Andrade said.

"Yeah, German State *Polizei* says if we can give them one intruder alive, they can break the organization."

"And you were the lucky winner to start the ball rolling," Andrade said, smiling.

"You know what the colonel told me?" Williams said with a little chuckle. "He said since my outfit had done such a good job scouting out the route for the field maneuver location, he was giving me the first assignment."

"I see the irony," Andrade said with a wry smile. "They reward you for doing well on a difficult assignment by giving you another difficult assignment. Who do you plan to send down there?"

"Well, they've advised us that if there's a confrontation, it'll probably happen with the initial detachment," Williams said, looking down at the note he had previously made on the notepad. "And if this detachment can catch them in the act, they can stop the operation cold."

"Yeah, if something's coming down, it will most likely happen right off before the intruders know we're on to them," Andrade said. "Who do you plan to send?" he asked again.

"Who else?" Williams said, holding up the notepad for Andrade to view.

Sergeant Andrade could plainly see what the captain had written. "McBride," he said, nodding in agreement. "That would be my choice as well." They looked at each other in complete accord.

*   *   *

After the following morning reveille, instead of dismissing Second Platoon for its routine work schedules, Lieutenant McBride ordered them to stand in place. He had been fully briefed by Captain Williams on the Miesau mission, and he already had preparation plans laid out. He had a few days before his platoon would convoy down to Miesau, and this was ample time to get his men ready. Because of this special detail and the special weapons they would be issued there, he scheduled a half-day training session at the firing range. When he briefed the platoon on the mission and said they were going to the firing range for the first part of the day, he got some confused looks.

"Any questions?" he asked.

"Yes, sir," one of the soldiers began. "There's not a man in this outfit who's not trained and proficient with the M1 Garand, the .30 Carbine, and the .45. And we just qualified on the firing range last month. May I ask why we need additional training?"

"You need additional training because you won't be using a Garand, Carbine, or .45," McBride said. "We'll be assigned a special gun that some may not be familiar with."

"And what gun will that be?" another soldier asked.

"We'll be assigned trench guns," McBride said. "And any question you may have about that gun, you can address to the range master."

At the firing range, the range master gave a short talk on the specifications and history of the trench gun. He had a poster stand mounted before the bleachers where each soldier could clearly see the display as he talked. He related the gun's specifications in a clear, monotone voice, which was the style for military instructors. Everyone sat quietly and listened to his lecture.

"The weapon we're training with today is a Winchester model 12, 12-gauge, pump action, shotgun that has a six-round magazine," he began. "The ammunition you will be using for your mission is a cartridge with nine hardened '00' buckshot. It has a maximum effective range on a man-sized target up to seventy-five yards. At close range, it is a very effective weapon. From twenty-five to fifty yards, it has a hit probability of 45 percent greater than a submachine gun and twice that of the M1 carbine." He then paused a moment before he asked, "Are there any questions so far?"

A few men asked some routine questions. For the most part, they were so weapons trained that they didn't feel additional training necessary and remained quiet. Wade whispered under his breath that he fired his first shotgun at five and got his first deer at ten years of age.

Mark looked at Wade, smirking good-naturedly. "Just a Texas ranch hand, huh, Sam," he said, nudging him in the ribs.

"Yeah, that's for sure," Wade said. "I once got three quail from one covey in flight. Of course, I wasn't using buckshot."

"Just a cowboy bringing home dinner," Mark continued to kid Wade, suppressing a smile. "Did you shoot some potatoes to go with all that meat?"

"Well, didn't you ever go hunting growing up?" Wade asked defensively.

"Never fired a gun until I came into the army," Mark said.

"What a deprived childhood you Yankees have," Wade said, now chuckling and turning the joke back on Mark. "But if you lived where I did, you were expected to bring something home when you shoot. We didn't have a super market on the next block like you city slickers."

"Okay, listen up!" the range master started up again, bringing their attention back to the firing range. "To give you some history of the trench gun, it was first used in the First World War and has been used since then in special situations. It has been used in trench warfare, close combat, and house-to-house fighting. In peace time, it's most often used by the military to protect ships, airbases, and military installations from saboteurs. And any of you who might think of the 12-gauge as just a gun to hunt quail need to know that the gun was so effective at house-to-house and trench warfare that the Germans tried to get it outlawed through the Geneva Convention." He paused once again before asking, "Are there any questions?"

The range master waited for questions, and when none came, he continued. "Okay, we're going to line up by squads and fire from three positions. The three firing positions will be the standing, the kneeling, and the prone position. From each position, you will, on command, fire three rapid rounds."

The platoon went through the firing cycles with no problems and then returned to the bleachers. When everyone was seated back on the bleachers, the range master said that they had completed the familiarity session on the trench gun, but he wanted to leave the platoon with a special thought about the gun. "Of the many uses of the trench gun, it is especially effective for guard duty at night when visibility is limited, and you may have to fire at sound as opposed to sight."

On the trip back to post, Wade drove one of the three two-and-a-half-ton trucks they used to get the platoon to the firing range. He suddenly looked over at Mark as he drove. "You know what?" he said, as if he had just thought of something. "Down at Miesau, we're going to get stuck on guard duty at night."

"Yeah, I'm thinking the same thing," Mark said. "Guard duty at night, out in back country with trench guns. What fun we'll have."

"And we're stuck there for a week," Wade said as he pulled up to the post gate and stopped for the MP to check their IDs and post destination. "What a bummer!"

"At least we're not scheduled to go for a few days," Mark said. "I've got plans for this weekend."

CHAPTER 34

"WHY THE POST EXCHANGE?" LAUREN asked as she stepped down from the bus and stood next to Mark. She wore a light gray sweater over a white blouse with a navy blue skirt that was cut above the knee, as was becoming stylish in Europe. Her blond hair, as always, was combed neatly back, revealing a natural beauty of youth and health. In the fifteen months Mark had known Lauren, he had never brought her to an army facility or military event. This was partly because he enjoyed getting away from the military routine and partly because he felt she would be more comfortable doing activities within her own culture. But on this day, he had a special reason for bringing her to the army's Consolidated PX.

"Just something different to see," Mark said, taking her arm and leading her through the bus crowd into the large building. He smiled inwardly as two American soldiers in uniform walked by, their admiring looks resting long on Lauren as they passed. Mark had long ago gotten used to the attention she innocently attracted.

Any natural jealously he might have had was allayed by Lauren's behavior and attitude, which let him know he had no competition. She was strikingly beautiful in looks, and he was always proud to be seen with her. "This is the surprise I've been telling you about."

The PX was a large, open building that had several walkways running the length of the store with cross aisles that divided the floor space into the various departments. Multicolored signs and banners could be seen above the sections designating the variety of products each offered. It was the newest the US Forces had set up in Europe, and in the range of products and goods it offered, it would rival most department stores in the States. Mark took Lauren immediately to the camera department that displayed photography equipment of all types from several countries.

"I've never seen so much equipment at one time," Lauren said excitedly after looking around at the glass display cases. As she glanced from item to item in the display case, her look stopped on a particular zoom lens; she asked the clerk if she could examine it more closely. When the clerk handed the lens to her, she turned it in all directions, reading all writing on the case and lens mechanism. "This is the new zoom lens I've been reading about, Mark!" she explained, her expression showing her disbelief. "It's such a new release; we don't have it in our shop yet."

Mark nodded and examined the lens, appearing only casually interested but memorizing the model number and mentally noting the price. The reason he had brought Lauren to the PX was to find out exactly which lens she had been telling him about. In several previous conversations, she had mentioned a new lens coming on the market that she planned to save up for and buy. Now he knew and could purchase it for her. But when he asked the clerk about it, she told him they had sold out and only had the display unit left, which she could not sell. She went on to say they would have more in stock soon and would reserve one for him if he left his name and outfit. Since Lauren was engrossed in the lens documentation some distance down the counter, she was unaware of Mark's conversation. He then planned to bring her back to the PX and surprise her by purchasing the lens.

With his initial purpose accomplished, he let his interest focus on Lauren. Although her expression appeared pensive, her face quietly glowed as she read the detailed specifications from the documentation the clerk provided. He remembered Herr Clause telling him she read technical photography material like ordinary people read newspapers. And she not only reads everything on the subject, he had said, but she retains most everything she reads. Smiling openly at her, he handed the item back to the clerk.

Not wanting Lauren to notice his interest in the lens, he began to joke with her. "Now why would a professional photographer need a zoom lens?" he asked, smiling. "Why don't you just get closer to the subject?" Mark waited, grinning down at her.

Lauren, still holding her awe at finding the item, looked up at Mark with surprise. "But Mark," she said, "that's a 70-210mm zoom. It gives you the flexibility of studying your subject from a distance." Her attention again went to the documentation, but she added, "And I'm not a professional photographer yet." In her studious mood, she didn't immediately pick up on Mark's joking.

"I'd rather just get closer," Mark said, almost in a whisper. He bent forward slightly, as if reading over Lauren's shoulder. They had not seen each other in two weeks, and both strongly felt the other's presence.

"Sometimes we have no choice but to study the subject from a distance," she said, smiling and looking back over her shoulder at him. "When you have no choice, you take what you can get." She laughed and nodded her head to finalize and emphasize her point. But then, strangely, her laugh froze, and her expression faded. A distinct change in mood appeared. It could have been the result of spontaneous and paradoxical emotions brought on by his closeness and the sudden realization of something unpleasant. But her expression turned from joy to melancholy as her look fell back to the documentation.

Mark didn't understand the abrupt change. He had seen this bizarre behavior before. It had suddenly developed a couple of weeks back as they talked about her hopeful plans to attend the university. It appeared briefly and then went away as she forced the conversation away from that subject. He stepped back, and hoping to recover their holiday spirit, asked, "Do you need film? We may as well get it here."

"Yes, I need some black-and-white," she said. "One roll will hold me until I get back to the shop." Her expression remained thoughtful, and she wouldn't look at him.

Mark purchased two rolls of black-and-white film, and they walked away to continue their tour of the PX.

"How do they do it?" she suddenly asked as they moved through the crowd.

"Do what?"

"How does your PX store get German camera equipment before we get it in our shop?"

"Oh, I don't know," Mark said, smiling down at her, glad that she seemed cheerful again. "It's just the American way, I guess."

"Is everything back in the States this way?" she asked

"No," he said, laughing and pulling her around a crowd of people standing at a cosmetic counter. "Some things are better, and some are worse." He felt better with her cheerfulness, but the mention of the States caused him to grow thoughtful. When they stopped in the book section, he stood back, studying her closely. Lauren had picked up a magazine and was casually turning the pages.

"Lauren," he said after a moment. He waited for her to look up. "Have you ever thought about going to the States?" He asked the question quietly but pointedly while watching her closely. Lauren didn't answer immediately but stiffened slightly, so slightly it was almost undetectable. Mark felt the change and was again confused. Lauren continued to hold the magazine, but he sensed her attention was not on the pages.

"Mark," she said at last and almost in a whisper, "let's not talk about that." Her look stayed with the magazine.

Sorry he had brought up the subject, Mark unconsciously touched her arm, and she reflexively moved closer to him. He had often thought of them back in the States together, but he wouldn't dwell on the details of that situation. He knew it would be very difficult for her in his family and in his community. And he guessed that she knew it as well, the same as if he lived in her village close to her father. Although the subject of the States was something they had both given thought to, it was something neither one of them had discussed or was prepared to face. With the shopping, they had been in a lighthearted mood, and now, within a short time span, he had twice done something that spoiled their fun. They stood silent for a moment.

"Okay," he said, finally recovering. "I understand." He worked at sounding casual and pointedly changed the subject. "That's the latest issue of *Photography Magazine*; let's pay and move on."

They continued touring the PX but without enthusiasm on either's part. Mark, realizing their holiday spirit had ended, led the way out of the PX. The weather outside had grown cloudy with a low, gray ceiling, and nightfall was near. They took a taxi to a small *Gasthaus* near Lauren's train stop that had clean, warm rooms and served good food. They planned to spend the night there and take the trains to their respective locations the next Morning. Mark had duty at noon the following day, and he planned to see her off before returning to post. They only had a few hours together, and they both knew they should make the most of their time.

*   *   *

When the Frau working in the *Gasthaus* came to their table, Mark said, "I need something stronger than beer. I'll have cognac, please."

"*Ich auch, bitte,*" Lauren said without hesitating, obviously needing something stronger, herself.

They had a light but good dinner and retired to their room early. Their room was on the second floor overlooking the street. Lauren immediately kicked off her shoes, went to the window, and opened it, allowing the street sounds to come into their room. "Do you mind, Mark?" she asked. "I feel better when the sound of life is around me."

Mark, sensing her mood and wanting to cheer her, returned back down the stairs of the *Gasthaus* to find something that would lift their spirits. He brought back a bottle of wine that he knew to be mellow with a light boysenberry taste—it was one they had enjoyed before. There was only one chair in the room, and Mark pulled it next to the window for a view of the busy street. Lauren sat on his lap, and they sipped the wine and watched the people hurrying about below them. Lauren watched the street scene a few moments and then laid her head on his shoulder, settling into a comfortable position as she sat on his lap.

Mark held her close, her warmth and familiar weight bringing a deep pleasure, a pleasure so deep it hurt. He remembered their conversation about the states and how it seemed to disturb her. *I won't bring that up again,* he thought. A dark mood came over him, and he pushed it away by gazing down into her face. Lauren looked up and smiled, which made him feel better.

Soon the wine cheered them, and they both reclaimed a lighthearted mood. They went to bed early, and in the quiet of their small world, they tried to make up for the longing, the yearning, and the need they knew when apart. They made love with a quiet, deep passion that left them both exhausted and clinging. In that moment, they were happy just being together. But later that night as they drifted into sleep, Lauren seemed to hold Mark tighter . . . as if afraid.

CHAPTER 35

T EN DAYS AFTER FIRST BATTALION assigned Charlie Company the Miesau mission, Lieutenant McBride and his Second Platoon got their orders. Captain Williams, wanting to make sure McBride had sufficient manpower, added ten more men from First Platoon to the detail. All of Second Platoon made the trip except Myers; he was excluded because of his barracks arrest. When the fortified platoon of forty men plus one officer arrived in four two-and-a-half ton trucks at the post gate, the MPs were expecting them. The MP advised McBride that his men were to be billeted down the main street in the third building on the right and that the BOQ (the Bachelor Officers Quarters) where McBride would be billeted, was the smaller building on the left. McBride ordered Wade, who was driving the lead truck, to proceed to the billeting area and began getting situated for their stay in Miesau. He then left the platoon to report to the post commander.

In mid afternoon, they got their first briefing. An MP captain stood at a podium in the Post Auditorium and presented the orientation. He introduced himself as Capt. Gene Crane. With a close haircut and a thin mustache like the British officers are fond of wearing and dressed in starched and creased, tailored fatigues and highly shined boots, he appeared fit and very much military. He began by referring to a large flipchart mounted on a display board standing next to the podium. The first chart was a topographical map of the post, and he explained that the post's storage area contained the largest collection of military ordnance of any installation outside the United States. This ordnance included ample supplies of every caliber round from a .22 to a 105 howitzer, as well as chemical and biological weapons. "That's why post security is such a big issue here," he said, pausing for emphasis.

He went on to explain that the ordnance was stored in bunkers, or magazines, in remote areas of the installation. The storage sites were located in heavily wooded areas with bunkers situated along a network of roads. The bunkers were constructed of concrete and steel, and each was covered with several feet of soil and a grass covering that helped to maintain a stable temperature within. The bunkers were constructed a safe distance apart from one another, so if one exploded, it would not set off a chain reaction. Miles of chain-link fence with concertina wire at the top encircled the entire area.

Initially, the men from Charlie Company listened only casually to Captain Crane. But when he flipped a page of the chart and explained it was a map of the sector they would be responsible for, they all listened closely. The map showed a road running along a fence line with trees both inside and outside the fence. Bunkers were not visible on the map, but circled numbers indicated and identified each one along the sector. After turning the page, the captain stopped momentarily to take a sip of water from a cup within the podium. He then picked up a pointer stick and continued his briefing.

"Number twelve bunker, here," he said, pointing at the map, "is the last bunker they've hit, as far as we know." He paused a moment looking about the room as if to let that information sink in. "We caught it on a routine inventory when we found twenty cases of 30-06's missing. We feel they will return for more."

"How do they get into the bunkers?" someone asked. "Aren't they locked?"

"Yes, they're securely locked," Crane said. "And yes, it's obvious they have inside help. Someone on the inside with a key is helping them."

"How will my men be deployed?" McBride asked, getting right to his responsibilities.

"Well, there's a distance of more than a mile along this fence line that has been assigned as your responsibility. The bunkers in this area are closest to the fence line, and for that reason, they are the ones that will most likely be hit," the captain answered, again pointing to that area on the map. "Your men will be deployed along this road from 0000 hours to 0400 hours."

Low groans and mumbled complaints rose from the men of Charlie Company at hearing the time frame they would be out in the back country of the storage area. Lieutenant McBride immediately stood up, looking about the room. Although he didn't speak, everyone immediately quieted down. He faced the room a moment and then turned his attention back to the captain. "Are there any particular patrolling techniques you use after you deploy your men?" he asked. "I mean, do they just walk back and forth along the fence line, or what?"

"We use several deployment and patrolling techniques," Captain Crane said. "And we change them often so that someone on the outside can't easily determine the system we're using." He paused again, taking a sip of water. "The technique we've selected for this week, and the one you will be using, is as follows: You will transport your men to the designated area in your trucks. As the moving trucks slowly enter your sector, the MP sergeant in charge who will be with you will begin dropping off two men at three-hundred-yard intervals. The trucks won't stop completely for these drop-offs; it will only slow down sufficiently for each set to dismount. This way, someone observing from outside the fence will have less of a chance of knowing where our men are located. For each of these two-man sets, the drop-off point where they exit the truck becomes their station to patrol from on their hundred-yard rounds."

"I have another question," McBride interjected. "Is there any lighting out there?"

"No! There is no lighting," the captain answered quickly. "When the moon is behind a cloud or the sky overcast, it is totally black out there."

Captain Crane waited for further questions. When none came, he continued: "Now, keeping in mind there will be little or no visibility, each of the two men in a set will take turns patrolling in each direction from their respective stations along the road and fence line. The first man patrols for a hundred yards, and only for a hundred yards, and then he returns to his station. His partner then patrols in the opposite direction for a hundred yards and then returns to the designated spot where his partner waits. This way, each of these two men will always know the general location of their partner."

"I see," McBride said. "And there will always be approximately a hundred-yard gap between each two-man groups. That way, each man of a group is not as likely to confront a man from an adjacent group, and in the dark possibly draw friendly fire."

"What about those hundred-yard gaps that are left unpatrolled?" Wade asked.

"As in all nets, some things may pass through," the captain said. "But an intruder or saboteur doesn't know where our men will be, so he would have to get lucky to get past them."

"What about confrontations?" McBride asked.

"I was coming to that," the captain said. "There will be confrontations to deal with. Each time a man in a set leaves his partner and returns, there is a confrontation. We handle these friendly confrontations with passwords. For example, with the password Betty-Grable, one man challenges the unknown one approaching him with 'Betty.' The other must answer 'Grable,' or he is to be considered unfriendly."

"This brings up a crucial question," McBride said. "How are my men to deal with unfriendlies if they encounter them?"

"You will deal with that situation in the standard way. After the challenged person ignores or doesn't know the password, you shout halt at least twice. If they don't halt, bring them down." Captain Crane paused again, obviously to let what he had just said sink in. When he continued, he spoke in a slow, measured tone. "These men are hardened criminals or worse, saboteurs, and they'll play rough if they have to."

After the orientation, the men of Charlie Company were divided into two-person sets and given truck assignments. Mark and Wade volunteered for a set, and their truck was assigned the first position in the trucks leaving the debarkation point. Being the first truck to leave would put them the farthest out in the remote area.

*　　*　　*

After a few hours' rest in the barracks where sleep was fitful for most, the men of the 0000 to 0400 hour watch assembled in the streets before the trucks that were lined up, running, and ready to go. They had already checked out their weapons and loaded them to capacity, leaving the firing chambers empty. Along with the M12s issued, they received a bandoleer with additional loads for their weapons. The trucks moved out with Charlie Company's contingent in the last three trucks. After a short drive, the bunker area was reached, and the deployment began. Two men were dropped off at proper intervals by the MP sergeant until only Mark and Wade remained in Wade's truck. They drove another three hundred yards and then stopped. The MP sergeant was picked up by a jeep, and

Mark and Wade were alone. This was to be their drop-off location and their station to patrol from. Wade drove the truck off the road onto a driveway leading to a bunker. A small sign identified the location as Bunker 12.

Once Mark and Wade were established at their patrolling station, they began their watch. Because their truck stayed with them, their patrolling zone was a hundred yards along the fence line to each side of the truck. They were instructed to maintain total silence except when returning from their patrols, when they were to issue the challenge and wait for the password. This exchange was to be made no louder than necessary. After they stopped and the vehicle and motor sounds died away and the blackness moved in around them, Mark and Wade stood silently, somewhat awed by the vastness of the night in the wooded countryside.

The night sky was overcast and offered no starlight or moonlight, and the only sounds were those of the forest. Mark and Wade, even after their night vision developed, could only sense the other's presence. They stood in place for a time until finally Wade whispered to Mark: "I'll take the first patrol. I'll go past the truck and do my hundred yards. When I return, challenge with the password."

"Okay," Mark whispered back. "Password check."

"Password is pocket-knife."

"Correct!" Mark whispered. "Now don't shoot me when I challenge you."

"Same goes for you," Wade said, and they each gave a low chuckle.

They began walking their hundred-yard patrols. At first, the blackness made it hard to stay oriented with the road and directions, but they soon adjusted, and the hundred-yard sectors became clear in their minds, even without seeing what was around them. After awhile, they could distinguish dim images, but they mostly knew what was ahead and behind them only by their innate senses. It was only their intuition and gut feelings that they could use to know their place in their surroundings.

The night passed slowly. Walking a set path over and over is monotonous, and to make it worse, they couldn't talk freely. On their patrols, an occasional night sound or false awareness of something ahead would focus their attention sharply ahead. When this happened, they would freeze in place, starring hard at the perceived spot of the sound, their weapons ready. Once Wade was so sure he heard something ahead that he almost issued the challenging password. With his M12 poised and his left hand ready to pump a round into the gun's firing chamber, he starred at the blackness for a long spell before continuing on. These infrequent but adrenalin-charged interruptions in the patrolling routine were often welcomed relief from the monotony of the patrols.

Their first watch finally passed, and they remounted the deuce-and-a-half and retraced their steps, picking up the men dropped off at the beginning of the watch. Back at their billeting area and just before Wade dropped off into sleep, he said to Mark, "This is the most mind-numbing and dullest duty I've ever pulled. I'd rather pull KP than guard duty."

Their second night was the same as the first, and so were the following nights. The boredom became even worse as the routine became more familiar. Their after-duty time wasn't much better. After their four-hour watch, they were free the remaining part of the twenty-four-hour day. They would sleep a few hours and then get ready for their day.

After morning chow, they would wander about the post or walk down into the village. After evening chow, they always laid around in the barracks, napping or reading and relaxing. They were experienced enough to know better than to go onto their watch tired or sleep deprived.

The week finally passed, and they began their final watch, mildly excited about going back to their home post the following day. After Wade stopped the truck to begin their final four hours, they dismounted and stood around and talked in low whispers for a time. When Mark got ready to start his patrol, he said, "I'm going to take more time on my patrols tonight."

"Yeah, me too," said Wade. "There's no moon tonight, but there's starlight. If you stop for a time, stay in the shadows."

"Yeah, but don't stop too long. You might get sleepy," Mark said. "I don't want to have to come looking for you," he continued with a low chuckle.

"Password check," Wade said.

"Password is thunder-lightning," Mark whispered as he turned to start his patrol.

They began their patrols, alternating their hundred-yard walks and taking a longer time out away from their drop-off point. This continued throughout the watch. The four hours were almost over when Wade returned from his patrol to find Mark had already left in the opposite direction for his walk. This was not too unusual, for they sometimes got bored waiting on the other and would go ahead with their own patrol to break the monotony. He waited a time for Mark to return and then decided to walk a short distance toward Mark's direction and away from their starting point. He walked about thirty yards and stopped, waiting. He sat down and waited a while longer, listening to the night around him and thinking about returning to Charlie Company at Grahfenvern Post. When Mark still didn't return, he decided it best he return to the drop-off point and wait for him there. He stood up and had walked but a few steps when he thought he heard something ahead of him back toward the truck. He froze in place.

He stood motionless for several minutes. He knew he had heard something. But what? Mark's position should be behind him. But what if it wasn't, and he had stepped into the woods for a few minutes and was just then returning to the road. There was some starlight, but the tree foliage was so heavy that no light penetrated to the ground where he stood or ahead of him where he thought he'd heard a noise. He waited awhile longer, staring into the blackness. He could hear nothing, but he felt a disturbing awareness that something was just before him and very close. His gut feeling brought all his senses to a heightened state, his adrenalin high. He waited, but nothing happened. He then decided he had to make a move, to throw out a challenge and resolve the stand-off.

"Thunder," he said in a low but distinct voice. He waited for the proper answer to the password, but none came. "Thunder," he said again, this time louder and with more authority. On the second challenge, he now heard something louder. It was a thud, as if something heavy had been dropped to the ground. This was a sound he knew Mark wouldn't make, and he knew there was someone there. "Halt!" he shouted and then waited. "Halt!" he shouted again.

Almost simultaneous with Wade's second halt command, two rapid gunshots broke the silence of the night, and he saw the muzzle flash but a few yards directly ahead of him. He immediately went to ground, and pumping the trench gun as he rolled off the road, he swept the area ahead of him with the six rounds in the magazine, spraying the area with fifty or better lethal buckshot. The booming report of the M12 reverberated through the trees and echoed back through the night like close thunderclaps. He had just finished reloading when he heard light footsteps behind him and Mark saying, "Wade, where are you?"

"Here," Wade said. In an instant, Mark was beside him.

"Where are they?" Mark whispered.

"Twelve o'clock," Wade whispered back. "Straight ahead, about twenty yards."

In the distance, Mark and Wade could hear voices and motors starting up, and they knew the gunfire had aroused the entire watch. "The first two shots sounded like nine-millimeter," Wade continued. "Probably a handgun."

"Should we wait for the others?" Mark asked.

"If we wait, they might get away," Wade said. "Let's try to draw them out."

"How?"

"Move to your right a few yards," Wade began in a controlled whisper. "I'll fire a couple rounds to try to draw their fire. If they return fire, unload on the muzzle flash, and I'll do the same.

Two booming blasts rang out, again shattering the night sounds. This was quickly followed by several shots from a smaller caliber weapon. Almost immediately, the night erupted in gunfire from both Mark and Wade simultaneously unloading their M12s at the sound of the opposing weapon. The loud, deafening gunfire from their weapons exploded through the night and continued to echo through the trees long after the two men stopped firing. The smell of gunpowder hung heavy in the air. They lay quietly, reloading and listening and staring at the black void before them. For a brief time, they couldn't see or hear anything, but soon, footsteps could be heard coming up behind them and excited but low voices speaking softly, "Thunder! Thunder!"

"Lightning! Lightning!" both Mark and Wade whispered back simultaneously. "Come on up!" The two men could soon feel the presence of other bodies moving in and around them and taking up positions.

In no time, the place was crawling with soldiers. Some MP officer took charge and began directing the men with sharp commands. When a soldier reported to him that an opening had been cut in the wire in a dry wash a short distance away, he sent four men through the opening to find what they could in the countryside outside the fence.

Mark and Wade were taken aside and questioned thoroughly. The first officer questioning them said he was sitting in a jeep about a quarter mile away when he heard the gunfire. He agreed that the first two shots sounded like a handgun. He said he knew the booming reports following that of the handgun were from an M12. "From what I can ascertain at this time, you two acted exactly as you should have. You were fired on, and you returned fire," he said. "And that will be the crux of my initial report."

He turned to speak to another officer who had walked up. The second officer said, "We've found a case of ammo lying behind the truck and several cases stacked just outside the cut in the fence."

A sergeant then walked up quickly. "We've got a body!" he said gravely, pointing his flashlight back toward the truck. "And it's a mess, sir!"

They all followed the sergeant's flashlight beam to a form that lay crumpled before the cab of the truck. Several flashlights surveyed the scene, their beans sweeping back and forth across the body and nearby area. The dead man had worn all black clothes, and his face and hands were blackened. But across his chest and right shoulder, his shirt front had been blown away, revealing white lacerated skin and bloodied bone and body tissue protruding from the wound opening. Other than the massive wound, the form looked like a pile of old clothes lying in the dirt and leaves. One flashlight beam surveyed the side of the truck next to the dead man. It found and stayed focused on a large blood smear just behind the driver's side door. "The M12 round blew him against the cab of the truck before he fell to ground," a voice said.

"Check for pulse, Sergeant," the MP officer said. "Just in case."

The sergeant stooped down and felt the body at the neck then stood back up immediately, wiping blood from his hand. "There's nothing there, sir," he said.

After the officers had finished questioning Mark and Wade, they told them to stand by until dismissed. One officer said the investigation would continue the following day when they could look the area over in the daylight. As Mark and Wade waited, a soldier approached the MP officers. He had his M12 over his shoulder and a flashlight in his right hand. "Sir," he said, "we've found blood on the ground at the cut in the fence."

"Good!" the office in charge said. "We've got one dead and one wounded and running." He then sent a sergeant and four more men through the fence in pursuit of the wounded man. "We need him alive," he spoke sharply as the sergeant and his men were walking away. He looked down at the body on the ground. "Except for being dead, this one's no use to us now."

He then turned back to Mark and Wade and looked at them momentarily without speaking. "Well done!" he said finally with a positive nod.

Mark and Wade began walking around the truck, searching for other evidence that might have been overlooked. As they approached the rear of the deuce-and-a-half, Mark said, "I smell gasoline!"

"Yeah, it's strong too," Wade said. He reached into the cab's glove box to retrieve a flashlight. "We better check that out," he continued as he bent down to look beneath the truck at the gas tank area.

"There's glass all over the seat," Mark said after opening the opposite door. "We hit the truck when we fired."

"And the gas tank's leaking," Wade said. "What's going on here?" he continued as he walked about, examining the exterior of the truck with the flashlight.

"The door window glass is shattered," Mark said, "and so is the windshield."

"And some of the rounds went into the motor compartment," Wade said, walking around the front of the deuce-and-a-half and shining the light about the body of the vehicle. "My God, Mark! The truck's shot all to hell! It was right in the line of fire."

CHAPTER 36

A FTER C COMPANY'S MEN RETURNED to their home post, Lieutenant McBride turned in his report of the operation, strongly justifying the situation with the disabled deuce-and-a-half and the reasons for temporarily leaving it at Miesau. Evaluations of their mission and the results of the ongoing investigations back at Miesau would be forthcoming, but all felt they had done a good job. With this detail behind them, their daily training schedule returned to a normal routine.

It had been almost five weeks since Captain Williams gave Mark a lecture on writing his mom. "You have a duty to the home front as well as here in Charlie Company," Williams had said. It was Saturday morning, and being a duty-free day, most of the men were lying around reading or writing letters and just relaxing in the barracks. Mark, Wade, and Myers had decided they would skip their daily runs and use the morning to get caught up on personal things. Mark got his boots in order and made out his laundry list. Next, he worked on his locker, rearranging items to SOP in case of another one of the surprise, unscheduled inspection that had been occurring lately. He still hadn't written home, and he didn't plan to write. The stack of letters in the back of his locker had grown considerably.

"Bergner!" a voice suddenly shouted from the barrack's entrance. "Where are you, Bergner?" A soldier entered the barracks struggling with an armload of boxes and proceeded down the center aisle. "Bergner," he hollered again. Finally, seeing Mark standing by his bunk with nothing on but his skivvies, he walked toward him. "This came in late yesterday," he said, dumping three sizable boxes on Mark's bunk. "They're taking up too much space in my mail room, so I'm giving you a personal delivery."

"These are mine?" Mark asked. "What's this all about?"

"How should I know? "I'm just the mail clerk. I don't open people's mail," he said back over his shoulder as he turned and walked away.

Mark examined the first box and saw a return address of Queens, New York City. "Oh, no!" he said as he sat down at the head of his bunk, turning away from the boxes.

"What's up with the boxes?" Myers asked while making his bunk and looking over at Mark.

"Something from my mom," Mark said, shaking his head and grimacing.

"What's wrong with that?" Wade asked, coming around from his bunk and viewing the boxes closely. "What's in them?"

"I don't know what's in them," Mark said. "And I don't care what's in them."

"Why's that, Mark?" Myers asked, putting the final touches on his bunk and standing up to face Mark. "You should be glad to get something from home."

"No, I'm not glad about this," Mark said, walking to his locker, his eyes avoiding the boxes. "My parents and I are disagreeing about something right now."

"What are you disagreeing about?" Wade asked. He picked up one of the boxes and shook it gently, his curiosity aroused. "Um . . . maybe it's goodies from dear old Mom." He shook the box again, holding it close to his ear. He was interested because whenever someone got a cake or something similar from home, it was traditional to pass it around. Ownership of prized goodies automatically spread to other members of the platoon.

"Well, it's personal, and I don't want to talk about it," Mark said. He stood with his back to the boxes, seemingly looking for something in his locker.

"Can I open one of them?" Myers asked as he began to peal the tape from the edge of the first box. "Whoever wrapped these boxes knew what they were doing. This is professional wrapping."

"Be my guest," Mark said, retrieving his shaving kit from his locker. "But if it's something to eat, and you eat it and die a slow, agonizing death don't blame me," he continued as he walked away with his shaving kit and a towel around his neck.

Mark planned to shower and shave and get dressed in his civvies. Then around noon he would catch the train into the city and meet Lauren for her afternoon break. He knew she worked late on Saturdays and that they couldn't get together that day after her work. But he liked to be in the midst of civilians in the busy city and away from the routine of the army post. And the short time with Lauren on her break made the trip worthwhile. On occasion, he would take in a German movie. He was proud that his German language skills had developed to the point where he understood the dialogue as if it were in English. When he went into the city and had coffee with Lauren on her break, she always thanked him for going to so much trouble just to keep her company for such a brief time.

Walking out of the latrine, Mark could see a cluster of guys around his bunk. Wade had the box open and the flaps bent back, revealing rows of cookies. The neat rows were carefully arranged where each cookie had its own separate location and was securely held in place by meticulous attention to packing with paper separators. The assortment of sweets consisted of both white and dark chocolate, oatmeal, and sugar cookies, as well as brownies and small pastries of various types. Some were a crusty brown in color, some were a soft yellow, some had pecans on top, and some were sprinkled over with red and blue sugar. With the sealed box freshly opened, a sweet, sugary aroma rose up from the interior. The men gathered around the box and stared as if mesmerized at the colorful assortment of sweets; it was an unusual sight for the soldiers of Second Platoon.

"It's a work of art, Mark," Wade said, looking up to Mark, clearly amazed at the craftsmanship that went into the arrangement and packing. "And the lower layers are packed the same as this top layer."

"Well, see if they taste as good as they look," Mark said. "We don't want them to go stale while we stare at them."

Wade immediately picked up a chocolate chip cookie with an almond on top and took a small bite. He then mumbled something and tilted his head back in pleasure. This was the signal for the rest to do the same, and simultaneously, many hands reached in and grabbed what they could. With a rising chatter of voices reflecting a childish pleasure in consuming the sweets, the top row disappeared quickly. Wade removed the paper separator and found a second row just as appealing as the first. In no time, it was also gone, exposing the next row for eager hands.

"By the way, Mark," Wade said as he munched away, his mouth so full he could hardly talk. "There was an open note on top of the first row when I opened the package." He handed the note to Mark.

The note said: "Mark, I hope you and your friends enjoy these sweets. I'll be sending a box weekly for everyone. Love, Mom."

Mark looked at the note for a moment and mumbled under his breath, "She's changing her tactics. This is her version of a Trojan Horse."

"What did you say, Mark?" Myers asked while licking his fingers.

"Yeah, what do you mean Trojan Horse?"

"Nothing," Mark answered. "I didn't say anything—just mumbling to myself." Mark took the second box, opened it, and placed it at the entrance to the barracks for anyone who might want a cookie later. He saved the third box, thinking he would drop it off in the orderly room for others in the company. He hadn't eaten any of the cookies and didn't intend to eat any of them. "My mom would be pleased to know you all liked the cookies so well," he said, laughing, finally seeing the humor in the spectacle the cookies were creating.

"What's your problem with your parents? Your mom's a great person," Wade said as he picked up his third brownie. "Anyone who sends cookies gets my vote of approval."

"Hail to Mark's mom!" another soldier said, standing at attention and holding his cookie up like a Roman Centurion saluting Caesar.

"We disagree on some personal issues," Mark said. "But it's not something I can talk about."

"Aw, Mark!" Wade said. "Moms from the beginning of time have manipulated their kids to control them."

"Yeah, I know, and I know she means well," Mark said. "But this is one issue she's wrong on, and I'm not giving in."

"Don't be too sure of that," Wade said, laughing and reaching for a pecan-clustered chocolate wafer. "Moms with a batch of cookies can conquer the world."

"I know," Mark answered. *The Trojan Horse is working already,* he thought. *She's entered my protective bastion. What's coming next? Will Troy Fall?*

CHAPTER 37

L AUREN, NEARING THE END OF high school, began planning to work full time. For some time, she'd had a secret desire to work in the newspaper business as a news photographer. She knew this dream was highly unlikely and tried not to think about it, telling herself to think more practically. But reinforcing and enhancing her dream was the fact that Dieter was often in the shop buying supplies for the newspaper, and he always took time to talk to her about his assignments. She listened to his stories with keen interest and looked forward to his visits. And Dieter, obviously wanting to impress Lauren, embellished and inflated his stories to make a stronger impression.

"Interviewing interesting people and chasing stories is a fun and rewarding profession," he told her often.

One afternoon when business was slow and Dieter and Lauren were examining shots that Dieter had taken at a *Fasching* parade, Clause walked over and casually said, "Dieter, sometime when you have time, why don't you take Lauren on a tour of the newspaper building. Show her how the type is set and how the newspapers are run off and things like that."

"Good idea," Dieter said. Then, turning to Lauren, he asked, "What do you think, Lauren?"

"Thing are slow today, Lauren," Clause quickly said. "Why don't you go this afternoon? That is, if Dieter can work it into his schedule."

"That's fine with me," Dieter said.

"But, Herr Clause," Lauren said. "What about my duties here?"

"Oh, I can manage," Clause said. "And, Dieter, why don't you two go to an early diner afterward so you can further explain to Lauren details of the business."

"Excellent idea," Dieter said, looking at Lauren and waiting for her consent.

Lauren looked confused for a moment but then glanced at Clause and nodded her approval. She wanted very much to work at the newspaper. She knew the difficulty of becoming a reporter and wouldn't let her hopes get that high. But to just get any kind of work around the newspaper business would be a dream come true. She would sweep floors if she had to. She felt that if she was just on the inside at any job, she would have a better chance of submitting her best photo shots to the editors for use in the paper. She also thought that Dieter could help her get hired if he thought she had the talent for the business. For this reason, she consciously worked to be informative and accommodating with Dieter, and she always smiled and offered advice with the camera and his photo shots. She did this not only because Dieter could help her, but because he was a charming and attractive person and she enjoyed his friendship.

*   *   *

Clause smiled as the two left the shop. As they were walking out the door, Dieter was telling her that the circulation of the newspaper was growing and that it would in time be hiring in various departments. Clause followed them to the door and peered out, watching them walk down the street. He then went to his office and made a phone call. "Hello, this is Herr Clause from The Camera Shop. Please connect me with the chief editor, Herr Schmitt."

Clause knew the editor well. He had been a reporter and photographer for *Der Stern* before he set up his business with The Camera Shop. Before he left the newspaper company, he secured a contract to supply them with photography equipment, and he did these transactions at wholesale. Thus, he had a direct connection with the chief editor and was in a position to ask for favors. He requested an interview with the editor for Lauren, telling him that her ability to determine what was important in photographic scenes was phenomenal. As an example, Clause described the shots Lauren had taken of the motorcycle that had plowed through the pedestrians in the crosswalk. Herr Schmitt was impressed and set up a time for Lauren's interview.

As soon as Clause hung up from talking to the editor, he dialed the number for the headmaster at Ellenbach High School. "Hello, Headmaster Werner," he began with unsuppressed glee. "I'm happy to report that phase two of our master plan is underway."

He then explained to Werner how he had set up Lauren's tour of the newspaper building with Dieter and their plans afterward for an early dinner.

With this done, he said he had another announcement. "Also, my old comrade, you'll be happy to learn that I've managed to get Lauren an interview with the editor of the newspaper."

*　　*　　*

"So you want to work in the newspaper business," the chief editor said at the beginning of Lauren's interview.

Lauren had dressed as formally as she could manage. After Clause informed her of the interview, she had almost depleted her savings to purchase a blouse, stockings, and her first pair of high heels. On the day of the interview, she selected a black skirt and white blouse to go with the new stockings and heels to look businesslike and professional. Then, upon her entrance to the editor's office, she felt she had, in fact, made a favorable impression. She gleaned this with one brief glance as she entered the office and saw Herr Schmitt's face going from a stern, businesslike demeanor to one of surprised pleasure.

Schmitt had already reviewed her resume with her school record that showed she was top in her class. There were also glowing recommendations from several teachers, as well as from Herr Clause. Even one of his young reporters had provided an excellent report of her potential. He was obviously impressed with Lauren's recommendations. "I think we can find something for you when your school term is finished," he continued. "You realize, though, that you'll have to start at the bottom."

"Yes, of course," Lauren answered. "I fully understand that."

"And when I say start at the bottom, I mean at the very bottom," he emphasized. "Working around the presses is dirty work."

"I understand," Lauren said. "And I'm willing to work hard."

"I believe you are," he said, a smile beginning to form on his face. After a moment, he resumed his business manner, crossing his arms and leaning back in his chair. "There is something else," he continued finally. "I hesitate to mention this, because it's such a long shot." He again paused while studying Lauren. "Clause tells me you have one heck of a busy schedule. You attend school until noon, catch the train into the city to work at his shop until five o'clock, and then take the train back home to help your father prepare meals and do the house chores. And you maintain this schedule six days a week. You're obviously a serious and determined young woman. In view of this, I think you're a candidate for the scholarship program the paper sponsors each year."

"Scholarship program?" Lauren asked, surprised and not understanding his meaning.

"Yes," he continued. "The paper awards a scholarship in journalism each year to one highly talented and deserving individual. The program is very competitive, and there will be many applicants. That's why I hesitate to mention it. I don't want to get your expectations too high, too soon."

"I would be very interested in journalism," Lauren said. "My interest in photography would go well with journalism."

"Very well. I'll submit your resume to the scholarship committee with my approval. But don't let your hopes get too high," he emphasized. "There will be many highly qualified applicants—literally hundreds."

Lauren quickly agreed with the editor, including her name and record with the applicants in the scholarship program. Although she would love to study journalism at the university, she didn't place much hope in winning the scholarship. It was enough for her at this point in her life to have a chance to work at the newspaper when her schooling was complete.

"There's one more thing," he said as Lauren rose to leave his office. He watched Lauren closely for a moment before continuing. "And I hope you don't think I'm being too personal."

"Yes?"

"You're an attractive young woman," he said in such a way that Lauren was unsure of his meaning. "Most young women in your situation would have some special person, but I can't imagine you having time for that with your busy schedule."

Lauren paused in turning to leave. She studied the editor a moment. Her first impulse was to not answer his question concerning her private life. But then she changed her mind, thinking it best her social status be known. "There is someone special," she said finally with a quiet but firm voice. "We are very close, but we know our duties as well."

CHAPTER 38

"DID YOU WANT TO SEE me, Sergeant?" Mark asked, walking into the orderly room and standing before the first sergeant at his desk.

"Yes, Bergner," First Sergeant Andrade said, looking up from his reading. "I want to talk to you." Various papers were scattered across the top of his desk. Contrary to his normal strict and formal military manner, the first sergeant appeared introspective and weary. "I'm working on some paperwork of yours."

"What paperwork is that, Sergeant?" Mark asked, standing before the sergeant's desk, his field cap in his hand.

"You've done very well on the firing range each time you've qualified with the .50 MG," Andrade began. He picked up a sheet of paper and glanced at it briefly. "Plucked the eyes out of that target at five hundred meters," he continued, talking quietly but smiling up at Mark. "How do you do it?"

"Just like they tell you, Sergeant," Mark said. "Start low with your tracers and work up to the target."

"You must have extraordinary eyesight," Sergeant Andrade said.

"Plenty of guys have that," Mark said.

"I'm not so sure about that," Andrade said, staring keenly at Mark and nodding his head to emphasize his point. "In any case, the captain's impressed. Wants to change your MOS, your military occupation specialty, to include heavy weapons." He looked at Mark a moment as if studying his reaction.

Mark remained silent, showing no enthusiasm for the news. He had long ago learned to be noncommittal in all situations with the army until he knew all the facts.

"It might mean a promotion in a short time," Andrade said. "That is, if the Myers incident doesn't cloud the issue. It'll look good on your records."

Mark still didn't answer. He felt Andrade was either stalling or probing, and he didn't want to commit himself before he knew which it was.

"Have you thought about making a career of the army?" Andrade continued. "If so, I'm sure the captain will recommend you for Officers Candidate School."

"Sergeant, my enlistment is up in five months," Mark began. "I've submitted applications at several universities. I hope to be in NYU next fall." Mark waited. He knew that if the captain wanted to change his MOS to heavy weapons, he would change it with or without his permission. And making it clear he wasn't staying in the army would end that particular conversation, allowing the sergeant to get on to his next point if there was one.

"Oh well, that's that," Andrade said, laying the paperwork aside. He leaned back in his chair and crossed his arms and gazed out the window. "I hate this damn paperwork," he mumbled under his breath. "I'd rather be out in the field on maneuvers or preparing a bivouac than sitting here at this desk." His thoughts seemed to be somewhere else for the moment.

"Is there something else you wanted to see me about, Sergeant?"

"Yes, there is, damn it," he said, turning back to face Mark. "You know . . . I told you I'd keep you informed of PFC Myers's status." He paused briefly before continuing. His look went to his desktop and then directly back to Mark. "It's not good, Mark . . . The investigation board has recommended a court-martial."

When the news of the court-martial hit the barracks, everyone was shocked with disbelief. The consensus was the accident was just that—an accident. There was no gross negligence or intent to harm. It could have happened to anyone, and on occasion, it did happen to others without severe repercussions. And if the army was pushing it further than that, it was the result of some force beyond that of normal procedure. Myers was well liked by everyone who knew him, and the sense that he was being treated unfairly for some obscure reason created anger and discontent among the entire company the following week. But on Friday, an impromptu announcement came that deflected the men's attention in another direction. The Company was ordered to assemble in the post auditorium at 0900 hours the following morning instead of having their normal free Saturday. Mark was disappointed that he wouldn't be able to get into the city, but he knew that something big was up.

"All come to attention!" the battalion's sergeant major shouted as the battalion commander walked onto the stage. Col. Jesse E. Evans, dressed in Class A uniform with ribbons spanning the left side of his chest, paused at the podium while the loud rattling of chairs and shuffling of a full company of men stood and came to attention.

"At ease," the colonel said loudly. He paused, looked to his right and then to his left at the two rows of officers flanking his position, and he nodded in recognition. The officers were all dressed in Class A uniforms, and most wore their ribbons. Many officers wore the silver and blue Combat Infantryman Badge. The platoon leaders being in Class A uniforms instead of fatigues meant they had been notified the night before, which was another signal that something big was up.

Turning back to the rows of uniformed men before him, the colonel began. "You men in Company C are the first in my Battalion to get this announcement," he said in a drawn-out command tone. "Late yesterday I received orders that the First Battalion of the 457th Infantry Regiment would be relocating to Fort Bliss, Texas. The purpose of this relocation is for retraining and redeployment. The deployment assignment at this time is unspecified. We have sixty days to mobilize, and after that time, we will go on standby status waiting orders."

There was a shuffling of feet and a low rumble of voices as the men, turning left and right to talk to their fellow soldiers, assimilated the unexpected news. Retraining and redeployment could only mean one thing to an infantry outfit in the early 1950s. The police action in Korea was escalating.

"What do you make of that?" Mark asked Wade after they were dismissed and had returned to the barracks.

"It could only mean one thing," Wade said.

"My enlistment is up in just a few months," Mark said.

"Mine too," Wade replied. "I hope this doesn't affect that."

Mark remained silent. He removed his field jacket and dropped it on his bunk.

"I heard Lieutenant McPherson say the army would probably extend the enlistments of those whose MOS is classified as critical," Wade continued. "That shouldn't affect us, though."

Mark opened his locker and stood before it without seeing its contents. The heavy weapons MOS papers that Andrade was working on would classify him as critical.

"That shouldn't affect us, should it?" Wade asked, again. "What's critical about us? We're not important enough to be critical," he said, laughing out loud.

Mark stared at the interior of his locker and didn't answer Wade.

CHAPTER 39

DURING THE LAST IG INSPECTION, Charlie Company had received a gig for not having current their TSEs, their training schedule evaluations. Williams assigned Andrade to see that the evaluations were brought up-to-date and to get a copy to Regiment as soon as possible. Andrade finished the dreaded project late Friday afternoon and then instructed the company clerk to deliver them to Regiment Headquarters immediately. Corporal Wade happened to be sitting in for the CQ who was on leave, and he got the assignment to deliver the document to Regiment.

"It's going to be late in the afternoon when you get to Regiment," Andrade said to Wade. "If they're shut down for the day up there, get their CQ to sign that they're delivered, and we'll have proof we delivered them on this date."

Wade was happy with the task; it would get him out of the orderly room a little early and give him a chance to stretch his legs before evening chow. As he walked across post to Regiment, the wintry weather was cloudy with a low overcast that promised an early nightfall. He breathed the cool twilight air in deeply and enjoyed the walk. By the time he had delivered the document and had chatted awhile with the CQ at headquarters, it was already dark. Being hungry, he decided to eat evening chow at the consolidated mess that was close by rather than wait until he got back to his regular mess hall.

Making his way through the chow line, he recalled the last time he had eaten in the Consolidated Mess. It was the time Mark had been roughly pushed by Ricco, causing him to spill his food on the floor. Mark had been severely embarrassed and was furious when he found out it was Ricco who had pushed him. In remembering the incident, Wade surmised that Ricco must be psychologically unsound to carry a grudge for such a minor incident during a soccer match long ago. In that moment, he also realized that Second Battalion, Ricco's battalion, used this chow hall for their meals. He gave it only a brief thought as he went about eating and casually gazing about the busy chow hall. He recognized no one in the crowd of soldiers.

Wade had finished his meal and was sitting back, relaxing, and sipping his coffee when he suddenly began to experience a certain edgy feeling. It was a peculiar feeling—a feeling of a heightened awareness of something unexplainable. The feeling was mildly disturbing and caused him to glance about the room. His look could see nothing unusual, just soldiers eating and coming and going. He tried to relax and finish his coffee, but the feeling persisted. His attention suddenly became focused when he realized that his uneasy feeling was the same as that when he was on guard duty at Miesau. At that time when he confronted the intruders in the night, he could see nothing, but he sensed something, and he knew there was something there before him. He knew there was something now that was close-by and needed his attention. He looked more closely about the room, casually turning about to see what was behind him and scanning the faces around him. Finally, his casual, roving glance locked for a brief moment on two men standing at the section entrance before moving on.

The two men had no food trays and didn't appear to be leaving or coming into his section like other soldiers were doing. One man, a heavyset soldier, had his back to Wade and was talking to another soldier who faced Wade. Wade's glances calmly drifted around the room, but in short flickering looks, it continued to return to these two men. He soon determined that the man facing him was looking directly at him while talking to the other man. Wade then knew he was being observed; the man with his back to him was using the other man's eyes and voice to watch him. His roving but returning glances then closely studied the man with his back to him. His heart went cold with a sudden recognition—it was Ricco. He remembered how Ricco had caught Myers out alone and attacked him viciously. Wade then knew he would not only have to face Ricco but Ricco's friend as well. He prepared himself mentally for what was to come.

When he left the chow hall, it was completely dark with the night air promising rain. He started walking toward Charlie Company. First Battalion and Charlie Company were located to the opposite side of Second Battalion, making it necessary for him to walk through the rows of barracks of Second Battalion. The street in front of the barracks was well lit, but he had to walk between the barracks buildings, which had little light. He passed the first rows of buildings without seeing anyone, and with only one more row of barracks to go, he began to relax. *Maybe they won't try anything tonight,* he told himself. But just as he was about to clear the second row of buildings and enter the light of the street ahead, he saw the silhouettes of two men ahead of him. They faced his direction, and as he approached them, they began walking toward him.

He knew this was it—he would have to face the two of them. There could be no talking his way out of this, and no amount of threats or tactful talk could forestall what was coming. He remained calm, but his mind raced. He knew the type and guessed that as they came closer, one of them would step to the side to get in back of him. He was right. When the two were just in front of him, one moved to Wade's left, while the other stopped, held up a cigarette, and asked, "Gotta light, Soldier?"

"Yeah, sure," Wade said as he continued forward, holding his hand out as if he held a cigarette lighter. Instead of starting a lighter, Wade hit the man as solidly and squarely in the face as he could. He aimed straight for the nose, and his forward motion and weight were behind the punch. The man went down immediately. He then spun around to face the second man, who he knew would be Ricco. In turning, he deflected Ricco's blow, which was already coming at him from his blind side. Stunned but still active, Wade threw another punch that he knew was good by the impact he felt as it made contact with Ricco's face. He then squared off with Ricco, and they traded punches several times, each landing heavy blows to the head. But suddenly, to his surprise, Ricco held back. At that moment, Wade felt a crushing blow come from behind him. The first man he had knocked down had now gotten back up and came at him from behind.

The next thing Wade knew someone was helping him up and saying: "Are you okay? We heard a commotion and came out to see what was going on." Several soldiers had come out of the nearest barracks and were viewing him sympathetically. "We saw these two guys hitting and kicking you. We hollered, and they ran off. You're lucky we did; they were trying to kill you."

At the aid station, Wade's bloodied face was treated, and the medic said he may have a broken rib. When the doctor arrived, he took one look and told the medic to get Wade to the hospital for treatment and evaluation. Charlie Company was called, and McBride was there promptly. "Who did this?" he asked. "Did you see who it was?"

"The one man I'd never seen before," Wade replied. "I didn't see the other's face really good, but I know it was Ricco."

"Can you swear to that to a court-martial board?"

"Well, like I said, it was dark, and I didn't see his face really good."

"But without positive identification, we can't make a case," McBride said. "Aren't we ever going to get this psychopath?"

"Somebody will get him," Wade said. "Sooner or later, somebody will get that creep."

CHAPTER 40

TWO WEEKS AFTER MARK AND Lauren's Post Exchange trip, the PX clerk sent word they had received the telephoto lens Mark had ordered. Knowing it would take Lauren a long time to save up enough money to buy the lens, he planned to take her back to the PX and purchase it along with a carrying case for her camera equipment. The Consolidated PX served all the US Army posts in the district and was located in a suburban area of the city. Mark met Lauren at her train stop. She was dressed in a navy blue skirt, a white blouse, and an open light blue sweater. They took a taxi to the PX.

It was Sunday and a pleasant warm and sunny afternoon when they arrived. The PX was crowded with soldiers and their dependents as they entered the large building. As they worked their way down the aisles, Mark took Lauren's arm, hoping she didn't feel uncomfortable among so many uniformed soldiers. A beautiful young girl was an unusual attraction to young men who most of the time only associated with other male soldiers. Mark took only casual note of the attention she got from some of these soldiers looking back at her as they walked past them. At the camera department, there was one clerk working the counters and several people waiting.

"We're going to pick up the new telephoto lens you wanted," Mark said as they waited behind a tall soldier and a slightly plump woman who was obviously the soldier's wife. "I ordered it after we were here before."

"But, Mark," Lauren said with some concern. "I can't afford that now."

"I can," Mark said with a smile, moving closer to her. "It'll be your nineteenth birthday gift."

"But my birthday's not for some time yet," she objected.

The woman with the soldier in front of them smiled at Lauren and said, "How wonderful to be just nineteen." She glanced at Mark, smiling, then back at Lauren. "And so young and so pretty, I might add."

Lauren acknowledged the lady's compliment and struck up a conversation with her about birthdays. Lauren's English was flawless. The tall soldier looked at Mark and shrug his shoulders as if bored but tolerant with the girls' talk. The couple moved up to the counter as their time came before the clerk. They purchased several rolls of film then walk away, the lady smiling a good-bye as they walked past them.

When Mark and Lauren reached the counter, Mark identified himself, saying he had previously placed an order. The clerk then produced the new lens still in its shipping box with a tag specifying Mark's name. Mark then ask to look at some carrying cases, and the clerk placed several on the counter for Lauren to view. She looked casually at a couple then selected one saying, "This one's about the right size, and I like the color."

Mark stood by idly, letting Lauren choose the one she wanted. He took one glance at the items on the counter and then watched her, always fascinated with the way she could focus so intensely on something that caught her attention. She picked up a black leather camera bag, and turning it back and forth, she examined it closely. She then turned about while still holding the bag up as if to see it in a different light. She suddenly turned back to Mark while clutching the bag close to her. "Mark," she said quietly, in a concerned whisper, "there's a soldier over there who keeps staring at us."

Mark turned around to see, unconcerned and thinking she was just again attracting innocent attention. His looked scanned the crowds of people moving about, but he didn't see anything out of the ordinary. Turning back to Lauren, he said, "Over where?"

"There by the hunting and fishing counter," Lauren said, her look glancing that way and then quickly back to Mark. "He's still staring at us."

This time when Mark glanced toward the hunting and fishing counter, through the throngs of people moving about, he could see a soldier standing alone and looking directly at them. The heavyset soldier was dressed in fatigues with no stripes or rank insignia, meaning he had been busted and was a troublemaker. He wore his field cap, which made it harder to identify him from a distance. Mark looked a moment before recognition came. And when recognition did come, a cold and fearful anger also came. It was Ricco!

"I don't like his looks," Lauren said in a whisper. "Let's move on."

Mark paid for the lens and case and then took her arm and led her down the aisles to the magazine stand. He was angry and wanted to face Ricco, but his first concern was for Lauren. He didn't think Ricco would start something there in the PX, but he wanted to get Lauren as far away from him as possible. At the magazine stand, they stopped for a moment. He calmly asked Lauren if she wanted to purchase the current issue of *Vogue* magazine, which he knew she sometimes looked through on the stand. He acted as if nothing was wrong, attempting to put her at ease.

"Yes, this is the new issue," Lauren said. She picked up the magazine and began turning the pages. With her attention on the

TOUR OF DUTY

magazine, she no longer seemed concerned with the soldier staring at them.

"I'll get it," Mark said and started toward the magazine clerk. He had carefully scanned the crowd behind him and hadn't seen Ricco, but he remained calmly tense and alert.

"No, Mark, let me pay," Lauren said and stepped in line at the counter. "You've done too much already."

"Okay, I'll wait here," Mark said as she waited her turn to pay. Mark stepped back to the magazine rack and picked up an issue of *Time* that featured a recent Korean battle scene on the cover. He began turning the pages to view the war scenes the magazine was covering. He stopped at a page where a combat medic was working on a wounded soldier and viewed the scene closely.

Suddenly, a voice came at him from behind. The low, hoarse voice was crude but clear. "That's some good-looking *Schätze* you've got with you," the voice said.

Mark whirled around. Before he saw Ricco, he knew he was just behind him. He instantly went on guard and was ready for anything. Facing Ricco directly, his look cold, hard, and steady, Mark snapped, "So what?"

"I bet she's a lot of fun in bed," Ricco said with a twisted grin. "I could really have fun with her."

"Why would a lowlife like you care?" Mark said calmly, staring hard at the man. "You'll never get the chance."

Ricco only smiled his warped grin before turning to disappear into the crowd. Mark watched him go, his hatred growing and mind spinning. He knew this confrontation was a harassment tactic Ricco was using to rattle him. He also knew it was a tactic preliminary to something that was to come. Lauren soon joined him. Not wanting to upset her, he was careful not to show his anger and tenseness from the confrontation.

They headed out by taxi to the same *Gasthaus* by her train stop they had stayed at before. They planned to spend the night there,

- 213 -

and then Mark would return to post after seeing her off. He drank two cognacs before dinner and relaxed back to normal. Lauren, no longer aware of anything out of the ordinary, had her glass of boysenberry wine and was cheerful and lighthearted.

Mark knew that now that Ricco had seen him with Lauren, he would not hesitate to take advantage of this vulnerability by confronting her if he got the chance. He realized the Ricco situation had reached a level where confrontation was certain. Growing concern for Lauren and remembering Ricco's attacks on Myers and Wade caused Mark's anger to grow. But instead of being fearful, he became coldly calm and determined, eagerly anticipating what he knew was coming.

CHAPTER 41

THREE WEEKS AFTER WADE HAD the fight with Ricco, he met a soldier from Ricco's outfit. What he learned from this encounter worried him considerably. It happened one night after he and Mark had been sparring around at the post gym, and Mark had left early to return to the barracks to write letters. Wade had sparred around awhile longer with someone and was toweling off when a soldier walked over to him and said, "Now I remember where I saw you. It was in the Rocket Bar."

"Can't say I remember that," Wade said, wiping his face, which continued to sweat freely.

"Yeah, it was the Rocket Bar. I think you guys were celebrating a promotion or something," the other soldier continued. "You shoved this guy Ricco down when he was going after your friend."

"Oh, yeah," Wade said, now looking closely at the other soldier.

"Well," the soldier said, "remember someone telling you that the guy you shoved was from his outfit, and he was a bad dude?"

"Yes," Wade said. "I'm with you, now."

"Well, that was me, and let me give you more on that," he said with a serious face. "I'm from Second Battalion, Delta Company, and that guy's bunk is just a couple of bunks away from mine. I hear him talking all the time. He's obsessed with getting even with you guys. Says he's already paid back two of you, but he's after one more. Says he's got some special ways he's gonna work the last one over. He mentioned just last night that this last one has a cute *Schatze* and how he's gonna mess up his face where she won't look at him. He then laughed and said he'd love to get hold of his *Schatze*, that she's a real looker."

The Second Battalion soldier then looked around to see if anyone else could hear before continuing. "He's sick!" he finally said. "And there's another creep who now pals around with him sometimes. But this other jerk might have learned a lesson; he came in a few weeks back with a battered face that looked like someone had really worked him over. But Ricco will never learn a lesson. He's just bad! He's smart too; picks a fight with someone, catches him somewhere the army can't do anything about it, and then jumps him. CO's trying to build a case against him and get him kicked out of the army.

"Ricco's friend," Wade asked. "Was it about three weeks back when he came in beat up?"

"Yeah, that's right."

"Yeah, I heard about that," Wade said. *Glad I gave him something to remember me by,* Wade though with a strong sense of satisfaction.

"Watch your back and pass that on to the other guy," the soldier continued. "Your friend's the one Ricco's after now."

"I'll do that," Wade said. "Thanks again."

When Wade told Mark about the encounter and the comments Ricco had made about both he and Lauren, Mark didn't say a word. Although Mark never spoke, Wade noticed the cold look that came into Mark's eyes and a peculiar inner focus he seemed to assume. It was like his entire attention was suddenly concentrated on one certain thing in a determined and absolute way. This surprised Wade. He was expecting Mark's usual carefree comments, such as "He'll get over it" or "I'm not likely to run into him." This was the first time he noticed a change in Mark's reaction to his warnings, and it caused him to wonder if Mark had finally realized the precarious world he lived in. In spite of this subtle change in Mark, Wade still thought of him as being too easygoing.

Wade knew he had to do something. Mark was a capable fighter but slow to get going. It took too much to get him in a serious fighting mood, and Ricco would be on him and overwhelm him before that. Mark's good nature would be no match for a vicious animal like Ricco. Wade knew that something was coming, and he wanted Mark to be prepared. He not only wanted to protect Mark, but he wanted his own payback too. He knew Mark would be Ricco's next target and the best one to bring that about. If Mark could have the right mind-set and be prepared for what was sure to come, he could properly make that payback.

But he also knew that Mark was the type of man who left people alone if they left him alone. Mark thought that other people thought that same way. In spite of his background in contact sports, Mark still didn't realize there are those who will harm you regardless of how uncalled for it may be. He simply hadn't had the life experiences that teach one there are people who will do you harm just because they can, if they can.

The second time Wade noticed a change in Mark's easygoing manner was at the gym. The gym's SIC had set up a boxing tournament with the men competing and classified into three classes. There was one man who was classified in the B Class who looked like he should have been in the A Class. He looked heavier than the 180-pound limit for the B Class, and he had powerful arms and shoulders. He was from Third Battalion, and no one knew anything about him except what he provided as his weight, height, and boxing experience on the sign-up chart that was used to classify the competitors. Wade drew this guy for a bout when he, Mark, and Myers arrived at the gym one evening.

Wade started as usual by sparring around to get the feel of the gloves and ring. His opponent sparred for only a moment and then bore into him with both left and right roundhouse blows. Wade was confused momentarily, reeling and stumbling back against the ropes. He was taking a real beating when the referee stepped in. Wade waited in his corner a moment, and then returned to the ring. His opponent came at him the same way as before, flailing blows without letting up. Wade was ready for him this time, and they went at it heavily until their time was up. Wade got beat up pretty bad, but all he said to Mark as they sat drinking water was, "That guy's a brawler."

"That guy should be in Class A, Sam," Myers said. "He's heavier than you. Don't fight him again."

"You held your own when you caught onto his game," Mark said, handing him a cold Coke he'd retrieved from the break room. "But Dave's right. Don't go against him again. I don't believe he's an amateur."

While they sat talking, the SIC walked up and asked Mark if he would go a bout with the same guy. He said the man had requested another bout, and he was trying to find him an opponent. "I don't like this guy," the SIC said. "There's something about him I don't like, but it's my job to find him an opponent."

To Wade's surprise, Mark promptly said, "Why not." Wade knew this was unlike Mark. He knew Mark enjoyed the sparring and the sporting aspect of boxing, but he also knew Mark always avoided serious fighting, and this upcoming bout would be serious.

"Don't do it, Mark!" Myers said. "He's a brawler. You've got nothing to prove by fighting him."

"It would get me off the hook," the SIC said. "And Myers is right. He's a brawler, but I'll referee and make sure nothing dirty comes off."

"You can take him, Mark," Wade said, speaking up for the first time. It had occurred to Wade that this brawler may create the right situation for Mark to realize that some people think differently from him—that some want to hurt others. "If I was expecting his style, I would've done better."

In the ring, the brawler didn't come at Mark like he did with Wade. He met Mark in the center of the ring and slowly circled around him. He faked a couple of left jabs but continued circling. Mark waited, staying loose and throwing a few half-hearted left jabs of his own. Then suddenly, with no warning, the man stepped toward Mark and started viciously throwing punches. Mark was pressed to defend against the barrage of blows and was driven back against the ropes. The brawler didn't let up; he hit Mark with both gloves, one after the other, pounding him against the ropes. Mark could only cover up, protecting his head and body the best he could.

"Break!" the referee said, stepping between the two men as was the gym's rule.

The brawler was a good twenty pounds heavier than Mark and using vicious brute force, even more than he had against Wade. But to Wade's surprise, Mark didn't seemed to be rattled; he calmly waited for the referee's go-ahead.

Cool but obviously smarting from the heavy blows to his head and the crimson welts developing on his shoulders and arms, Mark reentered the match. Wade could see a grim determination on his face as he again faced the man. Wade watched closely as the two men began to circle each other. He remembered the brawler usually started his roundhouse haymakers with a left jab before flailing away with both arms. He hoped Mark had also noticed. When the man threw his initial left jab, Mark deftly feinted to the side just slightly, avoiding the blow, and then returned a left jab straight to the face. The blow, which had Mark's weight behind it, caught the man squarely on the nose as he was moving forward. The blow not only stood the brawler up but caused him to stumble backward a step. Instead of waiting for him to recover as Mark usually did in such cases, he followed the brawler's backward step with a jab to the headgear and then another well-placed blow to the other side of the head. The brawler stumbled back more.

Don't let up! Wade thought. *Keep punching!*

Mark pursued the brawler as he stumbled backward, methodically pounding him with powerful, well-directed blows. When the man covered his head, Mark pounded his body, and when his arm dropped, he pounded his head. The brawler went down on the mat and lay there, rising on one elbow momentarily before collapsing back onto the mat with a dazed look.

"That's it! That's the way you've got to fight," Wade said under his breath, an unconscious smile coming to his face.

"Okay, that's all!" the SIC said, pushing Mark back. Mark resisted his push. "This bout's over. Take it easy now." The SIC pushed Mark several more time before Mark would leave the center of the ring.

Later in the barracks when Mark had gone to the shower, Wade said to Myers, "You know, Dave, there's a change in Mark these days. Have you noticed?"

"Yes, I sure have!" Myers said. "Before, you couldn't have paid him to go after that brawler, but today he seemed to relish the challenge." Myers paused a moment as if remembering and then continued. "And man, did he punish him! What do you suppose has happened to make him change?"

"I don't know," Wade said. "It's like he's matured into seeing the world like it really is."

"Maybe so. Do you think it's for the better?"

"Well, we all have to face the truth," Wade began. "Something has caused Mark to become more aware of his world, and it's shaping his actions."

"Yeah, maybe, but do you think it's for the better?" Myers asked again, looking at Wade seriously.

"I don't know," Wade said thoughtfully. "In the long run, I think it's for the best, considering Ricco is out to get him. But in the short run, I'm not so sure. Seeing reality for the first time can be painful."

CHAPTER 42

MARK OPENED THE DOOR TO The Camera Shop expecting to see Lauren across the room behind the glass counter or near the magazine rack talking to a customer. He had not planned to see her this day because of a scheduled company detail that had put him on duty for the weekend. His detail was cancelled at the last minute with no further explanation than the OD, or officer of the day, said he wanted someone who he knew played poker to pull the duty. Mark had smiled at his luck and immediately changed into civilian clothes and caught the train into the city, hoping to see Lauren. Stepping inside the shop, he could only see Herr Clause hovering over a counter, arranging camera accessories in the glass case.

"Can I help you?" Clause said before he looked up and recognized Mark. "Oh, it's you," he continued, smiling warmly.

Clause continued to be polite and friendly with Mark in spite of the conspiracy he had initiated with Herr Werner. Dieter was coming more and more to the shop, and Lauren always seemed glad to see him. They often had coffee together on her afternoon break, and they always seemed to be at ease with each other. With his plan apparently working, Clause had told his friend Werner that there was nothing to worry about. Besides, Mark was courteous and during the time he had been coming to his shop, he had purchased a good deal of merchandise. And Clause was, after all, a businessman.

Mark returned the greeting as he glanced about the shop.

"She's not here," Clause said. "She had an appointment with the newspaper—a very important appointment."

"With the newspaper?"

"Yes," Clause said, nodding his head as if to emphasize the importance of the event. "She just learned a couple days back she won the journalism scholarship. They're officially presenting the award today. The newspaper has a ceremony. Her father will be there, and there'll be others from her high school as well."

"Oh, yeah," Mark said, as if he knew. *Lauren hasn't told me about the award because we've been out of touch a couple weeks,* he thought. Although he smiled and seemed pleased with the news, he was more than a little disappointed that she was not there at the shop, and the uneasy feeling that she had a life separate from his returned. He suppressed the feeling, knowing it was both unfair and selfish on his part. "Will she return, soon?" he asked Herr Clause.

"Yes, she'll be back soon. I can't wait to congratulate her," he said with unsuppressed enthusiasm. "She has such promise!" He paused a moment as in thought. "We've all worked so hard for this," he began again, his look going above Mark's head. "Her father, my friend the newspaper editor, her schoolteachers—all of us have been working and pulling for her to get this scholarship."

Mark nodded his understanding.

"It doesn't matter what talent you have, how intelligent you are, or how hard you work if you don't get the breaks," he continued, looking seriously at Mark. "In the beginning, everyone needs help in getting started. And this is such a rare opportunity for Lauren."

Mark could see Clause's pleasure, and he understood the satisfaction Lauren's supporters would receive by seeing their protégé receiving breaks. But he sensed there was more than Lauren's education involved with the scholarship. He intuitively sensed that Clause's enthusiasm for Lauren's scholarship was more than concern for her future. The deeper reason became more apparent as Clause continued to talk.

"Our country is rebuilding, Mark. Do you understand what that means? We must seek out our most talented youth, educate them, and bring them to the forefront of our societies, our economies, and our government." He paused again as if to catch his breath and then continued, almost talking to himself. "In Lauren, and others like her, lies our future. We must encourage them to strive hard and guide them along a path that is best for the country."

"I understand," Mark said. And he did understand. Lauren was part of something bigger than herself. It was the same in his case. By being obligated to the army, and after that to education, and then a profession and the family business, he was always a part of something bigger. Mark made no positive or negative judgments about these observations; he only felt a strong kinship to Lauren's situation.

At that moment, a young German man and woman entered the shop. They paused a moment at the door and then walked toward the counter, clutching several rolls of film. Mark knew that Herr Clause was about to get busy, so he excused himself, saying, "I've got some shopping to do. I'll drop back by later."

Mark left Clause and caught a taxi to a district in the heart of the city that was known for its exotic shops and unusual wares. He thought he might find something there for Lauren. After looking in several shops, he could find nothing of interest, so he browsed from shop to shop with no particular purpose. One shop caught his eye that had a front window cluttered with relics of all sorts. There were knives and old muskets and other assorted items. A chess set with ivory pieces shaped like medieval knights was placed in the lower window corner so that it would be readily seen. As Mark examined the set, he heard a small voice from behind him. "Everyone needs a chess set," the voice said.

Mark turned to see a very small man with white hair and spectacles that were almost falling off his nose. He guessed the man to be the proprietor of the shop and knew he was about to get a sales pitch. "Oh, yeah?" he said with a grin. "Why does everyone need a chess set?"

"It's the game of life," the proprietor said in a calm, quiet voice.

"Game of life," Mark said, his grin growing. "How's that?"

"We are all pieces in a universal game of chess," he said with a stern look at Mark, "being moved about by a higher power."

"A higher power, huh?" Mark said. "And what is this higher power? God?"

"No, it's not God," the old man said. "It's circumstances and fate."

Mark suppressed his grin so as not to offend the old gentleman. "Well, I like the set," he said. "I'll think about it and maybe come back and buy it."

The old man slowly nodded his head up and down. "Please do," he said. "It'll not only teach you about life; it'll teach you that you can't escape your fate." Walking away, Mark felt there was something important in the old man's words, but he couldn't decide what it was. He thought about it briefly but then let it go; he was anxious to get back to the shop and see Lauren.

Mark caught a taxi and returned to The Camera Shop. It had been more than two hours since he had left Clause, and he thought Lauren would be back from the ceremony. But when he entered the shop, she still wasn't there. When he inquired about her, Clause said she had returned and left again.

"Do you know where she is?" Mark asked. "Is she coming back today?"

"Yes, she and Dieter went on a coffee break," Clause said. "They're celebrating her award."

"Dieter?" Mark said. "Who's Dieter?"

"Dieter's a friend. He escorted her to the ceremony," Clause said. "Now they've gone to celebrate."

Mark left as Clause turned to wait on a customer. He thought he would return to post but then decided to look for Lauren. The first place he looked was the coffee shop where they always went on her breaks. The café was crowded with several customers waiting to get tables. He stood with the crowd just inside the doorway and scanned the room and the people standing around. He finally saw them through the crowd in a far corner. They were sitting facing each other and sipping coffee and chatting cheerfully. As he watched, they both raised their cups and clicked them together as in a toast. They were laughing gaily and obviously enjoying the occasion and each other's company. On one occasion she said something, laughed, and then laid her hands on his briefly. Mark watched them for several moments. He could see she was dressed formally in her white blouse, and her face was bright and smiling.

As Mark watched, he became angry. He first thought of going over to their table but then decided his anger might cause him to lose control. If that happened, he knew the situation would become very messy and unpleasant. He fought back the rage and disappointment, telling himself he was getting out of line. As he felt his self-control returning, he had to admit that Lauren had a life of her own, the same as he, and he had no right to interfere in their celebration. Disillusioned and resigned to this new situation with Lauren, he left the café and caught the train back to post.

CHAPTER 43

W HEN SECOND PLATOON RETURNED FROM Miesau
after their mission at the ammo dump, they returned
to post minus one deuce-and-a-half. This situation left
a loose end that had to be dealt with. All property assigned to a unit
has to be accounted for during periodic inspections, and an IG,
Inspector General, inspection would surely catch the discrepancy
between Charlie Company's actual and recorded inventories. They
had a deuce-and-a-half on their inventory, but where was it? A
missing vehicle would be a serious gig with the IG, possibly rising
to a criminal level. And just retrieving the vehicle from Miesau
would not completely solve the problem either. The disabled truck
with windshields shattered, bullet holes throughout, and other
damages would be even more of a problem with an IG. Thus, in
spite of an apparently successful mission at Miesau, the disabled
deuce-and-a-half continued to plague Captain Williams.

McBride had turned in a glowing report on the mission and
on Mark and Wade particularly. The report stated the two men
performed exceptionally well under unusual circumstances and were

a credit to Charlie Company and the US Army. He recommended that consideration be given for some form of commendation for them and that the entire platoon should receive some time off from duty. Captain Williams readily agreed with McBride and told First Sergeant Andrade to give each man in Second Platoon plus the others who were on the mission a three-day pass as they requested it.

McBride only mentioned the loss of the truck in his report by saying that one two-and-a-half-ton truck had become disabled while there and had to be temporarily left at Miesau. This didn't end the issue of the damaged truck, however.

Within a few days, the post commander at Miesau issued a request for Charlie Company to retrieve the truck. They had no paperwork on the vehicle, and to have a vehicle in their possession without documentation was not proper. Under certain conditions, it could appear as stolen to some detached and uninformed inspector general. Williams received permission from Battalion to send a five-ton wrecker along with another deuce-and-a-half and two mechanics to Miesau to haul the truck back to their own post motor pool. The motor pool sergeant put the truck in the back lot behind the tank section so it wouldn't be easily seen. But when word got out, curious soldiers would come around to view the truck to see what an M12 trench gun could do to a deuce-and-a-half. After awhile, it became a laughing stock and the object of post jokes. The colonel at Regiment knew that something had to be done.

The colonel was irritated with the entire affair, but his irritation was greatly mitigated by the report received from the provost marshal concerning the actions of the German *Polizei*. On the morning following the shooting incident at Miesau, the local *Polizei* had arrested a man who had staggered into a *Gasthaus* in the village closest to the post. He was shot up and bleeding baldly and desperate enough to turn himself in to receive medical treatment. The army's CID, Criminal Investigation Division, and the German *Polizei* had grilled him into revealing the identity of others involved in the operation. Preliminary reports from the provost marshal's office were that a significant breakthrough had been made in apprehending the gang of international smugglers. Company C of First Battalion was instrumental in bringing this about, and he had to acknowledge credit for that. He sent down a "Well done!" to Charlie Company that pleased Captain Williams immensely.

Lieutenant McBride was relentless in his efforts to get Wade and Mark some form of commendation. "Sir," he said to Captain Williams on his third meeting on the subject, "those two men have been with Charlie Company for roughly twenty months now and have been outstanding at whatever they've been assigned to do." He paused a moment before continuing. "They deserve some recognition."

"I agree," Williams said. "I just haven't decided what recognition yet."

"They're both sergeant material," Sergeant Andrade spoke up. "Wade is still a corporal."

"Rest assured," Williams said. "They'll both get something special out of this. I've already spoken to the colonel on the matter, and he agrees also."

"Very well," McBride said, nodding his agreement. "Now, what about the truck?"

"Aw, the damn truck!" Williams said. "That's the real problem right now. I've passed this up to Battalion, and they've passed it to Regiment, and Regiment is supposed to be working on it." He paused momentarily as if in thought. Then he continued: "You men get out of here. I'm going to give Regiment a call to see if they've came up with anything yet."

McBride and Andrade left the CO's office, and Williams immediately placed his call to Regiment. He was on the phone for several minutes and then hung up and shouted to the outer office, "Andrade! Get McBride and bring him back in here."

Andrade appeared a short time later with McBride. No sooner had they entered the captain's office than he began relating his phone call to Regiment. "You won't believe what they've come up with to deal with the truck situation," he began, smiling. "They've decided that the cost and trouble to repair the vehicle is more than the vehicle is worth, so they're going to junk it."

"Sounds reasonable to me," McBride said.

"But there's a problem with junking a vehicle," Williams said. "The paperwork to do this with no more miles and age than that truck has will be tricky, and junking a vehicle has to be reviewed at levels beyond Regiment. So you know what Regiment has decided?"

McBride and Andrade said nothing but looked at Williams, waiting. "So what they're going to do is instead of submitting a 'Request to Junk' order, they're going to just let it disappear," Williams said, his grin growing. "They hold the paperwork there at Regiment, so they're going to simply lose the paperwork, and the truck will disappear from our logistical inventory."

The two men looked at one another for a moment without speaking. Finally, McBride spoke. "Brilliant idea!" he said and began laughing. Andrade started laughing too, causing Williams to follow suit.

They all laughed out their humor on the outcome of the truck problem. After they stopped laughing, each man grew quite with his own internal speculations on the simplicity of the problem resolution that had so puzzled them before.

Finally, Andrade broke the silence. "Well, I hate to lose the truck," he said quietly. "We need it."

"Yeah," Williams said with a thoughtful look that dropped to his desktop. "I hate to lose it too. But as you know, we always have to sacrifice for the greater cause."

CHAPTER 44

P FC MYERS'S COURT-MARTIAL WAS INITIATED and completed in three days. His defense was organized and presented by two captains who had legal backgrounds and were competent in military law. They had skillfully re-created the situation on the night of the accident where the two men who were struck by PFC Myers's vehicle were intoxicated and walking down the middle of the road through heavy fog on an overcast night. The sporadic fog patches had accumulated in such a way that it was impossible for the driver of the vehicle to anticipate its presence until entering the thick patches. And, according to the testimony of the other passengers in the vehicle, PFC Myers had immediately begun to slow down upon entering the mist. Further, the two men who were struck by the vehicle were in the middle of the road near the beginning of the fog patch at the time of impact, giving the vehicle less time and distance to slow as it entered the fog.

"To sum up my presentation," Captain Barrett, Myers's chief defense counselor, said at the end of his presentation, "I strongly emphasize that on the night of the accident, PFC Myers was a competent driver who was not speeding, and the accident was unavoidable under the various and extenuating circumstances."

The prosecuting team did not contest the mitigating circumstances leading up to the impact where the two German citizens lost their lives. They based their negligent homicide charge on the fact that PFC Myers was intoxicated at the time and had attempted to leave the scene of the accident and only stopped when his vehicle became disabled at the intersection. They surprised the defense team by bringing in two witnesses to support their accusations. The testimony of Herr Kuntz and his daughter that Myers had consumed a large quantity of alcohol before he left their *Gasthaus* supported their case that Myers was seriously intoxicated. To support their hit-and-run case, they produced photographs of PFC Myers's vehicle that displayed the grill, hood, and windshield at the front of the car damaged to the point that it would have become inoperable shortly after impact.

"With this evidence," the court-martial officer began in summing up his case, "the fact that the vehicle did not stop immediately but was driven on for an approximate distance of six hundred meters and only stopped after becoming disabled, suggests the driver was attempting to flee the scene."

The surprised and furious defense team immediately contested the prosecuting officer's case. "If it may please the court," Captain Barrett began, his voice strained as if struggling to maintain control, "the heart of the prosecution's case is based on the assumptions PFC Myers was attempting to leave the scene because he stopped a good distance from the impact and that they produced photographs displaying the damage to the front of the automobile. I point out again that according to witnesses, PFC Myers stopped as soon as he was able to understand the situation. And the fact that the front of the automobile was seriously damaged does not prove he drove until the vehicle became inoperable. The photographs displayed would look the same if taken immediately after and ten feet from impact. I most ardently challenge this assumption PFC Myers was deliberately trying to leave the scene by this evidence."

Again, he paused briefly before continuing. "Also, I might point out that the two intoxicated citizens walking down the middle of the road on a fog-clouded night were actually the ones negligent and the ones who caused the accident."

The defense team's case was sound and logical. But in a closed-door consultation, Lt. Col. Charles Pearson, ranking member of the court-martial board, gave a long speech on the importance of this court-martial. He revealed that it had caught the attention of some important people, and the outcome was being watched. He went on to say there had been accusations of partiality in the way the US Military had handled some of the trials at Nuremberg.

"At the time of the Nuremberg Trials," Pearson continued, "even some of our law scholars were critical. Our own Associate Supreme Court Justice William O Douglas said something to the effect that the Allies were substituting power for principle with the trials. Lately, some of those old criticisms have resurfaced. As a result of these accusations, trials involving German nationals and American soldiers are under close scrutiny. Thus, it will benefit the US Army and the European rebuilding program in general to show the nations of NATO that justice is fair and impartial in a US Military Court."

Colonel Pearson then paused and looked around at the other members of the court-martial board. After a moment, he ended his speech with, "In others words, the good of the US Army and its mission in Europe must be of first concern."

"But, sir! What about the rights of PFC Myers?" Captain Barrett challenged. He then stood to continue his speech. "There's more than a little cause for doubt in the prosecution's case. The only witnesses were in the car with him, and they testified he was stunned at first but stopped on his own accord when he realized what happened. Isn't there more than ample evidence here to give the benefit of the doubt?"

"I was speaking of the army and the European rebuilding program, Captain, not the individual," the colonel said.

"But, sir, this trial is to determine the guilt or innocence of PFC Myers not the US Army," Captain Barrett continued, his face glowing red in apparent frustration.

"This trial is bigger than the individual," the colonel said coldly. "And you surly must know that sometimes we have to defer to what's considered the common good."

*   *   *

PFC Dave Myers was found to be guilty of negligent homicide and sentenced to one-year confinement. He would be held in temporary custody at the US Army Prison in Mannheim, Germany, and then relocated to the US Federal Prison at Fort Leavenworth, Kansas, to finish out the sentence. After the one-year confinement and with a clean record, Myers would be returned to civilian life with a Bad Conduct Discharge.

As soon as the outcome of the court-martial came down to Charlie Company, Williams ordered First Sergeant Andrade to break the news to Mark and Wade. When they appeared in his office, Andrade got right to the point. "Prepare yourself for bad news," he said.

"Bad news?" Wade said, looking from Andrade to Mark.

Andrade appeared to be in a bad mood, but he spoke softly. His look stayed on his desk for a moment and then went directly to Mark and Wade. "I know you two are close friends of Myers," he began, "Ss we wanted you to know first."

"Has something happened to Dave?" Mark asked.

"His court-martial is over, and he's been sentenced to a year at Leavenworth," Andrade said. He paused a moment shaking his head. "This could have happened to anybody . . . What damn, rotten luck!"

Mark and Wade were stunned into silence. Prison time for a happy-go-lucky kid who never meant harm to anyone was something they couldn't understand. They could only stare at the first sergeant in disbelief.

"What a lousy deal," Mark said finally, his face growing red. "How did the brilliant sons of bitches arrive at that conclusion?"

"They claimed it was a hit-and-run," Andrade said, shaking his head. "Said he was drinking heavily and trying to leave the scene when the car became disabled."

"How can those jerks say that? Wade said, almost shouting. "We're the only eyewitnesses, and we said he stopped as soon as he regained his senses."

"Yeah," Mark said, also beside himself with anger. "How did they come up with that stupid decision?

"We don't know what transpired at the court-martial," Andrade said, "who their witnesses were, or what information they had."

"What can we do at this point?" Wade said, turning and pacing to the outer door and back. "How can we help Dave?"

"I don't know of anything that can be done," Andrade said. "A court-martial verdict is written in stone." He looked hard at the two men, and his tone became serious. "But I do know you two should settle down. Your actions and language just now with the wrong people could put you in prison with Myers. Don't do anything foolish."

CHAPTER 45

I T WAS LATE SPRING WITH the promise of mild temperatures and pleasant, sunny days ahead when Mark and Lauren got an unexpected surprise. Herr Clause announced that he was taking a sabbatical and was closing the shop for a week. He was donating his time off to the Society for National Improvement, an organization that promoted education for talented students, and he would be traveling about to different cities giving speeches and soliciting funds for the organization. "Take a holiday," he said to Lauren when he made his announcement.

Since Lauren had completed her schooling, this would leave her completely free for the week. She and Mark had never had more than a day or so at any one time to spend together, and this would be a rare luxury and a grand opportunity for them. Mark had no trouble getting military leave, and he proposed she select a location that would be fun and interesting and one that would get them away from their daily routines. Lauren, after thinking about it, said she had always wanted to spend some time in Heidelberg but then added that it would be too expensive. She said she had a little money saved, but it wouldn't be enough for a trip such as that. Mark only smiled. Lauren wasn't aware of Mark's family's financial status or of the fact that his father often sent him money, even though he never asked for it.

"You won't need a pfennig," Mark told her, laughing at her concern.

In the old section of Heidelberg, they found a third-floor room in a charming, old-fashioned *Gasthaus* that had a clean breakfast nook and narrow, steep stairs leading up to each floor. They were pleasantly surprised to find their top-floor room had a window with a view of red and brown rooftops and spiraling chimneys extending off into the distance. The first few days they toured the ancient castle and took river cruises. In their spare time, they wandered about the backstreets, peering into store windows and exotic shops. This left their evenings for each other, and most days they would have dinner and retire early to their top-floor room where Lauren would always open the window for the view of lights and the clean night air. It had been twenty-one months since that first day at The Camera Shop, and they had grown completely at ease in each other's company, each sensitive to the other's needs and each happy when together. One morning Mark awoke to find Lauren wide awake and quietly watching him as she lay beside him. He smiled inwardly, for he had done the same many times with her.

The Frau that ran the *Gasthaus* was typically plump with rosy cheeks and a quick smile. She seemed to enjoy their company and fussed over them like they were her own. One morning at breakfast, she asked them, "Have you young folks been to the Roten Ochsen yet?"

"The Roten Ochsen?" Mark said. "What's that?"

"It's a restaurant that young people and students often go to," the Frau said as she put a second sweet roll on their plates and refilled their coffee cups. "It has good food and music and should not be missed while you're in Heidelberg."

"She refers to the Red Ox Inn, Mark," Lauren said. "Although I've never been there, I've heard about it. I would like to go."

That night at the Red Ox, Mark and Lauren found the inn already crowded and had to wait to be seated. While waiting in line in the entrance foyer and studying the walls decorated with old photographs and other relics of the past, Mark commented on how nice Lauren looked. She wore her standby navy blue skirt and white blouse with a light yellow sweater. She also wore flats instead of heels, because they always walked about after dinner. Mark wore his blue tweed sport coat with dark slacks. With Lauren in flats, he towered over her as they waited. She stood next to Mark but not too close. Her stance within Mark's space said she was independent and open, but at the same time, it left no doubt as to whom she was with.

While they waited, there became a slight commotion behind them as a waiter worked his way through the standing crowd leading a group of young people who obviously had reservations. As the group filed by, a tall young man with sandy brown hair suddenly stopped next to Mark and Lauren.

"Lauren!" he said, laughing with surprise. "It's you . . . here! What a pleasant surprise!"

"Oh! Hello, Dieter! Lauren said, laughing in return. "Yes, this is a surprise. Are you on assignment here in Heidelberg?"

"Yes, I'm doing a piece on student activity at the university," he said.

She introduced Mark and Dieter and then turned to Mark. "Dieter works for *Der Stern.* He's helping me in the hiring process."

"Yes, I check on her application daily," Dieter said. He shook hands with Mark, looking keenly at him momentarily and then turned his attention back to Lauren. "You're waiting to be seated," he continued, smiling warmly. He was cheerful and upbeat and obviously the leader of the group. "Waiter, these two are with us," he shouted.

"*Jawohl!*" the waiter said, shaking his head as if not happy with the request. He led them to a table across the room and added two more chairs to the already crowded table. Lauren sat between Mark and Dieter. Around the table sat several young men and women who were stylishly dressed and attractive in overall appearance. Although she was just a village girl, Lauren was as vivacious and physically appealing as any of the smart young people there, and many of those in the room whose gazes were drifting about stopped on her. Dieter carried on a spirited conversation, but in most cases, the object of his talk came back to Lauren. She laughed often and was obviously enjoying herself. She occasionally turned to Mark but didn't have time to say much before Dieter pulled her back into his conversation.

Mark sat quietly, drinking his beer and chatting with two students who sat to his right. He had recognized Dieter immediately as Lauren's escort when she had received the newspaper scholarship and the one celebrating with her that day at the coffee shop. He remembered watching them across the room as they laughed and toasted with their coffee cups and how she had laid her hand on his to emphasize something she had said. Anger again stirred within him, and it bothered him now as it had then.

When the students on Mark's right found out he was from New York, they asked many questions. "Are you a baseball fan? Do you go to the theater?" Mark politely answered their questions and chatted freely with them while smiling at their interest in New York. The young girl sitting immediately next to Mark had long, red hair and a seductive smile; she looked from Mark to others as she chatted with each. As she turned talking back and forth, Mark was well aware of the movement and sensual feel of her body since it was jammed tightly against his. When she laughed and turned from one to the other, her body pressed into his even more. His suppressed anger grew, knowing that Dieter had the same advantage with Lauren sitting jammed up against his side.

Drinks came, then food, then more drinks. The table got noisier as the cheerful spirit of the group grew. Lauren, looking around the room, asked, "Why all the photographs on the walls?"

"They're photos of famous people who have frequented the Roten Ochsen," a young, dark-haired girl spoke up from across the table. She spoke in French but then quickly made an apology and switched to German. Lauren answered back in French, and they conversed back and forth in French until Dieter interrupted.

"They're of people who were students here at the university and later became writers and philosophers and princes and kings going back a hundred years. There's many here you'll recognize." He stood up and, taking her arm, said, "Come, I'll give you a tour of the gallery of famous people."

In getting up, Lauren pressed her hand down on Mark's shoulder to help her stand. Mark turned from talking to someone on his right and glanced up. Their eyes locked momentarily and then Lauren let Dieter lead her away from the table. Working their way around the room, Lauren and Dieter were gone a good thirty minutes. Mark could see Dieter had his arm around Lauren's waist as he led her from picture to picture, stopping to give a short lecture on each one. When they returned to the table, Lauren nudged Mark with a questioning look. Mark's returned look said, *Let's get out of here.* Lauren then stood up to leave, politely excusing herself and Mark in both German and French and saying they enjoyed everything and everyone.

As they were about to leave, Dieter handed Lauren a note. "Here's the address," he said. "It's called The Cave. Please come tomorrow night."

On their after-dinner walk, Mark asked, "What's the note all about?"

"Oh," Lauren said casually, handing the note to Mark. "It's an address. Dieter says the group's getting together at a special place tomorrow night, and he's inviting us to join them."

"Do you want to go?"

"I think so," she said. "It sounds like fun."

"Sounds like more of the same."

"Probably," she said.

"I'd rather be alone."

"But, Mark," she said, "Dieter's been a good friend, and he's helping me with the newspaper job application."

*   *   *

The following day was the last full day of their vacation, and they wanted to pack in as much as they could. They revisited the ancient castle and took a second boat tour along the river. These sights were more factually interesting to them the second time. The first time on the tours they had just gotten together after a long separation and were so engrossed in each other they hardly heard the tour guides' lectures. They found a lunch stand on the street next to the river and bought *Bratwurst* on *Brötchen* and *Bier* in dark bottles. They purchased their lunch and found a park bench by the river walkway to rest and eat. As they were eating, Lauren suddenly picked up her camera and followed a young couple who walked with a toddler down the path. With their permission, she took several shots as they meandered along the path following their child. When she came back to the park bench to continue her lunch, she commented that she wanted to catch the attentive facial expressions and vigilant body language of the young man and woman as they hovered around their child playing in the leaves.

"What meaning do you see with those shots?" Mark asked, knowing Lauren always had a reason in selecting her subjects. She often surprised him with her insight with such matters, and he knew she liked to discuss encountered scenes worthy of photographing. "What's so unusual about a couple with a child?"

"Oh, Mark, don't you see how wonderful a scene a young man and woman standing next to their child makes?" Lauren said, looking at Mark. "Their protective stance and look of contentment as the child plays at their feet."

"But it's such a common scene," Mark pursued, a small smile developing on his face. Sometimes he played with her serious nature with his humor. "What can it represent from the viewpoint of a photograph?"

"Um," Lauren said, pausing as if considering the question. After a moment, she continued. "Sometimes I go with impulse and can't say immediately what's important about a subject." She paused again taking a sip of *bier*. "But in this case, I think what's appealing is that the scene of a young couple and child is so profoundly natural that it's beautiful."

"I see," Mark said as he stood up and collected the remains of his lunch wrappings to place in the nearby trashcan. "Perhaps it's family," he said, closely watching her for a reaction.

"Perhaps," she answered.

That must be it, Mark thought. *She may not realize it, but a young couple with child represents her longing for family.* "Hand me your lunch wrappings, and I'll put them in the trash can."

She handed him the empty bottle and paper wrapping, and he walked to the trash can. Dropping the trash into the can, he continued to think as he had before. *With Dieter,* he thought, *she could have her family and continue her education here in Germany.* He then hated himself for thinking that way and forced it from his consciousness by taking her hand and helping her up from the bench. "What should we do next?" he asked.

"You know, I told Dieter we might meet up with them tonight," Lauren said as she stood, putting the camera strap across her shoulder. "We need to get back to our room and get ready for that."

*   *   *

That evening, they found the location for the address Dieter had given Lauren. The building was down a side street, and the front entrance was closed up with a sign in German that meant "No Entrance." But following a group of young people around the corner, they could see in the alleyway a door with an attendant. A small sign said "The Cave." There was a five-Mark charge, and they entered the building to find only an open room with a spiral, steel stairway leading down into a lower room. Descending the stairway, they could see in each direction a long, cylindrical room that was at near capacity with people from one end to the other. At one end of the room, a bar stood across the back wall. At the opposite end of the room was located a low stage with a single entertainer playing a Spanish guitar. The chatter of voices and people moving around almost drowned out the music, and a haze of smoke filled the air. Someone ahead of them was saying, "This place was a bomb shelter at one time."

They were only halfway down the spiral stairway before someone shouted, "Hey, Lauren, over here!" It was Dieter, and he had obviously been waiting for them. "We were hoping you would come," he said, meeting them at the bottom of the stairway.

Dieter then took Lauren by the arm and, without looking at Mark, led them through the crowd to a location close to the stage. Working their way across the room was a precarious journey, as everyone was sitting on the carpeted floor around tables only a few inches high. There were no chairs. Mark was relieved when they got to Dieter's group without stepping on anyone's toes or fingers. Seeing them and recognizing them from the night before, the young people at Dieter's table gave a noisy and cheerful greeting and began shifting around to make room for them. Glasses appeared from nowhere, and someone poured wine from bottles atop the table. Mark was sitting pressed against Lauren on one side and a blond student from Norway on the other side. None could move without the adjacent one feeling the movement. The young blond told Mark she was from Oslo. She spoke in German, and Mark responded in kind.

The guitar player performed on, ignoring the chatter from around the room. Most all the young people sat respectfully listening, but the wine and holiday atmosphere promoted a low din of voices that rose and fell like the chant of a Buddhist monk. Lauren leaned in close to speak in Mark's ear. "Well, we said we came to Heidelberg to get away from the routine," she said, while laughing.

The music went on, glasses were refilled, and the chatter grew nosier as the evening progressed. Mark couldn't say much to Lauren. Dieter kept an ongoing conversation going with her, and the blond student from Oslo did the same with Mark. Mark was becoming uncomfortable sitting in such a close, crowded space, and he was growing more irritated with Dieter's attempt to monopolize Lauren. He immediately suppressed his irritation, not wanting to let something get started he would have to finish and later regret. He was relieved when a young man from across the table spoke up. "Hey, we're out of wine," he said as he tipped the bottle up to drain the last drop into his glass.

"I'll take care of that," Mark said, knowing there were no waiters in the place. He stood up, feeling a great relief in his muscles, which were used to near constant physical exercise. Taking a quick note of the brand names of the three wine bottles, he turned to speak to Lauren. But seeing she and Dieter were face-to-face in conversation, he didn't interrupt and continued on his way through the crowd to the bar.

"Three bottles of wine," he said to the bartender when the man finally worked his way around the bar to Mark.

"Any preferences?"

"Yes," Mark answered over the noise around the bar. "One Scheurebe, white; one Pinot, blanc; and one Dornfelder, red."

The bartender smiled as he selected the bottles that Mark asked for. "You must be a bartender," he said to Mark. "You seem to know German wines."

"Not at all," Mark said, laying out the stated cost plus a five-Mark tip. "I just memorized the brand names from the table." The bartender laughed and introduced himself. His name was Gunter, and he was from Bavaria.

Mark returned to the table and left the bottles to a loud cheer from those sitting there. "Bravo for Mark," a young man with an English accent said, and more cheers followed.

He noticed that another couple had joined the table, and the blond girl from Oslo was now jammed up against Lauren, and she was pressed against Dieter, leaving him nowhere to sit. He picked up the empty wine bottles and glancing at Lauren, who was still facing Dieter in a smiling conversation, said to the group, "I'll get rid of these."

He heard someone say, again, "Hooray for Mark," as he moved away.

Mark returned to the bar to talk to Gunter. He ordered a beer and stood leaning on the bar and looking around the busy room. While Gunter drew Mark's beer, he smoked, holding the cigarette in his mouth. Still drawing Mark's beer, Gunter took his free hand and wiped down the bar with a towel. Mark smiled at Gunter's dexterity and then glanced back toward the table he had left. He could make out Dieter through the crowd, but he couldn't see Lauren because of her lower silhouette. They were all laughing and talking and having a good time. He knew that Lauren was somewhat attached to Dieter, and he wondered just how much. With that thought, he felt his irritation progress to a seething but controlled anger.

"How are things down in Bavaria?" Mark asked as Gunter set the beer before him. With his anger growing, Mark attempted to keep it under control by talking. He forced his thoughts to stay on the conversation with Gunter.

"Bavaria's okay, but I like it better here," Gunter said as he nodded at the man next to Mark to take his order. "There are more

Fräuleins here," he said, laughing back over his shoulder as he began to draw the man's beer. "And they're available too."

"That counts," Mark said, laughing with Gunter as he moved back down the bar to wait on a customer. Mark's laughter belied his disposition. He was approaching the point of no return with his anger. He knew Dieter to be actively and aggressively pursuing Lauren, and he was reaching the end of his patience. He told himself to calm down and not do something he would regret. He had no fear of a confrontation with Dieter. For, although equal to his own size, he felt Dieter would be no match for him in a fight. Mark even felt a physical confrontation with Dieter would be like a big kid beating up a much smaller kid, and he didn't feel good about that. In spite of this sporting attitude, his anger continued to grow until finally he set his beer mug down hard on the bar, ready to go get Lauren. *And if Dieter objects,* he thought to himself as he laid money on the bar to cover his fare, *he'll find trouble.*

Just then, someone brushed heavily against his back. His temper peaked, his patience gone, his anger flared up, and he quickly turned to confront the person who had rudely bumped into him. His anger diminished immediately as he faced Lauren.

"You didn't come back!" she said as if displeased.

"I did, but there was nowhere to sit."

"I would have come up here to the bar with you."

"I thought you were enjoying the music."

"The music is good. I have been enjoying it."

"You can't hear it very well here. It's better back there," he said. He felt his irritation melting away as he faced her and talked to her. "You'll lose you place at the table."

"My place is here!" she said quickly, her look direct and intent. Mark felt the meaning from her look. His mood continued to soften.

"Let's get out of here," he said. Then, seeing her eyes flicker toward the stairway, he led her in that direction.

They left The Cave and walked about the streets arm in arm. His anger completely gone, Mark no longer thought of Dieter. He felt much better being in the cool night air and being alone with Lauren. They walked about for a while and then returned to their third-floor room. They made love immediately and then lay awake, talking quietly, telling stories of their daily experiences and intimate feelings since their last meeting. They then made love again, each not getting enough of the other and wanting to fully experience the other by touch and sight and taste and to immerse themselves in the other's warmth and aura.

*   *   *

"I have news!" Lauren said cheerfully, her attention going from the river to Mark across the table. They were having breakfast on the patio of a small inn by the River Neckar, a place they had been saving for their last day in Heidelberg. Their train schedule was for early afternoon, and they had already said good-bye to the Frau at the *Gasthaus* where they stayed. They planned to have a long, leisurely breakfast and then stroll along the river one last time before heading for the train depot. "I've been saving it for the right time."

"Saving news? You're keeping things from me," Mark said, frowning. He felt like joking with her. "Have you taken a new lover?" he asked, his frown breaking into a grin as he sipped his coffee.

"Actually, the news is about an old love," she said, picking up on the tease. She paused, awaiting his reaction, her eyes laughing.

He waited for her to continue, but she only looked around the patio as if she had lost interest in the subject. "Well, tell me about this old love," he said, impatiently.

"Okay," she said, leaning closer and resuming the conversation in a low voice to suppress her enthusiasm. "I've been accepted at the university in their school of journalism."

"What? That's great!" Mark said. "That is really great!" He could see how proud she was, and it didn't surprise him about the university. He had long been aware of her capabilities. She had excelled in all subjects at her school and ranked first in her class, and she had won the highly competitive scholarship sponsored by the newspaper. And, according to Herr Clause, who was a professional photographer, her eye for photography had developed to near-genius level. Recently, *Der Stern* had published one of her shots of a train-car accident she had happened upon where she had focused on the pained expression of a survivor instead of the wreck itself. Sometimes photographs that reflect emotions provide a broader and more complete meaning than the physical scene, she had explained.

"This calls for a toast," Mark said as he motioned for the waiter who hovered just off the patio.

"We'll toast with our coffee," she said, laughing, holding up her cup. "I'm very happy about the scholarship and the university."

"No coffee for this toast," Mark said, turning toward the waiter. "Waiter, two champagnes here!"

"For breakfast?" she said.

"For you," he said, "and for your promising future."

They toasted, clinking the thin champagne glasses lightly together and laughing quietly while the waiter turned back to his post, shaking his head. Mark was genuinely happy for her, but at the same time, he again felt that familiar uneasiness with the realization that she had a life separate from his and that she had a future of her own. His gaze went to the river where two boats from the University of Heidelberg's rowing team practiced, their oars rising and falling rhythmically in the water as they raced along side by side.

"One more," she said, holding her glass out to Mark, bringing his attention back to her.

"Lauren," he began slowly, "you know I'm set for NYU." He watched her closely.

"Yes," she said. She started to continue, but stopped, studying the small bubbles rising in the clear champagne. She grew silent and continued to gaze into the glass.

Mark quickly changed the subject. "Look!" he said. "The two rowing teams are altering their course." He felt badly that he had mentioned NYU.

"The barge! It's forcing them to break their stride!" She said, pointing up river where a tugboat pushing a barge headed directly toward the two teams. They both laughed as the two teams veered off course, the rowers shaking their fist at the tugboat as it passed between them. She raised her camera and took two quick shots of the frustrated rowers as they angrily shouted across at the passing barge. "That's life," she continued. "You always yield to the larger force."

They left Heidelberg by train in mid afternoon, both chatting lightheartedly and feeling happy. But when they grew quiet on the long train ride, his gaze drifted out the window to the passing scenes. The countryside and villages flashing by reminded him of the way movies sometimes showed a rapid flashing of scenes to indicate the passing of time between two major events. Lauren had placed her head against his shoulder and appeared to be dozing. He was glad she could rest, and he carefully shifted his body just slightly to better secure her position against his. When he turned, her head moved to rest against his chest. Her weight felt natural and comfortable, and her closeness and warmth made him happy. For some reason, a dark mood came over him briefly. The passing of time thought reminded him of the inevitability of his rotation back to the States, and he guessed that was the source of his mood. He knew it was not good to think about that. He pushed the dark mood away, intent on savoring the moment.

CHAPTER 46

FTER PFC MYERS'S COURT-MARTIAL, HE was brought back to Charlie Company to get his personal items in order before being transferred to the army prison at Mannheim. He was to be temporarily held at Mannheim until arrangement could be made to ship him back to the federal prison in Leavenworth, Kansas. When the MPs brought him back to Charlie Company, they turned him over to Captain Williams. The captain was to take responsibility for Myers while he got his personal things packed up and disposed of and to get him to Mannheim the following day. Williams ordered First Sergeant Andrade to take care of the details. Andrade assigned Corporal Wade to make sure Myers got everything in order that evening and to make sure he would be ready to leave the company the following afternoon.

"Damn, Dave," Wade said as they sat on their bunks facing each other. "I wish there was something I could do."

"I know you do, Sam," Myers said. "But there's nothing anyone can do now."

"I wish Mark was here too," Wade continued.

"Where's Mark?"

"He's on leave. Went to Heidelberg, I think."

"Well, tell him good-bye for me," Myers said.

"Sure," Wade said. "We'll come up to Mannheim to see you as soon as he gets back."

"I'd appreciate that," Myers said. He sat for a moment looking down at the floor and then stood up. "Well, I'd better get my things packed." He began to take items from his locker and put them into a box that Wade had gotten from the supply room. Several other members of the platoon came by and offered to help, but Myers said he could manage.

Wade busied himself with his own personal chores. He spent a couple minutes working on his boots and then went to the latrine to shave. When he returned to his bunk, Myers was sitting on his footlocker. His wall locker was cleaned out and packed neatly in the box. He was sitting there with his back to Wade and looking into his empty locker. Wade watched him a moment before speaking. "'Bout caught up?" he asked. "When you're ready, we can go to chow."

When Myers didn't answer, Wade walked around to stand facing him. He started to say something but stopped after seeing the look on Myers's face. Dave's face was expressionless except for a faraway look. And looking closer, Wade could see the beginning of tears in his eyes. He couldn't think of anything to say, so he turned away and stepped back to his bunk.

"You know what's so bad about this?" Myers finally spoke up. "What's so bad about this is what my dad and brothers will think."

"Yeah," Wade said. He remained silent for a moment and then added, "Say, would you like for me to write them and explain everything? Tell them it's all just rotten luck. I'd be glad to do that."

"Thanks, but that won't help," Myers said. He continued to stare into his empty locker.

"Well, I'm hungry," Wade said. "Let's go to chow. You'll feel better after eating something."

"I'm not hungry," Myers said. "You go ahead."

"But I'm supposed to stay with you at—"

"Oh, go ahead," Myers interrupted. "I've got to clean out my footlocker."

"Can I bring you something back?" Wade asked. When Myers only shook his head and continued to stare into his locker, Wade left the barracks and headed to the chow hall.

Wade returned to the barracks within forty-five minutes. He immediately saw that Myers was not at his bunk and that he had not cleaned out his footlocker. He checked the latrine and then began asking around. No one knew where Myers went. Most everyone said that they thought he was with Wade. Finally, one soldier said to Wade, "Myers left right after you. I thought he was leaving to catch up with you."

This is not good, Wade though. *It will only bring him more trouble if he's caught ignoring his barracks arrest.* Wade then walked around the outside of the barracks, looking to see if Myers had just stepped out to get away for the moment. The sun had set, and dark shadows enveloped the sides and the back of the barracks. Wade walked through the dark areas making sure he wasn't standing in the shadows. When there was no sign of Myers in the immediate area, Wade headed back to the chow hall, thinking Myers might have decided to eat after all and missed him on his way there. He spent some time in the chow hall asking several people if they had seen Myers in the past hour. When no one acknowledged seeing him, Wade then headed for the gym. *He might have wanted to exercise to work off his feelings,* Wade thought. But when he got to the post gym, which was a good walking distance from the barracks, no one had seen Myers. Completely confused now, Wade got a Coke and sat down on one of the benches next to the boxing ring to think out his next move. He knew he had to find Myers—and quick.

As he sat drinking the Coke and recalling the steps he had taken in his search, it occurred to him there was another place where they often went. The other place was the Post EM Club. *Why didn't I think of that before?* he thought. With that, he left the gym and headed for the club.

"Have you seen Dave Myers tonight?" Wade asked Louie the bartender.

"Have I seen him?" Louie said with a frown and wiping a glass with his towel. "He just left! But in the last hour, he has had six shots of scotch and washed each down with a mug of beer. He didn't say what was bothering him, but I know something was."

"Any idea where he went?"

"No, but you should find your friend before all that alcohol hits him," Louie said as he set the glass down and picked up another to dry. "He's going to be very tipsy for sure."

Wade knew he couldn't have left post, because he would have to show a pass to get past the MP's at the gate, and he didn't have one. Wade walked back to the barracks and asked around if anyone had seen him. No one had. He then left the barracks and began walking around in the company area. When he turned the corner before the orderly room, he saw Myers clearly in the bright moonlight.

Myers was sitting on the ground before the company sign he had installed a few weeks before. He had a rock the size of a brick in his hand, and occasionally he would pound the sign or rub the rock across it as if to eliminate the writing. Sitting before the sign and working with the rock, he was mumbling something Wade couldn't understand. Getting closer, Wade could see the plants and flowers that Myers had planted around the sign had been ripped from their beds and thrown about the area. With the exception of the sign itself, Myers had destroyed his work project that he had successfully completed weeks before. He now sat before the sign attempting to destroy it as well. But the sign was constructed of heavy oak and was secured to iron posts that were set in concrete. With only his bare hands and the rock, Myers's project was nearly indestructible.

"Dave! Dave!" Wade said as he approached Myers. "What are you doing?"

"Destroying this sign," Myers said, glancing back over his shoulder at Wade. "Destroying this sign and the writing on it," he continued. He then turned his attention back to the sign. And as he rubbed the rock back and forth across the writing, he mumbled over and over, "Out, damned spot, out!"

Wade stepped closer, and then he could see that Myers was trying to obliterate the company slogan written in red on the bottom of the sign. But as hard as Myers worked, the slogan *Duty First* continued to stand out clearly and plainly in the bright moonlight.

CHAPTER 47

WHEN CAPTAIN WILLIAMS REPORTED IN the following morning, he saw the tulips that were pulled up and scattered about and the damage to the sign. He immediately went to his office and shouted for First Sergeant Andrade. The sign had become an item of pride for the captain. When it caught the attention of the other companies in the battalion and they had followed suit and installed their own, he got credit for being innovative and professional. It was a feather in the captain's hat that he had thought of it first, and he was furious that someone had deliberately and maliciously damaged it.

"Andrade," he said when the first sergeant entered his office, "I want an immediate investigation of that out there. No one is going to destroy army property and get away with it in my company."

"No need for an investigation, sir," Andrade said. "I know who did it."

"Who did it?"

"Myers did it, Captain," Andrade said. "He got drunk and did the damage."

"How did he get drunk?" He was on barracks arrest.

"He went to the EM Club and really tied one on, sir," Andrade said

"He's already in big trouble," Williams said, a serious look of concern coming over his face. "Breaking barracks arrest and destroying army property will just add to that. Why did he do it?"

"I'm not sure why he did it, Captain."

"How did you find out?" Williams continued. "Did you conduct an investigation?"

"No, no investigation. He walked into my office first thing this morning and told me he did it."

"And you don't know why he did it?"

"No, but I know he's under a lot of strain, Captain," Andrade said. "As you know, we're transferring him to Mannheim today. He got drunk last night and took his frustrations out on the sign for some reason."

"Hmm," Williams mumbled, tapping his fingers on his desktop. "I'll have to dispense some form of punishment, you know." He continued to tap his desk momentarily and then said, "I don't want to, but I have no choice."

"He got a rotten deal, Captain," Andrade said. "Everyone says that."

"I know, I know," Williams said. "And I went to bat for him. But what could I do against a court-martial ruling?"

"He didn't deserve what he got," Andrade said again. "Is there some way we can avoid adding insult to injury?"

"I wish I knew," Williams said. "This will get around. It'll be a dereliction of duty if I don't do something. And we only have this morning to do it."

Both Williams and Andrade grew silent for several minutes. Andrade walked to the window and stood looking out. Williams went back to tapping his desktop. At one point, Andrade turned back toward the captain as if he had an idea but then faced the window again without saying anything. Finally, Williams said, "Andrade, get with McBride, and you two brainstorm to see if you can come up with something. We need a way to mitigate this incident while keeping my neck out of the noose. Report back to me in two hours."

Andrade left the captain's office and immediately sent the company clerk to find Lieutenant McBride. Shortly, McBride appeared, and he and Andrade walked out of the orderly room to view the damaged sign and planter area. After viewing the site briefly, they began to stroll about the area talking quietly, obviously considering the options and possible solutions available to them. They ended up at the battalion mess hall where they entered, sat down with coffee, and continued to talk.

After about an hour, McBride said, "Well, that seems to be the best we can do. We're out of time, and we've got to get Myers headed to Mannheim no later than 1400 hours today."

They returned to the orderly room and reported to Captain Williams. "Captain," McBride began, "we've got a possible solution."

"It's got to be good," Williams said. "I can only go so far in protecting Myers."

"We've thoroughly considered the few options that are available to us on this matter," McBride said, "and we decided on the best one to suggest."

"What is it?" Williams asked, waiting.

"Sergeant Andrade and I think that the best thing to do is nothing," McBride said. "Not to forward any request to Mannheim for further punishment. If you do, they'll put him on bread and water for a spell."

"Well, doing nothing leaves me open to criticism from Battalion and Regiment," Williams said, scowling at McBride. "I won't go that far."

"But to cover your decision to do nothing, you can say that the Myers court-martial has had a negative effect on morale for the entire company, and that to punish Myers further would just aggravate that situation." McBride paused a moment as if to emphasize his point and then continued. "And you could further say it's your opinion that the best that can be done for the good of the army would be to show leniency, because the man obviously broke under pressure and acted irrationally."

"But that will be just my opinion," Williams said. "And if I say it's the considered advice of my first sergeant and Myers's platoon leader, they can say you two were just acting as 'yes-men' for your company commander. Not good enough, McBride."

"We've got something to address that too, Captain," McBride said. "We suggest you conduct a plebiscite of the men of the company concerning their opinion of Myers—his dedication to his duties, his ability to get along with others, his overall performance as a soldier, etc., etc."

"Hmm, a plebiscite, huh?" Williams said, looking from one to the other. "Assuming the plebiscite is strongly positive, it would add credibility to such a decision."

"I know how the men feel about Myers and this situation, Captain," McBride said. "I can assure you that it will be positive."

Andrade nodded his agreement.

"I'll say this too, Captain. Your esteem with the men will go up several notches, which will also boost morale."

"Hmm, you may be onto something here," Williams said. He paused a moment, thinking, and then continued. "Okay, I'm willing to give it a try. But here's how I want this plebiscite conducted. First, I want you to develop a form with the three questions concerning Myers's character and dedication to the army that you just mentioned." He paused again, obviously considering the best way to conduct the plebiscite before continuing. "Next, I want you to do this. As the men come in for noon chow, have the company clerk standing at the entrance to the mess hall. Have him quiz each and every man on these questions and check a plus or minus for each and every answer. When it's completed, I want this document witnessed by you two and certified by someone present from the provost marshal's office."

"Excellent idea," Andrade said. "We can accomplish this plebiscite and have Myers on his way to Mannheim by mid afternoon."

"It's not the strongest defense for doing nothing," Williams said, "but company morale is important. I think it'll work."

"I'm confident, Captain," McBride said, "that your actions will keep Myers off of bread and water, as well as serve the best interest of the army."

The plebiscite was taken at noon chow, and every man questioned spoke well of Myers. Using this information Captain Williams briefed the battalion commander on his decision, stressing heavily the advantage it would offer to his company's morale and the positive effect it would have on the army's image. The battalion commander agreed with the decision, saying justice must promote the common cause. Myers was taken to Mannheim that afternoon and turned over to the prison commandant to begin serving his time. There was nothing in his 201 File calling for additional punishment.

CHAPTER 48

A FTER HEIDELBERG, MARK WAS TIED up for two weekends on duty. The following Saturday, he phoned Lauren at The Camera Shop to let her know he could see her on Sunday. But Lauren said she had obligations that day. She said a friend of hers was getting married, and she was part of the wedding. But when she thought further about the timing, she said the wedding would be over early Sunday afternoon and that she would be free after that. Since time would be short, they decided to meet at her village square where they had had coffee in the early morning the time Mark had come to her home before dawn.

"I will be with friends from the wedding for a while, but after that, we can walk around and have dinner and spend a little time together," she said.

On Sunday, Mark's train arrived early, so he took the time to get a beer at the local *Gasthaus*. After promising the owner he'd return the mug, he walked across the street to the same bench in the park they had sat at before. The weather was good, with the mid afternoon sun lying yellow and warm on the grass and trees and outlining the war memorial across the park. He sat in the shade, sipping the beer and feeling good with the moderate temperature and his anticipation. He sat where he couldn't see the war memorial but facing the direction where Lauren would be approaching the square.

His thoughts drifted back and forth between army life and a life living in a German village. He had wanted to find the right time to talk to her about her father, to see if his attitude toward her American soldier had softened. But he knew her father hadn't changed, or she would have told him. He knew that her father was just like his parents and that they would never change. That was the cold, hard facts, and he wouldn't ask her about it. He wouldn't mention it, because it would put her in a difficult position to explain, and he didn't want to do that.

He looked up to see a group of young people coming up the street. They were dressed in better-than-everyday clothes, and he knew it was the wedding crowd heading for the village *Gasthaus* to celebrate. Lauren walked next to a tall, sandy-haired young man he recognized as Dieter. *Lately he seems to always be around her,* Mark thought. Remembering Heidelberg, he experienced a flash of hostility. But catching it immediately, he told himself to slow down. This was not the same as Heidelberg, he reminded himself. In Heidelberg, he was paying the fare, and that gave him certain rights he didn't have here as Lauren's guest. And he knew she had the right to choose her friends. When she saw him, she broke free from the group and turned in his direction.

He stood up to wait for her. His reaction to her coming on the scene after he had waited was always the same as that of seeing her the first time. She saw him waiting under the tree in the park and turned and walked in his direction. Dressed in a light blue blouse and a navy blue skirt cut stylishly at the knees, she appeared youthful and trim as she walked toward him. Her walk was casual and confident, and she began to smile as she approached him.

With her blond hair perfectly combed and appearing yellow in the sunlight, she walked up to stand before him.

"Hello, Soldier," she said, her face beaming. "Are you waiting for your *Fräulein*?" Sometimes they joked lightheartedly after one had waited for the other.

"Not anymore," he said. "My *Fräulein's* here."

"And this is where she belongs," she said, embracing him warmly.

"Well, how was the wedding?" Mark asked, smiling and holding her at arm's length.

"The wedding was fine," she said, smiling and eager to talk about the affair. "They were very happy, so happy they made us all happy." She then went into the details of the ceremony, explaining how the bride and groom were dressed and laughing at how the priest had to gently break then apart after he said, "You may kiss the bride." Mark smiled, letting her talk. He felt good seeing her happy and wanted her to keep that mood. When she had filled him in on the wedding, she asked him if they could join the others in the *Gasthaus* and join in with the celebration.

In the *Gasthaus* music was playing on the juke box, and a din of animated voices filled the room. No one was sitting down. All were standing, talking, laughing, and milling about. One couple was dancing but soon broke apart, stopping their dance but still standing close and talking and laughing. The room was almost at capacity, filled with young, excited people enjoying their day of celebration. There were several mugs of beer already drawn and setting on the bar for the group. As they entered the room, Lauren picked up a mug and handed it to Mark. She then took him by the arm and led him from one to the other, introducing him to her friends. When she came to Dieter, she stopped and said, "You already know Dieter. He's been such a good friend. He wanted to come to the wedding because he does human interest articles for the newspaper." Dieter shook hands with Mark, but he kept a straight face.

Several in the group were in Lauren's class at school and remembered Mark from his visit and his gift of 45 rpm records. Mark was an immediate hit with them. They gathered around him, thanking him for the gifts and asking questions just as they did when he spoke to them at their school. Two girls got Mark by each arm and led him through the crowd to the juke box for him to select some music. As they pulled him through the crowd, Mark looked back over his shoulder at Lauren. She laughed and shrugged her shoulders as if all was well. Dieter stood just behind her.

"What is most popular in America?" one young girl asked Mark as she beamed up at him, her face aglow in the light of the juke box.

"I don't know," Mark said, laughing. "I haven't been there lately." He turned to see Lauren, but he couldn't find her in the crowd.

"What is your favorite song?" another girl asked Mark. "Just tell me, and I'll play it for you."

"Well, let's see," Mark said, scanning the selection panel. "How about J3?" He continued to glance back over his shoulder, looking for Lauren. She wasn't in sight, and he wondered where she had gone.

"J3, oh that's 'TD's Boogy Woogy'!" she said as she dropped a coin into the slot. "I love that!"

Someone pulled at Mark's shirt sleeve, and he turned to see a young boy of about seventeen years of age. He was looking up at Mark with wide eyes and a big grin. "I've played the records you gave me many times," he said. "I would like to personally thank you."

"You are very welcome," Mark said, shaking his hand, man to man. "It was my pleasure." The young boy's grin grew even bigger. He gave a slight bow and backed away, obviously not wanting to intrude too much on Mark's time. The girls were arguing over what to select next on the juke box, and Mark saw his chance to break away and look for Lauren. He returned to the bar and ordered a refill on his mug. Standing there looking around the room, he could see Lauren was not in the room, and neither was Dieter.

"There he is," someone said. Mark turned to see the group of girls from the juke box headed his way. They surrounded him as before. "Tell us more about America," one girl said.

"Yeah," a chorus of voices agreed. "Tell us more."

Not knowing what to say, Mark could only produce a frowning smile. He was relieved when the volume of voices raised a pitch higher as a young couple holding hands entered the *Gasthaus*, and all eyes turned their way. Mark knew this must be the newlyweds who had come to join in the celebration. They had obviously taken time to go home and dress in regular clothes and were now dropping in briefly to join the celebration before heading out to their honeymoon. Someone shoved a beer into the hands of the groom, and two young men led the bride to the dance area.

Mark finished his beer and walked out of the *Gasthaus* to see if Lauren was on the outside. He walked around the park in the square across the street and saw only a caretaker empting a trash can. He walked around the park again, looking down the side streets but saw no one.

"Damn it!" he said out loud. "This is too much!" His irritation this time with the situation with Lauren and Dieter was more than he could suppress. The mystery of their whereabouts and Dieter's persistent attention to Lauren was more than he could handle. He headed back into the inn in a high state of irritation and anger.

Reentering the *Gasthaus*, Mark was surprised to find Lauren and Dieter at the bar. They were watching the commotion next to the juke box where the young men were taking turns dancing with the bride. The young groom stood by smiling and holding his mug of beer. Lauren was sitting on the bar stool facing away from the bar, and Dieter stood very close as they watched the happy occasion. He occasionally bent over to her and said something, and she would look up to him and nod. Mark walked up to the bar several places down the counter from Lauren and ordered a beer from the middle-aged Frau working there. There were several empty seats between where he stood and where Lauren sat.

When the Frau brought Mark his beer, she faced down the bar to Lauren and Dieter. "Thanks again, you two, for helping me back in the kitchen."

Turning toward the Frau, Lauren then saw Mark. "Oh, Mark! There you are," she said. "I'm sorry you got kidnapped by my classmates. I wanted to rescue you but was out numbered."

"I'm okay," Mark said. He had his anger under control, but he still didn't look at Lauren. Instead he took a sip of beer and then turned his attention toward the celebrating crowd gathered around the bride and groom. Lauren watched him for a moment without speaking. Dieter bent down again and said something to her, but she ignored him this time.

"Aren't they happy, Mark?" Lauren said again, looking down the bar at Mark. "Doesn't it make you happy for them?"

"Yes," Mark said. He continued to watch the commotion of the crowd, not looking at Lauren. Lauren continued to look Mark's way. She had turned her back to Dieter. After a moment, she stood up and walked to stand before Mark.

"Mark, will you please come with me?" she asked.

Mark didn't respond immediately. Finally, he picked up his beer. "Where?" he asked.

"No, please leave your beer," she said, taking his hand and leading him out the door of the *Gasthaus*. On the outside, she took his arm in both of hers and said, "Let's walk."

She set the stride, and they casually strolled down the street without talking. Coming to the edge of the village, Lauren finally broke the silence. "That was getting to be a little too much celebration back there for me," she said with a little laugh. Mark agreed but didn't say anything further.

Just outside the village was a meadow with short summer grass that allowed easy walking. Lauren continued to set the pace and direction, and they walked across the meadow until they came to a cluster of pines and oaks on a rise above the meadow. They found a spot under a tree with shade and soft ground cover. Mark sat down and leaned back against the tree. Lauren sat down beside him and collected her skirt around her. Before them, lay the yellow and green meadow they had just walked across. Beyond that, the brown and gray buildings of the village loomed in the clear sunlight. The air was comfortably cool, and the clean woodsy smell of earth and trees was pleasant and calming.

"This is better, isn't it?" Lauren said.

"Yes," Mark said, gazing out across the meadow and avoiding Lauren's look.

Mark sat on the grass next to the tree and leaned back against the trunk. Lauren moved to sit between his legs and leaned back against him as they often did when outdoors and relaxing in the countryside. With both facing the scene of the open meadow, Mark laid his hand on her shoulder, but he didn't put his arms around her or pull her closer to him as he usually did. He remained quiet and tense, his demeanor distant. Lauren sat silently for several moments, then stirred slightly, and then suddenly shifted her position around to face him. She looked at him with a serious face.

"It's Dieter, isn't it," she said quietly, as if the thought had just occurred to her. She faced him, her look direct and firm.

"Dieter?"

"You're uncomfortable with Dieter."

"Why do you say that?"

"I can tell," she said. "I didn't realize it at first, but now I know."

"Oh, no, it's—" Mark said. He didn't finish his sentence, and his eyes dropped.

"It's what?" she demanded, her face serious.

"Well, it's that he's your friend, and you have every right to choose your friends."

"Yes, he's been nice to me, helping me with the newspaper job. But I think of him only as a friend," she said. "No more."

"I understand."

"But he's presenting a problem for us, isn't he?"

"Whether I like it or not, I can't tell you who your friends are," Mark repeated. "Let's not talk about it."

"But, Mark, there must not be something between us that one of us doesn't understand," she said.

Mark remained silent then. His eyes swept the meadow below.

"If it's important to you, I'll keep Dieter at a distance."

Mark didn't say anything but continued to gaze out across the meadow.

"Okay, it's done!" she said decisively. "I'll be polite to Dieter, but you won't see him with me again." She studied his face for a moment and then continued. "Now, Mark, look at me."

Mark glanced up at her but then looked away again. "I understand," he said. "Don't worry."

"Mark, look at me!" she said again, her voice low but firm, her look sincere and unyielding.

Mark met her look. She held his gaze momentarily. "There is no other me and you. There is only one us. Me and you individually are just two people, but me and you together are unique and special. We must not have any misunderstandings between us, ever. There will always be others, but they'll always be separate from us."

"Okay, I get it."

"Do you?"

"Yes."

"It's important that you do."

"And I do." His eyes dropped again but then came back to hers. She had not broken her look. The blue in them seemed depthless and so compelling he could not look away. Once again, he was amazed at her understanding of things and how she could articulate her feelings. His gaze stayed with hers, and he felt, as he had many times before, that each could perceive the other's thoughts without speaking.

"It's all right," he said finally, the tension going from his face. "I'm okay now."

"Are you sure?" she said. "You must be sure."

"I'm sure," he said, and he smiled at her and pulled her closer, adjusting his body to hers. She turned back toward the meadow and relaxed back against him. In their closely huddled position, with each feeling the warmth and the breathing rhythm of the other, they sat quietly, happy now to be together and away from the world and its problems that existed across the meadow in the village and beyond.

CHAPTER 49

FOR SOME TIME AFTER THE guard duty at Miesau, Lieutenant McBride followed the ensuing developments closely. While at the Miesau Post, he had made friends with several of the officers, and they kept him up-to-date on the unfolding investigation of the smugglers and their operation. The CID, the MPs, and the German *Polizei*, all working together, had identified and arrested several of the front men for the group, and these men were providing information about the gang's method of operation. It turned out, as expected, that there were some local civilians working for the US Army tending to the ordinance who also worked for the smugglers. These inside men would, on specified nights, leave certain bunkers unlocked. On these designated nights, the intruders would slip past the sparse MP patrols and quietly remove certain quantities of munitions and pass it through a cut in the fence. They never took large quantities from any one bunker, and they always repaired the cut in the fence in order to make discovery of the missing items more difficult for the army.

It seemed that the gang operating in Miesau was just part of the total picture. Other small groups were operating in both France and Italy and stealing military supplies from bases located in these countries. Political unrest in the countries of Africa was creating a huge market for the gun runners, and one of their suppliers was the gang stealing from the military bases in Europe. The entire investigation unfolding for the US Army began with the arrest of the wounded man who staggered into the *Gasthaus* the morning after the shootout with the post guards at Miesau. McBride made it known that it was the act of two of his men that made the entire investigation possible, and McBride was a man who believed in giving credit where credit was due.

"Sir, I'm again recommending that both Bergner and Wade get a stripe out of this," McBride said to Captain Williams a few weeks following their return from Miesau. "If not for them, that situation down at Miesau would be unchanged."

"I agree," Williams said. "They have certainly made Charlie Company look good. The post commander at Miesau recommends some form of commendations for them as well."

"There's one problem with these promotions," First Sergeant Andrade said with a calculating look.

"What's that?" both McBride and Williams asked simultaneously, facing Andrade.

"The problem's not with promoting Wade," Andrade said. "His time-in-grade for an E-5 sergeant is sufficient. The problem is with promoting Bergner. He's already an E-5 sergeant, and his time-in-grade in not sufficient for an E-6 sergeant."

"It wouldn't be fair to promote one without the other," Williams said, tapping his desktop as he usually did when considering problems. "They were both in that firefight, and they both deserve something."

"I agree completely," McBride said, facing his first obstacle in getting the two men promoted. "We can't reward just one and not the other. We've got to be fair for the good of the whole company. Morale is high now, but if we appear unfair, it could go down quickly."

"Okay, here's what I want you to do," Williams said. "I've got a meeting at Battalion and can't spend any more time on this now. You two take a few days and see what you can come up with. We'll discuss this again later in the week."

*   *   *

At the battalion meeting, Captain Williams was first congratulated for the work his Second Platoon had done at Miesau. The word had spread rapidly about the Miesau operation, and the other company commanders spoke their agreement with the "well done" from the colonel. Things seemed to be going well for Williams until the colonel said that Regiment had asked for some help in getting the last two companies through their annual field training maneuvers. Since Charlie Company had led off the year's maneuvers and had been successful in getting their convoy to and from the designated areas without incident, the colonel asked Williams to provide someone to act as a liaison officer in getting the last two companies to and from their field locations. Williams had no choice but to assign his best platoon leader, Lieutenant McBride, to the task. Having McBride out of the company for two weeks would leave Sergeant Andrade alone to come up with a way to reward Mark and Wade for their work at Miesau.

For two days, Andrade kept the problem in the back of his mind as he went about his duties. He thought of not promoting either man and rewarding them in a different way as a means of being fair. But this wouldn't be fair to Wade, who deserved a promotion and was a grade behind Mark. And it would be a shame to pass up this opportunity to justify one. But then Mark deserved recognition as well. With this conundrum, Andrade struggled with finding a way to be fair and appropriate with the two men. Because there wasn't a question of promoting Wade, Mark's recognition was the only problem. Finally, he decided to call Mark in to discuss Miesau, hoping he could glean something that would help with the situation. He didn't want to put Mark on the spot, but he would be alert to anything useful that might develop out of the conversation.

"Did you want to see me, Sergeant?' Mark asked when he reported to Sergeant Andrade.

"Yeah, Bergner, come in and sit down," Andrade said. "I'd like to talk about Miesau for a minute or two."

"What about Miesau, Sergeant?'

"Well, I've read Lieutenant McBride's reports," Andrade said. "But I'd like to hear your version of what happened."

"Miesau," Mark began, with a thoughtful look. "Miesau was just one of those boring details that turned out to be intensely exciting." A smile slowly developed on his face. "But I could do without that type of excitement," he continued, his smile becoming a spirited laugh. Andrade followed suit. They both laughed out the humor of the moment, and then Andrade got down to business.

"As we've already said," Andrade began, "both you and Wade performed well in that situation. You've made Charlie Company look good."

"All in a day's work, Sergeant," Mark said. He laughed again lightly, as if the event was just another work detail.

"We're considering ways to reward you two," Andrade said, watching Mark closely. "But we haven't decided exactly how to do that."

"Reward!" Mark said with a look of surprise. "Sergeant, we were just doing our job, and there were about forty other guys from Charlie Company with us."

"True, but the sword of responsibility fell on you two."

"Just coincidence," Mark said. "Besides, let me make something clear about this situation. It was Wade's show. I just backed him up at the end. He had already confronted the intruders by the time I got back to him."

"Maybe so, but you were in the line of fire as well."

"By the time I got to Wade, he had already reloaded and was ready for another barrage," Mark said. "I just did what he told me to do after that."

"You're being modest, Bergner," Andrade said with some scorn in his voice.

"I'm being honest, Sergeant," Mark countered. "If there's any reward coming, I suggest that Wade get it. I wouldn't feel comfortable getting something equal to Wade."

"What do you suggest?" Andrade asked, still watching Mark closely.

"Um," Mark began. "I don't know . . . Wait! You know, Sergeant, Wade is in an E-4 grade. I think he has time-in-grade for an E-5. I think that would be an appropriate reward for him."

Andrade laughed. "And what about you, Bergner?" he asked. "What would be appropriate for you?"

"For me?" Mark said. "For me, nothing! Oh well, maybe a three-day pass. I could use that."

"A three-day pass? Hell!" Andrade said, the scorn back in his voice. "The captain will give you a three-day pass anyway."

"Well, that's all I can think of at the moment," Mark said, nodding his head firmly. "It's always been a little uncomfortable for me being a grade higher than Wade. If you want to reward me, give Wade that E-5 grade and me a three-day pass."

First Sergeant Andrade didn't immediately respond to Mark's statement. He could only look at him in amazement. Finally, he said, "Always self-denial, huh, Bergner. Don't you ever think of yourself?"

Mark didn't answer immediately. He felt good with the attention he was getting. In spite of this, he was uncomfortable with being singled out for reward that excluded the group. Long before the twenty-two months he now had in C Company, Mark had adopted the group-think that the captain had insisted on that first day he reported in. *There will be no individuals in my company,* the captain had said then. *I want only team players.*

Finally, Mark threw up his hands slightly and said flippantly, "Duty first, Sergeant." He then shrugged and laughed, as if it wasn't that important.

When Captain Williams reported to duty the following morning, First Sergeant Andrade met with him immediately. He related to the captain verbatim his conversation with Mark. The captain listened to his first sergeant without saying a word. He then leaned back in his chair and looked up at the ceiling for a long moment. "You know," he finally said, "this younger generation we're getting in these days are just as good as our own generation. They don't have the same burden as we had. But if they did, they would perform just as well, I'm sure."

"No doubt, Captain," Andrade said. "And Bergner's selfless attitude has solved our problem of promoting Wade."

"Yes," Williams said. "Issue him three-day passes whenever he requests them and it's appropriate. Also, work up a suitable letter of commendation for his 201 File. I'll sign it and then forward it to Battalion for the colonel's signature. When this comes back to us, I'll present it to him at retreat time so the entire company will witness it."

"Very well, Captain," Andrade said. "That'll be good for morale and appropriate for Bergner." He paused a moment and then continued. "You know, there's something about the good luck these two are having that's troubling to me."

"What's that, Sergeant?"

"Well, you know how sometimes when things are going unusually good, but you feel it's too good to be true and begin to worry that something is going to happen?"

"Don't get that feeling often," William said. "But I know what you mean."

"It's nothing specific," Andrade said quietly, his demeanor thoughtful. "But as you know, Captain, fate ain't usually so good to us mortals.

"Amen to that," Williams said.

CHAPTER 50

ONE MORNING AS THE PLATOON was preparing to fallout for reveille, the company clerk came hurrying into the barracks. "Bergner," he hollered excitedly as he walked down the center aisle. "Bergner, where's Bergner?" he continued, looking left and right at each soldier.

"Take it easy, man" Mark said. "I'm right here." Mark was in the process of getting ready for the day's duty. His bunk was already made and his locker was in order and shut and locked. "What's up?"

"Report to the orderly room, Captain's orders," the clerk said, stopping before Mark. "You've got a visitor."

"I've got a visitor? Who?"

"A civilian," the clerk said back over his shoulder as he turned to leave. "And he looks important."

Mark immediately left the barracks and walked to the orderly room and entered the captain's office. As he saluted and reported in, he only half noticed the gentleman standing off to the side. "Sergeant, you have a visitor," the captain said as he returned Mark's salute, a smile forming on his face.

Mark turned and faced the visitor for the first time. He was stunned into silence as he faced his father. "Hello, Mark," his father said, a broad smile across his face. Mark paused a moment, and then his hand went out reflexively to shake hands, but his father grabbed him and embraced him with a strong, manly hug.

"Pop! What? . . . Why?" Mark said, finally finding his voice. "Is everything okay?"

"Everything's fine," his father said. "I just flew over for a brief visit."

Captain Williams spoke, saying it was a rare honor having someone from the States visit his company and added that Mark was excused from duty for the day. He suggested they find someplace where they could talk.

Mark led his father outside. The weather was fair with mild temperatures and scattered clouds that allowed sporadic sunshine to break through. They strolled about the post talking, finally coming to the parade grounds. The parade grounds consisted of a grassy area bordered by a row of wooden bleachers on one side and a monument made up of a concrete base topped with a battery of NATO flags on the opposite side. Sitting on the bottom row of the empty bleachers, they talked about home and family and Mark's old neighborhood. All was well on the home front, his father had said, except his mother was worried sick that he might not return home after the army.

"What are your plans?" his father finally asked, watching Mark closely.

"I'm really in no position to make plans," Mark said. "The army is making all my plans for now."

"I understand," his father said, his face showing concern. "But soon you'll be discharged and can come home, won't you?"

Mark nodded but didn't say anything. His father seemed to have aged in the almost two years since he had last seen him. His face was darker as if he had been spending more time on the construction sites instead of in his office managing the projects. And his father's appearance no longer had that confident, authoritative demeanor it had before Mark had joined the army; he seemed somewhat desperate in his appeal for Mark to agree with him.

His father waited a moment, giving Mark time to answer. When Mark didn't speak, he continued. "As far as the business goes, we're doing really well," he said. "We have several renovation jobs in Queens and a major project over in Brooklyn constructing a sizeable school complex. Uncle Abe, whom I have made my executive manager, has all but landed a contract in upper state to build a shopping mall that will take more than a year to complete."

As he continued to relate the details of the business, Mark began to realize why his father had come to Europe to visit him. He wanted a face-to-face encounter to understand Mark's intentions after the army. "Mark," he finally said, looking at him with a serious face. "We're booming! I need you in the business with me."

"But, Pop," Mark said. "How can I help? I have no experience in the construction business."

"You don't now," his father began with a knowing smile, "but you will. I've got a plan all worked out."

"A plan?"

"Yeah," his father said with growing enthusiasm. "Here's my plan. We'll get you situated at NYU, but in your spare time, you can work on the sites. I want you to take the projects one at a time, getting to know the men and their jobs, working shoulder to shoulder with the carpenters and the bricklayers and getting tired and dirty with them just as they do, and just as I did when I was your age. If I know you, you'll like that."

"Yeah," Mark said, an unconscious smile developing on his face. "But, Pop, it'll take me years to learn enough to help out at your level."

"Yes, that's true, Mark," his father said, his face growing more serious. But it's the distant future I'm looking at for you and me." His father paused momentarily, looking sternly at him. "My goal is to have you at my side making executive decisions sometime down the road."

"But can't you hire the right people to help you manage?"

"Of course. I do that already," his father said and turned away as in thought. When he turned back to Mark, he spoke slowly and directly. "Mark, I've spent more than forty years building my business. It was slow at first, but now it's really moving. But more importantly, it's my life. It's like a family member, and that's what this is all about. I want it to stay in the family."

Mark was beginning to understand his father and could sense his father's need for reassurance that he would be joining him in his business and family life. Mark's father wanted him to pick up where he would leave off. He could do that, except his life wasn't his to choose the direction it would take. There was the army and the possible extension of his enlistment and the results of that. More importantly, there was Lauren and the reality of their situation that he'd refused to face so far. When it came to Lauren, he knew that no matter what developed, she was now and would always be a vital and essential part of him. But even with this knowledge, he refused to see beyond the next time he would be with her. At this time, the situation was too big for him to grasp and take charge of, but how could he tell his father all this?

"Pop, sooner or later, I plan to return home," Mark said, hoping to reassure his father. "I'm looking forward to NYU and working in the business, but I can't say exactly when I'll do this."

"If you're going to build a successful business, Mark, you have to sacrifice something," his father said, obviously detecting in Mark's demeanor thoughts of other plans. "You have to give up something in order to get something."

Mark instinctively went on guard. He knew his father saying he would have to give up something in order to get something implied more than the business. He was beginning to think that all the talk about the building business was a front for what he really wanted to talk about. "All I can say now is that sooner or later I plan to return home."

"That's good," his father said. "We're all looking forward to that day." He grew quiet for a moment, but his eyes never left Mark's face as if he wanted to say more. "There's something else, Mark." He finally began. "Your mother thinks you're having a relationship with a German girl."

That's it, Mark thought. *Now he's getting into what he really came to Germany for.* Mark now knew what was coming next. "Yes I am, Pops," he said. "There is someone special here."

"Your mother wanted me to talk to you about that," his father began. "I think you mentioned in an earlier letter that Lauren was her name." He paused a moment and then continued. "Your mother's worried about that. She's worried that you might have some serious plans with Lauren."

Mark was silent. He looked at his father blankly. *Now it's out,* he thought.

"Mark," his father began, placing his hand on Mark's shoulder. "Do you know what this would mean in our community?" His father's face revealed genuine concern and sympathy as he faced Mark. "There's a deep, deep hatred there for Germans. I know that some of this may be unjustified, that there's good and bad in all races. But at this day and time at home, there exist this all-prevailing hatred that you must understand. I think you know that, but I'm not sure you have really faced it."

Mark continued to be silent. He knew what his father said was true; there was an attitude and frame of mind back home that was firm and unchanging. He also knew that this attitude came from much suffering and loss and was justified in many ways. But at the same time, he knew his father and others to be wrong to condemn all Germans for what some had done.

The older man waited a moment. When Mark appeared to have nothing further to say, his father began again. "Mark, I know you to be someone who has his own mind and will think things out and act according to your own best judgment. But let me leave you with one thought." His father paused again as if to give Mark time to absorb what he had said and to prepare himself for what he was going to say. "Think seriously about this, Mark . . . With your feelings for Lauren and your concern for her welfare, would it be fair to bring her into the environment that you know exists there? And in considering this question, you should not only think of yourself but of her, foremost."

Mark listened but would not comment further. Although he remained silent, his father's words sank deep into his subconscious. Finally, his father gave up talking about Lauren, and they talked in general about life in Germany. They talked until the sun reached the treetops across the parade ground, and then they left the post.

Mark accompanied his father back to his hotel. They had a light dinner and afterward had several rounds of scotch while chatting about the family, the business, and the community. Although Mark was polite and respectful, he refused to further discuss Lauren. In spite of this, he knew his father to be right in one way; he knew he was right when he said Mark had not faced the reality of Lauren in Queens. He knew this but pushed it to the back of his mind and would not think about it.

His father's flight back to New York was early the next morning.

CHAPTER 51

S INCE HER SHOWDOWN WITH HER father months earlier,
life at home for Lauren was strained, and her father's
uncompromising rejection of Mark was the cause. She
searched for ways to soften his mind-set, but he wouldn't listen to
her attempts to justify their relationship. He was simply too rigid in
his ways and attitude to accept Mark. At first, she tried to resume a
normal routine by doing the house chores while offering a cheerful
chatter about their daily life, but her father remained distant.

After she stopped associating with Dieter, he seemed to get even
more distant and silent. They didn't speak about their disagreement,
but the tension was there. Her father only spoke when necessary to
get the house routines accomplished, and then his conversations
were short and to the point. She didn't know which way to turn or
who to talk to until she thought of the priest at her village church.
She decided to meet with him, hoping to get advice and support.
She went to the church and asked for a confessional. After she took
her seat and the elderly priest took his outside the confessional, she

sat silently for a moment, collecting her thoughts. She tried to see the priest through the small opening but couldn't.

Finally, the priest spoke. "Yes, my child, why have you come, today?"

"I have come to confess, Father, for I have sinned."

"What is your sin, my child?"

"My sin is I think of myself—often. I am selfish."

"Selfishness is not God's way, child," the priest said

"I know, Father."

"You must do penance," the priest said. "God will absolve you of your sins when you do your penance."

"What must I do, Father?"

"Help others and prey for them," the priest said.

"Yes, Father."

After her confession, Lauren asked for an audience with the priest.

The priest agreed to the audience, and they went into his office, which was located at the back of the church. The office was small and dimly lit. It contained a desk with a chair and one more chair in front of the desk where Lauren sat. On the wall to the right of the priest's desk stood a bookcase of considerable size. The bookcase contained numerous large books bound in dark brown covers. The books were perfectly aligned and straight in their rows, as if they were not often disturbed. There was little light in the room, the only light coming through a multicolored stained glass window located directly behind the priest and facing Lauren. The light from the window was at the priest's back and did not reveal his facial features. She could only see a shadowy silhouette as she sat before him.

"And what would you like to talk about, my child," the priest began.

"Father, I feel bad because my father and I disagree on something," Lauren said, straining to see the priest's face.

"People often disagree," the priest said. "What does he ask of you that you disagree about?"

"He wants me to stop seeing someone whom I want to see."

"Hmm," mumbled the priest. "Do you understand why your father doesn't want you to see this person?"

"Yes, I think so."

"Do you believe you father has your best interest at heart?"

"Yes, I think he thinks that what he wants is in my best interest."

"Um," the priest mumbled again and then grew silent momentarily. Shortly, he continued. "Do you think your father's a wise man?"

"Yes, I think he's very wise."

"Then if he has your best interest at heart, and he's a wise man, wouldn't it be prudent for you to consider his advice?"

"But what he wants is not what I want," Lauren said.

"But what you must understand is that what you want must come only after you do what God wants."

Lauren hesitated a moment. "And what does God want?" she asked.

"In most cases," the old man began in a low but serious monotone, "God wants you to obey your father."

"But, Father, do I not have the right to follow a path set for me, set by my own mind and nature instead of one set by circumstances and factors from the past?"

"When it's God's will, you do."

"But when does what I want count, Father?" Lauren said with some concern.

"Child, to be in good with God, you must deny the self. You have your duty to your father, your country, and your church. Always think of them and give of yourself to their causes."

"But, Father," Lauren began, her voice becoming more serious and rising higher. She then stopped her speech, as if to gain control of her feelings. Pained and bewildered, she looked a long time at the man before her. Finally, in a low and pleading tone she said, "How can I give of myself if I have no self?"

The priest was silent for some time. When he spoke, his voice continued in a confident monotone. "Pray, and God will show you the way."

Lauren became silent. She tried hard to see the priest's face, to see if she could find sympathy in his expression. But no matter how hard she tried, she could not see his features well enough to gain any meaning other than from what he had said. She could only sit silently before him, staring at his silhouette.

The priest paused a moment waiting for Lauren to speak. When she didn't say anything further, he continued. "Pray long and hard and often on this matter, and God will give you guidance."

"Yes, Father," Lauren said. She then stood up, thanked him, and left the church.

CHAPTER 52

SINCE MYERS WOULD BE HELD at the army prison at Mannheim only a short time before being shipped back to the States, Mark and Wade asked permission to visit him right away. Captain Williams granted permission, and the necessary orders were prepared. First Sergeant Andrade bullied the motor pool sergeant in charge of transportation into issuing them a jeep for the trip. The round-trip would take up much of the day in driving, so they left early to travel to the prison at Mannheim.

When they arrived at the prison, they found it to be a facility surrounded by a ten-foot high wire fence with concertina wire at the top. Inside the fenced compound were several two-story wooden buildings and several smaller buildings. The buildings were painted dark green, and all had heavy gauge, wire mesh coverings over the windows. At one side of the largest building was another fenced enclosure that bordered the building. Within this enclosure, several men stood around talking and smoking or just gazing about. These men were sloppily dressed. Their fatigue pants were not bloused in their boots, and their fatigue shirts were not tucked in. All had a white letter *P* painted on the backs of their fatigue shirts. The gate at the entrance to the compound had a guard shack manned by two MPs, and a third stood by the street curb. A sign above the gate stated "USAREUP STOCKADE."

When they approached the gate, the MP at the curb asked them in a clipped, formal manner to state their business. Mark and Wade produced their orders requesting permission to visit inmate Dave Myers. The first MP looked at the orders and passed them to one of the MPs inside the shack. This MP read the orders and asked Mark and Wade to follow him. He walked them across the yard without speaking and into the first building where they were told to report to the sergeant there. They stood in a small waiting area facing a solid wall that had a steel door and a four-by-four opening situated some three feet above the floor. The opening was protected by a heavy gauge wire mesh and thick glass. This thick glass enclosure had a smaller opening where the first MP inserted their orders, and the sergeant behind the enclosure picked them up to read.

"This place is hard to get into," Wade said to Mark.

"But I'll bet it's harder to get out," Mark said as he surveyed the inside of the sergeant's station. The sergeant stood at a small shelf facing them through the glass and wire mesh opening in the enclosure. On the shelf before him lay what was apparently a log book. To the right of the log book and within easy reach was a M1911 .45 caliber semiautomatic pistol. Behind the sergeant sat several other MPs who seemed relaxed but who looked them over carefully. Mounted on the wall behind these men sat a gun rack containing what Mark knew to be 12-gauge riot guns. All the MPs were dressed in starched fatigues and wore olive drab helmet liners with the white MP emblem stenciled on each side. Each man wore a web belt that supported a holstered .45 ACP sidearm and a packet in front holding two extra loaded clips for the .45s.

"These aren't parade MPs," Mark said under his breath.

"Not my kind of place," Wade replied quietly.

The sergeant turned and spoke to one of the other men, and this man opened the steel door. "Follow me," he ordered. He led them down a hallway and out a side door into the yard with the fenced enclosure. "Wait here."

Shortly, Myers appeared at the side door, and the MP took a seat on a bench near the fence, facing them. Mark and Wade shook hands with Myers and jostled him about playfully. He was dressed like the men they had seen in the first fenced in area.

"So, how's the chow here at this exclusive resort?" Mark asked, laughing.

Obviously glad to see them, Myers laughed, but his laugh lacked mirth, his eyes were dull, and his face had a sallow look. "The chow's lousy, and the waiters are gorillas with big sticks."

"Skimp on their tips," Wade said, laughing at Myers.

The three friends wisecracked and joked around a few minutes, and then the conversation began to slow. Myers became tentative and only talked when they pressed him with questions. He stood with his hands in his pockets and looked down at the ground most of the time. Mark and Wade worked at keeping a lighthearted dialogue going.

"Sergeant Riley," Mark began, "you know, the motor pool sergeant you did the stenciling for?"

"Yeah," Myers said. "Sure, I remember old Riley."

"He said to hurry back," Mark said. "He said he needs some good help."

"Ha!" Myers exclaimed, perking up a little. "That's a laugh. All Riley did when I worked for him was gripe about my work."

"Can't please the army," Wade said, laughing lightly. "All you can do is play the game."

"Amen to that," Myers said. "Play the game."

The conversation began to lag again. Mark tried to think of a joke he hadn't already told. Not coming up with anything, he glanced at Wade who only returned a blank look. Having no follow-up to their lighthearted talk, Mark began in a more serious tone. "Dave, you know we think you got a raw deal." He paused a moment and then continued. "If there was anything we could do, we would. You know that, don't you?"

"Everyone thinks you got a raw deal," Wade said, now finding his voice and beginning to back Mark in his attempt to support Myers. "All the guys in the platoon said to tell you good luck when we saw you."

"Thanks, fellows," Myers said. "I know you're behind me, but this is my problem. I got myself into this, and I'll tough it out." He was quiet for a moment but then perked up. "I'm just glad they couldn't find anything to charge you guys with."

Mark and Wade exchanged glances. They looked at each other and then quickly looked away. Wade seemed to become occupied with a large black bird as it slowly glided down on a chimney a short distance away. Mark studied the MP standing at the gate to the exercise yard as the MP lit a cigarette.

"These MPs look tough," he said, glancing up at Myers.

"Okay, guys!" Myers said quickly, looking from one to the other. "What are you not telling me?"

"Not telling you?" Mark said, looking around at Wade. "What do you mean?"

"I know there's something!" Myers said, firmly. "Come on, out with it."

Mark and Wade stared at each other for a moment. Finally, Mark said, "We might as well tell him, Sam. It'll come out sooner or later anyway."

"Go ahead, tell him," Wade said.

"Well, Dave, we didn't want to add to your worry, but here's what's transpiring now," Mark began. "The captain called us in late yesterday. He said he had just gotten word from the provost marshal that the same investigation board that worked your case was to reconvene next week to consider charges against us."

"What charges?" Myers said loudly. "What are the sons of bitches trying to do to you guys?"

The MP at the gate turned to watch Myers, obviously alerted by his angry voice. He took a short draw off his cigarette and continued to watch the three men. He watched them a moment and then turned his attention to adjusting his web belt.

"We told them you were not really drinking that night," Mark said. "We each swore that you had only one beer and passed the rest around to others."

"Yeah, and they brought in Herr Kuntz and his daughter to counter that," Wade said. "Old Kuntz testified that you drank many beers. That set us up for giving false testimony."

"Were you under oath?"

"Yes."

"My God!" Myers said. "Why did we go with that story? Now you can be charged with perjury!"

"I'm afraid so," Wade said. "We thought it best to say you only drank one beer to head off a charge of negligent homicide."

"I wish you hadn't done that!" Myers said. "They'll come after you now!"

"That's right," Mark said, "but there's a glimmer of hope. Andrade told us that McBride, Williams, and our own Colonel at Regiment have all appealed to the colonel in charge of the investigation to forego a court-martial recommendation in lieu of punishment at company level."

"Now I've got you guys caught up in my mess," Myers said, his face contorted with concern and pain. "Won't my bad luck ever end?"

"Now listen," Wade said. "Don't start putting yourself down because of us. We did what we thought we should have done at the time. It just didn't work out, that's all."

The three of them were silent for a time. Each withdrew into his own thoughts, obviously considering what might have been if they'd done things differently, if they'd had enough information and wisdom to make sounder decisions, and if fate had given them a different path to take.

Finally, Myers spoke. "You know, I've given this whole thing a lot of thought. And the more I think about it, the more I realize something."

"What's that?" Wade asked, looking at Myers closely.

"The way I look at it now," Myers said, with a faraway look. "I was destined to end up like this." He nodded his head slightly as if sure of what he had said.

"Destined?" Mark said. "What do you mean?"

"You know," Myers said, beginning to talk more freely. "It's just my ordained fate. Everyone is fated in some way, and this is mine."

"Your ordained fate!" Wade said incredulously, looking at Mark. "How do you figure that?"

"Well, I didn't think so at first, but then Captain Barrett told me what the court-martial board decided in my case."

"Who's Captain Barrett?" Mark asked.

"And what did he tell you?" Wade asked quickly.

"Captain Barrett was my defense counselor," Myers said calmly. "Good man too. But after the court-martial, he told me the board decided the case was bigger than the individual."

"What the hell does that mean?" Wade asked with visible and growing irritation. "Did he sell you out?"

"No, no," Myers said. "Captain Barrett was furious at the board, and he told me why."

"I'm not with you on this," Mark said. "What did he mean bigger than the individual?"

"Just that," Myers continued. "The army's mission in Europe is bigger than the individual. At first, I didn't understand, but now I do."

"And you're okay with that?" Wade exclaimed. "You're not upset about that?"

"At first, I was really mad about everything," Myers continued. "I hated the army and all those sons of bitches, but now I know that only makes things worse. Now I'm beginning to feel differently. I'm beginning to feel I'm part of something that's bigger than me. I know it's going to be tough these next ten months, but I'll make it. My situation now is just my place in the big picture, and I'm okay with that."

Mark glanced at Wade. As much as he wanted to boost Myers's moral and show support, he felt hopelessly skeptical and could think of no way to deal with Myers's logic. He couldn't think of anything further to say and looked at Wade for help.

Wade just returned Mark a blank look. Then, as if frustrated and seeking relief, he suddenly grabbed Myers in a headlock and began mussing up his hair in a playful manner.

"Ten months will pass before you know it, Shrimp," he said, laughing. "You'll be coming home fat and sassy."

The MP by the fence stood up again, watching the three men closely. When he saw it was a good-natured jostle, he sat back down. He watched the three men a moment and then took another cigarette from his fatigue shirt and lit up.

"I've got an idea," Mark said. "Let's get together a year from now. We can swap addresses and phone numbers, and a year from now, we'll drop everything and meet somewhere."

"Great idea!" Wade said, slapping Myers lightly on the shoulder. "We can tie one on and talk all this over like there was nothing to it. We can better understand this whole mess by then."

"You know what's so bad?" Myers said, ignoring their plans to meet in a year. "What I hate the most?"

"Come on, Dave," Wade persisted, obviously trying to lift Myers's spirit. "Don't you think we can have a blast a year from now remembering all this?"

"Yeah, I guess so," Dave said. He pause a moment and then continued. "When I left home, they told me to come back home a sergeant."

"Then it's settled," Mark said, glancing at Wade with a worried look. "One year from this date we'll have a reunion. We'll set it up before hand and get together and rehash all this. We'll find us a friendly bar and celebrate and philosophize about the way it was."

They swapped home addresses and shook hands. On the return trip back to post, Mark and Wade were mostly silent. But just as they exited the autobahn to take the shortcut to post, Wade said to Mark, "Man, is Dave mixed up."

"Yeah," Mark said, glancing over at Wade. "And even though he's acting like he's taking it okay, you can tell he's scared and depressed."

"Yeah, he sure is," Wade replied. "He doesn't seem to think he counts anymore . . . just a part of the big picture."

CHAPTER 53

IT WAS A THURSDAY AFTERNOON when Second Platoon received the good news. The captain himself had presided over the noon chow formation and made the announcement. He said that Charlie Company had performed exceptionally well in their training exercises for the previous month and that the battalion commander had taken note, sending his congratulation to Williams and suggesting some special treatment for the men. During the formation, the captain instructed First Sergeant Andrade to announce that all training for the remainder of the day was cancelled. It was to be a free afternoon for everyone. His advice to the men was to get caught up on things like letter writing and to relax in general. This unexpected free time created a cheerful enthusiasm among the men, and they streamed back into the barracks laughing and playfully kidding around.

Wade immediately went to his locker and retrieved a book he had been reading. It was a fictional account of the Texas War of Independence in 1835. As he flopped down on his bunk, he said to Mark, "You need to read this book, Mark, after I'm finished with it."

"Why?" Mark asked.

"Well, the battle at the Alamo will show you New York Yankees something about bravery and self-sacrifice," Wade replied, looking over at Mark and grinning.

"Um," Mark said as he poked around in his locker. "Rather than be brave and dead, this New Yorker would rather be a coward and live to eat hotdogs at Yankee Stadium and watch baseball."

"I'm with you, Mark," Corporal Peterson, a native of San Francisco, said as he walked by their bunks, heading for the showers. He was stripped to his skivvies and had a towel around his neck. "Retreat and live to love another day," he continued, stopping by Wade's bunk.

"Ha!" Wade exclaimed, laughing loudly. "Only your mother would love you, Peterson."

"Don't insult my mother, you loud mouth Texan," Peterson said, taking his towel and snapping it at Wade.

"Children, children, behave!" Mark said, laughing and looking from one to the other.

"Take that, Cowboy!" Peterson continued as he snapped his towel toward Wade again.

"You know where that towel's going if you don't stop that, don't you, Peterson?" Wade had laid his book aside and was now sitting up in his bunk.

"No. Tell me where it's going, Cowboy." He snapped the towel toward Wade again, getting close to his face.

"I'll show you," Wade said jumping up from his bunk.

"Remember the Alamo!" Peterson shouted and ran toward the end of the barracks where the showers were. Wade grabbed his own towel and ran after him. They both disappeared into the shower room, but a noisy clamor of howls and oaths and snapping of towels could be heard.

Mark found his letter-writing material and flopped down on his bunk, laughing at the commotion from the shower. Soon his facial expression lost its amused look and became pensive as he began writing. He wrote but then stopped, looked up momentarily, and began writing again, seemingly oblivious to the tumult still coming from the shower.

"Ahh . . . . take that, you Tex Mex," said an energetic voice simultaneously with a raucous yell that rolled down the long barracks building like a train through a tunnel.

Mark had just turned the page of his writing tablet to begin on the next page when he heard his name called from the barracks entrance. Looking up, he saw the mail clerk headed his way with his arms full of two large boxes.

"Bergner, you've got these boxes again," the clerk said, dropping them at the foot of Mark's bunk. "And, as I've said before, I don't have room for them in my mail room."

A shout came from the shower room. "So you wanted a shower, eh?" said the voice. "Well how about this?" The sound of spraying water could be heard.

"Ahh . . . that's cold . . . Let me up!"

"You like the temperature, eh?"

"What's going on back there?" the mail clerk asked, nodding toward the shower room.

"Turn it off, turn it off," came the voice again.

"It's just a couple of Second Platoon nutcases expressing themselves," Mark said nonchalantly, as if nothing unusual was going on. "If you'll open that box, you can have a cookie," he continued, pointing at one of the boxes.

The clerk took out his pocketknife and opened the box. Then, with a surprised but delighted look, he took out a cookie and began to eat. As he munched, a look of pleasure came over his face. He sat down at the foot of Mark's bunk with his eyes locked on the top layer of multicolored cookies.

Mark sighed, as if he knew the clerk was there to stay as long as he could get the cookies. Mark got up from the bunk and grabbed the box. "Let's put these on the table at the front entrance so the other guy's can have some," he said as he carried the box to the entrance; the clerk followed. "Help yourself to more," Mark continued. "Take a few back to the mail room. I know you've got work to do there."

As the clerk carefully picked out several of the colorful sweets, another loud yell came down from the opposite end of the building. Then, still in his skivvies and soaking wet, Peterson came running full speed down the aisle. Wade, also soaking wet and fully clothed, was right behind him, snapping his towel at Peterson's backside. As they ran through the entrance door, they knocked Mark aside, causing him to spill the box of cookies. Outside, Wade tackled Peterson a short distance from the building, and they rolled around in the grass, each struggling and making grunting threats.

"Remember the Alamo," Wade said as he pinned Peterson down and sat on top of him. As he rubbed the wet towel in Peterson's face, he said, "I'll give you West Coast Bohemian something to remember."

"Time for me to go," the clerk said with a startled look on his face. He cautiously walked around the two men wrestling in the grass, staying far to their side. Mark smiled at the two wallowing on the ground and then reentered the building. After cleaning up the spilled cookies, he returned to his bunk and resumed his letter writing as if nothing had happened. Presently, Wade reentered the building and went straight to the shower. A short time later, Peterson casually walked by Mark's bunk. He was covered with grass stains and dirt but was calmly composed like nothing had happened. He also headed for the shower.

When Wade returned to his bunk, he had showered and put on dry clothes. Without a word, he picked up his book and resumed reading. Mark gave him a couple minutes and then asked, "Want a cookie?"

"Sure," Wade said. "They come in today's mail?"

"Yeah."

"Good old Mom," Wade continued. "You know, you're a lucky man . . . having a Mom who sends you cookies."

Peterson soon joined them and helped himself to a cookie. He and Wade, having spent their rowdy energy, acted as if nothing had happened. All three were sitting on the bunks eating, talking, and joking when the charge of quarters entered the barracks and approached them.

"Bergner, Wade," he said immediately seeing them, "the first sergeant wants to see you two right now."

"Yeah, what about?" Wade asked.

"Beats me," the CQ said. "Probably knows you've been goofing off," he teased.

*　　*　　*

When Mark and Sam entered the orderly room, they found it empty except for Andrade. The normally active room presented none of its vibrant activity that controlled and directed the actions of Charlie Company. The door to the CO's office was closed. The closed door usually meant he was out and presented a sense of a lack of immediate leadership. The vacant company clerk's desk indicated he was off duty. With the clerk's desk light off and none of the usual paperwork scattered about, his desk offered a strange abandoned look. The room in general appeared still, like the quiet of an early morning river fog. Andrade stood with his back to the room as he looked out the back window. As the two men approached the first sergeant's desk, he turned and nodded, acknowledging their presence and then turned again to gaze out the window. He stood without speaking for some time while Mark and Wade waited. They waited with no one speaking, as in respect.

Finally, Mark spoke up. "You sent for us, Sergeant?"

"Yes, I did," Andrade said and then was silent again. The two men continued waiting, standing before the first sergeant without speaking. In time, Andrade turned and straighten up, almost to attention, and looked directly from Mark to Wade. "Brace yourself. I've got bad news."

"Bad news?" both Mark and Wade asked in unison, obviously confused.

"Bad news about what?" Wade added.

"Myers is dead!" Andrade said bluntly.

"What!" Wade exclaimed. "What did you say, Sergeant?

"Battalion called a short time ago," Andrade began, his voice low but steady. "They were notified by the command at Mannheim."

"How?" Mark asks, finally finding his voice. "When?"

"Seems he fashioned a noose by tearing up a blanket and hung himself," Andrade continued as if to get all the facts out.

"No! No!" Wade said, turning and pacing several steps away before turning back to face the first sergeant. "We knew he was depressed . . . sad, but this?"

Mark remained silent, blankly staring at the first sergeant. Andrade said no more but turned and walked to the window again. He stood straight, his arms locked behind his back as if at parade rest, and continued gazing out the window. Wade shuffled about a moment and then stiffened, also staring at the first sergeant's back. All three men remained in place for some time without speaking, the silence allowing each to absorb the news in their own way and giving each time to collect his composure and take the next step in their reaction to what had happened. It was as if they knew the event didn't provide information they could assimilate and organize in their minds with a sense of conclusion but an irrational something with an absolute finality that could only be accepted in time.

Finally, Mark asked, "What can be done, Sergeant? What can we do?"

"Nothing," Andrade said quietly without turning around. "Everything will be taken care of."

The three men again stood silent for a time. Finally, Wade asked, "Is there anything else, Sergeant?"

"No, you can return to whatever you were doing."

Mark and Wade started walking back to the barracks. As they approached the building, Mark stopped.

"I think I'll walk around a bit," he said. "Catch you later, Sam."

Mark began walking aimlessly about post. He walked up to the front gate, turned and walked to the EM Club, and then doubled back to gate two. At Second Battalion, he looped the buildings three times and then proceeded to the parade grounds where he walked the entire perimeter several times. At one point during his walk, he began to run, and he ran around the edge of the parade grounds until his breathing became fast and heavy. Finally, he headed back to the barracks where he found Wade sitting on the front steps.

"You know," Wade began as Mark approached him. "I was just thinking . . . I was thinking that now he's free of that big picture he seemed caught up in."

Mark nodded, and they went into the barracks.

CHAPTER 54

WITH THE BATTALION MOBILIZED AND on standby to rotate in thirty days, routine training schedules were cancelled, and work schedules were organized that focused on various rotation details. Mark got an assignment to take two officers who were on temporary duty with Charlie Company back to their permanent post some fifty kilometers to the south. They were experienced in mobilization procedures and had assisted in the planning and logistical phase of the operation. His round-trip put him back at Charlie Company in mid afternoon. He checked the jeep back into the motor pool and then reported to Sergeant Andrade, saying he had completed the detail. The first sergeant, who worked on a stack of paperwork scattered across his desk, waved him off. "Take the rest of the day off," he said. "Go to the EM Club or something."

Mark's disposition was not good. For days, he had felt a deep melancholy that left him gloomy and irritable. Myers's death and his relationship with Lauren preoccupied his mind; he was saddened with the loss of his friend and confused with Myers's self-sacrificing attitude the last time he saw him at Mannheim. And to add to his worry, he had promised Lauren they would go back to Martinschule on their next outing. But with the endless demands of the mobilization process, he was apprehensive about getting a pass. He longed to be by himself, but when he was alone, he felt even worse. Knowing there would be no one in the barracks in the early afternoon, he decided to go to the EM Club and have a quiet beer as Andrade had suggested. Feeling edgy and tense, Mark entered the EM Club to find it deserted with Louie, the bartender, half asleep next to the radio at the far end of the bar. He nodded at Louie. Louie gave a half salute and then turned back to his radio. Mark decided to go to the latrine before having a beer. That's when it happened.

As fate would have it, an old nemesis came out of the past. As Mark entered the long, rectangular latrine with mirrors and white sinks and urinals lining the walls above a wide concrete floor, he came face-to-face with Ricco, the man obsessed with doing him bodily harm.

Seeing Mark, Ricco let out a guttural howl and charged like a crazed man. Mark reflexively dodged the first blow, but the second one caught him squarely on the side of his face, stunning him severely and driving him back against the wall. Taking advantage of Mark's surprise and catching him off guard, Ricco moved in quickly, pounding him viciously. Pinned against the latrine wall, Mark couldn't dodge the blows; he covered his head with both arms and tried to roll to the side. Ricco moved with him, striking his body with blow after blow. Mark, dizzy from the blows to his head, dropped his arms to protect his body; Ricco then moved in to finish him off. But instead of punching, he grabbed Mark's throat with both hands, holding him helplessly in a death grip.

Mark frantically tried to break the hold but was too stunned and weak to pull Ricco's hands away. As Ricco's grip tightened, he grew weaker and began to lose consciousness. It was almost over for Mark, but just before the light of his awareness dimmed completely, something from deep in that imponderable abyss of his primal psyche stirred—a spark flared in that impenetrable darkness of the inner world of his subconscious. The spark sizzled only momentarily and then quickly burst into flames that instantaneously spread throughout his entire being. With this instinctive force rapidly emanating outward, every part of his consciousness and subconsciousness, as well as his entire physical self with all its capabilities, came acutely alive in one last, desperate attempt to continue to exist. It was a life or death struggle, and Mark's survival instinct emerged with all its ramifications.

He grabbed Ricco's head, forcibly pulling it toward himself and simultaneously slamming his own forehead hard against Ricco's face, directly between his eyes. This jarring action distracted Ricco just enough to cause him to loosen his grip slightly. Mark then tore Ricco's hands away and, moving quickly, landed a hard blow straight into Ricco's face, which caused him to stumble backward a step. With this advantage, Mark quickly landed more blows against Ricco's body and head, driving him back into the wall with the line of white sinks. Ricco seemed momentarily confused, but Mark didn't let up. His blows were instinctive and precise, honed from the many hours of boxing and sparring in the gym.

He wasn't thinking or calculating; he wasn't even aware of what he was doing. He fought mechanically, like some programmed robot that had only one agenda and would follow that program until the end. One well-placed punch drove Ricco back between two sinks, wedging him there in such a way that he couldn't move to either side or backward; he could only come forward, and that forward movement positioned him to receive the blows coming at him from Mark's fury. With Ricco stuck between the sinks, Mark methodically pounded him time after time, each punch leaving skin breaks and bloody contusions.

Dazed and with his survival instinct in control, Mark was not himself, not conscious of his actions. He continued pounding

Ricco, staining the white sinks and mirrors with crimson. Finally, weakened and exhausted, he could no longer raise his arms. He swayed awkwardly, stumbled backward, and would have collapsed if not for Louie who had just entered the latrine and caught him before he fell.

"Stop! Stop this madness!" Louie shouted. "I've called the MPs."

*   *   *

Lieutenant McBride was in the orderly room getting Second Platoon's training schedule for the following week when the MPs called, saying one of Charlie Company's men had been in a fight and was in the ER at the post hospital. McBride dropped everything and immediately went to the hospital. As he walked hurriedly through the emergency room door, he could see two MPs talking to an officer with a clipboard. He recognized the officer as Lieutenant Kelly from Second Battalion. Kelly turned to face McBride as he approached the door where they stood.

"What've we got here, Kelly?" McBride asked as he walked up to the three men.

"Well, since a picture's better than a thousand words, take a look," Kelly said, turning his head toward the room behind him.

McBride peered into the room where a man lay on a stretcher. He was naked with a sheet covering the lower part of his body. Fatigue shirt and pants and socks and boots were lying scattered about the room as if the medics had quickly removed his clothing to see the extent of injuries. A doctor clad in a white smock covered in bright red blood smears hovered over the man's face, intently focusing on his task as he worked sewing up one of several deep, jagged cuts about the man's face and head. A female nurse and a male medic assisted him as he worked. The man moaned and stirred slightly.

"He's in a lot of pain, Doctor," the nurse said calmly. "Can't we give him morphine?"

"Not with all that alcohol in him," the doctor said just as calmly. "I'll continue with this, but you get on the phone. Get me an orthodontist down here; he'll have a challenge with these battered teeth. And alert them that I'll need an ophthalmologist sooner or later to check for vision problems."

The nurse acknowledged the doctor's orders and turned immediately to leave the room. On the way out, she stooped and deftly scooped up some of the scattered clothing lying about as she hurriedly walked out. The male medic moved to replace her position across the table from the doctor.

"Clip the line here," the doctor said, holding the two ends of the surgical cord up for the medic to clip. "I'm going to tie this section off and begin a new one lower down."

McBride stepped into the room and peered around the doctor at the man on the stretcher. He didn't recognize the soldier and was relieved that it wasn't someone from his platoon. In spite of his relief, he was shocked at the sight of the man's battered face. Both upper and lower lips were severely swollen with long splits that were already sewed up, the ends of the surgical cord as yet unclipped and protruding upward. Both eyes were purplish red and swollen shut, and his nose had an odd slant to it, suggesting that it was broken. There were several significant lacerations about his forehead on the right side, but the most serious wounds were several jagged cuts that started above his left eye and extended down the side of his face. The doctor and the medic were intently working on these lacerations as McBride looked on; they paid him no mind.

"My God!" McBride said under his breath, as he reeled back and turned away from the sight. "I've never seen anyone beat up so bad,"

As he walked from the room to again face Kelly and the two MPs, he was thinking that the man on the operating table must have been crazy wild and the MPs had to use extreme force. "He's beat up pretty bad," he said to the MPs, looking from one to the other. "Did you guys have to subdue him with your night sticks?"

"No, sir, Lieutenant," the first MP said. "He was out when we got there. Lying flat out on the latrine floor."

McBride paused a moment and then looked at Kelly with a knowing look. "Did what I think happened, happen?" he asked Kelly.

"Yes," Kelly said decisively, slowly shaking his head up and down and returning McBride's knowing look. "Your guy did that."

"Where is he?" McBride asked,

Kelly motioned further down the hallway where three MPs stood just outside an open door, talking in low mummers and tapping their night sticks against their legs.

McBride walked to stand at the doorway where he could see Mark sitting upward on an emergency room table. He walked into the room and faced Mark.

"Okay, Bergner," McBride began as Mark sat on the table stripped from the waist up. "Fill me in with what happened from the time you entered the EM Club to the time I got here."

Mark's fatigue shirt and T-shirt lay across a nearby chair, and large red blotches stood out against the white of his undershirt. His upper body revealed multiple reddish lacerations with bluish outlines, and the area around his eyes was swollen and puffy with the skin cut and broken in several places. Dried blood remained in his eyelashes and hair.

"I first went to the latrine, and that's where I ran into this psycho-jerk," Mark began.

"Look this way, please," the medic requested as he swabbed the cut above Mark's right eye. "Wallowing around on a latrine floor is a good way of contacting germs and bacteria, so first I have to make sure the cuts are cleaned and sterilized."

"Then what happened?" McBride asked.

"He took one look at me and started swinging," Mark said, turning back to face the lieutenant. "I took a couple blows before I knew what was coming."

"Hold still, now," the medic said, bending around to apply the antiseptic, coming between Mark and McBride. "This is going to sting. Brace yourself."

"I know there's been bad blood between you two," McBride said, stepping to the side to look around the medic. "What was that all about?"

"Yeah, it started at a soccer match shortly after I joined Charlie Company almost two years ago. He took a swing at Myers, and I stepped in. No big deal for me, but he's held a grudge," Mark said, wincing from the medic's antiseptic and trying to look at McBride while still facing the medic. In addition to the cut above his right eye, his face was badly bruised, displaying reddened, skin-scraped patches on his chin and forehead, and a dark purple area was spreading around his left eye. His neck had red and blue bruises and scratches on both sides and across the throat. "I was able to avoid trouble until now."

"There . . . that'll take care of the face until Doc can get here and sew up the cut," the medic said, stepping back as if to admire his work and smiling at Mark. "I must say, I do beautiful work. Now, let's see about those hands."

At that moment, Kelly walked into the room. "This is Lieutenant Kelly," McBride said, nodding toward the lieutenant. "He's platoon leader for your friend down the hall."

"Yikes! These hands have been busy," the medic said, holding up Marks hands to view them closely. He seemed to be enjoying his work as he took one hand and began gently cleaning the swollen and broken skin with antiseptic. He ignored the two officers. "All cut up and maybe some broken bones," he continued. "Flex your fingers for me, please."

"Sorry to meet under these circumstances," Kelley said to Mark, nodding.

"Uh, fingers all working," the medic said, continuing to ignore the officers. "No broken bones. Good! This is going to be fun."

"You guys are ghouls," McBride said to the medic.

"All in a day's work, Lieutenant," the medic said back to McBride without looking at him. "We see this every weekend. Looks like it's starting early this week."

Mark nodded at Lieutenant Kelley but said nothing. Kelly motioned for McBride to follow him, and they stepped out into the hallway. The two officers conversed in a low, rambling conversation. Mark leaned toward the door, trying to hear their talk, but their discussion could not be heard back in the emergency room. He winced again as the medic began cleaning his hand with antiseptic.

"Sorry, but this has to be done. Infection has to be headed off at this stage of the game," he said as he gently swabbed Mark's hands, his attention closely focused on his work. "If not, you'll have big trouble later on."

Out in the hallway, the two officers spoke in a low, confidential tone. "We've got to be careful here," McBride said, nodding his head back toward the room with Mark. "That's a good man in there, and these cases sometimes rise to court-martial level. It'll be a shame if he gets into trouble over this when he didn't ask for it."

"I can't say that for my man," Lieutenant Kelly said. "He's been trouble since he came to my platoon, always fighting, can't get along with the others . . . He's hurt a couple of my guys pretty bad." He paused a moment. "I've tried to get him transferred out of my outfit but haven't had any luck so far."

"Did you get a statement from the bartender?"

"Yeah, he said the first soldier had been in the club drinking for two or three hours," Kelly began. "Said he had drunk quiet a lot and that he seemed mad at the world, cussing everybody from his platoon sergeant to his CO."

"What'd he say about the second soldier?"

"Said the second soldier had just walked in and was minding his own business."

"How do you see it? In a legal sense, I mean?"

"My guy attacked your sergeant, unprovoked," Lieutenant Kelly said. "There are several charges that can be made from that alone. In addition, he shouldn't have been in the EM Club in the first place. He was still on duty and had bugged out from his detail. I'm writing up the whole nine yards against him."

"He'll get a court-martial for sure," McBride said.

The two officers then reentered the room where the medic was still working on Mark's hands.

As they stood watching the medic work on Mark, the medic from down the hall brushed in and began assisting the first medic. "How's the one down the hall?" the first medic asked the second one.

"Not good," the second medic said. "The nurse has returned, and they're both busy with him. They're calling in more doctors."

"How is he compared to this one?" the first medic persisted, talking as if Mark and the two officers were not present. "This one has some serious bruises and a cut above the right eye but no broken bones that I've found yet."

"Much worse," the second medic said. "In addition to what I see here, the other one's going to need more stitches; he's got multiple facial lacerations that go all the way to the bone; plus, he needs some serious dental work, and his nose appeared to be broken." Looking up at Mark, he asked. "From the looks of the other guy, you know how to use these hands. Are you a prize fighter?"

"No!" Mark said flatly.

With that, McBride gave Mark an okay nod, and the two officers left the room. As they walked down the hallway, McBride said, "So we both agree who was at fault here."

"Yes, it was unmistakably my guy who started the fight."

"Okay, let our reports be clear on that," McBride said. "Sergeant Bergner was defending himself and not at fault in any way."

"Agreed," Kelly said. "I've now got a solid case against my guy. I'm sure the CO and the provost marshal will view this as we do."

"Somebody had to stop Ricco before he killed someone," McBride said as they left the building. He stopped for a moment on the sidewalk, gazing at Kelly with a thoughtful look. "I'm just sorry it had to be Sergeant Bergner. He's a good soldier."

CHAPTER 55

THE FOLLOWING WEEKEND, MARK HAD duty, but the next one he was free. On Friday, he called The Camera Shop and talked to Lauren from a phone booth at the EM Club. When asked if she would like to make the return trip to Martinschule, she said yes. They agreed to meet at the Martinschule train stop at ten o'clock in the morning as they had some twenty months before. The battalion was scheduled to rotate in two weeks. Both he and Lauren knew this but had never discussed it.

Mark had recovered well from the fight, spending only one day in the hospital before being released back to Charlie Company for light duty. Other than being considered somewhat of a hero by both officers and men, his daily routine returned to normal. By the day of his Martinschule trip, his face had mended to be clear of the bruises and the purple eye, and his hands had lost the puffiness and soreness. The only evidence of the incident was the cut above his right eye that had an inch-long reddened scar with small red dots around its edges where the doctor had removed the stitches the day before.

Arriving early at Martinschule, Mark waited on the platform until Lauren's train arrived. Although it was a clear day, the temperature at the Martinschule altitude was cooler than where he had come from, and he paced the platform to counteract the chill and ease the heaviness in his chest. A train going in the opposite direction came by, stopping with a loud jerk and then continuing on in a noisy commotion while releasing sporadic clouds of steam. Mark recalled the first time he waited on the platform. That now seemed far away in time. Much had happened since then, but he didn't want to think back or ahead. He wanted only to think and value this day, this moment in time.

Mark caught sight of Lauren as she stepped down from the train car following a short, heavyset woman with two children in tow. She paused on the platform, looking around and headed toward Mark once she spotted him. Carrying a backpack and dressed in her tan walking shorts and a loose-fitting, blue cotton sweatshirt with "Forest Grove Athletics" emblazoned across the front, she looked as a college student might appear coming home from school. Her blond hair stood out strikingly against the blue of her shirt, and Mark could only smile as she walked toward him. The shirt was the second one he had given her many months before when she had asked for something of his she could sleep in. Although she appeared as youthful and attractive as the first day he met her, her eyes didn't seem as bright as usual or her greeting as carefree and cheerful.

"Here, it's your turn to carry this thing," she said, laughing lightly and handing Mark the backpack before reaching up to kiss him. She immediately recoiled back, looking at the scar above his right eye. "Mark! What's happened to your face?"

"Oh, I had an accident," Mark said nonchalantly. He lied, not wanting to go into the details of the story.

"How? When?" she asked, stretching on tiptoes to get a closer view of the wound. "That's a big cut and so close to the eye," she continued, looking so closely that Mark could feel her breath on his face as she talked. He had a strong desire to hold her, but he held back.

"I was moving some equipment," he said with an easygoing laugh and instinctively stepping back to resist temptation. "It's nothing."

"Why didn't you let me know?"

"It's nothing," he repeated, throwing the backpack across his shoulder and taking her arm to leave the train depot. "We'll talk about it later."

In the foothills above Martinschule, Mark and Lauren found their old spot unchanged. The air smelled crisp and clean and cool, and the September sun warmed them as they approached the same tree and found a spot in the grass that had comfortable shade.

"*Déjà vu*," Lauren said as they paused under the tree and looked back at Martinschule, then south to the distant valley.

Lauren had led the way and had set a lively pace for them on their trip uphill. Mark had followed, marveling at her strong stride and glad he could exercise his legs on the uphill climb. He had learned the mental benefits of strenuous exercise from jogging and boxing. He discovered that by exercising to the point of exhaustion, he could drive away the black moods that had been coming over him more frequently lately. Thankful for the mildly heavy backpack and Lauren's strong pace, he felt better when they reached their spot on the crest of the hill.

"What have you got in here?" he asked as he set the pack down with a thump.

Lauren smiled. "I'll show you," she said as she began to unpack the contents. Spreading out a white cotton blanket, she then placed the pack at the head of the blanket and began unpacking the rest of the items. She first placed a bottle of white wine and two small glasses upright against the pack. "There are also apples and bread and cheese in the pack and a thermos of coffee."

"Good," Mark nodded. "All the comforts of home."

"And there's my camera and my new zoom lens and plenty of film," she continued. "I want to try a time-exposure against the mountains when the sun gets in the right position."

"Did you bring the kitchen sink?" Mark asked, smiling. He didn't feel like being witty, but he wanted to keep the conversation light. Lauren smiled and shrugged her shoulders. She seemed to be happy, but when he could see her eyes directly, he saw in the blue a matured depth, a kind of resignation that wasn't there before. He wanted her to be happy, and he wanted her to enjoy the day, and he was determined to work at that. Any dark thoughts he might have of his own, he could block out just by looking at her and being near her. He uncorked the wine and poured some in each glass and then set the corked bottle back against the pack. The subtle, earthy aroma of the wine briefly filled the air around them.

"Let me see that place again," Lauren said, reaching up to touch Mark's face just off the cut. They sat cross-legged on the blanket, facing each other. When she leaned forward to get a closer look, he could detect that clean, delicate scent that he knew so well. "Does it hurt, Mark?" she asked.

"Not a bit," Mark said as he turned his face to meet her touch. He then took her hand and held it in his own. He wanted to get the conversation off the injury. "I've missed you."

"And I've missed you," she said quietly, her voice dropping to almost a whisper and her face becoming soft and clear of expression.

It was a look that Mark knew well, and one that he found irresistible. "We need more time," he said almost unconsciously. He touched her face gently. He could feel her breath on his fingers as they lightly moved across her chin, the touch so soft as to be hardly felt.

"Let's don't talk about time," she said.

Realizing what he had said, Mark was immediately sorry. He had wanted to keep the mood light. "Yeah, you're right," he said.

"Sorry." Then to change the subject, he added, "Aren't you going to set your camera up for the valley shot?"

"Yes, I suppose," she said. She handed Mark her glass, which she had not drank from, and then stood up and began removing camera equipment from the backpack. She took out a small adjustable tripod and walked a few feet to set it up next to the tree. She worked confidently, deftly attaching the photo lens to the camera, then the camera to the tripod, then bending down and aiming it toward the village in the valley. She adjusted the camera settings, and after taking one shot, came back to the blanket and resumed her place facing Mark. Her face had taken on a serious look.

"It looks the same," she said

"What looks the same?" he asked, adjusting his own position to better accommodate hers and to view the scene before them.

"The valley there," she pointed to the valley below with the brown and green and yellow checkerboard fields and the black winding road that ran up to the village. In the distance, the village appeared small and unreal, like in a photograph. It had but one street and only a few brown buildings with red roofs, but a prominent looking church with a tall steeple stood at its center. After a short distance, the road leaving the village split in two different directions as each branch meandered off toward the mountains. They both gazed at the scene momentarily. Then suddenly Lauren said, "Let's play a game. Let's make a story about this scene."

"Okay, you start," Mark said. He could see she was working at keeping the mood light, the same as he was.

"I will," she said. "Let's see. Two weary travelers met in Martinschule and traveled up that winding road to find rest and food at an inn in that village in the valley," she began her story.

"Maybe they find a little wine and music there also," Mark said with an amused smile.

"Maybe," she said. She grew silent then, quietly gazing at the landscape below. Her look went past the village, up to the distant mountains, and then back to the village. "The mountains represent the future and hardships for the two travelers," she continued.

"But there's also fun and adventure there," Mark said, smiling.

"Maybe," she said again and then grew quiet.

Mark waited a moment for Lauren to continue. When she didn't, he said, "I'm enjoying your story." He put his arm around her, briefly pulling her close. His longing grew, but she was not looking at him. He turned back to the scene below. "What else do you see?"

"I see the two travelers in the village," she continued finally. "And they laugh and sing and have a wonderful time. They stay as long as they can, but then they must leave and continue their travel on the road toward the mountain. At the point where the road separates—" Lauren suddenly stopped talking, her look fixed on the distant scene. She seemed held to it by some inner force.

"Yes, go on," Mark said finally, causing her to break the look.

"No, let's talk about something else," she said. "Let's have some lunch."

"Okay, I could go for some bread and cheese," he said. "I'm hungry."

"*Jawohl*, Herr Mark," Lauren said, feigning a waiter's demeanor. From the backpack, she retrieved a small blue tablecloth and spread it out on the blanket. She then took a plate and knife and sliced several pieces of cheese and placed it before them. They ate the bread and cheese and sipped the wine, chatting and making small talk. They ate slowly, enjoying the simple meal and being careful to keep their conversation light.

"I've often thought of this place since we were here before," Mark said as Lauren picked up after their meal. He felt their mood had lightened, and he wanted to keep it going in that direction. And he knew he must focus on this day and this place, that their hilltop above Martinschule was special for both of them. Although he had all along felt the aura of that day long ago, he had not fully grasped the importance of this second visit until now. "I'm glad we've come back," he said quietly.

She didn't answer for a moment, and then looking around, she said, "This place will always have a special meaning for me." Her voice was low, and her eyes dropped to her lap.

"*Prost!*" he replied quickly, not wanting to let her mood fall. Their eyes met over the glasses, their look holding as they sipped, each savoring the dry sweetness and warming effect of the wine. Again, Mark noticed the rhythm of her breathing beneath the soccer shirt as it rose and fell ever so slightly. His desire to hold her increased.

Her eyes dropped briefly and then came back up to meet his. This time, her look stayed with his and did not waver. This time, Mark could not look away. They had not had a chance to be completely alone for several weeks, and the longing that grew with that separation and their awareness of the moment and of each other grew quickly. He reached for her, pulled her to him, and softly laid her down on the blanket. She shifted her position to adjust to his, and her arms came up to embrace him. They kissed eagerly and passionately, repeatedly; each responding in kind to the other as their breathing and movements and touch became their sole awareness, blocking out all else.

The intensity of their lovemaking grew rapidly, their emotions and instincts controlling their physical and mental selves. Each knew the other well, knew the other's wants and desires, and related to these in the other as much as their own. Each immersed themselves in the sound and feel and taste of the other, savoring the other's responses, reacting to the other's needs, and yielding to the other's wants, absorbed by their synergy of passion.

Later, they lay exhausted and clinging, drifting into and out of light sleep before stirring and awaking to the consciousness of their desperate capacity to hold on to the moment.

After a time, Lauren sat up and gazed out across the valley to the mountains. Mark turned to see what she was looking at.

"It's almost sunset," she said.

"Yes," Mark said as he repositioned himself to sit beside her. They sat quietly as if mesmerized for a time. Suddenly, Mark turned to Lauren, speaking slowly and deliberately. "Lauren . . . do you want to talk about it?"

She looked at him, hesitating for a moment, then spoke softly, "No, do you?"

"No," he said. They then turned their attention back to the west as the bottom of the orange glow approached the mountaintop.

They watched the glow settling toward the mountaintop a moment longer and then gathered up their things and left their spot on the hill.

CHAPTER 56

"**A**T EASE, MEN!" CAPTAIN WILLIAMS said as Sergeants Bergner and Wade stood at attention before the captain in his office. "You men have been brought before me to administer company punishment under Article 15 of the US Army Military Code of Justice."

Captain Williams spoke quietly, officially, without enthusiasm. Mark and Sam had been called out of morning formation by the first sergeant and told to report to the CO after the formation broke up. The two men stood at ease before the captain, and the first sergeant stood to the right of them. The company clerk stood behind the first sergeant with a notepad in his hand, recording the process.

"You are being punished for complicity in the vehicle incident in which two German citizens were . . ." The captain's voice droned on as he restated the incident in a formal manner and without much effect on the two men. They had known for some time what they were in for. After the testimony under oath that Myers had consumed little alcohol on the night of the accident was given to the investigation board and later proven to be false, the officers of the court-martial had no choice but to proceed with due process in a matter of perjury. It didn't matter how sympathetic the members of the court-martial board might have been toward the witnesses' reasons and motivations in providing the false information; once the facts go into the records, they must be addressed. If the offense revealed by the recorded facts is not addressed, then the ranking officer of the court-martial board is liable and can be charged with dereliction of duty.

Colonel Pearson, the ranking member on the Myers court-martial, at first said they had no choice but to set up a subsequent court-martial dealing with a charge of perjury. But when Captain Williams and First Battalion's Colonel Evans had an official meeting with the court-martial colonel and pleaded the case of the two men to be charged, Colonel Pearson listened to their appeal with interest. After Williams pointed out that the two men charged were outstanding soldiers and had impeccable records, the colonel began to waver in his attitude toward the court-martial. With this step forward, Williams went on to say that the two men charged had just turned twenty-two years of age and had been indoctrinated and influenced by army tradition and culture to defend members of their outfit. It was the soldiers' code to protect each other. Colonel Evans then spoke up, saying he hoped they could find a way to have due process without a court-martial.

After giving the situation serious consideration, Colonel Pearson said they could have due process by administering company-level punishment in lieu of a trial by court-martial if the company-level punishment was appropriate to the charge. To Mark and Wade's advantage, plans for a court-martial were cancelled.

As Williams spoke, Mark was well aware of how close he and Wade came to being tried by court-martial and having that serious black mark on their records. He was strongly appreciative and respectful of his CO and the others who had supported them. In spite of this respect for his superiors, he was becoming resigned to whatever was coming next. He felt that he had no individual control over events, and to try to change them was not only a futile affair but a risky one. It was best to play the game; that way, there would be less trouble and fewer disappointments.

"And so I have no choice but to reduce both of you in rank and sentence you to thirty days barracks arrest with hard labor as extra duty. This, of course, suspends your Class A Pass privileges and limits you activities to post details as assigned," the captain was saying as Mark's attention returned to his place before the CO. Williams paused a moment as if considering what to say next. "Sergeant Bergner, you are being reduced two grades in rank, because you were ranking man at the time, and the army holds the most senior man more responsible." Mark sensed regret in the captain's voice as he finished his official duty.

The captain then paused again before continuing. "Off the record now, men, this is not my doing. I'm a soldier like you and following orders, and the army always comes first." He then turned to the first sergeant and ordered him to dismiss the men back to their duties.

As they left the CO's office, Sergeant Andrade called Mark aside, saying he wanted to speak to him alone. He told him he thought that it was bad luck and unfortunate circumstances that had put the three of them in such a rotten situation. "As far as I'm concerned," he said, "you're all good soldiers. You were doing what good soldiers do—protecting each other."

Mark merely nodded. He had already accepted the worst. Myers had died in the army prison at Mannheim; this had left him both saddened and hopelessly pessimistic, leaving him expecting his own punishment and Wade's as well. Being busted in rank back to a PFC didn't bother him for some reason, and the barracks arrest and hard labor didn't matter much because of the impending rotation. As a matter of fact, it seemed proper and correct in view of the way things were. If you were unlucky and got caught between the good of the military and some lesser force, the lesser force would most likely be sacrificed. And if you were somehow associated with the lesser force, you would also be sacrificed. It's the way things were. It's the forces beyond our control that shape our lives. And often it is chance and circumstance that bring these forces to bear. Mark held no animosity or regret toward the army, just resignation to his luck. He knew, though, that the CO pulling his pass would not keep him on post.

As Mark turned to walk away, Sergeant Andrade said, "Hold up, there's one more thing I want to say." He turned to the company clerk, who always hovered near him. "Go to the chow hall and bring me back a cup of black coffee." The clerk pointed out there was a fresh pot of coffee in the orderly room. First Sergeant Andrade barked a quick, "I want chow hall coffee! Move!" The clerk hurried away.

"You know how I hate paperwork," Andrade began, turning back to Mark. "Well, that MOS change of yours to heavy weapons has somehow gotten pushed under the pile on my desk." He then moved closer and spoke a little lower. "With all the commotion and excitement of mobilization, I doubt seriously if I'll be able to work my way to the bottom of that stack before rotation." He then looked closely at Mark for emphasis and to let his words sink in.

In that moment of exchanging looks, Mark knew the first sergeant was giving him a break but didn't realize its full significance. He would delay the MOS change until after rotation. But why? So what?

"I can tell you now that it will be chaos when we hit Fort Bliss, getting ready for retraining and redeployment," Andrade continued. "Nobody will think about those MOS change papers. More than likely, I'll just lose them in the shuffle."

"That's okay with me," Mark said, working to get his full meaning.

"I know you're due to be discharged shortly after we arrive stateside. I also know the army will be extending the enlistments of those who hold a critical MOS."

"Yes, I've heard that," Mark said, beginning to understand the significance of losing the paperwork

"And something else—the captain, without realizing it, did you a favor by taking away your stripes," Andrade continued. "Being busted in rank and not possessing a critical MOS, you're less likely to be considered desirable army material by those clowns in personnel."

Mark was beginning to understand. The first sergeant was going out of his way, even sticking his out neck out, to help him. He wanted to say something. "I appreciate this, Sergeant—"

"There's nothing to say," Andrade said, stopping him midsentence. "The army is supposed to take care of its own, Mark. And it does in most cases. But this is a special case. When it comes to the good of the individual versus the good of the army, the individual always loses."

"I understand," Mark said firmly. "I see now." And Mark did understand for the first time how the first sergeant's simple but deliberate act of losing the paperwork could impact his life so profoundly. It would deflect the forces driving him toward an unknown fate to one toward civilian life.

"You men were doing what all good soldiers do," First Sergeant Andrade continued. "You were holding the line by protecting the man on your left and the man on your right, the fundamental nature of all good soldiers down the line of all generations of good soldiers in all wars and in all countries."

Mark was grateful when he fully realized the sergeant's intentions and the break it would offer him, but he was astonished by what it revealed about the sergeant himself. Here was a real soldier performing his duty, and this duty was not only the official version of formal military procedure and behavior but the version adhering to the core and essence of what makes soldiering work. First Sergeant Andrade, to compensate in his own eyes for the army's miscarriage of justice, was protecting the dignity and honor of the vision he held of the army.

With that, the first sergeant stiffened, resuming his military bearing. Mark thought he was through talking, but he spoke again. "Now back to your duties, Soldier."

CHAPTER 57

TWO DAYS BEFORE THE BATTALION was to rotate, the men of Second Platoon decided to get together at the EM club to have their short-timer's party. Everyone went to the club, and the drinking and the clowning around began. This lasted but a short time, for most wanted to go off post to their favorite *Gasthaus* for the last time. Everyone left except Mark and Wade. This suited Mark very well, for he didn't feel like celebrating, and the fact he and Wade were doing company punishment and didn't have a pass gave him his excuse to separate from the rest of the platoon.

When the others left, the club quieted down. Only a few soldiers from another outfit remained sitting at the far end of the bar. These soldiers drank and chatted, laughing occasionally, and kept the juke box going. Mark and Wade sat at a table next to Louie's end of the bar and had several beers. After a few beers, Mark grew quiet and preoccupied, but Wade stayed in high spirits and talked freely.

"It's been two years," Wade said. "It'll be good to get back to the states."

Mark didn't respond. He glanced up at Wade and then back to his beer. Wade watched him for a moment. He seemed concerned with Mark's moodiness. "Cheer up, Mark!" he said with enthusiasm. "We're going home! Think of that!"

"Yeah," Mark answered.

Wade was silent as he studied Mark. "You don't want to go, do you?" he finally asked.

"It's not something I want to talk about," Mark said.

Wade again grew silent. When he continued, he spoke quietly. "Well, look. There comes a time when we have to move on," he began. "I said my good-byes. Ursula had me out to her place a few nights back, and we had dinner and a few drinks and tied up all the loose ends. I'm looking ahead now."

"That's good," Mark said. "That's good for you."

Wade paused as if searching for something more to say. "Okay," he said finally. "What's the problem? We're getting discharged soon after we hit the States. Your tour of duty will be over. You can send for her, can't you?"

Mark didn't answer and wouldn't look at Wade.

"Well, can't you?"

"My tour of duty won't be over," Mark said with finality. He still wouldn't look at Wade.

"How do you figure that?"

Mark glanced at Wade. Seeing that Wade was waiting for his response, he said, "There's duty to family, tradition, profession, and whatever else life may find to trap you. It never ends. That damn bucket-of-water crap of the captain's never ends. It never ends for me, and it never ends for her." He paused a moment and then continued, almost in a whisper. "And it leaves nothing for us."

"I don't understand, Mark," Wade said. "I know you two have special problems, but can't you get together and talk it out?" Wade paused, waiting. When Mark didn't answer, he continued. "Have you two ever really talked about it and tried to work it out?"

"No, we've never talked about it."

"What! You've never talked about it?" Wade said incredulously. "Then how the hell can she know what you know if you never talked about it? Tell me that, Mark!"

"Some things—the important things," Mark began slowly, patiently, "if we had talked about them, would have been painful to the other. But I knew and she knew what they were, and each of us knew that the other knew. So we never talked about them."

"Oh hell, Mark," Wade said, as if scolding him. "When you get home, send for her, and you two get on with your life. That's all there is to it."

Mark looked up at him, but he didn't answer. He knew Wade couldn't understand. He took a long drink, emptying his mug.

"Well, can't you?"

Mark stood up ignoring the question. "I need a refill," he said as he walked to the bar.

At the bar, Louie handed Mark's refilled mug back to him. "Going home? That's great for you," he said. Louie was a German national who had worked at the EM Club for some time and had made friends with many of the soldiers. In the past two years, he had become close friends with Mark and Wade. As the time neared for them to rotate, he often said he would miss them. He seemed genuinely sad they were leaving. "This one's on the house," he said.

When Mark sat back down, he quickly said to Wade, "Louie's buying. He said to bring your mug."

Wade took his mug to the bar for the refill. He got his refill, and after shaking hands with Louie, he returned to the table. As he sat down, he repeated, "Well, can't you?"

Mark didn't answer. He looked at Wade a moment and then said, "We've had some times here, haven't we? I'll never forget the way we shot up that deuce-and-a-half down at Miesau."

"Yeah, good times, bad times," Wade said, giving Mark a puzzled look.

"I still think of Dave," Mark said. He obviously wanted to change the subject.

"Yeah, me too," Wade said. Wade continued to watch Mark with a serious face. Then, as if to cheer up the conversation, he said, "You know, there's a lot about this place I'm going to miss—the *Gasthauses*, the camaraderie, the beer drinking. And after it's all over, I'm sure I'll miss Andrade, McBride, and even Captain," he continued, laughing as if to influence Mark with his cheer.

"Sam, I'm staying," Mark suddenly said, staring straight at Wade.

"What!"

"Yeah, I'm staying," Mark said decisively. "I'm tired of the army and all its self-sacrificing ways and traditions, and going home is just more of the same."

"You can't stay," Wade said. "You'll be AWOL."

"So be it," Mark said with determination.

"And after three days, they'll declare you a deserter," Wade said, looking hard at Mark.

"So be it," Mark said again.

"And sooner or later, they'll find you, and you'll go to prison," Wade continued. "With the war in Korea, they can get you for desertion in time of war. That's damn serious. You'll get twenty years or maybe more—spend the rest of your life in a federal prison."

"I don't care. I've made up my mind," Mark said. "Besides, they won't find me."

"If you desert, they'll find you," Wade said flatly. "But it doesn't matter. If you miss reveille in the morning, I'm coming after you," he continued, growing angrier as he talked. "I'll get McBride to give me a couple guys, and we'll find you, and we'll drag your ass back here. I'm not going to let you go down like this."

Mark stared at Wade. Although he knew Wade wouldn't come after him, he knew he was right. But in his frame of mind, Mark could see no other way. They both sat without speaking for a time and slowly sipped their beers. The club's juke box was playing the German song "Lili Marleen." Mark understood the lyrics and hoped the song would end quickly. Just as the music stopped, Mark spoke. "I'm not leaving, Sam, and that's it."

CHAPTER 58

THE FOLLOWING DAY WAS THE day before the battalion would leave Grahfenvern Post for good. Mark knew he couldn't get a pass, but he applied for one anyway. "Permission denied," First Sergeant Andrade said. Orders were posted. The battalion was ready and on standby status. The next morning, twelve hundred men of the reinforced First Battalion would begin to move. Orders stated they would travel by bus to the Frankfurt Bahnhof and then travel by train north to the port of Bremerhaven to load onto troop ships. "No passes for anyone under any circumstances," the first sergeant continued.

"Colonel's orders."

Mark left without permission. Late in the afternoon, he traveled to a village two train stops past Lauren's stop as they had planned, acquired a room, and then returned to the depot. By the time her train arrived, it had begun to rain in a slow, steady drizzle, the type of weather that would last for days. They immediately went to the *Gasthaus* where he had secured the room.

"It's the best I could do," Mark said as he opened the door, revealing a small, dimly lit room with one bed, one table with a lamp, and a small window on the wall next to the bed. The table lamp cast a dim yellow glow across the bed and up one wall, leaving the remaining space in dark shadows that pressed against and merged into the lighted space around the bed. "It's the only room they had available."

Lauren didn't speak but looked around as she removed her wet coat and draped it across the chair. "There's only one *Gasthaus* at this train station," she finally said absently. She walked to the window and opened it. The soft patter and dripping sounds rose up from the street two stories below their room. The cool air from the open window filled the room, and the rhythmic patter of the rain projected a confining oppressiveness. She sat on the bed without speaking or looking at him.

"Shouldn't we close the window?" he asked gently. "The rain's not coming in, but the outside air is cold and damp."

"No . . . please leave it open," she said softly, still not looking at him. "The room's so small . . . I feel closed in."

Mark opened his overnight bag and took out a bottle of cognac and two glasses and poured a small amount of the dark, red liquid into each glass. "Sip this slowly," he said gently. "It'll warm you."

She took the glass, took a small sip, and then held the glass in her lap. He removed his raincoat and sat across from her on the bed and sipped the cognac, his eyes resting on her back where her hair fell across her sweater. He wanted to say something but didn't know how to begin. He wanted to hold her, but he knew it wasn't the right time. With only the low, steady hiss of the damp night coming through the open window, they sat silently for a long period of time.

"Lauren," Mark finally said, "we need to talk." He spoke as quietly and gently as he could. He then waited. When she didn't answer, he continued. "We need to talk about us."

She seemed at first not to have heard him. Finally, she said, "What can we say at this point?" She spoke quietly and without looking around. "What can be said that would change anything?"

"I'm not going tomorrow, Lauren," Mark said decisively, nodding to emphasize his point. He spoke up as if his raised voice could make it more plausible. "I've thought it over, and I'm going to leave the army and stay here."

Lauren didn't respond immediately. Then she slowly turned to face Mark across the bed. Her face registered a deep concern as she looked directly at him, holding his eyes with hers. She didn't speak for a moment as if carefully considering his words. Her eyes at first reflected a brief brightness, as if something pleasant had occurred to her, but then dimmed noticeably with obvious recognition of something very wrong. Without breaking her look, she began to gradually turn her head from side to side in unshakable and unmistakable disagreement.

"Oh, Mark," she said slowly, "that won't change our real situation. It will only bring you trouble."

"I can handle the trouble," Mark said. "I'll find a way to make it work. I can speak the language. I'll find work and we can make it. You'll see."

"Mark, sooner or later they'll find you. And when they do—" Lauren cut off her speech as if she didn't want to think about it.

"They won't find me!" Mark said, his voice growing desperate. "I'll see to that."

"Mark, stop!" Lauren said, putting her hand on Mark's lips and holding his eyes with hers. "Listen to me! Listen . . . I understand what you're trying to do, and I wish it would work, but it won't. It won't!" she continued, stressing her words. "It will only bring you trouble, and you'll be doing it because of me, and I'd have that on my conscience the rest of my life." Lauren held Mark's face, not letting him look away, her eyes locked to his as if passing to him thoughts and feelings that let him think as she did. "I won't agree to this. I won't let you do it!"

Mark stared at her, shaken by her passionate opposition to the plan he had so carefully worked out. He had never seen her so serious and determined before. And seeing her distress and agitation and wanting to calm her, he quickly said, "Okay, okay, we'll talk about it. Just don't be upset."

At first, he only agreed with her hoping to make her feel better so he could get on with his argument. He thought if he could get her to relax, he could convince her his plan would work. But the more he tried to sell her on his idea, the more adamantly she opposed the plan. Slowly, with her persistent and unyielding objection, Mark's argument began to weaken. Finally, realizing her mind was firmly and decisively set and that no matter what he said or did she would not give in, he began to listen.

As he listened, he slowly began to realize her opposition came not only from fear but from an awareness of what the outcome of the act of desertion would mean. To desert his unit would mean having to live in secret with constant fear of the authorities and always suspicious of everyone around them. With a clearer understanding of the trouble his plan to desert would bring to them, his resolve and determination to leave the army began to waver. With his attitude changing, his plan to abandon his unit and stay in Germany suddenly seemed foolish and unworkable. Feeling hopeless and dejected, Mark turned away, staring into the darkness of the far wall. He gazed into the darkness for a long time, his mind racing trying to find a way.

Finally, he stood up from the bed and went to the table to refill his glass with cognac. Taking a long drink, he welcomed the strong, sweet aroma and the harsh, burning taste of the alcohol. For some reason, the image of the war memorial in her village crossed his mind. Mark turned back to the bed where Lauren had now reclined on her side, facing the window and away from him. *She's one of them,* he thought, draining the glass. Then it struck him that they both were victims of what that memorial represented. *Sacrifice and duty . . . it's our heritage,* she had said. He lay down on the bed and held her close, comforted by her familiar feel and the warmth of her body.

They lay quietly, neither one speaking, both staring out at the darkness and listening to the methodical, relentless whisper coming through the open window of the room. *It's like a vague and distant voice calling*, he thought, as his mind desperately sought a way for them to stay together.

They neither made love nor slept. Far into the night, they arose and talked more. His new plan disregarded the idea of deserting, but he said he would stay with his unit until discharged. At that time, they would reunite according to whatever plan they worked out at that time.

"Okay, then this is our plan," Mark said, after considering all practical options. "After I'm discharged, we'll talk it over and decide whether you'll come to New York or whether I'll come back to Germany." He went on to say they would say good-bye and stay in touch by letters. Mark done all the planning and was upbeat and positive and assured her all would work out well. Lauren quietly listened but was noncommittal.

The following morning, Wade breathed an unmistakable sigh of relief as Mark walked into the barracks in time to make reveille. The outfit had been packed and ready for days. That morning, they were shipping out.

CHAPTER 59

WHEN MARK'S BUS MOVED UP in the line of busses in front of the Bahnhof, the front door opened, and the soldiers began to unload. Mark moved to the door and turned sideways, balancing the duffle bag high on his shoulder, and stepped down into the light rain that had been falling since the previous day. The cool, wet air washed over his face, clearing his mind of the mental dullness of the bus ride and the hurry-up-and-wait routine of the military moving masses of troops. He had hardly slept in the past forty-eight hours, and the exhaustion and numbness increased his melancholy.

The man in front of him stopped, and Mark bumped into him, pushing him forward in the line. Someone shoved into Mark as more soldiers poured out of the buses. A mass of olive drab uniforms formed in the street, which was black with shiny spots of rainwater. The mass slowly moved forward as if a single entity. Having little individual control, each soldier moved at a pace and direction dictated by the amorphous mass. Hardly anyone spoke or complained. More busses pulled up from the line of dark green busses stretched out down the street and began unloading. Soldiers streamed out of the busses into the wet street, milling about momentarily, but quickly forming together, adhering to the will of the mass. A sea of army-green uniforms formed around the Bahnhof's entrance and gradually flowed inside.

Moving on the outside of the mass, working his way toward the entrance, Mark saw her standing in a doorway next to the Bahnhof. As their eyes met across the distance, his resolve to shut out everything except moving with his outfit melted away. For days, his thoughts had dwelled on remaining in Germany when his outfit rotated back to the States. But Lauren had made him face the harsh reality of that plan. The only way he could stay in Germany was to abandon his outfit, and desertion was something he couldn't do. To protect himself, he had framed his mind around the mechanics of the troop movement, blotting out all consideration of that possibility.

With one glance, the decision to think only of what lay ahead vanished, and he felt the futility and the dull sickness of this truth. But even with the thin blanket of protection gone, he knew what he had to do, and he knew he would do it. With the crowd of soldiers moving forward slowly, he felt he had a little time. He broke free and walked to her.

"Lauren," he said. "You came!"

"Yes, don't be angry."

"But we agreed last night you wouldn't."

"I know . . . I wanted to come." She stood facing him, her face expressionless, her eyes clear and blue and shiny, her tan raincoat turned up at the collar and dark and rain-soaked around the shoulders.

"You shouldn't have . . . It's not good."

"It doesn't matter."

"It's not good," Mark said again. But his eyes revealed an understanding and empathy of things they both knew and shared— things that no matter what happened would always be with them.

Lauren didn't answer, her look staying on his face.

"I don't have much time," Mark said, dropping his duffle bag just out of the rain in the doorway foyer and glancing back at his outfit clustering at the Bahnhof's entrance.

"I know."

"You're wet, and you look cold," he said. "Can I get you something? A cup of coffee? It's just next door."

"No, nothing."

"It'll pick you up," he insisted. "You need something warm for this weather." Mark turned to go to the café next door.

"No, I'll be okay," she said. "We don't have time for that."

"But you need something!"

"I'm okay," she said again. "I'm fine." Her look told him more than her words, and he resigned himself to her finality and the situation. He gently guided her further back into the short passageway, shielding her from the blowing mist. The passageway had no lighting, and the daylight from outside had little effect on the black-and-gray stone walls. She yielded to Mark's push, but her look went past him back out into the light of the street. The rain came in only a few feet, and they stood in the dim light of their temporary world and out of the rain.

"You need to go home," he said.

She glanced at him and then back to the light of the street. "I'll go when it's time," she said. Mark sensed there was something more wrong than they had talked about.

She continued to face the street a moment and then turned back to him, grasping his arm. "Mark, I've got something to say." Her voice was low and serious and trembled slightly. Her eyes were locked to his.

"Yes? Are you okay? You look cold!"

"Mark," she said, ignoring his questions. "I want you to listen to me. I've got something to say that's very painful. I couldn't say it last night even though I thought I should have. Then I thought about a letter, but now I think it best to say it here." She then stopped, turning away and facing the stone wall as if to collect her thoughts.

"Lauren, what is it? What are you trying to say?"

She continued to face the stone wall a moment. Suddenly, she turned, looking at him intensely as if forcing herself to continue with something she had previously planned to say. She again paused, fixing his eyes with hers and holding them.

"Mark, I've known this day was coming . . . from the beginning," she began slowly. "I've faced it many times, but I wouldn't accept it. I just pushed it away. But now I'm prepared." Mark started to speak, but she stopped him, pressing her fingers against his lips. "We've had our time together, almost two years," she said in a soft, steady voice. "Now, what has to be, has to be. There's no changing that. What we've had has been wonderful. These memories will be like photographs in an album, and they will always be with me."

She continued to hold his eyes, and with that unwavering look, he knew she was pleading with him to understand what she was saying. But in spite of her pleading, he didn't understand.

"What? Don't talk like that!" he said, grasping her shoulders firmly and holding her at arm's length. "We've got things worked out! We'll be separated for a while but then we'll be together again," he continued, shaking her shoulders slightly, his voice and eyes showing deep concern. "Lauren, we can make it work!"

"Oh, Mark, we both know—" She paused then, her face revealing her pain as she looked up at him.

"What do we know?" Mark said, shaking her slightly. He stared at her a moment and then released her and turned away, as if rejecting her words. "I only know I can make it work."

"Make it work," she began. "Mark, we both know how much there is to overcome. The improbability of it working and the terrible struggle we would face only to have it end up badly anyway. Mark, we have our memories. Let's keep it like that and hold to those memories."

"No! Memories are not enough!" Mark said. "Lauren, why do you say that? Why are you talking this way?"

"Mark, it's more than just us," Lauren continued softly, her eyes pleading. "It's so much more. We're inseparable parts of different worlds; we have different paths to follow with different obligations. And we both know we can't escape what life has set for us. All along we've known it. I felt we each came to that conclusion somewhere along the way. But we couldn't face it, so we each pushed it down and lived for the day. I thought that you knew, so I didn't think we had to talk about it."

"We should have talked about it," he said, angry with himself and shocked with her dark mood and words. "We should have worked at things as we went along."

"We didn't talk about it, because we knew we couldn't change things," she said pleadingly, as if begging him to understand. "You know it to be true, don't you? Oh, please, Mark, please understand. We have so little time."

"Okay, let's make firm plans right now," Mark said, ignoring her question and pleading, not able to grasp and accept what she was saying. "Forget about firming up plans until after I'm discharged. Let's say right now that I'll either come back to Germany or send for you. That's firm," he said, his voice growing desperate. "No ocean can keep us apart."

"Oh, Mark," she said, shaking her head while taking his hand and holding it tightly against her face. She looked up at him, her eyes brimming. "We both know there's more than an ocean between us."

Mark didn't answer her this time. He only stared at her, struggling to grasp it all. The truth she spoke of was still not quite to the surface of his mind, but it was coming. He knew what she was saying, he understood what she was saying, and he even knew it all to be true. But he hadn't had time for it to sink in and spread throughout his subconscious and then well up into his consciousness in order to bring him to grips with its reality. His mind sought arguments and reasons, but slowly the accuracy of her words began to weigh on him and to take hold of his thinking. And then suddenly, he knew what she knew; he knew the truth and the stark reality of that truth. They both had known this day would come, and she had faced it first. As he gazed blankly in his own astonishment, a slight, almost undetectable nod told her he now knew what she knew.

CHAPTER 60

A BLOWING GUST OF MIST suddenly blew up into their small space, and Mark pulled Lauren to him, wrapping his open coat around her. She yielded, pressing her body against his. They stood motionless, clinging and silent for the moment. He could smell the moist air warming on her forehead and the familiar scent of her hair. He lost himself momentarily, allowing her presence to blot out the world around him. The tempo of the rain picked up, blowing harder and obliterating the activity at the Bahnhof, leaving them alone and isolated. Both knew now what they had to do, and both would do as they should. They expected nothing, each holding to these moments in time, moments that silently slipped away as they stood in the wet shadows.

He could feel her occasional shudder under his raincoat. He pressed against her to pass his warmth to her. Finally, during one of the wind lulls, he pushed her back slightly and looked down into her face. "Lauren," he said. When she looked up, he continued gently. "You need to go home."

She didn't answer immediately; her look dropped downward. He thought she was going to ignore what he had said. Finally, she looked up to meet his eyes. "I will, when it's time," she said firmly.

He felt her tremble again, and he pulled her closer. "You need to go somewhere and get dry," he repeated. "You're going to be sick." She didn't answer but stirred slightly under his raincoat and continued looking out at the rain and the people in the street.

Standing in the passageway that had become their temporary world, they took the time left the best they could. There was not much they could say and not much they could do. They only clung to the moments left, and the rain and the clamor outside didn't matter to them. More buses pulled up in front of the Bahnhof and began unloading. The soldiers grouped up around the entrance like the others, the mass of military uniforms swelled out into the street and then slowly shrunk as the mass oozed through the narrow entrance. Mark and Lauren stood and watched, speaking little and holding to each moment.

"Your shivering is worse!" Mark said, sensing another chill run through her body. "Damn it, I've got to get you a taxi! You've got to get back to the shop or go home."

She didn't answer but gazed vacantly down the street where crowds of people rushed along in raincoats and carrying black umbrellas—a continually moving mass of people, determined in their efforts, and each person held and encased within the demands of his own particular life, and each person hurrying to his own destination.

"No, I'll wait awhile longer," she finally said.

"This is not good," he said. She didn't answer but continued looking vacantly out at the rain and the people in the street. He then realized what she meant when she said she would go when it was time. She intended to stay until he was gone and that the best thing for her would be for him to leave. He waited a moment longer and then spoke gently. "Lauren, they'll be looking for me."

She slowly began to pull away, but he stopped her at arm's length. He tried to smile but couldn't. He wanted to say something, but nothing came to mind. Unconsciously, he touched her face, his fingers moving lightly across her mouth and cheeks.

She looked long at him and then pulled away, speaking softly, so quietly that if he hadn't seen her lips move, he wouldn't have heard. "*Auf Wiedersehen*," she whispered.

He hesitated, not knowing what to say, not able to acknowledge her words. She turned and quickly walked away, her stride steady and strong as she merged into the crowd of black umbrellas and raincoats moving up and down the street. He watched until he could no longer see her, looking at the point where she had disappeared. He picked up his duffle bag and walked to the cluster of GIs at the entrance to the Bahnhof. Stopping at the beginning of the cluster, he turned back to look once more at the point in the street where she had disappeared.

He had a strange feeling, as if some mystical force was in control, and the street scene of umbrellas and raincoats suddenly clicked in his mind, leaving a black-and-white image. He remembered her saying once that photographs were our way of holding on to things we valued that time had taken. But soon the crowd of soldiers enveloped him, pushing him forward, and he disappeared into the moving mass of army-green uniforms.

CPSIA information can be obtained at www.ICGtesting.com
Printed in the USA
LVOW07s1212251115

464123LV00035B/54/P